Praise for the Novels
of Carol Berg

Flesh and Spirit

DISCARDED

"In Carol Berg's engrossing *Flesh and Spirit*, an engaging rogue stumbles upon the dangerous crossroads of religion, politics, war, and destiny. Berg perfectly portrays the people who shape his increasingly more chaotic journey: cheerful monks, crue'   us warlords, and a whole cast of fanatics. But it's the vividly r   ings to life every stone   ety, describing the difficult dirty work of ordinary life as beautifully as she   s the heart-stopping mysticism of holiness just beyond human perception."

—Sharon Shinn, national bestselling author of *The Thirteenth House*

The Bridge of D'Arnath Series

"A very promising start to a new series."

—*The Denver Post*

"Berg has mastered the balance between mystery and storytelling [and] pacing; she weaves past and present together, setting a solid foundation. . . . It's obvious [she] has put incredible thought into who and what makes her characters tick."

—*The Davis Enterprise*

"Berg exhibits her skill with language, world building, and the intelligent development of the magic that affects and is affected by the characters . . . a promising new multivolume work that should provide much intelligent entertainment."

—*Booklist*

"Imagination harnessed to talent produces a fantasy masterpiece, a work so original and believable that it will be very hard to wait for the next book in this series to be published."

—*Midwest Book Review*

ntinued . . .

Song of the Beast

Winner of the Colorado Book Award for Science Fiction/Fantasy

ALSO BY CAROL BERG

The Rai-Kirah Series

Transformation
Revelation
Restoration

Song of the Beast

The Bridge of D'Arnath Series

Son of Avonar
Guardians of the Keep
The Soul Weaver
Daughter of Ancients

Flesh and Spirit

CAROL BERG

A ROC BOOK

ROC
Published by New American Library, a division of
Penguin Group (USA) Inc., 375 Hudson Street,
New York, New York 10014, USA
Penguin Group (Canada), 90 Eglinton Avenue East, Suite 700, Toronto,
Ontario M4P 2Y3, Canada (a division of Pearson Penguin Canada Inc.)
Penguin Books Ltd., 80 Strand, London WC2R 0RL, England
Penguin Ireland, 25 St. Stephen's Green, Dublin 2, Ireland (a division of Penguin Books Ltd.)
Penguin Group (Australia), 250 Camberwell Road, Camberwell, Victoria 3124,
Australia (a division of Pearson Australia Group Pty. Ltd.)
Penguin Books India Pvt. Ltd., 11 Community Centre, Panchsheel Park, New Delhi - 110 017, India
Penguin Group (NZ), 67 Apollo Drive, Rosedale, North Shore,
Auckland 1311, New Zealand (a division of Pearson New Zealand Ltd.)
Penguin Books (South Africa) (Pty.) Ltd., 24 Sturdee Avenue, Rosebank, Johannesburg 2196, South Africa

Penguin Books Ltd., Registered Offices:
80 Strand, London WC2R 0RL, England

First published by Roc, an imprint of New American Library,
a division of Penguin Group (USA) Inc.

First Printing, May 2007
10   9   8   7   6   5   4   3   2   1

RoC REGISTERED TRADEMARK—MARCA REGISTRADA

LIBRARY OF CONGRESS CATALOGING-IN-PUBLICATION DATA:
Berg, Carol.
   Flesh and spirit / Carol Berg.
     p. cm.
   ISBN: 978-0-451-46088-2
   I. Title.
   PS3602.E7523F64 2007
   813'.54—dc22   2006032044

Set in Perpetua • *Designed by Elke Sigal*

Printed in the United States of America

For Pete and the greatest of all fantasy adventures

Acknowledgments

Best thanks to my ever-attentive muse, Linda, for prodding my thinking. Heaps, mountains, and really awfully luminescent thanks to Susan, Laurey, Glenn, Brian, Catherine, and Curt for refusing to let me slide over those tough details, to Markus, the Fighter Guy, for combat review, and to the doc-on-the-net, Doug Lyle, for a few gory consultations. And, as always, to my readers for the words that get me through the tough days and my family for their forbearance when I go into hermit mode.

The cusp of autumn arrives untimely. Dun haze. Tarnished gold. Leaves . . . glory dulled . . . whipped from their branches. Wolves gather, howling, gnawing the light. No more the culmination of summer, but harbinger of bitter blue days and ever longer nights. The dance is finished, and my heart aches for the waning season. Hollow. Wanting. Dare I sleep?

—Canticle of the Autumn

PART ONE

The Cusp of Autumn

Chapter 1

On my seventh birthday, my father swore, for the first of many times, that I would die facedown in a cesspool. On that same occasion, my mother, with all the accompanying mystery and elevated language appropriate for a prominent diviner, turned her cards, screamed delicately, and proclaimed that my doom was written in water and blood and ice. As for me, from about that time and for the twenty years since, I had spat on my middle finger and slapped the rump of every aingerou I noticed, murmuring the sincerest, devoutest prayer that I might prove my parents' predictions wrong. Not so much that I feared the doom itself—doom is just the hind end of living, after all—but to see the two who birthed me confounded.

Sadly, as with so many of my devotions, some to greater gods than those friendly imps carved into the arches and drainpipes of palaces, hovels, latrines, and sop-houses, my fervent petition had come to naught. I'd been bloody for two days now, the rain was quickly turning to sleet, and I seemed to have reached the hind end of everything . . .

"I've no quarrel with ye, Valen, ye know that." The hairy brute stuffed my sweetly chinking leather purse into the folds of his cloak and returned to burrowing in my rucksack. "Ye've been a fine comrade these months. But ye've need of more care than I can give ye, and I've told ye, I can't be hallooing with no monkish folk. If I thought so much as a slavey's hovel lay within thirty quellae, I'd drag ye there."

"And as you're going to abandon me here, well . . . no use wasting good plunder on maggot fodder," I said bitterly, teeth chattering, lips numb. The cold rain sluiced down the neck of my sodden jaque and collected about my knees in the ruts of the ancient road. My elbows quivered as I tried to hold my chest above the muddy water. This damnable goat track had likely not been used since they hauled in stone and wood to build the ghostly abbey tucked into the misty, folded land below us. "I've watched your back for a twelvemonth, you devil. Not a scratch have you suffered since Arin Fay."

One by one Boreas pulled out the remaining carefully wrapped bundles: the onyx jewel case crammed with chains, bracelets, and jeweled brooches, the gold calyx, two daggers with ruby-encrusted hilts—the finest prizes of our infamy. Just one of the daggers could outfit a man with a decent horse, a sword, a thick wool cloak with no holes in it, and a pleasant trimonth of meat, drink, and fair companionship. I'd paid a pretty price in blood and flesh for collecting this bit of plunder, and—Magrog's demons devour this beast I'd foolishly called friend—I wasn't even to profit from it.

He stuffed my goods into his already bulging sack. "None o' this lot'll do ye no good. Wasn't a monk bred won't steal whatever he lays an eye on. And yer in no fit state to argue with them . . . or me neither, come to that."

The arrow point embedded deep in my thigh and the fist-sized gouge that had started seeping warm blood on my back again bore ample witness to his verity on the last point. I *did* need help more than I needed my booty, and a wounded man could do far worse than a monastery. These concessions did nothing to ease my mind, however, as I was not yet at the abbey gates and not at all sure anyone would be traveling this particular road with night coming on and a three-year civil war and a sevenday's deluge to keep folk by their own hearths.

I ought to have been angrier with Boreas. But gods knew I'd have done the same were he the one collapsed in the muck, wailing that fire-eyed Magrog himself could not make him take one more step. And I was certainly in no fit state to forcibly reclaim my belongings.

"Just get me down to the gate," I croaked, another wave of chills washing me closer to the grave. "My share ought to pay you for that at least. And leave me one luné for an offering."

"I daren't. The baldpates'll have me swinging ere I kiss ye farewell. No worry, lad. One of 'em'll pass by here and see to ye. And their Karish god teaches 'em to give alms to them with naught, so you're better off with no silver in your pocket."

He shook his head and shrugged his massive shoulders as if the entire mystery of the holy universe was puzzling him at that moment. Then he pulled one last bundle from my rucksack—a flat, squarish parcel, two handspans on a side, wrapped in multiple layers of oiled cloth—and peeled open one flap.

"Have a care; the rain will ruin that," I said, attempting to draw one knee up high enough that I could slide my foot underneath me. If I could just get back to my feet, find a thick branch to lean on, perhaps I could stagger down the hill a little farther on my own.

"Is it plate?" he asked, shaking the bundle and getting no sound. "Heavy enough, but it don't feel right. I don't remember nothing this shape."

My left boot squelched into place under my hip, jarring the festering wound in my thigh, shooting bolts of white-hot fire up and down my leg. "Aagh! It's a book. More valuable than plate. More valuable than those daggers to the right people. And I can send you to the right people if you'll just get me to a leech."

Boreas shifted backward, just out of my reach. "A book! Ye're twinking me, right?"

He poked his dirty fingers into the corner of the parcel, and then glared down at me dumbfounded. "You donkey's ass! Have ye an arrow planted between yer ears as well? All the rich stuff we had to leave behind and ye hauled out a blighting book?"

He threw the parcel and the empty rucksack to the ground and laid his boot into my backside. My shaking elbows collapsed, and I fell forward into the mudhole. Though I twisted enough to avoid a direct hit, I jarred the broken-off arrow shaft protruding from my thigh. Lifting my face from the muck and spewing mud from my mouth, I bellowed like a speared boar.

Unconcerned, Boreas crouched beside me, rifling my clothes. He tossed aside my bracers and the rag I had used to dry my long-lost bow, stuffed my knife into his own belt, and unwrapped the last bite of sour bread I'd hoarded for more than a day and crammed it into his mouth. Fumbling at the waist of my braies, he pulled out a small bag the size of my palm—a scrap of green wool I'd sewn myself and soaked in tallow until it was stiff. "What's this?"

I grabbed for the little bag, but he snatched his hand out of my reach. "By Mother Samele's tits, Boreas, you've got to leave me something."

He yanked it open, sniffed at its contents, and then gaped at me as if I had sprouted three arms of a sudden, shaking his shaggy head until the drips flew off it. "Nivat seeds! But you've no bent to use such stuff . . ."

"Of course not, you clodwit. Would we have scraped and starved this year past if I were some misbegotten spellcaster?"

Lips curled in disgust, he pulled the silver needle and the jagged fragment of mirror glass from the little bag. "By the night lords—"

"The bag was hid in the jewel box." I jumped in quickly to stop his thick head pondering too much. "The nob was surely pureblood. Richer than a prince. And surely Magrog's henchman to practice such perversion." I could stanch my babbling no better than I could stanch the blood from my shoulder.

He dropped the things back into the little green bag and crammed the bag into his pocket. "So you decided to sell the nivat on your own and jupe me out of my share. I thought I knew you, Valen. I thought you were my comrade."

Rain pounded the soggy ground. My gut sent a warning, like a lightning flash beyond the hills. "I thought we could use the seeds to make feast bread come season's turn. Offer it to the Danae. Change our luck. Come, you wouldn't take everything."

"Ye said yerself a man makes his own luck. I'm making mine."

No plea could induce him to leave anything he thought he could sell. Nivat was very expensive, as were the quickened spells worked from it. Only nobles, pureblood sorcerers, or desperate twist-minds without any choice could afford either one.

Boreas straightened up and kicked the book parcel and the ragged rucksack toward my head. "The monks'll heal your hurts if anyone can. Pay 'em with your *valuable* book."

I dragged the rucksack under me, lest the slug-witted ox change his mind.

"You're a coward and a thief, Boreas!" I shouted as he trudged off. "You stink like a pureblood's midden!"

Only moments and he was gone, the heavy footsteps and ponderous breathing that had been a passing comfort at my side for a year's turn were swallowed up by the pounding deluge. He couldn't go far. The light was failing. I could scarcely see the slender arches of the abbey church through the sheets of rain. Monks—especially these pious fellows out in the wilderness—put themselves to bed before a meadowlark could sing. Before a whore had her skirts up. Before an owl had its eyes open. Before . . .

Alehouse riddling threatened to squeeze out more useful thoughts. Shaking my head, I stretched out my forearms, dug my elbows into the muck, and dragged myself forward on my side perhaps one quat—the length of a man's knucklebone. Ominous warmth oozed out of the gouge on my back. My leg felt like a molten sword blank awaiting the smith's hammer.

I rested my head on crossed forearms. One moment to catch my breath . . .

Much as I pretended elsewise, even to myself, I *could* shape spells, of course. Mostly destructive things, minor illusions, a child's wickedness. Nothing that could heal a wound. Nothing that could summon help. Nothing useful.

The driving rain splashed mud in my face. Sleet stung the back of my neck. The cold settled deep in my bones until I wasn't even shivering anymore. I hated the cold.

"Magrog take you, Boreas," I mumbled, "and give you boils on your backside and a prick like a feather."

Groaning shamelessly, I jammed my left foot into the rut and rolled onto my back. The dark world spun like soup in a kettle, yet I felt modestly satisfied. I might be doomed to blood and water and ice—madness, too, if breeding held true—but by Iero's holy angels, I would die face*up* in this cesspool.

Rain spattered softly on my cheeks and the ground, on the puddles, the leaves, and a large rock, each surface producing a slight variant of the sound, defining the world on the far side of my eyelids. The scents of rotted leaves and good loam filled my nose . . . my lungs . . . seeped into my pores. My body blemished that vast landscape like a fallen tree, soon to be rotted, dissolved, and completely one with that cold, dark, and very wet place.

Soft padding steps rustled the wet leaves, stirring up smells of grass and moss and sea wrack, everything green or wet in the world. Paused. *Fox? Rabbit? Mmm . . . bigger.* Cold rain and warm blood had long washed away fear. Moments more and I wouldn't care what kind of beast it was. A faint shudder rippled through my depths. *Terrible . . . wonderful . . . to dissolve in the rain . . .*

Creaking wood and iron sent the beast scuttering away. Soft yellow light leaked around my eyelids—a lamp spitting and sprizzling in the rain.

"You heard him at the sanctuary gate? From all the way up here?"

"By Iero's holy name, Brother Sebastian. His cry sounded like the seven torments of the end times. When I poked my head out the shutters and saw none lay at the gate, conscience forbade me to lie down again without a search."

"Never use the One God's name lightly, boy. And in future you must seek Father Prior's permission to go beyond the walls, even when on duty."

A warm weight, smelling of woodsmoke and onions, pressed lightly on my chest. If I could have moved, I would have wrapped my arms about it. Kissed it even.

The weight lifted. "He breathes. I'd call it a miracle you found him, but now I look, I'm coming to believe you heard the fellow, after all. For certain he's been *through* the seven torments. Here, lend me your hand."

Hands grabbed me behind my left shoulder, where Boreas had extracted a second arrow and a sizable hunk of flesh. I left off any thought of joining the conversation. Breathing seemed enough. Keeping some wit about me. Listening . . .

The two mumbled of Iero and Father Prior and Saint Gillare the Wise, as they laid me on my side on a wooden platform that stank like a pig wallow and then proceeded to tilt it at such an angle that all my painful parts slid together in one wretched lump. The cart bumped forward, causing me to bite my tongue.

"Was he left by highwaymen, do you think, Brother?" The eager young speaker labored somewhere in front of me, expelling short puffs of effort.

"Highwaymen don't leave boots with a man, even boots with soles thin as vellum. No, as his outfit's plain and sturdy underneath the blood, I'd name him a soldier come from battle. Doesn't look as if he's eaten in a twelve-month, for all he's tall as a spar oak."

"A soldier . . ." The word expressed a wonder that comes only when the speaker can't tell a pike from a poker or a battle from a broomdance. "One of Prince Bayard's men, do you think?"

"He might serve any one of the three, or this mysterious Pretender, or the Emperor of Aurellia himself. Such matters of the world should not concern you. Once Brother Infirmarian sees to the fellow, Father Abbot will question him as to his loyalties and purposes."

Bones of hell . . . one would think an abbey so out of the way as this one might not care which of the three sons of King Eodward juped his brothers out of the throne.

The cart jounced through a pothole. The older man grunted. I sank into mindless misery.

Anyone might have mistaken the cold uncomfortable journey for the everlasting downward path. One of the two fellows—the younger one, I guessed, not the wise Brother Sebastian—chirruped a psalm about running with Iero's children in sunlit fields, a performance so cheery it could serve as proper torment on such a road.

Eventually we jolted to a stop. Above my head arched a stone vault of uncertain height, not an ever-raining sky, though a round-cheeked aingerou carved into a corner spat a little dribble of rain water onto the wagon bed. The yellow lamplight danced on the pale stone.

"Run for Brother Robierre, boy, and tell him bring a litter."

"But I'm posted sanctuary, so I must give—"

"You've walked me halfway to Elanus. I'll stay right here and give the fellow his blessing."

Elanus. A small market town. South? West? Ought to know. How far did we run? I'd been more than half delirious on the road.

Bells clanged and clamored from the church towers, and out of the night rose the sound of men singing, plainsong, clear and strong like a river of music, quickening my blood like a fiery kiss.

"Brother, it's the call to Matins!" said the boy. "You have to go!"

"All right, all right, my hearing's not so bad as that."

Matins—morning at midnight. A perverse custom.

The wind shifted the lantern so that its beams nearly blinded me. I squeezed my eyes shut again. The night's edge seemed sharp as a razor knife. I'd always heard the Ferryman's mortal breath *dulled* the senses.

A dreadful thought shivered my bones: Had the Ferryman himself been breathing at my ear? He'd even smelled of sea wrack. I'd never truly believed . . .

"I'll send Brother Infirmarian," said Brother Sebastian. "When he no longer requires you, hie you to prayers yourself. The good god excuses no green aspirants."

"Of course, Brother."

Footsteps trudged away. A warm hand touched my brow. "By Iero's grace, find safety here, thou who fleest sword or hangman. By the saint's hand, find healing here, thou who sufferest wound or sickness. By gift of holy earth, find strength here, thou who comest parched or weak. And by King Eodward's grant and his servants' labor, find nourishment for thy flesh and spirit. God grant thee ease, traveler."

An interesting prayer . . . gift of holy earth . . . King Eodward's grant . . . all mixed in with the Karish god Iero and one of his saints. For the most part, the Karish dwelt peaceably side by side with the elder gods, but I'd never before heard a joint invocation.

I lifted my head. "Perhaps, if you could just help me out of this corner . . ."

An uncomfortable ricketing tilt of the cart brought a pale, narrow face above me. The lamplight revealed the thickening brows and downy upper lip of oncoming manhood, and such delight and amazement as could only emanate from the same soul that sang cheery psalms while slogging a manure cart down a mountainside in the rain. "You're alive!"

I didn't feel at all sure about that, having come so close as to hear the Ferryman's footsteps. "Not dead. Thank you."

"No need to thank me, sir. It's my duty, you see, assigned me by the prior, who was given the task by the abbot, whose authority is from the hierarch and the One God in Heaven. I sleep above the sanctuary gate, ready to hear the bell and open the gate for any who come. You're the first since I was given the task. You *do* beg sanctuary, don't you?"

His eagerness exhausted me.

"Yes. Certainly."

"Thus you must have broken the law of God or king, or someone believes it so . . ." He tilted his head and drew his brows together. Clearly his excitement at receiving a supplicant was now tempered with consideration of my soul's peril. My offenses were, indeed, countless, and my peril ever present.

"If you could just help me sit up." So long tipped downward in the stinking cart had my belly mightily unsettled, not that there was aught left in it to spew.

The untonsured boy was as diligent with his wiry arms and gentle hands as with his words. By the time a gray-haired monk with darkish skin about his eyes, something like a badger's markings, dropped a bundle of long poles on the paving, I sat across the lip of the three-sided cart, my head bent almost to my knees and my lip bloody from biting it.

"Jullian, unfold the litter. Let me examine what we have here. Ooh . . ." A glimpse of the broken, dark-stained shaft protruding from my black and swollen thigh was clearly the most interesting thing the fellow had seen that day.

"I hope you've a sharp knife, Brother," I said, my voice shaking, "and a steady hand."

Then he touched it, and the world slipped out of my grasp.

Chapter 2

"How do you feel this morning, my friend?"

I cocked one eye open. The smudge-eyed monk peered down at me, his arms overflowing with bundled linen and wooden bowls. Plastered walls hung with strips of green-dyed cloth rose up behind him to a timbered roof, and an array of narrow windows, paned with horn, admitted murky light. A smoking rushlight clamped to an iron tripod revealed ten more beds lined up neatly in the long plain room. From my odd vantage—I lay on my left side, some kind of bolster propping me up from the back and legs tipped higher than my head—the beds appeared unoccupied.

"I feel like Iero's wrath," I said. Every particle of my flesh felt battered; my leg throbbed as if the arrow point were grinding its way into the bone. My shoulder might have had rats chewing on it. Damp all over, I shivered helplessly despite a pile of blankets.

I had known better than to pull the damnable arrow out of my thigh when I had no help but Boreas, who was convinced that burying a live cat under an oak at the full moon would cure his crabs, and that spitting over a bridge rampart while wearing a moonbird's feather would speed the healing of his broken hand. I knew little of the body's humors. But one of a man's great veins lay in the thigh, and I'd seen men bleed to death faster than a frog takes a fly while removing an arrow point carelessly from just the same spot as my wound. And we hadn't been able to stop moving. When the Harrower priestess had thrown her legion of madmen against us, the battle had gone completely to the fiery pits, and six thousand other bloodied soldiers who had wagered their fortunes on the wrong side in this cursed war were soon to be right on our heels.

A halfwit would understand what the delay would cost me. Though I had weighed bleeding to death likely preferable to sepsis and amputation, in my usual way I had postponed the decision, figuring it was better to die tomorrow than today. Now the payment was falling due.

Mustering my courage, I broached the question gnawing at my gut. "You'll take the leg, I know, Brother. But think you I'll live to raise a glass again?"

The monk dropped his bundled linens atop a wide chest pushed against the end wall of the infirmary, then began arranging the wooden bowls on shelves already crowded with ewers and basins, jars and bottles. "If the One God's mercy continues to hold sway, your leg will heal with no ill result. Your fever's broken just this morn. Young Jullian will be certain his prayers are answered. You'd think the boy had delivered you from the gates of hell bearing sword and shield like the Archangel himself."

"But it's putrid, and when you remove the arrow——"

"The nasty bit of iron is two days out, lad, and for certain, you've the constitution of an ox. You're on the mend." The monk was a strapping fellow. Despite his circled eyes and his stubbled cheeks that drooped excess skin about his jaw, his face expressed naught but good cheer. He spread out an array of bundled plants on a long table that stood between the last bed and the stack of shelves. Perching his backside on a backless stool, he began picking leaves from the array. "I'm Brother Robierre, as it happens, by Iero's grace the infirmarian of Gillarine Abbey."

"Oh!" Astonishing how much better I felt straightaway. As if the jagged bits of a shattered mirror had put themselves together again. As if I'd pulled the veil off my contracted bride and found some girl I loved. I dropped my head on the pillow and crowed like a banty rooster. "May the angels scribe your name, Brother! The moment I'm afoot, I'll dance you a jig and carry you to heaven on my back!"

A stoop-shouldered monk with piebald hair and a gray scapular over his cinched black gown scuttered out from behind me, casting a mildly shocked glance my way. The steaming crock he carried past my bed to the table left a scented trail in the air. Chicken——holy Mother, could it be?——and onions and carrots and thyme and savory. My stomach rumbled uproariously.

Months had passed since I last tasted meat. In early summer Boreas and I had shot an aged squirrel, three bites apiece and broth from the boiled bones with little more than grass to throw in it. Then and since the Ardran legions had been squatting on land long raided, gleaned, and stripped. We'd had only bread like dried leather made from shriveled peas or even acorns ground into flour. And never enough. No planting or harvest this year in any of western Ardra. The summer campaign had been only one of Prince Perryn's gross miscalculations in pursuing his father's throne. Not even the worst.

"Thank you, Brother Anselm," said Robierre. "I do believe our patient's going to appreciate the soup today. Inform the abbot that our supplicant is awake, if you would."

Piebald Brother Anselm nodded solemnly to the infirmarian and scurried away. To my delight, Brother Robierre put aside his activities and selected a wooden bowl from the shelf. I almost moaned as he filled the bowl from the tureen, acquired a spoon, and dragged a low stool to my bedside.

The good brother insisted I drink some concoction that tasted like boiled scrapings from a stable floor first of all. But after the first spoonful of the soup, I would have knelt to kiss the hairy toes that peeked out from his sandals had he but asked.

"Abbot Luviar has been most concerned about you," he said as I reveled in the savory broth and tiny bits of succulent poultry deemed suitable for an invalid. "He's had prayers said, asked blessings as we sit at table. He'll be in to see you now I've sent word you're awake."

"Mmm," I said, holding the last warm spoonful in my mouth before I let it trickle down my throat. "Iero's holy angels . . . all of you." I was feeling quite devout.

He grinned, an expression distinctly odd for a badger. "I'll get you more."

I had never shared Boreas's horror of monks, but then I had never been fool enough to creep over a priory wall with a bursar's coffer on my back. Boreas had been sentenced to the loss of one hand, a flogging, and a week in pillory, but managed to escape before suffering any of the three. Now he was convinced that every monk and lay brother passed his description about the realm tucked in sleeves or under scapulars, and that every abbot and prior was determined to hang him.

Sadly, my own direst peril had less to do with lawbreaking or sin than with birth and blood, circumstances for which no sanctuary could be granted. But I had no reason to believe that my loathsome family or the Pureblood Registry could find me here or anywhere. I'd shed them both at fifteen and had long since drowned myself in a sea of anonymity. I had no intention of bobbing to the surface. Ever.

Two more bowls of the brothers' heaven-kissed soup and I took even the changing of the dressing on my thigh with good humor. Warm, fed, and clean—indeed someone had washed me head to toe while I slept—and out of the weather, and no one coming after me with arrows, pikes, lances, or hands outstretched for money . . . perhaps the boy Jullian was indeed the archangel who guarded the gates of Paradise. The truest wonder was that he had let me in.

I fell asleep as promptly as a cat in a sunbeam. When my eyes drifted open again sometime later, a long-limbed man of more than middling years sat on the stool at my bedside. A golden solicale dangled from his neck—the sunburst symbol of Iero's glory worked in a pendant so heavy it must surely be an abbot's ensign. Instead of effecting a modest tonsure like the infirmarian's, he had shaved his head entirely clean.

Holding in mind my present comforts, I bowed my head and shaped my greeting in the Karish manner. "In the name of holy Iero and his saints, my humblest gratitude be yours, holy father. Truly the One God led my wayward footsteps to this refuge when the world and all its ways had failed me." I didn't think it too grovelish.

"Iero commands us offer his hand in charity," said the abbot, "and so we have done. It remains to be seen what he has in mind for you." His full-shaven pate, fine arched nose, and narrow, pock-grooved face made his cool gray eyes seem very large.

I squirmed a bit, suddenly feeling even more naked than I already was under my lovely blankets.

A younger monk, full-shaven as well, but with unmarked skin and dark brows that made a solid line above deep-set eyes, stood a few steps behind the abbot, hands tucked piously under his black scapular. Though his expression remained properly sober, his brow lifted slightly and his mouth quickened with amusement as he observed me under the abbot's eye.

"What is your name, my son?" The abbot took no note of his attendant's improper levity.

"Valen, holy father."

"Valen. Nothing else, then?"

"Nay, holy father." No title to mark me as nobility or clergy. No town or profession to mark me as a rooted man even if my father was unimportant. No association with any of the three provinces of Navronne—Ardra, Morian, or Evanore—or with their contentious princes. And certainly no colineal surname to proclaim my family pureblood, and thus my future beyond even an abbot's right to determine. Especially not that. "Just Valen."

"Valen Militius, perhaps?"

Another dangerous topic. The young attendant monk's dark brows lifted slightly. Attentive. At the worktable, Brother Robierre's head was bent over his mortar and pestle, plants and vials, but his hands grew still.

Though I tried to dip my own head farther, being propped on my side made it difficult. "Not a professional soldier, holy father, far from it, nor even a worthy freeman-at-arms. But I once carried a pike for King Eodward, Iero cherish his soul, and stood behind him as he drove the Hansker barbarians back across the sea. He called us his men of light, and so we all felt more than what we were born." All true. And now the test would come . . .

"And what of noble Eodward's sons?" He touched the clean linen that wrapped my shoulder and made a blessing sign upon it. My flesh warmed beneath the bandage. "Which of the three princes owns your fealty? Or do you hope for this ghostly Pretender of current rumor?"

"None of them, holy father. Though the sign of three speaks of heaven, these three sons are so far from worthy of their kingly father that an ignorant lout such as I am cannot choose. And though I reverence any issue of good King Eodward, I fear that naught but tavern gossip has delivered him a fourth son."

Unless I could discover with which prince this man's favor rested, I dared not say more. Perryn of Ardra, whom I *had* chosen as being the most intelligent and least openly brutal of the half-brothers, was surely dead by now, or in chains, babbling his plans and the names of his noble supporters to his brother Bayard's torturers. In either case, my oath to him was moot. He had shown himself mean and so stubbornly inept that my loyalty had been ruined much earlier. He certainly was not worth dying for.

I glanced up. The gray eyes held steady, the long, slender bones of the abbot's face unmoved. "So your wounds were not earned in battle, then?"

Well, the battle had been over months before we'd charged Prince Bayard's line at Wroling—in the spring when Bayard of Morian had allied with Sila Diaglou and her Harrowers. But such quibbling wouldn't carry weight with this abbot. Not with a wound in my back, and the admission requiring me to declare not only that I had run away, but which side I had deserted. I needed a better story.

"Nay, holy father, rather my wounds stem from a private dispute with another man regarding property that belonged to me. Though right was with me in the matter, I believed I was going to die and so confessed my sins to a village practor. He sent me on the road with my wounds untended as penance, saying the One God would put me in the way of death or life as was his will."

I held still and listened carefully, fighting the urge to add more words to this collection of nonsense, such as what village I'd come from or why I had suffered the strikes of arrows rather than knife or club. It seemed a very long time until the abbot spoke again.

"Was this, by chance, the disputed property, Valen?"

The dark-browed monk stepped forward, pulled a book out of his black gown, and passed it to the abbot. The abbot laid it on the bed in front of my face, a squarish book some three fingers thick, its brown leather binding tooled in gold with gryphons and dragons, long-limbed angels, roundels, vine leaves, and every flourish of the leather gilder's art. Slightly damp at one corner, but I quickly verified that the dampness had not touched the fine vellum pages enough to damage them or smear the ink.

"If so, and if you have any idea of what you carry and can tell me how you've come by it, then I may believe your story."

I swallowed, puffed out a strong breath, and touched my finger to the golden letters on its cover and the familiar sigil of a gryphon carrying a rolled map in its claws. "Of course, holy father. This is the original volume of *Maps of the Known World*, created by the pureblood, Janus de Cartamandua-Magistoria, the most famous cartographer in all of Navronne's history." That part was true, of course. My mind raced. "It was given me . . . seven years ago . . . when, with Iero's grace, my service . . . scouting . . . preserved the Mardane Lavorile's troop from capture by the Hansker. Knowing a scout would understand its worth, his lordship said it was fitting recompense for the lives I had saved. One of these wild Harrowers tried to take it. They think to burn all books, you know."

"So you are familiar with the book, studied it no doubt, used its guiding spells when you served the mardane?"

Monks valued books. New initiates often brought them. And the Karish would certainly want this one. Legend said it could lead men to the realm of angels.

"Of course, holy father. I used it often in the mardane's service. I treasure each page." Though my valuing had more to do with the gold coins of pawnbrokers than the gold crowns of angels.

The gray-eyed abbot nodded. "I'll accept this tale for now. Brother Robierre is scowling, for I promised not to tire you. Tell me, Valen, what do you ask of Gillarine Abbey beyond your fortnight of sanctuary?"

This answer was much easier than the previous ones, requiring no instant work of the imagination. "To join your holy fraternity, holy father. To repent my licentious life and serve the god Iero, if I may." That is, to eat and stay warm, dry, and anonymous until I decided where to go and what to do next to revive a fortune that seemed to have reached its nadir. Soldiering, the only work I'd found in two years, had decidedly lost its attractions.

"Granted," said the abbot with astonishing speed. "Brother Sebastian will be your mentor, instructing and guiding you in our rule and custom. Brother Gildas, you will inform Sebastian and Prior Nemesio of our new aspirant."

The dark-browed monk bowed respectfully from the hip.

Once prayers and blessings had ushered the two of them out, Brother Robierre appeared at my side, bearing a clay jar into which I took a grateful piss. He then passed the jar on to the piebald Brother Anselm, who settled at the worktable and began to dip and pour and examine my output as if it were the waters of the heavenly rivers. I recited my stories over and over in my head so I'd not forget them if questioned again.

After a while, the infirmarian provided me with a thick posset, not so savory as the chicken, but sweet, warm, and filling. Setting the empty mug aside, Robierre reached his hand toward the book that still lay on the bed with me. Hesitating. "May I?"

Eyelids heavy, I smiled. "For thou, blessed angel of the infirmary, anything."

He chuckled and lifted the book from the bed and ran his thick fingers lovingly over the binding. "A Cartamandua book of maps . . . to have such a thing come to Gillarine . . . You will be besieged with pleas to see it. Few of our brothers, even those who labor in the scriptorium, will have glimpsed so rare and precious a work or one so storied. The very book that led the Sinduré and the Hierarch to discover young Eodward in the realm of angels, the book that shows the hidden places of the world. What strange roads it must have traveled. Who would have thought that one like you would possess a sorcerer's finest—? Ah, I'm sorry." His sagging cheeks flushed in kind embarrassment.

"You're not the first, good brother, not the first."

Strange roads indeed! Until five days ago, when I'd discovered the book in a deserted manse I happened to be looting as I ran away from a battle I'd sworn to fight, I'd last touched it eleven years before at a bookshop in Palinur. I'd been desperate for money—a state less familiar then than now. I'd had to settle for less than its full worth because the book pawner refused to believe I'd come by it honestly. Neither the good Brother Robierre nor the pawner would believe—nor would I ever tell anyone, could I avoid it—that old Janus de Cartamandua himself had given it to me, his ill-behaved and unappreciative grandson, on my tumultuous and unpleasant seventh birthday. My parents had been furious.

Chapter 3

The bells in the abbey tower fell silent. Brother Robierre had hurried off to the chapter house for the monks' daily meeting, and Brother Anselm had retired to his herb garden, closing the infirmary door softly behind them so as not to wake me. I heaved a deep and pleasurable sigh.

On this second day of trying to sleep away my wounds in Gillarine's infirmary, I had only three complaints of any substance. Firstly, the bells. Bells banged every hour day or night and set off a cacophony whenever the brothers were called to services, which seemed fifty times a day. Second, the shy lay brother Anselm devoutly believed that one window must always be left open in an infirmary to allow ill humors to escape the room, which caused a frigid draft whenever the outside door was opened. And third, endearing as I found Brother Badger, as I called the good infirmarian, a sick man should be exempt from excess praying. Feigning sleep was my only reprieve.

I tugged the blankets over my bare shoulder, luxuriated in the returning warmth from the hearth, and speculated about what delicacy the good brothers would bring from the abbey kitchens to fill my invalid's stomach. I had always been a quick healer, but the brothers didn't need to know that. Life was good.

"Comfortable, are you?"

My eyelids slammed open to reveal the abbot's attendant sitting on the bedside stool. I'd heard not a step or a breath.

"Brother Gildas! How did you——?" Recalling my position as aspiring novice and the tedious duties that were like to involve the moment I was well enough, I checked my tongue and allowed my breath to quaver bravely. "Well,

Brother, I'm as comfortable as a man can be with fever shakes and septic blood and holes in his flesh where there should be none. Bless you for asking."

His dark brows lifted, and he pulled a wedge of cheese from under my pillow. "We'll feed you even when you're healed, Valen. And you needn't fear I'll tell the abbot that your devotions are perhaps more directed to his kitchen and his bed than his church at present. Every man here has his own reasons for piety."

"The bounty of the good god is a fit occasion for thanksgiving," I said a bit defensively, tucking the rest of my cache more securely under my head. "And surely he expects us to conserve that bounty for harder days."

Perhaps it was their shaven heads that made this man and the abbot appear so intensely focused, their eyes dominant in their hairless skulls as if they might read a man's very soul. Not that my soul was all that interesting—a man of seven-and-twenty summers who scrabbled from one job to another, doing as he needed to wrest a bit of enjoyment from a world that seemed worse off by the day. But at least this fellow was near enough my own age that he might remember something of a man's needs.

"I do hear Iero's call to the prayerful life quite clearly. But, in truth, Brother Gildas, I am yet a sinful man who enjoys the pleasures of bed and board overmuch. No matter how devoutly my soul yearns to reform, my body forever backslides."

"And yet our abbot, whose eye is infinitely wise, judges you worthy of initiation. I've never known him so precipitate in judgment. He'd have you vowed before Saint Marcillus's Day, scarcely a fortnight hence." His head tilted as if to examine me from various angles, his deep-set eyes unwavering. "Well, neither you nor I may see the right of it, but the god scorns none with a good heart. We must have faith that he will illumine yours as he sees fit. Brother Sebastian has been charged with your guidance and instruction, but Father Prior has dispatched him to Pontia to investigate the rumor of two books brought in by traders. So I was asked to bring you these."

He laid a worn book and a roll of parchment on the bed in front of me. "Your psalter, left by good Brother Horach, who passed to his next life not long ago. And a summary of Saint Ophir's Rule, which you must commit to memory ere you take your novice vows. Brother Sebastian will discuss them with you upon his return."

"A dead man's book?" I said, drawing back from it as far as the heavy bolster allowed.

"He was not diseased, if that's your worry."

"No, no . . ."

I had long abjured the soldiers' maxim that wearing a dead man's boots or cooking in his pot would see your own life forfeit within a year. Books, as it happened, raised other problems.

"It's just that . . . a holy saint's book . . . for my eyes that have looked on so much of the Adversary's wickedness to rest upon such precious pages seems sacrilege. Until I have confessed and labored out the days . . . months . . . of expiation, I doubt I could look upon a holy work without it bursting into eternal flame. And such a waste of a precious book that would be!"

Brother Gildas laughed—a pleasant, resonant sound—and shifted the book and scroll to the bedside table. "We must certainly get you up and working hard to soothe this burdensome conscience of yours. Do you not know that those who cross our threshold for sanctuary are cleansed of past offenses? You are a new man, Valen, whether you like it or not, as pure as a new-dipped babe. The only marks upon your soul will be those you scribe there from this day forward."

The Karish hierarchs pronounced many tenets to admire, but this one— that an unwatered babe could be marked with evil, whereas a failed man of the world who had no intention of repenting his iniquities could be somehow purified by crossing a brick threshold—had always struck me as untenable.

I sighed deeply. "Oh. Well then, when my fever allows my blurred sight to clear, I'll study both book and scroll."

"If Brother Sebastian fails to return by tomorrow, I'll come myself to quiz you on the Rule," he said, rising from his stool. "And, of course, Father Abbot will require the details of your birth. We care naught for high or low, pureblood, noble, or common at Gillarine. But neither bonded men nor natural sons nor purebloods lacking dispensation from their family are per-mitted to join our order."

"Of course." I had the disconcerting sense that the monk felt my mind racing. "Tell me, Brother Gildas, where is my own book, the book of maps?" After the odd chance of happening onto such a rarity, I'd be a fool to lose track of it.

He smiled in a knowing fashion that I found somewhat annoying. "Safely locked into the abbot's own book press. Father Abbot would not see such a treasure splattered with blood or possets. If you choose to leave before you take vows, of course it will be returned to you."

He offered me a sip of the spicy caudle Brother Badger had left on the stool. I downed it gratefully. My awkward drinking posture left drips enough on my bed linens to make Brother Gildas's point.

I would need to find the book. If this Elanus was a good-sized town, perhaps it had a knowledgeable pawner. A few weeks and I would suffer for my lack of silver. Of a sudden the beery sweetness of the caudle tasted of brine and bitter. Some of life's unpleasantness could not be so easily evaded as Registry investigators or my family's bloodhounds.

"Thank you, Brother. Iero grant you like mercy." I licked a stray drop from my lips and let my eyelids sag, hoping the soft-spoken Gildas might forgo the prayers sure to accompany his departure. Like flies about raw fish, prayers seemed to cluster about every monkish activity.

But when his soft whisper came in my ear, it bore no pious sentiment. Holy words, nonetheless. "Mutton broth today."

My laughter disrupted all my feigning. He smiled and vanished through the door as quietly as he'd come. I would have to watch my step with this man.

With the skill of long experience I banished all thought of the future. Perhaps these good monks would solve all my ills—body and soul together.

My head had scarcely touched the pillow again when a clank of the latch and a damp, chilly whoosh of the draft signaled another arrival. A warm body hovered a handsbreadth from my face like a restrained pup awaiting my word to begin licking. This one smelled of rain and mud, onions and innocence . . . and boy.

"Could this be the Archangel Jullian?" I said without opening my eyes. "He of the exquisite hearing and golden tongue, who shall have whatever service he needs of me from this day forward as thanks for preserving my feckless life?"

"Aye, it's Jullian," he said softly. "Are you asleep, then? I shan't stay if you're asleep. But I'm off sanctuary watch and on to kitchen duty as of this day's chapter, so I've more time to see to you. Brother Robierre told me you're healing astonishingly fast and are ready for visitors."

I lifted my heavy eyelids and grinned. "Not asleep. Indeed I'm pleased for cheerful company. As long as you don't make me pay for it by draining my wounds or poking my bruises." Besides, the sooner I knew the ins and outs of Gillarine, the better, whether I chose to stay a season or not.

"I've brought you something to aid your healing. Water from Saint Gillare's holy spring." The boy held out a flask of amber-colored glass as reverently as if it held the saintly woman's tears.

I drew back a little. "Water? Uh . . . I don't . . . not usually . . ." I didn't want to offend the boy, but I'd been leery of that ruinous beverage since my mother's divination when I turned seven. Certainly many a soldier came to grief from it. "So kind. Thank you. But we'd best wait for Brother Bad—Robierre. I'm sure I heard him say my stomach was too weak for water as yet."

He set the flask on the stool, then hiked up his coarse brown tunic and plopped down on the tile floor, leaving his face on a comfortable level with mine. Though the damp, matted hair cut bowl-shaped to his ears could have been any color, the fluff on the boy's full lip and bony chin was red-gold in the lamplight and his skin ruddy. I judged him wholly Ardran. Most Navrons, especially the Moriangi of the riverlands to the north, bore some trace of either the black-haired Aurellian invaders of past centuries—my own ancestors—or the flaxen-haired Hansker who plagued our coast.

"I just wanted— Is there any further service I can offer? Something else I could bring you? A prayer I could offer? Whatever you need." His voice belied his coarsening features and remained clear and boyish, putting him nearer twelve than fourteen to my mind. The ripe stench of less than diligent washing assured me he was entirely human male and no angel in disguise.

I propped my elbow on the bed and supported my head with my fist. "Mmm, I've a wagonload of curiosity. As you may have heard, a penitential pilgrimage led me here, but I was in such a state of sin and remorse that I've no idea what roads I walked or where I ended up."

The battle had begun at Wroling Wood in southwestern Ardra—a damnable, confusing, twisted region of forested gullies more akin to god-cursed Evanore than the fertile hills and vineyards of gentle, golden Ardra. And between my delirium, the impenetrable trees, the wretched weather, and the lack of human habitation along the way, naught had illumined our location since. The desolation was almost enough to make one believe the Harrowers had succeeded in their mad quest to erase all trace of human works from the land. In truth, that our flight had ended near any sanctuary but a bandit's hut, much less by a house so prosperous as to have sheep bones to boil, was enough to make a man a devotee of Serena Fortuna.

Closing my eyes, I offered a quick apology to the divine sister of Sky Lord Kemen for my doubts during those wretched days, promising a libation next time I was blessed with a cup of wine. I thought it prudent to honor all gods and goddesses until someone wiser than me sorted out the contention between Navronne's elder gods and the Karish upstart Iero.

"Gillarine lies eighteen quellae north of Caedmon's Bridge and three quellae south of Elanus, which itself lies one hundred and seventy-four quellae southwest of Palinur. We sit ninety-three quellae east of Wroling." The boy recited his numbers as if they were an alchemist's formula.

I gave his information little credence. Boreas and I might have traveled ninety-three quellae in two days afoot when well rested, with full stomachs and the wrath of the gods scorching our heels. But we'd never come so far after months of poor rations and the soldier's flux, and with my leg threatening to collapse the entire way.

At least it seemed I'd managed to keep us in Ardra. Even ravaged by war and fiendish weather, my birth province was yet the fairest of Navronne's three. Morian was flat and ugly, its sprawling ports and trade cities infested with rats, mosquitoes, woolen mills, and rapacious trade guilds. And our proximity to Evanore, that land of devils' mountains, yet left me queasy. Evanore's duc, Prince Osriel, forbade purebloods entry into his lands. I'd been taught that his border wards would boil a pureblood's brains until they leaked out his ears.

I grimaced and rubbed my shaggy head.

Jullian hunched his thin shoulders and dropped his voice. "I've heard a battle was fought at Wroling a sevenday since, Prince Perryn's army routed by Prince Bayard and the Harrower legions. Gerard, another aspirant who took up the sanctuary watch after me, was told to watch for survivors, though Brother Porter said he'd heard they were all captive or dead, every one."

Disgust at the waste raised my bile. As far as I was concerned, they could give the cursed throne to the Harrower priestess, Sila Diaglou—or to this Ardran child Pretender whom no one sober had ever seen. "Does your abbot favor Prince Perryn, then, to be willing to take in what's left of his men?"

"The abbot holds Gillarine as a neutral field," said the boy. His wide blue eyes shone, declaring his faith that a sainted man could make even such a ridiculous thing be true. "King Eodward built the abbey years and years ago. On holy ground, the story says. He gave the Hierarchs of Ardra dominion over it, but only as long as they fulfill the terms of his grant—to preserve and protect all knowledge and all supplicants—even those who know naught of Iero or his holy writs. He said the angels themselves, sent forth to journey among men, would know of this place, and might find their way here in their need."

I couldn't imagine the warring princes honoring so magnanimous a legend. But it sounded very nice. Far better than any number of places Boreas could have abandoned me.

"Holy ground this might be," I said, "but alas, no one will ever mistake me for an angel. Your wise abbot can tell you." Which left open the question Gildas had brought to the fore. Why would a perceptive holy man admit a stranger to his household so readily? Were his stores so plentiful he could afford to take on any vagabond who happened by? Serena Fortuna had ever been kind, but sensible caution had kept me free.

A blast of wind rattled the horn windows, ruffling the parchment and plants on Robierre's worktable and setting his hanging herb bundles to swaying. The spring auguries taken by Prince Perryn's pureblood diviners predicted the coming winter would be the worst in living memory. Of course, a blind birdwit could predict that did he but bare his skin to the wind these past days. And the Reaper's Moon had not yet shone.

I scooted a little deeper in the bed. The more I considered a house full of kindly fellows given to charity and good cooking, the better it sounded as a winter haven, prayers and bells notwithstanding. If I'd imagined it so easy to join up with a Karish brotherhood, I might have done so years ago. Best keep the path smooth.

"So, Jullian, clearly you are not some villein boy sent here to be a mere kitchen drudge forever . . . but schooled. An aspirant . . . preparing to take vows yourself when you're old enough. Perchance . . . being a scholarly boy . . . of course, you can read?"

He sat up proudly. "Both Navron and Aurellian, though my Aurellian is not so fine. I read it as well as any in the abbey, but to think out the words to write a new text and set them together with proper variants is very hard. Not that my writing hand is ill. Abbot Luviar says I could scribe for the saint at heaven's gate. He's even allowed me to help in the scriptorium. Not to write, of course, not yet, but to clean the pens and brushes, help mix the inks, and even to rule and prick the pages. With so many books to copy, and new ones coming every month, everyone must help. And I try to read them all. The learning is a wonder." The boy's expression shifted as easily as light in an aspen glade.

"Well then, there is one boon you could grant me."

"Anything."

"My illness clouds my eyes, so that reading makes my head ache and all the letters swim together. Yet I must commit this scroll of your Rule to memory before Brother Gildas tests me, else I'll be thrown out of Gillarine ten days hence to languish again among wolves and sinners to the peril of my soul. So if you could aid me . . ."

One might have thought I had asked Jullian to polish my heavenly crown. He carefully untied the ribbon that bound the scroll and proceeded to recount the fifteen laws of Saint Ophir's Rule. Among the expected admonitions to abjure fornication, gambling, excessive drink, and the lures of worldly wealth, to forgo the practices and use of magic and other earthbound power, to pray the holy Hours and give absolute obedience to the commands of prior, abbot, and hierarch, lay the small requirements that declared a novice must be a free man of sound body and legitimate birth and be schooled so far as to read and do simple sums.

"Am I reading too fast, sir?"

"No, no," I said, swallowing a curse. "I'm just fixing the holy words in my head."

Of necessity, my memory had developed exceedingly keen. The balance of the world had never seemed fair to me—that reading was placed so high in the scheme of virtue while the skill to remember what others read or to make some use of it languished far below.

When he had finished the scroll, he picked up the psalter. "I could read you a psalm, to soothe your tormented humors."

"Truly my head is so weighted down with words, it will not lift from my pillow. My tormented humors must get along as best they can."

He thumbed through the book, paused for a moment, then slapped it down on the stool and snatched his hand away as if it had scorched his fingers. "This is Horach's book."

His anxiety surprised me. Karish held no squeamish notions about unquiet ghosts. "I've heard the fellow has no further need of it. You don't think his spirit minds me using it?"

"It's just . . . whenever I fetch water from the font, I can't help but see . . ." He averted his face.

"See what?" I dragged his chin around again. "Come on, lad. Get it out. It's not healthy to bottle up a story that turns your face the color of sour milk. And you've set up a keening curiosity that needs relieving, else my humors will be more tormented yet."

"He was *murdered*," said the boy in a solemn whisper. "Not a twelveday since, I found him in Saint Gillare's shrine . . . in the font. Someone slashed his skin to threads and left him bound in the water until he bled out every drop in his veins. Brother Robierre said they had pricked his throat so he couldn't scream."

Spiders' feet tickled my spine, and I felt an uncommon urge to ward my soul against Magrog's incursions. I touched the book gingerly—not that I could have said what I was expecting. "Who did such a thing? Not a monk . . . surely!"

"Certainly not!" the boy sputtered indignantly. "Father Abbot questioned every one of us under pain of hell's fire. He even sent to Pontia, and the magistrate brought his pureblood investigator. After three days here, examining us and the abbey grounds and questioning every villager within ten quellae, the sorcerer could say only that a nonbeliever had walked the cloisters. The magistrate said the killer must have borne some tormented grievance against Karish folk and sneaked into the abbey in the night to act it out."

"Such a killing seems more than random grievance. Likely this Horach had made some enemy in his life—before taking vows, of course."

Jullian shook his head vigorously. "Brother Horach was but sixteen, newly vowed, and had lived here since he was five—an aspirant like Gerard and me. Gerard hasn't slept properly since, and he'll not go into the shrine except in company." The boy sat up proudly and straightened the water flask he'd brought me, as if to demonstrate he'd conquered such fears himself.

I nodded in sympathy, but could not shake my disturbance. Common disputes among those who lived in close quarters rarely caused such savagery. And a boy of sixteen . . . Ugly.

To make sure murder was no disease festering in these halls—like mold or pox that clings to old stone—I asked the boy to tell me more of the abbey and its works, and he was soon chattering cheerfully about the scriptorium and library, sheep and barley, and thirty-three holy monks and twenty lay brothers who were all that were left to occupy an abbey built for five times that number.

Before very long Brother Robierre blustered through the infirmary door with a mournful monk named Brother Cadeus, who needed a decoction of rose bark to bathe his filmy eyes. Cadeus, as it happened, was the abbey porter, who sat at the gatehouse in the daylight hours, dispensing alms and regulating entry to the inner and outer courts of the abbey. While Cadeus shared news brought by a starving mason in search of work—of a Harrower riot that left half the city of Montesard in ashes and of a new outbreak of murrain in a sheepfold near Avenus—piebald Brother Anselm arrived with a vat of mutton broth. They propped me up on pillows so I could feed myself.

"This world's in a proper hellish season," I said when Cadeus finished his news. I regaled them with tales I'd heard the previous winter—of Ardrans frozen in their beds, of ice rivers consuming Evanori villages in a day, of Moriangi chopping frozen fish from the rivers and eating them raw as the wood was too cold to burn. ". . . and then in spring I dragged myself half starved down to the Cumbran vale, hoping to hire on for planting, only to wonder at the evil-smelling cloud hung down in the vale. Turns out the crofters had found their seed stock rotted in the bins, and their lord had burned every one of their women as Magrog's whores . . . begging your forgiveness, good brothers, for the unseemly language."

While Jullian drank in every word, eyes as wide as if my reports were hero tales of Grossartius the Revenant, Brother Robierre repeatedly made the sign of Iero's sunburst on forehead and breast as if the Adversary himself sat on my shoulder. Brother Cadeus nodded as if he had expected nothing else. "The roads are fraught with sorrow. Iero punishes humankind's sinful ways."

"Of course, sorrowful roads can lead to interesting places," I said, swallowing another savory bite. "When the late blizzard hit Cumbra, a shepherd took me in. The snow buried his hut until only a spelled candle he'd got from a witch gave us light. We ate naught but milk and cheese for seven days and taught his favorite goat to walk on her hind legs and play ball games with us. And he taught me twelve new stanzas of 'Caedmon's Lay' . . ."

My tales were not even the worst I'd seen or heard. For eight or ten years now, self-named prophets had roved the length and breadth of Navronne crying out that our spate of cold stormy summers and savage winters foreshadowed the end of the world. Magistrates flogged the doomsayers, which succeeded only in making more who spent their days in a frenzy trying to placate the gods. I'd seen a man walking the length of the kingdom naked. I'd seen a cadre of women throwing burnt sheep in the sea. Villeins dangled so many charms and amulets from their wives and children, the whole countryside jingled like a tinker's wagon, and painted their lintels or their foreheads with mule droppings to stave off ill luck.

A man could say what he would of such activities—and I had scoffed at the general foolishness as much as any—but two years had gone since I'd tasted wine from Ardran grapes, though war had never touched the precious vineyards. The vines had now frozen two winters in a row, and folks said they would never recover. Perhaps the bowl of the sky had slipped askew as Sinduri astrologers claimed.

One thing was certain. With grain fields burnt by soldiers or afflicted with smut from the cold damp, with plants unable to thrive in the changing weather, and herds dead or sickly, famine would surely strike again before the new year. And I'd been perilously close to starving three winters running—which unhappy counterpoint with the delectable soup reminded me that I could likely tolerate a few monkish restrictions.

I'd certainly no wealth or earthbound power to give up. Gambling held no allure but for the coin it could provide. And so long a time had passed since I'd experienced the pleasures of excessive drink or fornication that they were easy to bargain away when tucked in a warm bed with a full stomach. Magic was another matter.

I lopped off that consideration faster than a farm wife could wring a chicken's neck. Did I allow thoughts of my worst troubles to take hold, my life would shrink to a hard black knot exactly the shape of a nivat seed.

Once Cadeus had gone, Brother Badger held his hands under his black scapular and peered into my rapidly emptying bowl. "When you've sopped up the remainder of your supper—not long it would appear—it will be time to take a walk. A man with such an appetite as yours must, of necessity, be getting stronger."

"But it's only been—"

"—four days since I took out the fiendish bit of iron. I know. But you've wallowed in your blankets long enough. Damaged sinews need using or they'll knot or wither. You'll thank me."

The infirmarian snatched away my empty bowl and dropped a short brown tunic on my lap. He watched as I eased it over my head and bandaged shoulder and relinquished my lovely blankets. The air felt dreadfully cold on my bare legs. Indeed, as he eased me to my feet, my excessive height left the skimpy tunic excessively short, exposing half my rump and privy parts to Brother Anselm's open window. "You are the Adversary's lackey, Robierre," I mumbled, shivering.

Brother Robierre was a mere half head shorter than I, and built with the sturdy bulk of a smith. Even so he called on Brother Anselm to help propel me up and down the long infirmary. I clutched at their shoulders, scarcely touched my right foot to the ground, and moaned and gasped, only muting my groans when young Jullian looked ready to pound the infirmarian for his cruelty.

"To feel the wound is only to be expected," said the good brother, inspecting my bandages when he at last allowed me to sit again. "See? No fresh blood or drainage." Adding insult to insult, he then insisted I drain Jullian's flask of water from the abbey's spring, swearing that the holy font had been resanctified since Brother Horach's gruesome death.

"You're a proper villain, Brother," I said, wincing as I rolled over and let them prop my leg up again. "I'm not thanking you as yet. This activity has surely stirred up the poisons in my blood. And this drink fit only for dogs and horses, tainted by ill-let blood, will compound them. I could die from it."

"You'll not die today, Valen." Chuckling, Brother Badger tucked me in more gently than my mother had ever done. This was indeed a fine and friendly place.

Chapter 4

"I need to be gone now," said Jullian, scrambling to his feet not long after the bells for the Hour of Compline—night prayers—fell silent. "I've duties."

The door banged behind him. He had been regaling me with descriptions of the various monks, while the infirmarian and his assistant hied off to pray again. Though guileless as a newborn calf, the boy had a wit about him. I felt as if I knew the denizens of Gillarine already.

Left alone, I wormed my way down into the bedclothes, more tired than I ought to be from another day of sleeping and eating and taking Robierre's enforced exercise. Before I could settle, a draft from the door set the rushlights wickering. Another visitor. Boots, this time, curiously enough. Quiet, measured steps.

"Yes, I'm awake," I said over my shoulder, wishing I could lie facing the doorway at least. "And pleased for visitors." The infirmary was beginning to feel more like a public marketplace than a house of healing.

"Good. I've no wish to overtax you."

The quiet boots and low, pleasant voice belonged to a gaunt man soberly dressed in secular garb and a round-brimmed felt hat. As he came round the bed, he grabbed one of Robierre's stools. Under his other arm, he carried my book of maps.

My welcome froze on my lips, and I set myself ready to muster a host of ailments if the conversation grew dangerous. Jullian's talk of magistrates and pureblood investigators still had me twitching.

"My name is Gram Scriptor," he said, inclining his back and extending his open palm in greeting as southerners do. "My employer is visiting Gillarine and got wind of this magnificent volume. He's an educated man of wide-ranging interests and bids me learn what I can of it while we bide here that I might record the information in his journals. Abbot Luviar graciously permitted us to view the book and suggested I consult you with my questions, if you felt up to it." *Scriptor* . . . a secretary, then, of unnotable family.

"I don't know that I could tell you aught you'd not read from the book itself," I said as he settled himself on the stool.

He was something near my own age, and not a bad-looking fellow, save for an unhealthy gray hue to his complexion. His close-trimmed black hair, beardless chin, and conservative attire—ash-gray cape over an unadorned knee-length tunic of dark gray—accentuated the hollows in his cheeks. His eyes sat deep, dark, I thought, though that could just be shadows from his hat.

"If nothing comes of my questions, so be it." A grave, modest smile softened his severe appearance. "At the least I can report to my master that I did as he asked, which is often quite enough to satisfy him once the . . . mmm . . . storm of displeasure . . . is past. Just tell me if I press too much or if you tire."

I had to be careful. To refuse this fellow might offend the abbot. And I'd not wish the abbot—or this man, whoever he was—to conclude I'd stolen the book after all. Likely I knew enough to satisfy a besieged secretary. "Ask what you will. I'll do my best."

"I'm ever grateful." He scooted his stool closer to the bed, so we could view the book together. He leafed through several pages. "Of course I've seen common maps—a few scratched lines and place names and perhaps a landmark or two. But I've no experience of such fine maps—a sorcerer's maps—and so great a variety of them. The written explanations in the book itself are confusing. I thought perhaps that the lord who'd given it to you might have explained what kinds of maps these are and how their magic works."

Gram offered me the book, and I turned a few pages, opening to a leaf displaying four small maps of different kinds. I stared at the page—its lines and symbols evoking far too much of memory. On his random appearances at our house, my grandfather had forced me to sit with him and look at his book, whispering in my ear of its importance, of its perfection, of its cleverness and magic, and how I must learn to use it. His breath had smelled of cloves, onions, and black ale, his body of unwashed skin and horses despite his fine clothes. Disgust rippled through me alongside the recollection.

Those sessions had lasted only as long as it took me to spit on his shirt and wriggle out of his grasp. But his lessons had always begun with this page.

"My— Mardane Lavorile told me that every variety of map is represented in this book," I began. "Most, like this one, are fichés." I pointed to the rigorous little rendering of roads, mountains, and rivers—very like the great maps stretched and mounted on the walls of my father's library. "It is accurate in heading, scale, and proportion, so that a lesser distance on the map implies a lesser distance in truth. And the details are as precise as the cartographer can make them . . ."

The secretary listened intently, as I explained about keys and compass roses, and interpreted some of the symbols—for mountains, water features, towns and cities, shrines and temples, and the like. He asked me to clarify a few points, but otherwise did not interrupt.

"This map, on the other hand"—I indicated a fanciful colored drawing of a town with buildings and bridges and roads all mismatched in size—"is of the type known as a grousherre. The streets and structures are drawn with proper connections and relative positions, so that you can know which road leads to which, or which house stands beside which bridge. But the size and proportion of each object is determined by its importance not accurate measure."

"That seems a strange way to make a map." Gram pored over the drawing for a moment, his face drawn up in a puzzle. "Makes me think the maker was an odd sort of fellow."

I grinned. "Exactly my own thought. I've never seen the purpose of them, save for making a page where the cartographer could show off and splash around all his colors of ink."

"So what about these other two? This one looks to be a coastline, but I don't understand the markings." The little map detailed the fanlike outlets of one of Morian's great rivers and the creneled inlets and channels on either side of it. Tiny numbers littered the expanse of land and sea.

"That's a portolan," I said. "A navigation map. The marks are winds and tides and notations for sailors' instruments. I've no skill with ships to be able to tell you more than that. And this last is an example of a mappa mundi—a rendering of the wider world as if viewed from Iero's heaven. You can always tell them by their oval shape." My grandfather had included three mappa mundi that spanned two pages each. "The one in the very back of the book shows the trade routes to Aurellia and to Pyrrha, the land of volcanoes."

"Now, what of the magic? I've heard tales of Janus de Cartamandua's maps . . ."

"Well . . ." I bit my lower lip, a reminder I often used to watch my mouth. This visitor had set me too much at ease. "I know little of that. I used only a few of the maps, as the mardane needed."

Supposedly, unlike those created by my father or my brother, Max, or any other cartographer in Navronne, my grandfather's maps showed the earth's most secret and holy places—magical pools, sacred groves, the earthly dwellings of spirits and angels, places that no traveler would ever "happen" upon. Places that could be found only by using these maps. So I had been told.

"But the abbot says you used the guide spells that unlock their power. I'm sorry to press. My master is"—he cleared his throat and ducked his head, his gray skin taking on a rosy cast—"excitable. So I beg your indulgence. Whatever you can tell me would be valuable. I'm afraid he's going to ask me to copy one of these before we leave the abbey."

Though I didn't begrudge him the knowledge, I sincerely wished the fellow would stop asking questions. Yet he was gently spoken and seemed a mournful sort. And I knew well of *excitable* masters who asked the impossible.

"You see this oval banner on the larger map," I said. "It's called a cartouche. Look carefully and you'll find the words of the guide spell scribed there, or if the map is too small to have a cartouche, you'll find it buried in the border decorations. But copying won't give you any use of it. The mardane told me that the cartographer's magic is in the *rendering*, not just the words and symbols."

"Ah." He sat up straight and sighed. "Well, that's good news for me, if my lord will believe it. So how would you *invoke* the spell?"

"Speak the words of the spell while tracing your finger along your desired route. With the aid of the spell and a bit of common wisdom, your mind and senses will tell you when you stray from the path. It's useful enough." So I had been told. Endlessly.

"And that's all?"

I sagged back onto my pillows. "If a fellow like me can do it, I've no doubt anyone can."

Gram smiled again as he closed the book and stood to go. "I think you speak yourself an injury, sir. Your explanations were very clear, and you've surely a good head for maps and scouting. Someday perhaps I can return this favor."

I appreciated his effort to be kind. Old resentments about family and books and written words could not but taint my answers. He had no way to know that maps were of no use to me. "Your employer . . . he would like to own such a book as this?"

"In truth, not. He gives all his books to Gillarine." Gram cocked his head to one side, curiosity blossomed like a daylily at dawn. "But I thought you were taking vows. Don't initiates give—?"

"Yes, yes, I am," I said, gathering my wits. "But I wasn't sure what to do with the book . . . or whether the abbot would actually *want* such a valuable one when the price of it could do so much in the way of almsgiving."

Gram nodded and held out his palm again. "Abbot Luviar is very wise. He'll guide you rightly. Heal well, friend, and thank you."

Once he'd gone, I longed for some other visitor to break the evening's quiet. Not right that such a gentlemanly fellow should lance old boils and leave me to suffer the stink.

No one came.

Rain entirely inappropriate to Ardra's driest season drummed on the roof all night, slowing only when the blackness beyond the horned window yielded to gray. I slept fitfully, seeing far too much of both night and dawn. Daylight brought Brother Gildas.

Brother Robierre waved a wooden mallet he used for crushing seeds and pods, as he talked over my head with the dark-browed Gildas. "Ignore his complaining. Any man who can talk and eat as he does is fit enough to take wherever you will for an hour. Keep him moving, and send for me only if he collapses altogether."

"Am I to have no say in this?" I said, spitting out the detritus of hulls and stems that showered from his implement. "My leg—"

"You have applied to take vows, including strict obedience bound by punishments both in this life and the next. If you insist on 'having your say,' perhaps you'd best reconsider your future." Brother Gildas held up a white wool shirt he'd pulled from a black and white bundle in my lap.

"He's not broken his fast as yet this morning," said the infirmarian. He retreated to his worktable, where he dumped a bag of dried seedpods into a large wooden bowl and attacked them with his mallet as if they were a nest of Iero's detractors. "Never saw a man relish our victuals as he does. Point him toward the kitchen, and he'll keep apace."

Shivering in the cold damp, I thrust my head and bare arms into the thick shirt. "There's more folk eating bark soup than mutton broth of late, Brothers," I mumbled. "Must I go barefoot?"

"Wear your own boots today. You'll receive your cowl and sandals on the day you take your novice vows, which we do sincerely hope will be your choice." Brother Gildas smiled as if to soften the sting of his earlier rebuke, while I fumbled with clean white woolen trews and black knee-length hose. When my tight shoulder bandage hampered me, he knelt by the bed like a trained manservant, smoothly tugging the stiff, heavy boots onto my big feet, tucking in the hose, and tightening the laces up my legs.

"Up now," he said, rising and offering me his hand. "Don your gown. Then we'll go walking to stretch your limbs, I'll ask you a few questions for Father Abbot, and we'll find sustenance before you wither."

Ah, the questioning. No one had come to the infirmary on the previous day to test my knowledge of Saint Ophir's Rule. Jullian, who had taken it upon himself to visit me at least three times a day, had reported that Brother Sebastian had not yet returned from Pontia, and Brother Gildas had been closeted with the abbot and "visiting abbey benefactors" all day "except when they went to see the progress on the lighthouse." The presence of a lighthouse here, at least six hundred quellae from Navronne's northern seacoast, struck me as an oddity, even allowing for my usual morning dullness.

The prospect of interrogation damped my already soggy spirits. Awkwardly I wrestled the common black wool gown over my head, not at all sure I could bring myself to take vows here—even for a season. Rules and restrictions and righteous preaching curdled my stomach like vinegar in milk. If I could find a buyer for the book of maps, then perhaps I could find a less restrictive haven, perhaps a lornly widow who needed pleasuring.

The heavy garment enveloped me from neck to ankles, an unlikely happenstance as I had never failed to be the tallest man in any gathering since I had reached my full height at nineteen. But even more extraordinary was the sense of safety that enfolded me with the thick black wool, the same as that worn by every other monk throughout Navronne. Sweet, blessed anonymity.

Most ordinaries viewed pureblood life as god blessed and couldn't imagine why any of us would choose to forgo it. They didn't understand about contracts and protocols, submission rules and breeding laws, all the things that had made me feel as if someone had bound me head to toe with silken cord and locked me blind and deaf in a coffin.

Under the oversight of the Pureblood Registry, pureblood families contracted out their magical services for a great deal of money. As Navronne's nobles, magistrates, and clergy profited handsomely from the magic of our undiluted Aurellian blood, these parties had devised an inviolable compact a century ago, requiring every knight, magistrate, reeve, and sheriff to enforce the Registry's rules. Not even a Karish abbot would dare disobey the fugitive laws. Harboring a common fugitive—a thief or a deserter—past his fourteen days of sanctuary would cost Abbot Luviar disgrace and ten years' income—everything his abbey collected or produced—meaning ten years' groveling to the local magistrates to return enough to allow the brothers to eat. But if the abbot was judged to have knowingly hidden a pureblood renegade—a *recondeur*—those magistrates would burn his abbey and his fields, and then they would hang him.

So they just couldn't know. A *recondeur* with any sense learned quickly to keep his head down, his lies consistent, his past private, and his appearance unremarkable. I smoothed my warm, unremarkable wool layers and felt a grin split my face.

After fumbling briefly in the folds of his own gown, Brother Gildas pressed an alder walking stick into my hand. "A gift from Brother Horatio, our carpenter. Welcome to our brotherhood."

He slipped his shoulder under my right arm, and we stepped through the infirmary door into a chill, watery daylight. The infirmary sat off by itself, separated from the abbey proper by a patch of wet grass and a soggy herb garden. Far across the sea of gray slate roofs and the warm yellow stone of sturdy walls, the vaults of the abbey church soared heavenward.

"We'll visit the cloister garth first," said Gildas, pointing toward the grander structures beyond the infirmary garden. "The abbey's heart."

A flagstone path led us across a rock-lined channel that funneled water under the infirmary and past a squat wooden structure with two massive stone chimneys. Its jumbled wood stacks and the heaven-blessed scent of hot bread proclaimed it a bakehouse.

The place seemed inordinately quiet. Water dripped from roofs and gutters. A fat, cold splatter on my head made me even more grateful for my wool layers. In his unending quest for cleanliness, Brother Anselm had bade me shave my face and trim my tangled hair the previous day.

Once we passed the bakehouse, the infirmary no longer blocked our view to the south. I shook loose of Gildas's arm for a moment and stopped to savor the spectacle. Mists and smokes and occasional pools of pale sunlight drifted over the green, steep-sided valley and the river, a flat band of silver that looped around the abbey precincts. Beyond the sheen of the river, a field of barley rippled gently in the soft rain, as healthy a crop as I'd seen in five years. My throat tightened at the beauty of it, and my eyes filled with more than raindrops, which left me feeling a proper weakling fool. Since I'd left the nursery, I'd never wept but when I was drunk.

"I'm assuming you've seen grain fields, tanneries, mills, and sheep, all those things we'd find in the outer courts and south of the river—the River Kay, this is. If Father Abbot judges your calling that of a lay brother—suitable for manual labor, rather than the more challenging studies of a choir monk—you'll live out your days in those surrounds."

Ranks and privileges—even in a brotherhood. I shouldn't have been surprised. Gildas offered me his shoulder again, but I shook my head and hobbled along beside him.

As we rounded the corner of the garden, the monk walked faster as if to keep up with his thoughts. "The true peace of the monastic life is found in prayer and contemplation, study and scholarship. We don't allow speech in the cloisters, library, or scriptorium, but sign to each other for necessary communication."

"Peace will be welcome," I said, working to keep up with his brisk pace. "There's little enough to be had in this world, and talking never seems to improve matters. Though truly, telling stories of an evening or singing chorus to a bard are fine pleasures . . . holy gifts . . . as well. I'll wager you brothers come from everywhere and have much to share in that way—after all your studying and contemplating, of course." Surely they talked of something besides gods and holy writs. Surely they talked. All this broody silence seemed unnatural.

"Within the framework of our discipline, certainly we converse—some of us more, some less. Brother Infirmarian says you've traveled all over Navronne and are overflowing with curious tales. I'd like to hear of your experiences."

"No denying I've had restless feet . . ." My mind sorted through my spotted history like a washwoman picking through soiled and ragged linen. Sadly, I found little fit for display. Gildas wouldn't be looking for adventures and oddments like those Jullian teased out of me on his daily visits. "I followed King Eodward all the way to the Caurean shores. After he died, I hired out on the docks in Trimori for a while, but the Caurean storms frosted my bones worse than Ardran winter. I think the Adversary's domain is surely ice, Brother Gildas. Not fire at all. Is that false doctrine? The holy writs say the wicked will burn, and I've found that cold burns worse than fire."

"I've not heard that point argued," he said. Though he knit his solid brow, his face was not so sober. "Perhaps Brother Sebastian will pursue the question in your studies. Go on. Tell me more."

"Well, I moved on to Savil and apprenticed to a tanner—honest work, but the stink is poison to a tender stomach such as mine . . ."

At the far end of the walk a plain rectangular building stretched off to our left. On the littered muddy ground behind it, three lay brothers, their gray scapulars tucked up in their belts, wrestled the trunk of a sturdy oak from a donkey dray. Another of the brethren was shifting a pile of new-split logs to the wood stores stacked neatly in the building's undercroft.

"The lay brothers' reach," Brother Gildas said, nodding to the busy fellows when I paused in my babbling. "Their sleeping quarters and refectory, and the food, oil, wool, and wood stores for the abbey. So did you stay in Morian?"

I moved on carefully. "Nay. After the winter in Avenus, cutting stone in the quarries, I heard the call to labor on the hierarch's new cathedral in Palinur. A fine thing to build for Iero's own house . . ."

. . . and excellent pay on a sacred project, intended to proclaim Iero and his Karish church as triumphant over the elder gods and their Sinduri council. I had worked in Palinur only one season, though. The labor had been grueling, the hours long, and the punishments for any lapse in workmanship severe. And indeed, the proximity to my family and the attendant risks of being identified had made the royal city unpalatable. Once I'd padded my purse enough to last a season more, I was off to try something new.

It was not fear of discovery made me move so often. *Recondeurs* were rare, and every one of them was recaptured within half a year, hauled up for public flogging or humiliation, and then vanished from sight and speech, save for horrified whisperings among pureblood families about "close confinement" and "unrestricted" contracts. Every sorry soul of them failed in rebellion because the fool could not forgo using the bent to soften the hardships of ordinary life: hunger, cold, hard work, uncertainty. The Registry would never search the places I lived, because they'd never imagine a pureblood forsaking his duties or his comforts for a life where he'd not know when he'd eat next. I had refused to learn much of spellworking as a child—as I had refused to learn much of anything they tried to pound into my head—so I'd little to give up.

As it was, I'd just never found any occupation worth the bother of staying in one place. Restless feet, just as I'd told Gildas. Incurably restless feet, in fact. A disease.

The path turned sharply back toward the river. We left it behind and angled right into a brick alley.

"Gillarine seems well constructed," I said, seizing an excuse to divert the conversation from myself. "What building is this to have windows so many and so fine?"

"The monks' refectory," said Brother Gildas. "You'll be happy to hear that novices get meat three times a week and half again the portions of the rest of us. We use all our wiles to lure the worldly into harmony with the god."

As I picked my way across the uneven bricks of the pooled and puddled alley, I caught a merry glint under his sober brow. Cheerful humors can redeem even excessive piety. I liked him.

"Gillarine must truly lie on holy ground to produce such bounty," I said. "The patroness of travelers led me here, no doubt of it."

"We've exceptional soil and water here. The font in Saint Gillare's shrine is said to be rooted in a holy spring." All the monks and friars I'd ever met seemed to wear a secret pleasure beneath their holiness, like gamers who carry skewed dice up their sleeves. Gildas was no different.

The brick passage squeezed past a coal store and kitchen building and then widened as we approached a colonnaded walkway that extended right and left and all the way around the broad green garth beyond it. The walkway's tiles had been laid in intricate coiled patterns like those on Aurellian urns and doorposts, with the trilliot, the three-petaled lily of Navronne, tucked into its loops here and there, alongside the golden sunbursts reminding us of the One God's glory.

Gildas laid a finger on his lips. I had not actually noticed the bustle of kitchen and bakehouse, the whacks and grunts of the wood choppers, or the complaints of distant sheep as we walked from the infirmary . . . not until we stepped into the cloisters of Gillarine and all such common sounds dropped away. The place was so quiet, I could almost hear my own blood flowing.

We crossed the cloister walk and paused at the edge of a vast square of healthy green. The garth was bounded on four sides by the slender columns and graceful roof arches of the cloister walks, and dominated by the church's vaulted roof and slender towers, directly across from us. To our left loomed the unadorned bulk of the lay brothers' reach. On our right, a round-domed structure with lancet windows of colored glass and a number of other fine buildings with many windows crowded the cloister walk. And in the center of the garth stood a small shrine, its interlocked arcs of delicate stonework looking very like a large birdcage.

Few monks were abroad. One sat reading on a narrow bench enclosed on three sides, one of forty or fifty such carrels tucked under the cloister by the church. Another hooded brother halted and bowed before passing into the shrine beneath a stone lintel supported by two lithe stone angels who had somewhere lost their wings. He quickly reappeared, a copper ewer in his hand.

Gildas pointed toward the shrine and stepped onto the cobbled path that led across the grass. I dutifully followed . . .

Darkness engulfed me. I staggered sideways, limbs quivering, joints turned to jelly. Weak . . . sick . . . gasping . . . starved for air and sound, as well as light. *Gods of mercy, what have I done that I should be struck blind?* Guilt and horror, the surety of death and vengeance wrung my neck like a hangman's noose, while remnants of old sins chased each other through my conscience like brightly colored birds, only to be swallowed in the blackness.

And then, as quickly as the night had fallen, all was consumed by light, as if the unsullied sun of summers past shot its beams straight into my eye sockets. As an avenging angel come down from heaven, the light swept away terror and in its place left a bright and sharp-edged tenderness that wrenched my heart. I cried out and stumbled backward.

A sharp crack on my skull brought the world—the green garth, the shrine, the cloister walk, the dull morning light—into focus again. I gulped air into my starved lungs. A cherubic rump protruded from the low arch where I had whacked my head. I spat on my middle finger, slapped the little aingerou, and prayed its friendly spirit to protect me from collapsing or exploding. No battle wound or shock had ever afflicted me so precipitously.

Brother Gildas's gaze flicked from my face, to the serene enclosure, to my hand that now gripped the carved sprite as if seeking only its structural support. I half expected his lip to curl and his mellow voice to denounce me immediately as a heathen blasphemer. But he merely gripped my waist securely and assisted me back into the alley, looking a bit puzzled.

"Perhaps we've overdone," he said when we were outside the cloister bounds again. "And you with an unbroken fast. Can I help?"

The world was so bright. So sharp. I pressed my head to the cool stone of the refectory wall and drew a ragged breath. "A drink of something . . . ale . . . or wine . . . please."

Anything to dull the glare that yet vibrated behind my eyes like a fresh knife wound, to soothe the ache that throbbed in my chest as if I had lost my last friend or heard the last song ever to be sung.

Gildas pried me from the wall and assisted me down the alley, through a wooden gate and a muddy herb garden, and into the steams and smokes of the abbey's kitchen. Two lay brothers, half obscured behind hanging baskets and vermin safes, stood at two long tables, trimming or chopping vegetables—turnips, garlic, carrots, and leeks—while a wizened, stoop-shouldered monk worked alongside them, grinding herbs with mortar and pestle. A slight figure in a layman's hooded cloak of brick red deposited a flat, covered basket on one of the tables and retreated toward a far door.

"Thank you, Squire Corin," called a ruddy-faced, leather-pated monk who stirred an iron vat that hung over the great central hearth. "We'll hope poor Gram finds more appetite at supper. Brother Cellarer will send better wine for your master."

"Jerome!" my companion called across the stone-floored vastness.

"What can I do for you, Brother Gildas?" said the ruddy-faced monk as he emptied a wooden bowl of chopped cabbage into his pot. With the efficiency of long practice, he set the cavernous bowl aside, snatched a long-handled spoon from a rack on the soot-blackened wall, and poked at the cabbage that sizzled and spattered in his pot.

"Have you a bit of something mild and sustaining for our newest aspirant?" said Gildas, steadying me as I sank onto a pine bench beside the door. "I fear I've overtaxed him on his first excursion from the infirmary."

Brother Jerome spun around, his wooden spoon raised as if it were a hierarch's crozier, ready to assert his holy authority in this domain. "The supplicant who brought the Cartamandua maps?"

The whole world seemed to stop and stare just then, even the departing layman, who paused in the half-open doorway across the room and lifted his red hood slightly as if to see me better.

"Aye, the same. Still recovering from his injuries and unfed this day. My misjudgment." Gildas returned his sober scrutiny to me. "And I beg forgiveness for that," he said quietly. "Unworthy of me to assume . . . uh . . . that your strength was greater than you showed."

I waved off his concern. My leg and back had contributed naught to my weakness that I could judge. Yet if I told Gildas what I had experienced, surely nothing good would come of it. The monks would call it a sign of Iero's displeasure, pile on penances or rituals to reform me, and likely send me away. If some god or spirit or magical being *did* live within that garth, it must—

The likely truth stung my skull like a pebble from a sling. The shrine . . . the font . . . the murdered Brother Horach! Some people said that spirits loosed in savage torment would linger in the place of death, become revenants. Had I somehow invoked his wrath . . . or his benevolence? The contrary nature of the encounter left it open to myriad interpretations.

The world moved on again. The monks were back to chopping and grinding. The beardless servant vanished through the door. Forgoing fruitless speculation, I breathed deep, pleased to smell the garlic and to feel the steam that hissed from the wilted cabbage as Brother Jerome tossed aside his spoon and emptied a crock of liquid into his pot.

Brother Gildas filled a wooden cup from a nearby barrel. I drained it before his hand had moved away. Lovely ale, new made, not old. "Iero's grace," I said, and he brought me another.

"I've a barley loaf and syfling cheese will suit a fragile constitution," said Brother Jerome, once he had tamed his soup. Thick gray hair fringed his leathery tonsure. He rummaged briskly in the flat basket and extracted a wrapped bundle and a small crock. "Sent back from the guesthouse untouched. Father Prior says Lord Stearc's secretary Gram is a sickly sort and I thought to bolster him, but all the fellow took this morning was Robierre's strengthening tea."

Ah, Gram—the mournful fellow who'd consulted me about the maps. He'd had an unhealthy cast to his skin. A lord's secretary.

The loaf was chewy where it should be and tender everywhere else, and the soft cheese tasted of almonds. Unflinching, I ate every morsel of both and buried my disturbance in the homely comforts of a well-run kitchen. Jerome and his minions, as with all who worked in kitchens and brewhouses, wielded power I understood.

Brother Gildas and I bade the kitchen staff farewell and trudged slowly past the lay brother's reach in a light rain. I felt almost myself again. Likely Brother Gildas's estimate of my collapse had been right, naught but hunger and healing. I'd had little experience of common sickness.

"Gillarine seems a vastly holy place," I said. Healthy grain, plump vegetables, untainted sheep, spirits in its garth . . . I doubted any house in Navronne could boast such bounty.

"Many in our brotherhood have found it so. I have discovered my own destiny here—against every expectation of my life."

His words left an offer hanging in the air, something more generous than tavern friendships. More honest. I was gratified, and a bit astonished, at such trust. But if I probed deeper, he would rightly expect to do the same. And that could not happen. Of all the protections I had built over the years, the surest was to keep my secrets close.

Fumbling about for a new topic, I hobbled across a cart track that led from the lay brothers' reach southward along the Kay. The view of the wide, shallow river and the mist-shrouded valley, bound by forested ridges and the high mountains far to the south, recalled Jullian's odd tidbit. "Tell me, Brother, why would anyone be building a lighthouse so far from the sea?"

Even the broad River Yaronal that separated the kingdom from the brutish herdsmen to the east could be no nearer than two hundred fifty quellae, and likely unnavigable at that nearest point. Indeed, I wasn't certain people *built* lighthouses on rivers, much less in green vales like these.

My inquiry, posed in all innocence, halted Brother Gildas in midstride. "Who spoke to you of a lighthouse?"

One never reveals one's sources when queried with such severity. "Mmm . . . I don't recall. So many people come in and out of the infirmary."

After a moment, he smiled and nudged me onward. "Well, of course, you haven't yet seen the church windows on a day when the sun shines, else you'd grasp the reference. Come now, tell me more of Palinur."

A nice recovery, but I didn't believe him in the slightest.

As we crested a slight rise between the cart track and the infirmary garth, a cloaked horseman barreled up the track through the increasing drizzle, passing just behind us. He vanished in the cluster of buildings behind the lay brothers' reach.

Brother Gildas halted again, glancing after the rider and then to the infirmary, squatting peacefully with its back to the river. "Can you make it the rest of the way on your own, Valen? The hour is Sext, and I've duties before prayers."

"Certainly. The air has done me good. I was beginning to feel like sheep in a pen, shut up in that infirmary."

With an admonition to inform Brother Badger of my weakness at the cloister garth, Gildas hurried off, not in the straightest path to the church, but in the same direction as the rider, soon lost to sight as well. A departure as enigmatic as his excuse. No bells had rung for the holy Hour. This place seemed to nurture mysteries: lighthouses, savage murders, an intelligent abbot who welcomed vagabonds like me, and a spirit in the cloister garth who did not.

Monastery life moved slowly, so I understood. Though abbots might be required to heed the winds of politics, their flocks of holy brothers sat outside of the stream of time and events, wrapped up in scholarship that spanned centuries and prayer and contemplation that spanned the boundaries of earth and heaven. So why, of a sudden, did I feel as if I were being rushed down a dark alley by a gang of smiling jacklegs who would pick my pockets and plant a shiv in my spleen before dawn? I hobbled quickly toward the infirmary.

Chapter 5

Vesper bells clanged and hammered. The monks were gone to prayers again, the lingering draft from their departure my only company in the quiet infirmary. Robierre had left me a brimming posset, dosed with extra honey in apology for sending me out walking too strenuously.

In truth my leg felt better recovered from the day's adventure than my spirit. I could not shake my thoughts free of the murdered monk. Had this Horach truly made himself known to me? Surely of all residents of this abbey, I knew the least that might ease a tormented soul. But a man left himself open to mortal peril did he ignore the demands of the dead.

My fingers traced the smooth curves of the turned wood mug. The bells fell silent. The monks would go to supper after prayers, which meant near two hours alone here with naught to think of but a youth left in agony to bleed, unable to cry for help.

Before I knew it, I'd thrown my damp gown over my dry shirt, pulled my boots over my bare feet, and retrieved my walking stick. Guided by the church towers and wafting smoke that smelled pleasantly of onion and garlic, I limped across the infirmary garth and through the puddled passage between the kitchen and refectory, retracing our path of the morning. Pigeons' cooing and the fading echoes of plainsong accompanied me into the deserted cloisters. Thick clouds had stolen the early-evening light.

I shivered. Saint Gillare's wingless angels gleamed pure white against the dusk. The chill air, heavy with moisture, clung to skin like mud and smelled of rich earth and green grass. To retreat felt stupid and cowardly, yet now I was here, I couldn't steel myself to step wholly into the garth. My hand squeezed the smoothed knob of the walking stick. There were other ways to approach uncertain ground than just blundering in.

Though I had denied it for years, adamantly avoiding occupation as a scout or guide as if to prove that denial, I *had* inherited the familial bent for route finding and tracking. My Cartamandua bloodlines were well documented, of course, enshrined in the Registry in Palinur before my birth and witnessed on the day I took my first breath. I'd always felt like a prized cow, bred to supply Navronne with the cream of sorcery.

I wandered down the south cloister, past the kitchen wall and around the corner into the walk that fronted the lay brothers' reach. Dared I release magic here? Whether I used it in formulated spellwork or to trigger my family bent, it would leave traces, detectable by a Registry inspector. Or perhaps an abbey sanctified to Iero, its Rule forbidding use of magic, might be warded to prevent spellcasting and give off noises or explosions if I breached its protections. Every instinct said not to risk it, but then again, my instincts were unused to the requests of unquiet spirits.

I tossed some of Robierre's stock of bergamot onto the grass that young Horach might use it for the Ferryman's tally, apologizing that I'd naught better to offer. Then, clutching my walking stick, I eased myself to kneeling. Crouched at the verge of the west cloister, some halfway down its length toward its meeting point with the church, I laid my palms on the cool wet grass, shaped my intent, and released just a spit of magic.

My limited experience of such trials led me to expect an image of the square to resolve itself in my mind: the grass and stones, the shrine, the bounding columns and walkways, the size, shape, and source of the font. Not a visual image, but more of an understanding of structure, composition, direction, and history, and if I was fortunate, a sense of what obstacles, spells, or spirits might lie here. But the sensations confounded all expectations.

The earth pulsed beneath my hands, warm and living, its lifeblood a deep-buried vein of silver, as plainly visible to my eye as the shrine itself. The memory of all who had walked here wove a pattern in the earth, each path sharp edged against the clarity of a long and reverent quiet. The understanding of the garth's composition and direction existed, not as some separate image to be analyzed, but embedded in my flesh as plainly as the skill of walking or speaking. And even beyond these marvels, something more teased at my spirit . . .

I breathed deep and tried to quiet my trepidations, to open my senses and push deeper. Just on the edge of hearing, the sighing notes of a vielle quivered in the stillness, and a woman's clear voice intoned a haunting, wordless melody that swelled my soul with wonder and grief. A memory . . . and yet a presence, too . . . if I could but sort out the music and its meaning—

The unseen bludgeon struck again. *Saints and angels!* I toppled backward, landing hard on my backside. As on my first encounter with this place, the blow slammed me square between my eyes. Dizzy and befuddled, I pressed my fingers to my forehead, sure I'd find a bruise swollen the size of a cat. But, though my wounded thigh complained loudly that it was twisted to the point of tearing Brother Badger's stitches, both brow and temples seemed intact.

If Brother Horach wanted my attention, he had gotten it. But did he want me to see what lay here—something far older than a youthful monk—or was he the one who so forcibly forbade my intrusion? I rubbed my brow and tried vainly to recapture the moments before the blow: the warmth of the earth, the silver thread of an underground spring, the music—so beautiful, so dreadfully sad.

I had long speculated that Iero was just another name for Kemen Sky Lord, Creator of Earth and Heaven. But neither Kemen, nor Iero, nor any god or spirit had ever made himself known to me so forcefully. I didn't like it. My hands trembled and my stomach shifted uneasily.

As I stumbled to my feet and untwisted my gown, a brief burst of plainsong from the church intoned the *perficiimus* that ended every Karish prayer and service. Someone threw open a side door that opened onto the east cloister walk, directly across the garth from me. The monks would soon be filing out on their way to the refectory. Unwilling . . . unable . . . to explain what I had just experienced, I hobbled quickly through an arched passageway that divided the undercrofts just behind me.

The sturdy simplicity of the clustered buildings behind the lay brothers' reach implied design for use rather than devotion. Lingering scents of roasted barley, yeast, and sweetly rotting refuse named the rambling structure with arched doors a brewhouse. The tall, windowless building set on stubby stone piers was likely a granary, its floor raised to discourage vermin and damp. Twilight had already gathered in the warren of wood and stone, and a light drizzle fell from the heavy sky.

The sudden sounds of a slamming door and a horse's whinny, just as I reached the corner of the brewhouse, flattened my back against the stone wall of the deserted alley. No question the evening's events had set me on edge. Heart galloping, I peered around the corner. A small muddy yard fronted a well-built three-story house with a steep-pitched roof and many fine windows. Soft light from the upper windows and a single torch in a door bracket illumined three saddled horses tethered by the stoop.

A man in a brick-colored cloak darted down the steps and wrestled a leather satchel onto one of the saddles, buckling straps to hold it. But the horse sidestepped nervously, the fellow's arms were too short, and the satchel slid back onto his shoulders, dragging off his red hood. Fine boned and fair, he was younger than I'd guessed from his height. A tight braid bound his thick bronze-colored hair.

Blundering into strangers' urgent business violated my usual practice, so I did not step out to help. In moments, Brother Gildas appeared on the stoop, holding open the heavy door for two other men. These two descended the steps slowly, one supporting the other. The more robust of the pair, a big, hawk-faced man with a narrow beard and meaty shoulders, barked an order at the squire—for the red-cloaked youth was surely Squire Corin from the kitchen. The house must be Gillarine's guest quarters, these strangers the abbey's noble benefactors.

The squire yanked his strap tight and hurried around to help the others lift the weaker man into the saddle. The gaunt, dark-haired fellow, racked with coughing as he gripped the pommel, was none but the gentlemanly secretary Gram. The hawk-faced man's cloak fell back as he shoved his charge into the saddle. The sleeves of a hauberk gleamed from under his holly-green surcoat, and his jewel-hilted great-sword sparkled in the torchlight. A warrior, then, as well as a lord—Gram's "excitable" employer.

Horrid weather to ride out. The faint drizzle had become an insistent shower, pattering on the brewhouse roof and dribbling from the gutters and downspouts. To get back to my dry bed in the infirmary, I had either to return through the cloisters or cross this courtyard, inviting Brother Gildas's perceptive examination. If they would all just go . . .

Relieved, I watched as Brother Gildas gave the squire a hand up to his mount and retreated to the sheltered stoop. The warrior swung his bulky body into the saddle, exposing a device on his surcoat.

I uttered a malediction—under my breath, so I thought, but the lord's head jerked up and twisted in my direction. Snatching my head out of sight, I slammed my back to the wall. Water sluiced down my neck. My skin felt as if swarming with midges.

Once, when I was eleven or twelve and lay in my bed bleeding from an encounter with my father's leather strap, my elder sister, Thalassa, had chosen to break her long-standing habit and be civil. She told me of *obscuré* spells—certain patterns created in the mind and infused with magic that could cause one to be overlooked. In my usual way I had spat at her, called her a *vyrsté*—a pureblood whose parents had not paid enough attention to breeding lines—and ignored her.

Not for the first time, I regretted that choice. Embroidered in silver thread on the lord's holly-green linen was a howling wolf with a lily under its paw—the device of Evanore and its sovereign duc, Osriel the Bastard.

Lords of the night! Afflicted with a sudden case of the shivers and a raging desire to hide, I hobbled back down the alley and around a corner of the brewhouse, doing my best to keep my stick and my booted feet quiet. Behind me, a man issued a sharp command. In moments, the three horsemen rode right past me.

"Teneamus!" Brother Gildas's call followed them through the alley.

One of the three called an answer, softly enough no one but his companions and I could possibly hear. *"Teneamus!"*

Once the riders had vanished into the rainy gloom, I exhaled and took out as fast as I could down the alley. Though the torch was extinguished, lamps yet shone from within the guesthouse, but I saw no sign of Brother Gildas. As I hobbled across the yard and down the cart track that led through the lay brothers' workyard, inside my sleeves I splayed the three middle fingers of my left hand, and inside my head I recited three saints' names three times each. Whyever would a man of Prince Osriel's party be welcome at a Karish abbey?

Chilled to the marrow, I stripped to the skin before diving gratefully into my bed. By the time Brother Robierre and Brother Anselm returned from supper, bringing me leek soup and hot bread, I had managed to stop shivering. As the two men changed my dressings and fussed about their evening duties, I put my mind to an escape plan should I need to abandon the abbey in a hurry. I would winter in a cave before crossing paths with King Eodward's crippled bastard.

I ought to have had some sympathy with the youngest of Eodward's progeny or at least with his pureblood mother. Though not strictly a *recondeur*—she had not actually run away—Lirene de Armine-Visori had defied her family and the Registry's breeding laws by mating outside the pureblood families, an unforgivable offense, no matter that her lover was a king. Lirene had died when the boy was quite young, and stories named the halfbreed Osriel, raised out of the public eye, twisted in both mind and body.

Veterans who had served in Prince Perryn's ill-fated campaign to wrest Evanore's gold mines from his bastard half-brother displayed wicked burn scars from Osriel's mage-fire arrows and told of comrades snatched in the night and returned without balls, tongues, or hands. They described plagues of nightmares that afflicted their encampments, and men and women found wandering the tangled forests naked and mindless, their privy parts blistered from forced breeding with gatzi—creatures from the netherworld, pledged to Magrog's service. And they swore that on every battlefield near Evanore, what dead were left to lie through the night were missing their eyes on the next morning. Which seemed not such a dreadful thing in itself compared to being dead, save that most Navrons believed a man's soul resided in his eyes. Without a soul, a man was left with no hope of an afterlife, for the Ferryman had naught to carry.

It's a soldier's wont to top the next man's tale. For years, I took no more stock in the stories of Prince Osriel's evils than in legends of angelic visitations or of the Danae whose dancing supposedly nurtured fields and forests. Gods knew battle left enough mutilated bodies for every demonic purpose. The pox from unclean whores was a scourge could flay a man's loins, and drinking raw spirits squeezed from agueroot could scour a mind to blankness for a week. Yet over the summer as Prince Bayard's march across Ardra drove us toward Evanore, one comrade and then another swore me to find him should he fall in battle, and to pierce his heart before nightfall to ensure he was well and truly dead before Osriel the Bastard came for him. Such stern belief cannot but wear upon a man's mind and take on the likeness of truth.

When the lay brother Anselm had hurried off to bed and the choir monk Robierre to the church for another bout of praying, I prowled through the infirmary stores. Using scraps of twine and linen from Brother Robierre's baskets, I wrapped up small amounts of his powders and herbs—anything he had in plenty that I might sell or need. I discovered an herb knife with a nicked blade shoved to the back of a shelf, and I took that, too, bundling it with the medicines in a rag and stuffing the bundle under my palliasse with the bits of cheese and bread I'd saved from every meal.

As I worked, a lesser puzzle nagged at me. Pureblood families flaunted their unbroken descent from the decadent Aurellians by speaking Aurellian and Navron interchangeably. It was a useless skill that only they and hide-bound scholars set store by now Aurellia was reduced from a great empire to a walled city a thousand quellae distant. But such childhood training penetrates very deep. Even after twelve years away from pureblood society, I could not have said in which language I articulated my thoughts. Therefore, I could wonder at the Aurellian farewell that Brother Gildas had exchanged with the Evanori lord. *Teneamus*—we preserve.

The infirmary was dark, a single tall rushlight left burning. After returning from his prayers, the yawning infirmarian had retired gratefully to his own bed in the monks' dorter, declaring me well enough to survive the night with only Iero's angels to watch over me.

The weather had taken a turn for the worse. Sleet clicked on the roof and the stone path outside the open window, threatening to freeze and rot what scanty harvest might have ripened in the disastrously short, cold summer. A month or more remained till Saldon Night, and I ought to be basking in Ardra's golden summer, pleasuring a milkmaid out of her chastity in a haystack instead of shivering in my bed.

Unnerved by the day's events, I was infernally restless. When my breath became visible in the air, I dragged the blankets over my head, abandoning my toes to the cold draft left by the waning flames in the infirmary brazier. My wounds itched and throbbed, more annoying than sore. But deep in my gut sat a small tight knot, cold and quiet for the moment, the threads that linked it to every particle of my being slack.

A disease had gnawed at my gut since I was seven, probably longer if one assumed the rebellious temper and indiscipline that caused my parents to despair of me in the nursery were its first manifestations. Every day of my life I had lived with an unrelenting restlessness. On occasion it would worsen, exploding into a tormenting fire in the blood and a virulent overexcitement of the senses—everything I heard or smelled or looked on exaggerated until my body felt raw. By the time I was ten these attacks had become a regular occurrence, and as I got older, the symptoms grew worse and lasted for days at a time. Even soft candlelight would blind me, whispers set my nerves screaming, and any smell stronger than porridge leave me nauseated. The knot in my gut was ever the precursor of an attack.

I lay wide-eyed, sated with the days of sleep, wishing I had been able to convince Brother Robierre to give me poppy extract again. He hoarded it so carefully. Said their plants were not propagating well in the foul weather.

That the abbey had any healthy plants at all was a wonder. Perhaps their god had powers enough to protect his holy place.

Matins came and went, allowing me to forget myself for a while in the beauteous surge of their singing—fifty-three strong male voices honoring their god. What deity could fail to manifest himself with such power at his beck? Yet in the ensuing silence, the warning in my belly grew more insistent, and hot, as if Brother Robierre had made another incision and implanted a burning coal inside me.

I slammed a fist into the thin pillow wadded under my head. *This is far too early. It's scarce been a fortnight.* I buried my face in the pillow, unable to stop the calculation. We had abandoned the battle before its second day and spent two on the road, then I'd lain two days insensible in this infirmary, and four more recovering . . . and I'd last dealt with this a twelveday before the battle. Twenty-one days. Since I'd first chosen to control my disease with magic, I'd never felt its waking sooner than twenty-eight days. The problem, of course, was that the remedy had become its own disease, and I could no longer distinguish one from the other.

So think of something else. The wind whined in the cold and lonely blackness outside the infirmary walls. The blanket wool tickled my nose. Propped up on my elbow, I drained the last of the weak ale Brother Anselm had left me, and then threw the mug across the square red tiles. The clay vessel shattered. No rushes on the infirmary floor. No straw. Brother Anselm thought them unclean. I curled my arms over my head.

This is no battlefield with the stench of death all around. No whorehouse after the women have moved on to other customers. No stinking back street with rats and refuse your only company. Nor even is it that wretched house in Palinur where your existence was an offense to those who birthed you. You're fed and warm and healing. You've friends here already. You don't need this. Let the cursed sickness burn itself out.

But the coal took flame in my gut, its fiery wounding spreading rapidly into my chest and limbs, into my head, my eyes, my dry tongue. I shoved off the blankets and lay there naked and exposed, unbearably hot as I tried to breathe away the pain. The light seared my eyes. The rain drummed like thunder; the wind bellowed like maddened oxen.

Why had I thought of my parents? If ever the gods had played a wicked prank on human folk, it was on the day they quickened my father's seed in my mother's womb to produce me. From the distance of so many years, my parents' hatred seemed wholly out of proportion to my misdeeds—at least in the years before I learned to detest them in equal measure and was old enough to demonstrate it.

A spasm contorted every sinew in my back, as if a giant played knotwork with my spine. Cascading cramps wrenched my shoulder, legs, and belly. *Ignore them. You've been abed too long.*

On a small painted chest near my bedside lay my torn shirt, stained padded jaque, ragged braies, and hose, neatly folded and stacked. The monks had cleaned or brushed them as I lay insensible, and set them alongside my rifled rucksack. They wouldn't have examined the bag too carefully. Surely. I just needed to see.

I grabbed the rucksack, knocking the stack of clothes onto the floor. Every object I touched seared my skin as if it were iron new drawn from a forge. Jerking the scuffed leather bag onto my lap, I prayed that what I needed would be there. I turned the bag inside out and fumbled at the thick seam. Intact. *Blessed be all gods.* Now for a knife . . .

Holding on to the wall, the rucksack looped over my arm, I hobbled across the tiles to Robierre's worktable. I dragged the stinking rushlight close only to find it on the verge of guttering death. Muttering epithets, I snatched another from the stack under the table, set the fresh one aflame from the stub, and clipped it in the iron holder. Then, seated on the brother's stool, I used his well-honed herb knife to rip the long stitches that held the newer layer of leather to the bottom of the rucksack. *Great Kemen Lord of the Sky, Mother Samele, Lord Iero and your angels or Danae or whomever you dispatch to watch over your children be thanked.* The little green bag—the one Boreas had *not* found—fell into my trembling hand. And the craving swept through me as a fire sweeps across a parched grassland.

In the pool of smoky yellow light I set out the shard of mirror glass, the silver needle, and the white linen thread, and spilled the tiny black nivat seeds—all that was left of my emergency store—onto the table. The fragrance of spice, dust, and corruption burst from the nivat as I crushed the seeds with Robierre's knife. I could not rush, could not afford to be careless, yet the first monk who saw what I was about would know me as a cursed twist-mind, Magrog's slave, a gatzé's whore, and boot me over the wall to languish in the darkness with the rest of the Adversary's servants.

A prick of the needle freed three drops of blood from my finger to mix with the aromatic powder, the pain of the bloodletting as exquisitely shrill as a virgin's scream. My sinews cramped and knotted. My hands shook. Sweat beaded my brow, my arms, my back. *Soon . . . hold on . . .* Perhaps my injuries had made the disease and the hunger for its remedy come upon me early and so dreadfully fast.

Holding one end of the thread between two fingers, I let the other end dangle into the reeking little mess, using the connection to channel every scrap of magic that lived in me into the patterned spell. Touching the mixture directly with my agonized flesh would sap the spell's strength before it reached full potency—a hard lesson I'd learned when first experimenting with this particular remedy. The black paste heated and bubbled. In the enchanted mirror glass I watched the otherwise invisible vapors rise from the unholy brew. Waiting . . .

A mixed-blood alley witch named Salamonde had given me the glass fragment on my fourteenth birthday. The disease had seared my gut and lacerated my senses with such virulence that day, I'd felt the Ferryman's breath on my neck. For the first and only time in my life, I had swallowed pride and hatred and begged my parents for help with my sickness. My mother, typically, retired to her bedchamber and drank herself senseless. My father tied me to his favorite grate and beat me until I pissed myself, insisting that my malady was naught but my vile nature festered in my soul. He said no remedy existed for it. And so, on that night, for the twentieth time that year, I broke the locks on my room and ran away. By the time they dragged me back home three days later, old Salamonde had introduced me to perversion.

The rushlight flickered. I squinted at the glass. One final wisp of vapor drifted upward, taking the last of the earthy scent. I scooped the dark droplets onto my finger and onto my tongue. The potent liquor spread quickly to my pain-wracked extremities . . . the satisfaction of cool ale on a parched tongue . . . the scent of rain after drought . . .

Groaning, I snatched up my rucksack and bit down on the leather strap, for the tasteless paste that was my salvation would not instantly quench the fire. The perverse remedy had first to feed the torment. As did I.

I gripped Brother Badger's grinding stone and slammed it, edge on, into my wounded thigh. Once. Again. Fiery agony swelled to monstrous proportion . . . devouring my organs, my limbs, my senses . . . threatening to completely unhinge my mind . . . until the moment body and spirit teetered on the verge of dissolution, and then . . .

O, elixir of heaven! Rapture! An explosion of exhilaration engulfed every sense, every limb, every part and particle of my flesh and spirit, transforming pain to pleasure as quickly and as absolutely as the ax of a skilled headsman transforms life to death . . .

. . . and then with the same abruptness, it was gone, the convulsion of sensation past. Fire quenched. Cramps dissipated. Throbbing wounds silenced. Every shred of my being quivered with release, the searing heat of my flesh yielding to languid warmth like the aftermath of carnal climax, lacking only joy or merriment. Not oblivion, but assurance that the world was right and ordered exactly as it should be. The rucksack dropped to the floor. My forehead rested on the scratched wood, my dulled mind fallow, my senses throbbing in gratification. The knot in my gut unraveled.

The spell was called the *doulon*. Legend claimed the nasty little enchantment was Magrog's wedding gift to Nemelez when he took his human bride to the netherworld—to ease the pain of their coupling. And more than just the ignorant believed that every invocation of the doulon opened a door to Magrog's kingdom and allowed a demon gatzé to crawl into the earthly plane. Such was no concern of mine.

Some of those enslaved to the doulon burnt or mutilated themselves before they succumbed, for the degree of pleasure in the release always matched the severity of the pain that preceded it. I had not fallen so far out of mind as to do that—not yet, at least. Nor did I use it for ordinary physical discomforts that I could anywise tolerate. I told myself that these practices delayed the inevitable consequence. Every doulon slave went mad eventually, trapped inside a ruined body whose perceptions of pain and pleasure were irretrievably tangled. Unfortunately, between the disease itself and the nivat hunger, the consequences of stopping were equally dreadful. Once in the year just past, I'd had to wait three days until I could get nivat, and I would throw myself off a cliff before doing so again.

Move, fool. Quickly, before losing all sense, I licked the thread clean and purified the needle in the rushlight flame, packed all away in the empty green bag, and stuffed it in the bottom of my rucksack. No time or means to sew the flap shut again.

The bent, the power for spellworking, was the only virtue of my pureblood birth I'd ever seen, and for good or ill, I had chosen to abandon the small magics I had learned as a boy and whatever greater uses I might develop as a man and spend it all on this. I hobbled away from the worktable and threw the rucksack onto the painted chest. Naked and shuddering, I crawled under the blankets and gave myself to dreams of pain and pleasure.

Chapter 6

Between supper and Compline, as the gray light filtering through the infirmary's horn windows faded, I was alternately dozing and perusing the intricate little drawings attached to the margins and headings of my psalter. Though lacking the elaboration and gold leaf one would likely find in the abbey's service books, the little codex had been created with the care always given holy books. Had Brother Horach himself inked the illustrations? The copyist had surely borne a fascination with the natural world, inserting energetic and sometimes fantastical representations of stags, foxes, and racing hounds alongside the angels and vines that graced the prayers and psalms. I speculated as to whether he had suited the beasts' postures to the mood or sense of the prayer, which struck me as a clever idea.

Yawning, feeling lazy and dull-witted as always on the day after the doulon, I traced my fingertips over the letters as I had so often as a child. In those days, believing I might remedy my persistent failure to decipher the mystery of written words, I had allowed magic to roar from my body's center into the confounding shapes on the page—scorching no few books in the endeavor. The fingers are the conduit of magic.

I no longer wasted my resources on that particular exercise. I had come to terms with my incapacity and managed well enough all these years. But if these holy brothers discovered my lack, they would surely pitch me over their lovely wall. That was damnably annoying.

I slammed the book shut and hunched deeper in the bed, warm and dry again after the previous day's unsettling excursions. Jumbled thoughts of murdered monks and abbey benefactors who just happened to serve unsavory princes had plagued me all the boring day—or at least when I could avoid thinking of my empty nivat bag and the difficulty of refilling it. I had trained myself to set that worry aside for a few weeks between necessity, refusing to allow the disease or its unhealthy remedy to set the course of my life. The attack, a full week short of the usual and with so little warning, had profoundly unnerved me.

Under the more direct beams of the rushlight, Brother Anselm worried over his colored chart that detailed astrological influences on the body's humors, certain he would find some correlation with my relapse in the cloister garth. Sooner or later the earnest fellow would approach the bed with his piss jar or his magnifying lens or his well-polished lancet, asking politely to examine my eyeballs or the underside of my tongue or to take some sample of my regenerating bodily fluids.

I was trying to decide whether to give in to sleep and thus keep good Anselm at bay, when a blast of cold air heralded Jullian's appearance in the infirmary doorway. The boy was as pale as an Ardran milkmaid's ass. "Brother Anselm, Brother Robierre summons you immediately with his medicine box and both litters. We've wounded soldiers at the gates!"

"Who?" I said, sitting up straight as Brother Anselm jumped from his stool and dragged litter poles from beneath the vacant beds.

"Ardrans. Fifty of them at the least. Or a hundred . . . bloody . . . torn to pieces . . ."

The boy's peaked complexion and strangled declaration indicated that the evening's events had already profoundly altered his understanding of the world. Exposure to ugly injuries such as mine was one thing, but four or five cadres' worth of battle wounds would be far different. Angels preserve the boy from ever seeing the battlefield itself.

It had required many a tankard to dull the images of my own introduction to the soldiers' mysteries. I had never subscribed to myths of noble purpose or personal glory in battle, but I *had* believed that shoving a spear into a twitching body busily shitting itself could make a man of me. I'd blundered through innumerable bloody days since, as much avoiding other fools' spears and axes as wielding my own, but I'd never grown comfortable with wholesale bloodletting or with humans turned more savage than wild beasts.

Brother Anselm wrapped the litter poles in their leather slings, dumped them into the boy's outstretched arms, and threw a stack of linens atop the load. After tossing a few loose items from the shelves into a wooden chest, he slammed the lid, fastened the latch, and hefted it onto his shoulder. Before you could blink, only the chilly draft remained with me in the infirmary.

The laws of sanctuary and the sanctity of abbey walls seemed suddenly flimsy. Why had I ever imagined them protection against the feral madness of this war?

Two of the royal brothers, Perryn, Duc of Ardra, and Bayard, Duc of Morian, had maintained a deadly balance for three years. As no one had produced Eodward's authentic writ stating elsewise, Bayard claimed the Navron throne by right and precedent as Eodward's eldest son. But Eodward had granted Prince Perryn regency in Ardra—the ancient seat of Caedmon's line—and Perryn insisted that this demonstrated Eodward's intent to name him king over his poorly educated elder brother.

The third and youngest brother, Osriel the Bastard, regent of Evanore, had taken no active part in the three-year dispute save his grisly reaping on the battlefield. Some said Osriel cared naught for ruling on earth, but aimed to supplant the divine Magrog himself as lord of the netherworld. Others claimed he was waiting only for his brothers to weaken each other so he could sweep them both aside with an army of gatzi.

Only in the winter just past had stories of a fourth brother—this child Pretender—risen, and as sure as dead men stink, before the rumor could gather strength enough to create him a rival, Bayard had made a devil's bargain that looked to win him the day. He had allied with the Harrowers.

The Harrowers denied both the elder gods and the Karish upstart Iero, claiming that Navrons had lost their respect and proper fear of the true Powers who ruled the universe. Their priestess, Sila Diaglou, said that our cities and our plowing had defiled the land and that our false religions had caused us to forget these Powers that she called Gehoum, and that was why the weather had gone sour and the plagues and wars had risen.

For years people had laughed at a woman speaking out as if she were the divine prophet Karus come back again, set on changing the ways of the world. Yet, in the last years of Eodward's reign, when pestilence and storms grew worse and the king could pay no mind to aught but Hansker raiders—Sila Diaglou's direst predictions come true—folk began to listen and nod their heads. More and more wild-eyed rabble, dressed in rags and orange head scarves, heeded her call for burning and destruction to "harrow" the land and appease the Gehoum's wrath. Scorned by priests and nobles, she had grown her ragtag band of lunatics into an army to rival those of Navronne's princes.

Throughout the summer campaign, while Prince Perryn dithered and regrouped farther and farther south, claiming that no rabble could stand against his knights and legions, the Harrowers burnt villages and fields and left us nothing to eat and nothing to defend. And then Prince Bayard and Sila Diaglou had joined forces and swept us up like chaff from a threshing floor.

The abbey bells clanged in an urgent rhythm. Distant shouts, mysterious door bangings, and running footsteps from the infirmary courtyard accompanied the summons. The evening reeked of danger. Unable to lie still, I threw off my blankets and pulled on my wool shirt, trews, and hose.

A brown-clad body burst through the door and pelted down the long room to Brother Robierre's shelves—the other young aspirant, Gerard, a soft, stammering boy of fourteen. He shoved bowls and basins aside, knocking half of them clattering to the floor, and slammed boxes and cases back onto the shelf after examining their contents. Then he whirled about, dark stains on his arms and in his eyes. "B-b-bonesaws. Where does he k-keep them? He said the far end . . ."

I was already on my feet, alder stick in hand. "In that great iron chest down below."

By the time I joined him, the boy's trembling fingers had scarcely got the lid open. Together we lifted out two trays of small, fine instruments—pincers, scalpels, probing tools of thin wire, and the like—laid out between sheets of leather. In the bottom of the chest lay a number of larger, linen-wrapped bundles. The boy knelt and dragged them out one by one: cautery irons, mallets, and strangely shaped implements of unknown purpose. But I'd seen enough use of such tools to recognize the wide blade and thin, squared handle of the bonesaw.

"There. That one. That's likely what he wants. And you'd best take the larger iron as well."

The boy looked up at me like a begging pup, raising a small key in his hand. "And p-p-poppy extract. He said you'd know where to find it."

"I'd guess that every wounded man who comes here learns where the good infirmarian keeps Iero's salvation . . ." I limped to the corner of the room where the roof truss lapped over the wall, forming a high shelf, well out of view, and lifted down the heavy iron casket that likely only Brother Badger and I could reach. I carried it under one arm to the worktable.

". . . but he chooses not to leave it loose about to tempt boys or weak-minded malingerers like me. It will be a boon to those you've seen, as will the care the brothers give them." Saints and angels, I didn't want the boy to start weeping.

I wheedled the recalcitrant lock open and handed over the precious brown flask. "Anything else?"

The boy shook his head, wiped his nose on his sleeve, and trotted out the door.

I stowed the nicked herb knife and the pilfered herbs and medicines in my rucksack and tied the bag around my waist with a length of linen bandage. Then I pulled my jaque over my woolen shirt, wrestled my boots onto my feet and my damp monk's gown over all.

Caution demanded I bolt. To strike out directly across the River Kay behind the infirmary would get me away from the abbey without involvement. But the church would hold valuables—calyxes of gold or silver used for noblemen's offerings, or the offerings themselves—rare oils, coins, gems perhaps, or other gifts from wealthy benefactors and pilgrims. I made Iero's sign on breast and forehead, vowing to take only enough to pay for my book. Stealing from a god's house was a risky practice.

Though twilight lingered in the outer airs, night had already settled in the confines of the inner courts. The wood-splitters' yard was deserted, the wood stacked in the voluminous undercroft, splinters and flakes neatly raked and dropped in weatherworn tinder baskets. The ripe stench of a latrine overlaid the scents of brewhouse and granary. All very natural. Yet I peered over my shoulder fifty times in that short journey, and gripped my alder stick so fiercely I likely put dents in the smooth wood. The guesthouse sat dark. I breathed freely only after I hobbled into the maze of gardens and hedges before the church.

I paused amid the overgrown yews, wondering at the quiet. Perhaps circumstances were not so dire as the fears of naive boys implied. Only a fool would pillage a church and abandon such a comfortable sanctuary without ripe cause. So instead of bearing right into the church, I headed left toward the abbey gates.

Just inside the massive outer wall of the abbey and its twin-towered gatehouse lay the walled enclosure the brothers called the Alms Court. In this pleasant space of fountains and mosaics, where, on ordinary days, Brother Porter dealt with visitors, five dead bodies lay wrapped neatly in linen. A lay brother sponged blood and dirt from a sixth corpse, while a white-haired monk droned prayers over the dead man's battered head. The mournful Porter, Brother Cadeus, filled a pail at a splashing fountain and dashed it over the paving stones as if to expunge the horror.

Save for these few and a trickle of monks hurrying through with blankets, soup crocks, or rolls of gray linen bandages, the courtyard was deserted. I had expected it to be overflowing with wounded.

"Could you take this, Brother?" An overburdened monk thrust an ale pitcher into my hand. Tucking the heavy pitcher in the crook of my arm, I joined the procession. The decorative gates of iron- and copper-work at the mouth of the gatehouse tunnel had been blocked open with stone urns. The gate tunnel itself was quiet, the sharp click of my walking stick and uneven clomp of my heavy boots on the stone paving far louder than the shuffle and swish of passing sandals and cowls. The thick wooden gates halfway along the tunnel had been propped open.

Beyond the vaulted entry lay a scene worthy of the Adversary's domain. The broad sky blazed with orange-edged clouds and swaths of gray and purple. Torches had been mounted on staves, illuminating, not a hundred, but surely sixty or seventy bloodied soldiers sprawled on the puddled apron of grass before the gatehouse. They didn't look to be in any condition to cause much trouble for the monks. I had seen the ravages a defeated army could work upon a town or village. And these men *were* defeated. The wounded huddled quietly, suppressing moans and gasps of pain while mumbling prayers and curses. Other men sat silent, twitching at every noise, each man closed into himself, glaze-eyed with exhaustion and hunger.

Monks moved among the crowd like bees in a clover patch, offering prayers, ale, bread, blankets, and strips of linen men could use to bandage themselves until others could see to them. Fires sprang up here and there as the river damp rolled in with nightfall.

Close by the gate tunnel, an Ardran wearing a ripped tabard and cloak over hauberk and mail chausses fidgeted near a small group of monks. His bearing proclaimed him an officer, as did the sword at his waist and the riding crop in his hand.

The moment the group dispersed, leaving only one stocky, bald-pated brother standing by the gate, the officer pounced. "An hour we've waited, holy father," he said, his tight-lipped sneer more honest than his address. "My lord asks again when the abbot will come and grant his right of sanctuary. Nor have my lord's wounds been attended as yet."

"All in good time," said the monk, his shaven head and the silver solicale that dangled on his breast gleaming in the torchlight. "Your arrival has caught us quite by surprise. Abbot Luviar works in our farthest fields today. Though we've rung summoning bells, we've no horses to fetch him. Perhaps you can explain to me: I've granted sanctuary to all comers, but none have entered. They say their officers will not permit—"

"No cowards or gutterwipes will pass this gate before their lord," said the officer through clenched teeth, "and he will *not* share a common blessing given by some underling friar. He will have his proper reception."

"Naturally, protocol must be followed." The monk spread his hands in helpless resignation. "We will offer everything Iero provides us to ease your lord and his men until Abbot Luviar arrives. I'll encourage our infirmarian to attend your lord immediately." One could not mistake a barb of indignation amid the proffered roses.

"See that you do, monk." The officer nodded stiffly and retreated to a knot of men in the very center of the field—a cadre of knights, twelve lances sprouting from them like a stand of needlegrass.

What lord lay there with no horses or banners? Some landless edane, no doubt, who thought himself Iero's chosen for surviving when mardanes, ducs, and princes lay dead or captive. None of the regular soldiers paid him any notice.

Nestled above the tunnel between the twin gate towers was the room where, as Saint Ophir had commanded, one member of the Gillarine fraternity remained ever alert for those in need of sanctuary—certainly to my own benefit. As I weighed the merits of avoiding even so slight an entanglement with the war against the efforts of finding another haven, someone poked his head from the window and yelled, "Hark, Father Prior!"

The stocky monk craned his neck to see the caller. "Must you shout so loud, Brother Cosmos? Even *underling friars* must maintain our wits and decorum." His politeness had shriveled like a currant.

"There are more men on the ridge, Father Prior. Coming this way." Brother Cosmos damped his volume, but he could not mute the quaver of fear that accompanied his report.

"Riders or foot?" said the prior, squinting into the murky evening beyond the firelit field.

"I'm not certain. They seem to move too quickly for foot. Perhaps one with better eyes should take up the watch. If we could just move these men inside—"

The prior sighed deeply. "The soldiers cannot move without their officers' orders, so we must await Father Abbot. The newcomers are likely more sad cases like these."

"But—"

The stocky monk silenced the protest with a warning finger. "Age does not preclude punishment for disobedience, Cosmos. Stay at your post. As the saint taught, good order will carry us through all earthly trials." He folded his arms and surveyed the field, dispatching the monks here and there as they bustled through the gates.

Perhaps innocent men were not primed to expect trouble when dealing with such ugliness as war. Or perhaps the prior was just a fool. I had soldiered on and off since I was seventeen and knew that unexpected company rarely brought any good. The monks needed to get these men behind the abbey walls.

If I were to avoid any ugly encounters, I needed to be on my way as well. But first I'd get a better sense of where these men had come from, lest I blunder into the war I had abandoned. Almost a fortnight had passed since Wroling Wood. Some other noble boil must have been lanced in recent days to spew commoners' blood.

A woodcart rattled through the tunnel. I stuffed the pitcher and my alder stick into the bed, gripped the cart rim for a support, and moved into the field. Once we reached the center of the crowd, I extracted stick and pitcher and wandered off on my own, searching for someone who could tell me what I needed to know. I stayed cautious. Little chance any would know me. But if, by chance, some had fought at Wroling, I'd not want it to get about that I'd arrived at Gillarine so much earlier than they.

"Brother, can you help me?" A scrawny man with one arm bound to his chest was trying to roll a bulky comrade onto his side. The pale, slab-sided soldier was retching and choking, half drowned in his own vomit. The heat of his fever could have baked bread.

"Iero's grace," I said, narrowly avoiding losing my own supper as the poor wretch heaved again, mostly bile and blood. I set my pitcher on the ground and helped prop the fellow on his side. A cold like deep-buried stone weighed my spirit as I touched him. The gore-soaked wad of rags bound to his belly oozed fresh blood.

"Where have you come from?" I said to the other man, snatching my hands away from his friend. "I've heard naught of this battle. Where was it fought?"

The scrawny soldier gaped as if I'd asked him to explain the thoughts of women or the intents of gods. "In the wood."

"The woods close by here? West beyond the ridge? Or more northerly, near Elanus?"

"A fearful dark wood." He could be no more than sixteen. "They kept coming at us. Knights. Halberdiers. And the mad ones . . . screaming like beasts and waving orange rags on their spears." He shuddered and swallowed a little twisting noise. I'd heard that sound before. Felt it. The terror that sat inside your gut and kept trying to climb out. The fellow didn't know any more. He'd likely never left his mother's croft until he was dragged off and told to kill Moriangi.

"Have you a cup or bowl?" I said. "And one for your friend?"

I filled two crude wooden bowls from my ale pitcher. The youth took a grateful sip, and I left him trying to give the bulk of his own portion to his friend. He ought to have drunk both portions himself. The wounded man wouldn't live past midnight. I'd known it when I touched him, known it with the certainty that always gave me the shudders—a hint of my mother's bent, I'd always thought, that showed up at random through the years, never biddable, never revealing matters I could do anything about. Control of death and life were beyond *any* pureblood bent.

On the near side of the field, a blood-slathered Brother Robierre sawed away at a whimpering soldier's thighbone. Young Gerard sat on the man's good leg to help keep the poor sod still, his gawking taking in every gruesome detail. Jullian, pale as a mist-dimmed moon, held the glowing cautery iron in a fire they'd built a few steps away. I gave the wretched proceeding a wide berth.

"Iero's grace." I approached a hollow-cheeked veteran who sat off by himself at the edge of the field, tending his feet. "Tell me, good sir, how close by the abbey was this terrible engagement? And in which direction?"

"Not so close as to threaten holy folk like you. We fought Bayard the Smith himself at Wroling Wood. The whore priestess of the Harrowers rode beside him."

"Wroling! But I thought—" I caught myself before blundering into any confession. "I'd heard rumor of a fight there, but days ago. You must have given Prince Bayard a noble struggle."

He spat and continued blotting his peeling toes with a scrap of dry cloth, pulling off bits of straw he'd used to stuff his boots. "Pssht. Three days' killing and what's left of Ardran honor is scattered to the winds. Unless Kemen Sky Lord brings forth this Pretender, the Prince of Brutes will be king in a fortnight, for all the good it'll do 'im. When the orange-heads finish burning Ardra, they'll burn Morian, too."

He was probably right. But I needed to understand his geography. "Here, if you've a cup, I can ease your thirst. For certain, you've had a long adventure to get here from Wroling. Perhaps you went the long way round and ran into another fight along the way?"

Looking up at last, he wrestled a tin cup from his belt. "Nay, good brother. We'd all be dead if we'd had to face aught since Wroling. If there'd been horses to commandeer, we could have nipped off to these fine walls in three days or less, despite our wounded. But even his Grace and his lordlings lost their mounts there at the end."

"Prince Perryn unhorsed!" Who'd ever believe the cowardly princeling would get close enough to combat to lose his horse? "He's captive, now, I suppose. Or dead."

"Aye, one or the other. At least that's kept the Smith off our backsides. With noble prey ripe for plucking, he needn't bother chasing dregs like us. A few unchartered knights is all they'd have to show for taking this lot."

"But your lord lies just over——" Unreasonably disturbed, I held the pitcher poised above his cup. "Prince Perryn . . . you didn't see him taken, then?"

"Nah. But he's likely squealing in Bayard's dungeons by now. Pompous prickwit." The soldier licked his lips and jerked his cup toward the pitcher.

When I'd heard of Prince Perryn's foiled plot to burn Navronne's fleet—our only defense against Hansker raiders—because his brother Bayard commanded the ships, I was done with the Ardran prince for good. Who of any mind could wish for either the Smith, the Pompous Prickwit, or Osriel the Bastard to wear good Eodward's crown? I feared the tales of a fourth brother, a Pretender, were naught but wishing dreams, wrought to hold off a kingdom's despair.

As I filled the soldier's vessel, my mind toyed with his news. If Prince Bayard had captured his half-brother, the throne was indeed likely his, no matter what Eodward's lost writ of succession had to say. In Evanore Prince Osriel squatted on the richest treasure in the kingdom—veins of gold to satisfy an Aurellian emperor's wildest dreams—but most people deemed his sparsely populated domain too small to mount a campaign for the throne.

Over the soldier's head the forested folds of hill and vale were enveloped in gathering gloom. With Perryn taken, Bayard would never chase down sixty wounded men, a few knights, and a minor lord. But if the Duc of Ardra had slipped Bayard's grasp, and some pureblood scout had detected royal blood on this rabble's trail . . . Brother Cosmos had seen riders on the ridge.

I shoved the ale pitcher into the startled soldier's hands. "Riders are coming from the west. Drink up, put on your boots, and set a watch. Remember, you've no sanctuary as long as you're outside the abbey gates. If by some chance a certain unhorsed lord were hiding here among you, and if by some chance the Smith were to get wind of it from one of his pureblood lapdogs . . ."

The soldier stared at me for a moment, and then over his shoulder into the darkness flowing down from the forested ridge and pooling in the valley on every side. "Yo, Tobit, Gerrol!" he called, snatching up his boots.

I sped away as fast as I could hobble. Thankful for the disguise of monk's garb, I kept my shoulders hunched and looked no soldier in the eye. No bed or board was worth involvement in the princes' bloody argument. I'd had my fill of killing. My leg was not up to running, but I needed no stick to propel me across the field toward the river and the cart road south—away from the oncoming Moriangi.

Did these monks understand what was going to happen here? Bayard, Duc of Morian, called the Smith for his crude and thuggish manner, would surely slaughter these men to take his rival and might violate the abbey itself. Sanctuary was only effective if the pursuers respected the concepts of mercy and salvation. And in such regards, I had no confidence in either Bayard the Smith or Sila Diaglou.

The stench of charred meat hung over the crowd of wounded surrounding the infirmarian and his assistant. Jullian and Gerard were wiping bloody implements with bloody rags and replacing them in Robierre's wooden chest.

I ought to warn the brothers. Of course, Robierre and Anselm would likely not come away from the field. And truly, as I thought of it, I owed them no debt, as their service had naught to do with saving me, but with their own gifts and obligations. But the boys . . . I'd given my word to protect young Jullian, and I didn't break my word.

I pushed through the listless press and crouched down behind the boys. "Father Prior bade me send the two of you into the church," I said quietly.

Gerard gaped at me blankly, as if too horror-sated to make sense of common speech. Jullian, though, snapped his head around. "Valen! What are you doing out here? Your leg—"

"I'm carrying Father Prior's commands. Everyone must help in such a desperate time, even such as me. Come now, leave your task for those more knowledgeable, and get you to the church. You're needed for . . ." My mind juggled to come up with anything that sounded reasonable.

"But we were told to help Brother Infirmarian."

The glassy puddles beside my feet shivered. Horses.

"Well, all that's changed. You're wanted in church . . . for the singing . . . as so many of the brothers are occupied and your voices and hearts are pure . . . and we will need Iero's grace very much with what's to come this night."

In an instant, Jullian's puzzled expression blossomed into the most profound awe. His voice dropped to a whisper. "The dark times . . . the long night . . . come so soon?" He glanced quickly at Gerard, who seemed to comprehend as little as I did of his meaning, and then back at me. Jullian jumped up, dragged the other boy to his feet, and gave him a shove. "Gerard, run for the church! Go! Begin the psalm for the end times!"

Gerard scooted away. Jullian crouched down again, whispering excitedly. "I wasn't sure you knew. This afternoon, Brother Gildas reprimanded me for my loose tongue . . . I mean, I had heard them say that your book could be the key and surely the god had sent you here, and so I assumed you knew of the lighthouse. But for this night to come so soon . . ."

My teeth thrummed with the approaching hoofbeats. Cries of dismay broke out from several sides. "Jullian, I've no idea what you're saying, but you must go into the church with Gerard and say whatever prayers you can think of. Don't come out until Father Abbot himself tells you it's safe. Do you understand?"

Face glowing with more than the ruddy torchlight, eyes pooled with determined innocence, the boy ducked his head and raised his hand. "I understand," he said, and then added softly, so only I could hear, "*Teneamus.*"

Chapter 7

I stared after Jullian as he sprinted for the abbey gates. But only for a
moment. Matters were deteriorating too rapidly. The first outriders thundered across the fields toward the abbey, swords raised, cloaks and pennons flying. The little cadre of bristling lances moved slowly from the center
of the field toward the gatehouse—*away* from the coming assault, which did
naught but affirm what I suspected about the lord they protected.

"Father Prior!" Abbot Luviar himself ran out of the gatehouse tunnel as I
picked my way across the uneven ground along the wall away from the gates.
"In the name of the Creator, Nemesio, why are they not within?"

"Their officers refused. Their lord insists on you—"

"Run, Nemesio! Get him inside now. By my command as your superior in Iero's service, under pain of your immortal soul, get the lord's party
through the gate. Do you understand me? Brother Broun, Fescol . . . ring
the bells!"

The prior dashed into the murmuring crowd. As the alarm rippled in
from the perimeter, Abbot Luviar strode straight out through the stirring
soldiers as well. "Rise up!" he cried, moving from one to another, the golden
sunburst on his breast glinting in the torchlight. "You must stand one more
time. Rise up and take arms. Support your comrades to stand as well. Navronne needs your strength. Your children and your children's children need
your courage. If good is to be made of your suffering, then these riders must
not find you asleep." He tugged on weary arms and laid his hand on bent
heads. "You are the men of Ardra, Eodward's men of light! Mighty Iero will
lift your arms, if you but stand. This fight is bigger than you know. The stakes
grander than all of us."

I was astonished. One by one, men who but moments before were ghosts of warriors, drained of blood and spirit, grasped pikes or spears and rose to their feet, drawing their fellows up to stand beside them and face outward. None of them seemed to notice the knights retreating toward the abbey.

I wanted to call after Luviar, "The one you protect is not worthy of more lives; he betrays his men for pride and greed!"

But the abbot was out of my reach. Like a tight eddy in the current of the shaping battle, he spun and touched and cajoled. "Rise up and the archangels will join you with their swords and shields. This cause you serve must not die this day. Show Navronne the strength of your resolve!"

Indeed, the abbot's voice carried across the sea of bloodied faces like an archangel's clarion, almost enough to draw me back into the conflict I had abandoned. Not for the cowardly prince I believed lay hidden behind the screen of his lancers, not for golden Ardra or industrious Morian or mysterious, mountainous Evanore. Yet, perhaps, for good King Eodward who had lived with the angels and dreamed of Navronne, the Heart of the World . . .

Even as I considered grabbing a weapon from one of the men too weak to use it, I shook off the fey notion and called myself an idiot. I was not ready to die for anyone or anything. To enter a fight at less than full strength was an invitation to the Ferryman.

I climbed the gentle apron slope of the wall and angled away from the gatehouse, resigned to a long and miserable journey. The abbey walls would lead me back to the river. Somewhere the monks would have built a bridge to open the cross-river pastures for grazing. The thick damp of the night resolved into cold spatters on my face. Unvowed, I had no cowl to shield me from the rain.

"Valen!" The call startled me, and I glanced over my shoulder. A pale face lined by dark brows appeared out of the night behind me. "You should get yourself inside the walls immediately, Valen."

Iero's bones, where had the monk come from? "Ah, Brother Gildas," I said, "perhaps you don't recognize the perils of this night."

My gait was slow and clumsy on the uneven ground. Gildas quickly caught up with me, grabbed my arm, and drew me to a halt. "This world is naught but perilous. Nothing is simple. Nothing is innocent. And sometimes, those who think themselves the most worldly are the most innocent of all."

I snorted at the concept of this monk telling me anything of the world. "Sometimes a man must look to his body's safety as well as his soul's. Bayard of Morian is hunting his brother, and any man who gets in his way is a fool. Soon to be a dead fool. Though Abbot Luviar seems to disagree, I doubt Iero would have us throw our lives away for nothing."

Purposeless death was not the only risk in staying. Bayard would surely have pureblood attendants. Any interrogation of Gillarine's inhabitants could be my downfall. Time only increased the Registry's determination to recover a *recondeur*.

I limped past Brother Gildas. He darted in front of me and gently, but insistently, blocked my way. "The god has given your safety into our hands, Valen. Please believe we take that very seriously. You must not leave."

I wanted very much to believe him. The drizzle had yielded to a downpour. My thigh ached. I was already shivering and had no provisions. All that awaited me in the dark and the wet were pestilence, Moriangi swords, and a hungry winter. "But these riders—"

"—will not find the one they seek. I swear to you they'll have no cause to broach our walls. The dangers of this night are outside Gillarine, not in. Come. Hurry. And have faith."

His grip was much stronger than I expected. And perhaps his faith, too. For it was more than the weather and my poor prospects that crumbled my resolve so quickly. Since I'd first taken up soldiering, I had hated the last moments before battle, when it seemed as if the boundaries between earth and body, between past, present, and future, between knowing and experiencing dissolved. But something about this place . . . every moment I stood on this field multiplied those sensations beyond bearing. As a wind blustering my hair and robe, I felt the sweeping onslaught of the Moriangi. As the sea crashing upon my knees, I felt the surging Ardrans step up to meet them. A horse neighed wildly in the distance and a cheer went up among the Ardrans. My soul ached, and I longed for wine . . . for mead . . . for hard spirits or poppy . . . for the doulon . . . anything so I would not feel all this.

As the cold deluge soaked my hair and funneled down my neck, I resentfully allowed Gildas to turn me around. "Answer me one thing, Brother," I said as the monk steadied my steps. "What would it mean if I were to bid you farewell with the Aurellian word meaning *we preserve?*"

Though Gildas did not miss a step, his arm suddenly felt like a post. Moments passed. "Well, of course, preservation of knowledge is our charter here at Gillarine. Many here use *teneamus* as a challenge when our spirits flag. A reminder of duty and service to the god. You never mentioned that you understood Aurellian, Valen. Most aspirants must learn it from the begin-ning. What other talents are you hiding?"

My spine froze. I should have known he would turn the question on me. *Stupid tongue-flapping fool. Come on. A story* . . . "I was schooled early . . . a Karish charity school near Ymir . . . took to the language. I've a gift with the pronunciations, I'm told, though not the writing of it."

Mumbling curses at my slip and thanking the gods yet again that my curling hair, light complexion, and excess height were so exceptional for pureblood stock, I hobbled back along the wall toward the gatehouse. The sloping apron gave a wide vantage. More riders broached the hardening Ar-dran perimeter. Arms clashed. Men and horses screamed . . .

"They should not shed blood upon that field," I said, shuddering. As the last rays of sunlight pierced the cloud and sculpted the surging sea of bodies with orange and scarlet, the very thought made my veins burn and my stom-ach heave as they had in the cloister garth. *Holy ground*, Jullian had called Gillarine. Perhaps that was what I felt.

"Shedding blood is a great evil," said Gildas. "Yet some causes demand it. Blood spilled in violence has great power for good."

"Some causes, perhaps." But not this one. I hobbled faster. "King Eod-ward could not have meant his sons to bring Navronne to ruin."

"So you've no loyalty to any of these princes."

"Loyalty never put blood back in a man's veins."

We reached the gatehouse just as the party of knights entered the arch, moving like a many-legged insect, stepping smartly around dented shields, bloody rags and bundles, and a few sprawled bodies that even the abbot's call had not roused. In the center of the lancers' spiked circle, shel-tered from the rain by a cloak held over his head, was a stumbling smudge of silver mail and white-and-purple satin, a tangle of fair hair that ladies called spun gold, a blur of maggot-colored skin, supported on the arms of servants. How like Perryn of Ardra to keep his men in danger while he awaited a triumphal welcome to his last refuge. And now, for the moment, they'd saved him. I'd wager my grandfather's book that he was more drunk than wounded. The cost of the pelisse his knights held over his head could likely have paid for a month's provisions for his legions or a troop of mer-cenaries to aid us.

"Brother Victor," called Gildas to a diminutive monk who stood in the vaulted entry staring, aghast, at the battle. "Could you please escort Valen back to the infirmary? My duties beckon . . ." Gildas planted a brotherly slap on my arm and jogged ahead alongside the lancers.

As Gildas and Prince Perryn's party vanished into the tunnel, the Ardran troops' brief resistance collapsed into a rout. Night and death rode pillion behind the Moriangi horsemen, as their central wedge plunged inward to slice the Ardran force in twain.

Brother Victor, a tight little man whose features seemed on the verge of sliding off his chinless face, wrenched his eyes from the field, took my arm solicitously, and urged me into the gatehouse tunnel. "Brother Valen? Why, you're the supplicant who brought us—"

"Yes, yes, the Cartamandua maps," I said, straining to see over my shoulder. "And you're welcome to view them at any time, if you'll just hold up for a moment."

Halfway along the tunnel, the great oaken gates yet gaped. I drew Brother Victor into the space between the leftmost gate and the wall, where I could peek around and see what was happening here. I dearly wanted to understand it.

The abbot stood at the outer end of the tunnel, outlined against the flares of torches and steel. "Here, brave men, hurry! By Iero's grace, find safety here, thou who fleest sword or hangman. By Saint Gillare's hand, find healing here . . ."

But the Moriangi had encircled the retreating Ardrans and quickly barred the tunnel opening with leveled lances. The snort and snuffles of agitated horses and the chinking of mail and arms could not drown out the shouts of anger and the lingering cries of the wounded.

Through the crush advanced a small party of riders, the foremost being a bull-necked man on a chestnut destrier. Both man and horse were cloaked and furbished in scarlet and blue—not the deep-dyed vermillion and indigo of Aurellian-style finery, but common madder and woad.

Bayard, Duc of Morian, called the Smith, relished his particular ancestry as dearly as any pureblood. He claimed that his Moriangi mother, daughter of a common shipwright, had reinvigorated Caedmon's royal line with uncommon strength. He made a great show of abjuring silks and jewels in favor of coarse woolens and hammered bronze and believed it made him one with his people.

Perhaps. I'd met those who honored Bayard as Eodward's eldest child, and thus, lacking evidence to the contrary, Eodward's rightful heir. Even in the king's lifetime, Bayard's ruthless campaigns against the Hansker were revered by those who lived in the vulnerable riverlands. But I'd met neither man nor woman, common nor other, who professed to love the man.

"Who has passed here, priest?" Prince Bayard's horse was at noses with the abbot. "I would know what men have sought your hospitality this night."

"Your Grace." The abbot inclined his head and spread his palms. "Alas, only the dead have entered our gates this night. I granted all these men holy sanctuary, but they chose to fight instead. How will Iero judge those of us in authority who fail to avert such horrors?"

Hypocrisy among the powerful, even the clergy, did not surprise me. But I was shocked at the abbot's blatant lie, especially in the absolute sincerity of its delivery.

Prince Bayard, of course, was experienced with both lies and hypocrisy. "Prove to me that no one has passed. My men were certain they saw knights at your gate. Surely your holy brothers have not been hiding swords or lances in their trews."

The squires in his party snickered.

The abbot ignored the crude jape and swept an arm in welcome. "Enter as you will, Your Grace, though I must insist you leave your weapons behind. Your noble father's grant specified Gillarine as neutral ground."

Was *that* it? Had the abbot and his prior kept the Ardran soldiers outside the walls apurpose so Luviar could maintain his claim of neutral ground and thus retain King Eodward's grant of this fruitful valley? He'd had an Evanori nobleman ensconced in the abbey guesthouse. But then why hide Perryn?

"Interfering with the capture of a traitor is hardly neutral!" Prince Bayard snapped, voicing my own thought. "All your pious mouthings these past months, bidding me negotiate with this poltroon my father sired . . . Now your true loyalties are revealed. You've set yourself and your holy brothers square in the sapless dandy's camp, and if you've sheltered him, I'll take this house down stone by stone while you hang by your bowels and watch." Bayard's destrier snorted, blew, and sidestepped. The prince drew rein with a heavy hand.

"Iero bids us open our doors in peace to those who request it, and we ask no questions as to past sins or future plans." The abbot yielded no ground, his every syllable precise and clear. "We would welcome either of your royal brothers here as we would welcome your own honored self or the lowliest of your warriors or even yon priestess, your ally, who denies king and god and human soul. I assert that no one has passed this gateway to my inner precincts save those of my own flock and the dead. Leave off your weapons and come see for yourself, or send one of your men. But I would remind you that to violate our precincts lays an interdict upon the soul, unworthy of a man who would be Eodward's heir and awkward for a man who desires the Hierarch of Ardra—my superior—to affirm his crown."

"You presume much, priest." I would not have been Bayard's horse at that moment. Surely the prince's ruthless hand on the reins must shred the poor beast's mouth.

Bayard flicked a gloved finger at those behind him. A man dropped from his mount, bowed to the prince, and strode through the tunnel toward the Alms Court. My heart stuttered when the shifting lamplight revealed his cloak to be the color of claret—the color mandated for a pureblood working among ordinaries. And there was something else . . .

I stared after him as he passed by me. A short, broad-shouldered man with thick black hair and beard, his face half obscured by a silken mask. His walk so like a cat's . . . smooth, confident, a touch of swagger . . . so familiar . . . Once inside the courtyard, he knelt and touched one hand to the earth, then rose and moved out of sight.

My feet shifted as if to follow. Brother Victor jerked hard on my gown. I came to my senses and shrank deeper into our niche behind the gates. Gods, if he saw me . . . I closed my eyes, not daring to so much as think until the firm footsteps passed us by again. Then I peered around the edge of the gate.

"The priest speaks truth, Your Grace." The pureblood's arrogance rang through that tunnel like struck bronze, his words properly blunt and formed entirely without passion. This was business. "The only Ardran soldiers in the courtyard are dead—six of them. I verified their state. Only one set of footprints in the courtyard beyond this tunnel is aught but monks' sandals. That pair of boots walked out the gates, not in. No path beyond the three inner gates showed evidence of either passing soldiers or princes. Your royal brother certainly escaped Wroling with this rabble, but he either abandoned them along the way or is out there with them yet." I would recognize Max's voice anywhere.

Unsubtle, Prince Bayard wheeled his mount and charged back to the field. My brother, Max, swung his compact and brawny bulk onto his horse and rode after him with the rest of the party.

Slowly I relaxed fists and shoulders. It was more difficult to banish the echoes of taunts and mocking laughter that would forever taint the air about my brother like the stink shrouds a midden.

How logical that Max called the Duc of Morian his master. My father was shrewd enough to bind his children into the most prestigious contracts offered, unswayed by sentiment or relative virtue or even hard coin, come to that. Max prided himself on his wit and intellect, and ever ambitious, would have made certain that the contracts offered for his service were to his own taste.

"Come on, then," said Brother Victor, tugging at my sleeve. "No need to watch what they'll do now. We must pray for mercy and for the souls of captors and captives alike."

No. No need to watch the macabre dance of victors and vanquished. Screams followed us into the now deserted Alms Court. I knew what Max had done here: crouched down and touched the stone, then let flow a bit of magic, calling on our family bent for a simple test we had learned as we learned to walk. Whereas roads and portals held the remembrance of all who had traveled them for a very long time—the abbey gates likely would reveal traces of Eodward himself—the lingering footsteps in a paved court-yard would tell the tale only of those who had passed this night.

I dared not read the footprints for myself, even assuming I could draw any magic on the day after a doulon. I dared not work *any* sorcery with Max nearby. My brother, a pureblood with more than ten generations of scouts and cartographers in his lineage, would not miss the residue of pureblood spellworking any more than he would have missed the invisible traces of soldiers' boots or a prince's tread.

So where *were* Prince Perryn and his lancers? As Brother Victor and I crossed the Alms Court and passed through the Porter's Arch, I whipped my head around to look back at the gatehouse and the tiny windows of the sanc-tuary room, tightly shuttered now. A pulse of satisfaction left me smiling. Of course, the monks would need access to the sanctuary room from inside the gate tunnel, somewhere in the dark nooks and niches along the walls behind the gates, so that the watcher could descend swiftly to open the gates for a supplicant. Brother Gildas would know. And I'd wager my arm that a second stair would lead to the sanctuary room by way of the outer wall walk, so a monk would not need to cross a busy Alms Court to take up his watch.

"Please go on ahead," I said to Brother Victor, slowing my already snail-like trudge. "My leg tires, and I'd like to . . . pray . . . as I walk. I can find my way to the infirmary on my own."

The small monk vacillated. I argued. He yielded. "Well, if you're sure, then. I do have duties. We must prepare to rescue those we can."

As soon as he vanished into the maze of yew hedges, I left the path, squeezed through the thick barrier of hedges, and hurried across the bridle path that led into the outer courts. Sure enough, a few hundred quercae south of the Alms Court, a steep stair led to the walkway atop the abbey's outer wall. Mumbling curses at my overtired thigh and at the cold rain that pelted my face and slickened the narrow steps, I hauled myself up the stair.

I limped northward along the wall overlooking the Alms Court. The walk came to an abrupt end at the south gatehouse tower. And snug in the tower wall sat an iron door, a convenient entry that would allow monks to take up their sanctuary watch or errant princes to slip into the abbey precincts without detection.

The wind blustered, flapping my gown about me like a luffing sail and bearing a nerve-scraping screech from the field below. Morbid curiosity drew me to the outer parapet where I could gaze down on the scene before the gates. Dark, still forms lay everywhere. A few shapeless creatures scurried among them on the peripheries where the rain had snuffed the torches—monks, searching for the living or blessing the dead, or perhaps scavengers, drawn from the forest on the trail of a war party like rats following a leaking grain sack.

The majority of Bayard's men, some mounted, some afoot, crowded near a great bonfire not far from the gatehouse. A small mounted party sat slightly apart—Bayard, Max, and a third rider, a slender warrior clad in silver mail and orange cloak, her long pale hair streaming in the swirling wind. The priestess of the Gehoum.

Gehoum were not comfortable gods, not at all like the bickering husband and wife, Kemen and Samele, whose lusty inclinations had peopled the world with lesser deities and whose devotion to the earth had created the guardian Danae to enrich and protect it. Nor were they in the least like the benevolent Iero, the father/brother god of the Karish, who had promised to send angels to carry us all to his heavenly realm did we but forsake our sinful ways. Gehoum were blind immortal powers who cared naught for mortal beings who existed only by their tolerance.

Sila Diaglou, once a temple initiate herself, had traveled the cities and villages of Navronne since she was seventeen, calling for a cleansing of the corrupted temples and a return to blood penalties for those who insulted the gods—beginning with the five members of the Sinduri Council, all Karish, and certain Navrons who had degraded their bodies past redemption, that is, harlots and nivat-crazed twist-minds. When the Sinduri condemned her as apostate, she had staged a public rite of repentance in the temple square in Palinur. Rending her garments and slashing her own face and arms with a knife, she had abjured the elder gods as false and named herself high priestess of the Gehoum. Some people had wept to see Sila Diaglou's fervent savagery. Some had laughed. No one laughed at her anymore.

Another soul-wrenching scream came from the center of the group. And then another. And another. My fingers gripped the gritty blocks of the wall until the hoarse, burbling cry abruptly ceased. The crowd shifted and surged. Then the screaming began again, but in a different timbre.

The Ardrans didn't know where their prince had gone. They thought him left behind on the field at Wroling Wood. How many would Bayard and the priestess kill before they believed it?

Why did I stay and heed such dreadful doings? I could not aid the poor wretches. I ought to get back to the infirmary. But some stray shred of honor forbade me seek the comfort of bed while men so near were screaming out their last hours on earth.

Nor was I the only observer. A tall, full-shaven monk stood before the Gillarine gatehouse, the gold solicale on his breast glinting in the scalding light. Was Father Abbot pleased with this outcome? Was soldiers' blood the price of his inviolate gates?

A chill shivered my flesh. Beyond the pool of firelight, the night shifted. I peered through the rain until my eyes felt screwed from their sockets. *There!* Another movement, like an inky worm slithering down the hillside. Of a sudden, a horn call pierced the night—no bright trumpet blast, but a low, hollow sound that settled like cold iron in the base of my spine.

The group by the bonfire disintegrated. Moriangi warriors raced to reclaim their mounts and with their leader—Bayard, I thought, from the size and shape of him—reinforced the pickets with a solid defensive line.

A wall of midnight taller than the gate towers swept toward the abbey across the dark plains, no surge of mounted knights or ranked halberdiers, but rumbling, roaring darkness itself. I'd never seen anything like it. Halfway across the plain, giant horses that breathed dark flames took shape and surged

out of the cloud wall as if straining to break free of the encompassing dark, drawing it along in their wake. Alongside them strode black-helmeted warriors thrice
the height of a man with mailed fists the size of boulders and lances as thick
as tree trunks. But these monstrous creatures were but phantasms—an unliv-
ing vanguard designed to instill terror and awe, like an Aurellian legion's
guide-staff hung with skulls and jangling bells, or the gorgons carved into
a Hansker longboat's prow. It was the warriors who rode behind the cloud
phantoms that struck my heart cold. Hidden as they were in roiling darkness, I glimpsed only a gray, twisted face here or a blood-streaked arm there.
But in that stomach-hollowing, knee-weakening moment before their strike,
I tasted a brutal hatred that could grind stone into dust.

The wall of midnight shattered the Moriangi picket line as an ax breaks
a dirt clod. Horses reared and screamed. Some riders fell; some slumped in
the saddle as their mounts ran wild.

Bayard's defensive line broke and fled, only to be snagged from behind
by the swift-moving legion of night. A few escaped by flailing their mounts to
a gallop before the wall reached them. Max's wine-colored cloak streamed
alongside Prince Bayard's blue and Sila Diaglou's orange, as they rode helter-
skelter into the night. Once at the top of a rise beyond the fray, Sila Diaglou
drew rein and turned to watch as the monstrous cloud forms lost cohesion
and the blackness settled over the battleground, extinguishing the bonfire
and remaining torches. But after only a moment, she struck out again and
galloped northward after the others.

The black fog enveloped the field, hiding the huddled prisoners, the
dead, the injured, and the laggards. Wails of terror rose in chorus. As the wall
of night rolled over him, the abbot dropped to his knees, arms extended.
"Stay thy hand, O Lord of Night!" he cried. "Have mercy on these that lie
before you! Let them pass!"

Suffocating with dread, I pressed my back to the parapet and slid downward to the wet stone walk, my arms flung over my head, praying the holy
stones would hide me.

Bells. A clear, measured cadence. Gray light penetrated the dark cave of my
arms and dangling sleeves. Dawn—wet, cold, and dismal. I unfolded my
stiff, aching limbs and peeled my sodden gown away from my sodden under-
garments. Was it possible I had fallen asleep? I remembered vividly where
I was and what had made me huddle in a quavering knot at the base of the

chest-high parapet. But the wall of night had overtaken the abbey well before midnight, and I could remember nothing since.

The bells changed from simple strikes to a pattern of changes: one-two-three-four, one-two, one-two-three-four, one-two. Prime—the dawn Hour.

Grabbing my stick and the edge of a granite block, I eased upward. My first tentative peek over the parapet propelled me to my feet. One harder look and I hurried down the stair and back toward the gates, ignoring the cold night's ache in my thigh. The dead had moved.

I limped through the gates and into the churned-up ruins of a once-grassy field. Abandoned weapons, packs, ripped blankets, battered pots and cups lay scattered amid blood-tainted puddles and dead horses. Close beside the walls, a muddy, disheveled Brother Robierre sat weeping alongside five other monks, all of them drenched and trembling, several with hands clenched in prayer. Abbot Luviar, seemingly uninjured, moved from one to the other, crouching beside each man to offer words of comfort. But what comfort could there be?

Save for the seven monks, no living man remained upon that field. But neither did the dead men rest where they had fallen. They had been separated into Ardrans and Moriangi, the two groups laid out in orderly rows six wide and stretching across the field. None of this was so dreadful, save when one gazed upon the ranks of fallen warriors and realized that beyond the usual grotesque battle injuries, their eyes had been plucked out, every one of them.

The Karish claimed that stealing the eyes of the dead did *not* remove their souls and forever bar them from the afterlife. Yet of all the battlefields I had walked, many with far more victims than this one, none had so twisted my heart. The gaping bloody emptiness where joy or fear, knavery or kindness, intelligence or dull wit had once lived was worse than any death stare. And the careful placement of the corpses, the cold deliberation of the deed, was far more terrifying than any barbarian battle rite.

At the head of this lifeless array, a lance had been plunged into the muddy earth and an ensign tied to it. The pennon hung limp and heavy, even its color indistinguishable in the gray morning. I stepped forward and lifted its edge. The tight woven fabric was the deep, rich green of holly and fir, and embroidered upon it in silver were the three-petaled trilliot and a howling wolf, the mark of Evanore—the mark of Eodward's third son, Osriel the Bastard, who purportedly had uses for the souls of the dead.

Chapter 8

On the morning after the assault—already referred to as Black Night—we buried ninety-three soldiers and one monk. Every able hand in the abbey, including my own, set to the grisly task. The cold mud weighed my spirits beyond grief, and as we laid the chilled flesh in the earth, I found myself mumbling, "Sorry. Sorry. Forgive." I could not have said why.

I asked Brother Robierre and others who endured that night before the gates what they had seen. Those who could speak of the matter at all agreed on the vanguard of flame-breathing horses and cloud warriors the size of the church. None reported aught else visible in the fog. I did not mention the gray faces I'd seen or the mortal dread that had afflicted me. But I could not let go of the memory.

On that same evening, everyone who could walk was summoned to church for a service of mourning and repentance. Brother Dispenser ladled ysomar, the oil used to anoint the sick and dying, into our clay calyxes—the expensive indulgence signifying the solemnity of the occasion. As we carried our votive gifts forward to empty into Iero's fire, the texts read from the holy writs were all of Judgment Night and the end of the world. The prayers did not sound at all optimistic.

Not allowed in the choir as yet, I stood in the nave with the lay brothers, wishing I could feel the same solace the brothers seemed to find in vague promises of a dull heaven. The music drew me through the hours like a strong current, and the scent of incense and burning ysomar evoked my childhood imaginings of divine mysteries. Candlelight reflected from jewel-colored windows, gleaming stone piers, and gold fittings, until the air in the vaults and domes of the church shimmered as if angels hovered there, the light and gossamer of their wings the evidence of their presence to us mortals below.

So much praying in this place. I'd not spent so much time inside a church on a single day in my life, save perhaps the day of King Eodward's funeral rites. For the first time since escaping my parents' house, I had donned a pureblood's mask and wine-colored cloak—both stolen—and haughty air—inbred. I had lied my way into the half-built cathedral in Palinur and promptly hid in the gallery, lest someone recognize me or attempt to unravel the family connections of an unknown pureblood. Only to honor King Eodward would I have risked discovery. His public glory had been but a part of what he was.

Though I had been presented to the king at three years of age, as were all pureblood progeny, I had met him only once. I was seventeen and feeling slightly giddy, having just survived two fierce days of fighting the Hansker invasion at Cap Diavol. One of my comrades took out a tin whistle and played to lift our spirits. The song moved my feet, and I stepped through a jig, faster by the moment, the surge of life grown wild in me, having been so close to death.

A man crouched by our fire for a moment to warm his hands and watch. When the song was done and I dropped breathless to the ground, drinking in the laughter and cheers of my comrades, I recognized the king. Though I'd heard he often wandered through the camp after a battle, I'd never believed it. But none could mistake the three trilliots blazoned on his breastplate—one lily the scarlet of Morian, one Ardran gold, and one the silver of Evanore. Despite deep creases about his eyes, his hair and beard yet flamed red-gold, scarce touched with gray.

He spoke a few words of thanks and encouragement to each of us seven, all that remained of our cadre of twenty. When my tongue flapped loose, as has always been my worst failing, spewing some foolish comment comparing a soldier's hardships and a king's, he smiled as if my nonsense cheered him in the face of three thousand dead and a worse battle facing us at dawn. And when I chose to take the measure of the only king I was ever like to meet, staring boldly at him rather than dropping my eyes in deference, he did not avert his gaze.

Before or since, I'd never known anyone who left his soul so exposed for another man, a stranger even, to view—and so I witnessed King Eodward's devotion to all who followed him and his grief for the price they must pay for their loyalty. Though I had already decided that the soldier's life was not for me, I vowed right then to serve him until one or the other of us was dead—an easy promise, of course, as he was in his sixtieth year and had few battles left to fight.

As he rose to leave our fire and move on to the next, the king cocked his head at me again, half smiling, half grieving. "Your quick feet and saucy mouth remind me strangely of some I knew in my own youth, lad. If you've happened here from Aeginea, tell them I don't think I'll get back. Tell them . . . *askon geraitz.*" The words, neither Navron nor Aurellian, made no sense to me.

I scrambled to my knees and bowed my head. "Of course, anything you ask, Your Majesty, but I know not this place—"

His hand raised my chin, silencing me. "No matter, then, lad. Just dance."

In the ten years since, I'd asked a number of people where a place called Aeginea might be, but no comrade or acquaintance had ever heard of it. Another of Serena Fortuna's jests—of anyone in the wide world, my grandfather the cartographer would surely know.

Not that I would ever ask the mad old man. He had appeared at our house at random intervals throughout my childhood, pawing at me with ink-stained fingers and babbling meaningless words in my ear, pretending we were allies in the household warfare. Then he'd disappear again without changing anything, abandoning me to my enraged father and hysterical mother. If a bleeding child's curses carried the weight of the gods, as some said, then the old gatzé had long since fallen off a cliff and taken a year to die.

Family. Not a topic to consider in a house devoted to the spirit's health. It was a marvel any of my bodily wounds ever healed with such poison in my blood. Family was long over and done with. I kneaded my scalp and tried again to lose myself in the monks' mournful music. Without result.

Max was the first member of the Cartamandua-Celestine household I'd glimpsed in twelve years. Contracted as Bayard of Morian's hound. Walking straight into my refuge. *Gods . . .* My urge to run blazed like a new-stoked furnace, even as I argued how unlikely he was to return here.

Truly, Abbot Luviar's role in this royal brawl ought to fright me more. Now *there* was a mystery worth the deciphering. If I, a man of thick skull and paltry skills, had come to see that the Duc of Ardra was an arrogant sham who would as soon sell the crown of Eodward as wear it, then why would the Abbot of Gillarine claim that prince's rescue to be the salvation of Navronne? Had Luviar fallen into the same magical stupor as his monks and I had done, or had he watched as the Bastard of Evanore stole the eyes of the dead?

Gillarine's safety seemed more ephemeral than I had hoped. Though not yet ready to abandon the place, I dared not relax the caution that had kept me free.

"Tell me, Brother Artur, do the Evanori warrior and his sickly secretary yet reside in the guesthouse?" I asked one of Brother Jerome's assistants when he brought supper from the kitchen two days after Black Night. The unsavory thought had crossed my mind that the abbot was brokering some alliance between Perryn and Osriel through this Evanori "benefactor."

"Nay, Thane Stearc and his party departed the day before Black Night," said the grizzled lay brother, uncovering the bowl of carrot and leek chowder he'd brought me.

A thane! Not just some landed knight, but an Evanori warlord—descendant of a family who centuries past, along with the gravs of Morian, had bound their lives and fortunes to Caedmon, King of Ardra, thus creating the kingdom of Navronne. I dropped my voice to a confidential whisper. "It seems a scandal to find Evanori in a holy place. I was taught they served the Adversary in their heathenish fortresses."

The monk's broad brow crumpled. "No, no! The thane's a scholarly man and Gillarine's greatest benefactor since King Eodward passed to heaven. Thane Stearc studied here as a boy and has visited the abbey every month for all these years, always bringing us new books and casks of wine, and donating generously to our sustenance."

"But he serves the Bastard Prince . . ."

"Indeed not!" Brother Artur blanched at the scandalous suggestion. "Though he wears the wolf of Evanore while in Ardra to proclaim his neutral state, his house is Erasku, which straddles the border. The thane claims both provinces or neither as he chooses."

Convenient, if one could get away with such juggling. The thane must be quite a diplomat or quite a warrior . . . or quite a liar. I hoped these monks were not so naive as to accept the lord's word without solid proof.

The lay brother carried his soup to the other patients——monks wounded on Black Night. I ate slowly, so that when he brought his tray around to gather up my bowl and spoon, he had to wait for me. "So, Brother Artur," I said quietly between bites, "I suppose you must carry a good lot of food to the guesthouse now."

He shook his head, puzzled. "None at all. We've few visitors in the best times. I doubt we'll see another till Lord Stearc returns."

I dropped my bowl on his tray and slumped back in the bed, disappointed and mystified. No infirmary visitor had dropped the least hint of Prince Perryn's presence.

The assault had left the abbey a dreary place. Brother Gildas did not show his face. Jullian spent a great deal of time in the infirmary, doing whatever small tasks the infirmarian assigned him, but scurried away whenever I so much as looked at him. Even genial Brother Badger wore a cloak of grief that lightened only slowly as the sun set and rose and set again, the life of the abbey taking up its plodding rhythm.

Though I had every reason to be satisfied with my prospects, Black Night and my odd experiences in the cloisters had left me on edge. I forever imagined dark shapes lurking in the shadowed corners of the infirmary. One night I broke into a nonsensical sweat when someone paused outside the horn windows with a blue-paned lamp and remained there for an hour.

To distract myself, I took to telling stories and reciting bardic rhymes in the hours between the monks' prayers, though indeed I had to search through my store of experiences and fables for those that would not shock celibate ears. I also began taking regular exercise around the infirmary garth. My leg felt well healed, giving only a bit of soreness and stretching when I took long strides. Though happy to be up and about—activity suited me better than indolence now I'd made up for half a lifetime's missed sleep—I was not yet ready to give up such a perfectly useful circumstance. I made sure to limp and grimace a great deal. I had a better chance of doing as I pleased if no one knew my true condition.

A tarnished silver medicine spoon I'd found in Brother Robierre's chest of instruments and a blood-crusted gold button he'd gouged out of a soldier's chest wound went into the packet under my palliasse—a pitiful lot of nothing. Memories of demon horses and gray-faced warriors left me chary of pilfering valuables from the church. Which meant, should I leave Gillarine, I'd surely need my book.

On one night in the quiet hours between Matins and Lauds, when my companions in the infirmary slept soundly, I tugged on boots and gown and crept through the darkened abbey. Three times I dodged around a corner and peered into the night behind me, imagining I'd catch someone following. But the only sign of life was a flare of light from the church. Someone's lamp illuminated a sapphire outline from one of the colored windows. The wavering light set the blue-limned figure moving. I signed Iero's seal upon my breast and took a long way around the cloister walk, offering a prayer for Brother Horach's spirit.

The small, many-windowed library building nestled in between the domed chapter house and the long, blockish monks' dorter in the east reach of the cloister garth. The scriptorium occupied the ground floor. One reached the actual library by way of an exterior stair.

A rushlight borrowed from the infirmary revealed the upper chamber to be unimposing. The white-plastered walls were unadorned, save for two tiers of deep window niches that overlooked the cloister garth. On the opposite wall, an arched doorway opened onto a passage linking the library with the adjoining chapterhouse and dorter. Backless stools of dark wood stood alongside five long tables, and deep, sturdy book presses with solid doors and sliding latches lined the side walls.

I opened the cupboard farthest from the door. A locked inner grate of scrolled brasswork revealed shelves crammed with scrolls and books. A careful examination through the grate indicated that the book of maps was not among them. I moved on to the next.

In the third book press, near the bottom of a stack of large volumes, I spied a leather binding of the correct color, quality, and thickness. No gryphon lurked amid the gold elaboration of grape leaves and indecipherable lettering on its spine, but then I'd never actually examined the thing edge on.

In hopes my search had ended, I assembled the spell components for manipulating locks: the feel of old brass tarnished by greasy fingers, the image of the bronze pins and levers that might be inside this type of lock, my intent in the rough shape of a key, ready to be filled with magic and applied to the lock. Then I began to step through the rules for binding these elements together to create an unlocking spell.

With lessons and practice the pureblood bent for sorcery could be used to shape spells that had naught to do with familial talents. Though my childhood indiscipline had prevented me learning the rules for many spells, I'd had a great deal of experience breaking locks as a boy and become fairly accomplished at it. Yet years had gone since I'd done much of any spellworking. Beyond my vow to forgo magic and thus avoid the fatal weakness of most *recondeurs*, I'd needed to hoard my power. Without sufficient time for the well of magic inside me to be replenished, I could find myself lacking enough to empower the doulon, and my nasty habit used almost everything my particular well could produce. But surely I could scrape together enough to break a lock.

I held the spell ready, touched my fingers to the keyhole, and released a dollop of magic. Nothing happened. The brass wasn't even warm to the touch.

I tried again, adjusting my expectation of the inner workings of the lock to something simpler. Feeling the press of time, I applied a much healthier dollop of magic. With a loud snap, blue sparks and bits of brass and bronze shot from the keyhole. The grate hung loose, a severely bent latch dangling from the brass frame.

"Holy Mother!" I waggled my stinging hand. Mumbling curses at my ineptitude, I twisted the latch back into shape the best I could, pulled off the most noticeably broken pieces, and brushed the metal chaff under the edge of the cabinet with my boot. Gingerly, I pulled open the overheated grate and extracted the book. It was not mine.

I stuffed the book back in the stack and slammed the grate, using a bronze shard to wedge it shut. Once the outer door was latched, I proceeded to the next book press. And the next . . .

So many books. Useless things. Searching those damnable cupboards felt as if I walked down a street of noble houses, where lamplight and singing spilled out the windows, knowing I'd not be allowed through any door. Not that I yearned to read about the world in place of living in it. It just would have been nice to know I could get in if I chose.

With nothing to show for my search so far but a broken lock and a stinging hand, I came to the last cupboard.

"We would be happy to provide you books, Valen, did you but ask." Pale light flared and died behind me.

I dropped my walking stick with a clatter and spun about, backing into a table that immediately began sliding out from under me. "Father Abbot!"

Abbot Luviar glided across the room and rescued the rushlight before I dropped it. "I'm sorry to startle you."

How the devil had he gotten to the far corner of the library without me seeing him? He'd certainly not been lurking there the whole time. I straightened my gown and backed away from him until blocked by the yawning door of the book press. "I was just . . . restless. I've slept so much."

"Understandable." Smiling, he set the rushlight on the nearest table and retrieved my dropped stick. He carried no lamp of his own. "This is a fortuitous encounter. I've been intending to thank you for your service on Black Night and since. Your warning saved lives. Your tales lift hearts. Even the digging—"

"I didn't help. Don't thank me." The last thing in the world I desired was any share of what this man had wrought on Black Night. "Perryn of Ardra should have stood with his men. Died with them."

"Indeed, he should have," said the abbot, using my rushlight to ignite a wall lamp, flooding one study table with pale illumination. "Events demanded otherwise."

"Is he still here?" Anger worked as well as strong mead to embolden my tongue.

Revealing naught but weariness, Luviar propped his backside and his hands on the table. "The prince is safe. I'll not say where."

"I'd have thought holy monks would stay removed from sordid politics," I said.

"Fleshly needs oft intertwine with the spiritual. How can a woman think of heaven while her children starve, or a man contemplate Iero's great love as his vines wither?" His furrowed gaze fixed somewhere in the emptiness between us. "We cannot always see the full span of history as it unfolds. Sometimes I fear that to attempt it is to infringe the role of the One who sees all, past and future. Yet, if the Creator *grants* us sight—"

His hypocrisy forced a choking sound from my throat. He jumped up and offered me his hand. "Here, Valen, are you ill?"

"Must have jarred my wound when I stumbled," I murmured, waving him off. "I'll be all right."

He passed me the rushlight. "You should get back to bed. Rest. Heal. Despite its current troubles, the world is a wondrous place, the earth itself God's holy book. Each man must discover his place in the great story. May you find your place . . . your peace . . . at Gillarine."

I bowed and hobbled toward the door. Behind me, Luviar unlocked one of the brass grates, pulled out a book, and sat down to read. His composure only pricked my fury.

Boreas had been right. Monks were naught but self-righteous thieves. No Cartamandua gryphon marked any binding in that library.

My days of sanctuary expired. As the only way a man of sixteen years or better could stay at the abbey beyond a fortnight was to take vows, that was what I resolved to do—at least until I could put my hands on my book. The monks insisted that my face revealed Iero's joy coursing through my veins. But truly, my good cheer stemmed from imagining the faces of anyone who had ever known me upon hearing of my intent.

"Good morrow, Valen! Iero's grace is full upon you this glorious morn!" Only two days after his return from Pontia, I had already learned that Brother Sebastian was excessively cheerful in the early morning. My mentor, a ruddy-cheeked monk with a round head, a neat fringe of gray hair bordering his tonsure, and an ever-immaculate habit, as might be expected of the son of a ship captain, had just come from chapter to disturb my morning nap.

"Brother." Bleary-eyed, I hauled myself to sitting, keeping the blankets up to my neck as the morning was damp and cold. Five more beds had been claimed by coughing, wheezing monks who had taken chills on Black Night. Jullian crouched by the brazier, stirring a cauldron of boiling herbs.

"What is great, you may ask?" Sebastian's face beamed as he snatched the black gown from the hook on the wall beside my bed. "Brother Robierre and I have decided that you may set sail from your sickbed today."

"But I thought—"

"Sorry to lose your good company, Valen. But you'll be healthier out of here." Brother Robierre pressed a rag across a spindly old monk's mouth as the poor fellow coughed up enough sputum to float a barque. Perhaps he was right.

Truth be said, I was a bit anxious at leaving my simple infirmary life behind for the mysteries of the monks' dorter. As a child in a house devoted to the elder gods, I'd heard outlandish tales of Karish monks who ate children in their secret precincts, of barbed tails grown beneath their gowns, all manly hair plucked out, or even privy parts removed entire. Being older than age ten, and having met a good variety of folk along the years, and having even practiced Karish ways when times made it expedient, I knew such talk as nonsense. Yet missing princes, murdered monks, and their unquiet spirits had left me a bit more wary of Iero and his holy precincts.

As Brother Sebastian exchanged blessings and gossip with the patients,

I donned my gown. My little bundle of provisions, medicines, and knife—now well sharpened—went into my rucksack along with my secular clothes. The empty green bag remained safely tucked away at the bottom.

"Until you take your novice vows, they'll send you here to sup, so we'll not lose you entirely," said the infirmarian, grinning as he dispensed one of his potions to another man. "And you must come down here every evening to let me examine your wounds . . ."

". . . and to finish your tale of that tin smuggler in Savil," called Brother Marcus from the bed closest to the door. "You can't leave us not knowing if the fellow got out of the cave."

I laughed. "I've a better one, about the time I fell in with a caravan of—"

"Be off with you, Valen, or I'll chase you out," said Robierre, beckoning Jullian to replenish an earthenware bowl with his steaming decoction. "We've our work to do."

"You've done well by me, Brother Infirmarian," I said, taking a jig step and twirling foolishly into a sweeping bow. "You are Iero's own artist with your lancets and caudles. I do thank you."

Robierre bobbed his head, flushed a little, and went on with his work. Jullian watched intently, a ladleful of his pungent liquid sloshing noisily into the fire. I winked at the boy, grabbed the rucksack and my alder stick, and joined Brother Sebastian at the door.

"I shall strive to do as well by you as Robierre has done," he said.

"You can stick your nose in *his* business, Sebastian," Brother Marcus called after us, "and leave off telling the rest of us when our gowns are untidy or our beds ill made." The red-haired scribe had taken a spear wound next his spine on Black Night and was dreadfully uncomfortable. He lay on his belly all day and all night, sketching odd little drawings on scraps of vellum laid on the floor under his nose. Robierre wasn't sure the man would ever leave his bed.

Brother Sebastian chuckled, held open the door, and waved me out. "Tell me if we set too fast a pace, Valen. Your leg seems to be progressing well."

We strolled past the herb beds and around the bakehouse. "I was thinking that I should go walking in the countryside to strengthen it and cleanse my lungs from the sickly humors of the infirmary . . ." *. . . and scout the possibilities for replenishing my supply of nivat.*

Brother Sebastian halted abruptly. "That would not be at all appropriate. Though yet unvowed, you must draw a sharp separation from the outer

world. Once your leg receives Brother Robierre's clearance, you will be assigned outdoor duties more than sufficient to cleanse your lungs."

"But—"

His raised finger ended discussion. We had reached the stair to the
monks' dorter, and he was soon busy showing me the rope bed and straw-
filled palliasse at the south end of the long, high-ceilinged room where I
would sleep.

The empty green pouch in the bottom of my rucksack soon became more
worrisome than midnight massacres, eyeless corpses, or monks who explained naught of lighthouses or vanishing royalty no matter what wheedling
I did. I had taught myself not to think of nivat or the doulon overmuch. The
need could come to shape all a man's dealings, his friends, his choices, until
life took shape from it every day and not just the one day in twenty-eight . . .
or twenty-one . . . that it devoured him. I swore I'd rather go mad from
the lack than let it rule me. But always the hour arrived when my bravado
withered.

I had already confirmed that Brother Robierre kept no nivat seeds in
the infirmary. An exploration of the bakehouse, while its denizens were at
Vespers, had revealed that Brother Baker kept his brick ovens clean, his floor
swept, his barrels of flour and salt sealed tight, and his wooden boxes of
herbs and seeds labeled neatly, though with no sketch or hint of their contents for any who had difficulty with letters. None of the boxes contained
nivat. I would have to go farther afield to replenish my supply.

My hopes of moving in and out of the abbey freely were quickly
squelched. Every hour of my day was scheduled: services in the church,
meals in the infirmary, washing, and walking. I suffered endless lessons, everything from how to fold my gown and place it in the wooden chest at the
foot of my bed, to the signing speech the monks used in the cloisters, to a
history of the brotherhood so detailed I could near recite what Saint Ophir
had for breakfast every morning of his four-and-eighty years. Even my times
of "study and reflection" in the church or the gardens were scrutinized. If I
dozed off, one or the other of the brethren would immediately walk by and
rap my skull with a bony knuckle.

And so I decided to slip out at night. The monks were abed with the
birds, and as the dorter had been built for a hundred and twenty, a wide gap
of empty cubicles separated my quarters from those of the thirty-one men

who slept at the end nearest the church. And in the main, I was well shielded from their view. Besides the common shoulder-high screen of carved wood that separated one monk's bed, chest, stool, and window alcove from the next man's, a folding screen of woven lath had been set across the central aisle to separate the novices' cubicles from those reserved for the monks. And I was the only novice.

But not only did Brother Sebastian poke his head around my screen twice each night, as the Rule advised, but the very structure of the dorter thwarted me. My cubicle lay between the monks' cubicles and the reredorter. Throughout the night, sleepy monks in need of natural relief made a constant procession down the central aisle, around the lath screen, and past my open cubicle toward the cold wooden seats of the rere.

Worse yet, I was expected to parade down to the church with the monks to pray the nighttime Hours. These interruptions came at such frequent and unholy times—Vespers before supper, Compline at bedtime, Matins at midnight, Lauds at third hour, Prime at sixth—I could not see how I would ever be able to absent myself long enough to acquire what I needed. The anxiety I tried to keep from ruling my life crept inevitably into every hour.

"It's come!" Brother Sebastian hurried down the path from the cloisters waving a rolled parchment. "I worried we might have to lie twixt wind and water for another month."

I slammed the wretched book shut. Excessive meditation was surely ruinous to good health and spirits. While my mentor had attended the chapter meeting that morning, I'd sat on this stone bench in the hedge garden, pretending to study. The characters on the page had tightened into seed shapes. Every scent—of yew, of grass, of smoke from the kitchen—taunted me because it was *not* the earthy fragrance of nivat.

"It's the letter from Palinur. The last impediment to your investiture is removed." Having been informed that I was schooled enough to comprehend Aurellian, Brother Sebastian had blithely deemed no further reading test necessary, and his oral quiz of my mathematical skills had been less taxing than a visit to any Morian trade fair. He had lacked only the proof of my birth.

Sebastian unrolled the parchment under my nose. I furrowed my brow and inspected the page as if I could comprehend it. His chattering implied the cathedral labor rolls had indeed confirmed my status as a freeborn and legitimate son of nobodies.

Neither bastards nor villeins were allowed to labor on holy works. When I'd wandered back to Palinur a few years before in search of work, I had assembled several tavern acquaintances into a poor but devout family, believable enough to testify and get me hired on at the cathedral. I had cheerfully imagined my mother's face if she ever learned she had been mimed by a whore who had serviced Palinur's garrison so often, she could identify the soldiers' pricks blindfolded.

Brother Sebastian's face shone brighter than the hazy sun. "The abbot has given his consent. And, most excellently, it happens that the Hierarch of Ardra himself has arrived for a visitation and will preside at your vesting! Come along with me, lad."

Before I knew it, we had collected my secular clothes from the dorter and a provision bag from the kitchen, and he was bustling me through the doorway of the very guesthouse where I had been certain that the Duc of Ardra was hiding from his royal brother.

"Tomorrow dawn I'll come for you, my son. Open your heart for Iero's guidance." Brother Sebastian pushed a canvas bag into my hands, and for a moment the animation of his round face yielded to a quieter sentiment. "You've a cheerful heart, Valen . . . yes, yes . . . Robierre has seen it as well, as has everyone who's met you. Our brotherhood will benefit greatly from the vigor you bring. But nothing sours a graceful spirit more than taking a path it is not meant to walk, so we would have you be certain of each step along the way." He grinned and retreated down the steps, waving as he disappeared past the granary. Guilt nudged my shoulder, but I quickly dismissed it.

The bag contained bread, cheese, and a traveling flask of ale, provisions for my journey should I decide to abandon the monastic life. An earthenware flask contained a liquid that had no smell. I wrinkled my nose. Water from the blood-tainted abbey spring was to be my only sustenance for my night of meditation. The bag did *not* contain my book. I wasn't sure whether to be insulted that they thought I was so stupid as to abandon my only possession of value, or gratified that they considered me worthy of their company.

I explored the guesthouse, speculating as to where the abbot had installed his royal supplicant if not here. Though its chambers were not elaborately decorated, it was more luxurious than anywhere I'd slept in many years. Plum-colored rugs warmed the bare floors. Brightly woven tapestries blanketed the walls, depicting the events from the life of Karus, the divine mystic from the steppes of far Estigure whose unruly sect had grown into Iero's Karish church.

A magnificent fresco in the dining room illustrated the familiar theme of the *ordo mundi*—the world's proper order. In sweeping bands of blue, yellow, and crimson, the artist illumined the three spheres: the arc of heaven, where the holy saints lived with Iero and Karus; the base foundation of hell, domain of the Adversary and damned souls; and in between, the earthly sphere with its righteous layers of kings and hierarchs, purebloods and peasants, its somber labors and abject wickedness so vividly depicted and its true delights so blatantly ignored. Though Iero extended his hands toward the earthly sphere in invitation, only the winged grace of angels bridged the gaping emptiness between the spheres of heaven and earth. A sad oversight, I'd always thought. In this respect, the Sinduri Council offered a more pleasing view: that every arch, tree, window, grotto, and mud puddle had its pesky aingerou, a messenger to the elder gods. Thus common folk could hold a discussion with our ever-quarreling divine family by raising a glass in an inn or taking a piss in the wood.

It was tempting to build a fire in the hearth, relax on the fine couch, and contemplate this profound and beautifully wrought statement of humankind's place in the scheme of things. But I dared not miss this chance to get out, acquire what I needed, and get back again without prompting uncomfortable questions from my hosts. Unfortunately the guesthouse held no valuables small enough to carry with me.

Though I had been instructed to leave my monk's garb in the dorter for my vigil night, pragmatism had prompted a minor disobedience. Those who prowled the roads of Navronne, whether soldiers, highwaymen, or even the most devout followers of the elder gods, considered it unlucky to touch a wayfaring monk or practor. Interference with traveling clergymen had been a hanging offense since the days of King Caedmon's Peace and the Writ of Balance. The Writ, a declaration of truce between the priests and priestesses of the Sinduri Council and the Karish hierarchs, had been proclaimed at Navronne's birth by King Eodward's great-great-great-grandfather—or his father, if you believed the legend that a beleaguered Caedmon, his beloved kingdom on the verge of annihilation by the Aurellian Empire, had sent his infant son Eodward to live with the angels for a hundred and forty-seven years.

As soon as darkness fell—the time when Brother Cadeus the porter gave up his post at the Alms Court—I downed one more swallow of ale, threw the black gown over my jaque and braies, and slipped out of the guesthouse. From the mouth of the gatehouse tunnel, I skulked northward along the outer wall, avoiding the track across the open field so as not to be observed from the sanctuary room. A wooded hollow near the junction of the track and the main road, where the tricky moonlight shifted shadows, provided a likely vantage for less benevolent observers. Prince Bayard would surely have set a watch on the abbey.

Only when I reached a lonely beech grove did I breathe again. I scoffed at my racing heart. What was wrong with me? These were *monks* after all, and they held no bond upon me. No matter what kind of exit I made, they'd likely take me back come morning if I vouched some saintly vision had changed my heart. This constant prickling of unease was wholly foolish—likely naught but my long-muzzled conscience thrown out of sorts in such a holy place. Laughing at the thought of *myself* shipped off to live in the realm of angels, I shouldered my rucksack again and set out along the mist-shrouded river.

Chapter 9

A quellé north from the abbey, the River Kay vanished into ripe-smelling boglands. The road, so firm and wide at Gillarine, dwindled into marshy tracks, scarcely distinguishable from the fen in the patchy moonlight. My steps slowed. No bogwight was going to lure me into a muddy death, doomed to take its place until the next unwary traveler set me free in turn! Unfortunately, a careful pace would never get me to Elanus and back in any sensible time, even assuming Jullian's estimate of three quellae was at all accurate.

Thus, I chose to risk using a bit of magic again. If I didn't acquire nivat, no amount of power would save me. As the moon darted behind a wad of clouds, I knelt to lay my palms on the earth and discover my way using my bent. I closed my eyes. The mud was cold and gummy and smelled of rotting timber, moldering leaves, and animal droppings. Softening the boundaries of my mind, I released magic to flow through my fingertips.

Inhale. The scents grew richer . . . stronger. Boot leather and greased axles, cut timber and hay had passed this way. Horses and donkeys. Flocks of sheep and pigs driven to town. *Listen.* Gurgles and trickles spoke of the river, not vanished, but merely hidden beneath and beside and around me, as powerful in its dispersal as in its joined form, just more subtle. I discovered traces of travelers . . . of voices. My youthful ventures in use of my bent had never been so vivid.

I stretched my mind forward and swept from left to right, as a draftsman ties his pen to a string and stretches that string from a fixed point to scribe a perfect arc. Within that arc I could sense the variance of terrain: puddles and gullies, sucking mud pits, submerged trees, plots of firmer ground, the tracks of thirsty deer and bears and skittering mice, and always the road like a band of sturdy cloth, woven of scents and earth and the quivering remnants of those who had trod or ridden or driven over it, talking, braying, singing.

So many sensations all at once . . . and the music . . . A number of singers had traveled this road, leaving behind telltales of their music. One of them . . . ah, what a gift . . . the plucked notes of a harp wound through present and past like a thread of silver, woven into the road for a while and then wandering off into the fens . . . a song to pierce the heart. A prickling crept up my arms, as if I were dissolving into the fens like the river and the road. Beneath my palms the earth swelled, as if a body lay beneath the mud and had begun to breathe. Somewhere eyes were opening . . .

Quickly, I scribed the shape of the land on my mind and yanked my hands away, rinsing the mud off them in a puddle and wiping them on my gown. A glance around the still, moonlit landscape revealed neither man nor beast. But as I set off again, I could not slough off the sense that my eyes were unreliable.

Forests and bogs were favorite haunts of spirits. Though aingerou preferred cities and other man-built habitations, and revenants preferred the places they'd lived or died, tales spoke of older beings who yet walked in the wild—the guardian Danae, whose dancing wove the patterns of the world and who could merge their bodies with ponds or groves, or demon gatzi, who were but Danae corrupted to Magrog's service. Both were said to whisk folk away from mortal life. I'd never run across any such creatures, so they didn't worry me all that much, but it never hurt to keep one's eyes open.

Holding the thread of path and direction in my head, I hurried down the road, humming the harper's song that still shimmered in my head. The cheerful melody swelled my heart and kept the night's terrors at bay.

The hour was not even Compline when the first glimpse of torchlit roofs and walls, and the first sounds of pipe, tabor, and raucous laughter set up a rampant thirst in me. I stripped off my monk's gown, stuffed it into my rucksack, and trotted the last few hundred quercae up the road and across the ditchwork to the cross-timbered gate. A good-sized town like Elanus should have a fine selection of taverns, sop-houses, pickable pockets, friendly barmaids, and gullible gamblers, not to mention an herbalist or apothecary with nivat seeds to sell. Not to mention a tankard of potent mead to warm away the damp and make a man forget politics, holy men, and conspiracies for an hour or two.

A closer look dampened my optimism. Though the earthwork surrounding the hillside town appeared substantial, the wooden palisade atop it was rotting and the town watch lax and slovenly. My claim that I'd come in search of a secure bed on a journey to visit my brother in Palinur easily satisfied the two half-soused guardsmen who carried but one serious weapon between them—an iron-bladed bill hook that would see its best use as a club. They seemed more interested in my assertion that my brother had a job awaiting me in a Palinur tannery than in the motley bloodstains on my jaque or how I had managed to travel any distance in these perilous times, carrying no weapon but a walking stick.

"Bog iron's failing," said one of the reeking pair as he cracked some aged walnuts with his bill. His blotched skin was peeling. "Half the smelts are cold. Roads too risky to bring in ore, and them as might haul it are fighting or dead. Elanus won't last a year more."

The second guard sneezed and wiped his nose on his sleeve. "Some Harrowers were through here yestereve, preaching. Lot of folk figure the orange-heads have it right. Won't take but another smelt closing down for them to have us all burning for the Gehoum."

"So they've gone now . . . the Harrowers?" I asked, glancing around uneasily, happy I'd taken off the monk's habit. I didn't need any ragtag from Black Night taking out their frights and vengeance on a monk. Harrowers didn't honor the Writ of Balance. "You're sure they weren't soldiers—Moriangi?"

"Nawp. Only orange-heads, but soldierly, especially the woman leading 'em. They're burning farms and outliers these last few days, them they say is offending their holy Gehoum. They burnt Mott's granary, saying his plow was a curse. The watch snagged one of her hags for the pillory. Rest got away."

"Mayhap I'll be on my way sooner as later, then," I said. "Wouldn't want to cause them offense. But I'm for a tankard first." I'd need to be careful leaving. The Harrowers would likely hang about the town to get their woman back. Perhaps theirs was the foreboding presence I'd felt on the road.

The town pillory sat just inside the gates. A frowsy woman, face streaked with ash and blood, yelled at me hoarsely as I hurried past. "The day of terror comes! The Gehoum will have their vengeance!" Her hair was strung up in a greasy wad atop her head and tied with an orange rag. She didn't sound so much crazed as excited.

I sloughed off the worry, waded through a knee-deep gaggle of muddy geese that blocked the town's main street, and happily inhaled the scent of civilization—dung, smoke, and burning fat. Just ahead of me, a ragged donkey boy leveled one whip and manifold curses, trying to get a charcoal-laden dray up the steepening lane.

The people of Elanus seemed a grim and unhealthy lot altogether, just like their town. At the edge of the road bony children dabbled sticks in the puddles, and cripples shook empty cups, bawling for a citré. Everywhere were hollow cheeks and peeling, unhealthy skin, and sunken eyes that would not meet mine. Orange head rags stuck out like bits of bright paint on a wall of gray.

As I strolled past an alley, trying to decide whether to locate a source for the nivat or the means to pay for it first, a burly man with a slack lip and a sinner's nose pawed at my sleeve. "A bed companion this night, traveler? Or an hour's pleasure?"

In the shadowed alley, a squint-eyed young woman opened her threadbare cloak to reveal a tight-laced bodice of ruffled lace. A slim, pretty boy with skin the color of milked tea leaned against the sooty brick, smirking as he shivered in naught but a stained silk tunic and a silver ankle bracelet.

"These two come all the way from Estigure. Blessed is the man who lies with divine Karus's kin. Lay away blessings lest the world's end catch you lornly."

I sighed and let my eyes drink in the sights. "Regrettably I've other holy business must come first."

The man waggled a finger and the girl spun in place, billowing her cloak and a filmy skirt, slit from hither to yon, offering glimpses of long, slim legs. The tasseled string that fastened her lacy bodice swayed most enticingly. My hands twitched as I imagined the smoothness of those long legs and the delights that lay underneath the shabby lace. Serena Fortuna had cursed me with overlong abstinence already, and now proffered the lonely prospect of winter at an abbey. No prayer I'd ever heard could sheathe a man's ache.

With apologies to the goddess Arrosa for refusing her sweet gift, I worked to cool the growing heat in my loins. *Think of battlefields, Valen. Winter. A starving belly. Monks. Nivat seeds. Family.* "Perhaps later."

His pitted, leaking nose twitched, and he licked his sagging lip, revealing stained teeth. "Five citrae will hold the girl for you until midnight. Ten for the boy. I've others as well. Locals. Cheaper, but blessed, all the—"

"I'll come back if Serena Fortuna is kind."

Even if I'd had the price, I wasn't fool enough to give it on a promise. But I bowed to the girl, which brought a lovely flush to her pale cheeks and set her licking lips much finer than the procurer's, and I winked at the youth, which replaced his smirk with a soft and subtle eagerness. Perhaps four years older than Jullian, he stretched an arm behind his head and thrust out one slim hip just enough to make a graceful curve.

I cleared my throat and dragged my eyes away. "Tell me, goodman, where in this sober town might I find good mead and honest dice?"

"Cross-hill toward the smelts, you'll find the Blade. Tell Holur that Tigg sent you for a game and a taste from his cask. He'll see to you." He shrugged and turned his attention back to other passersby.

My stomach rumbled as I meandered down the lane that leveled off westward, "cross-hill," rather than taking the steeper way that climbed the rounded mound of Elanus. A few tight-shuttered houses lurked among others collapsed into weedy ruins. The sweet pale smokes of peat fires laced with pork fat hung over the lane like mist over the bogs. At the far end of the lane, darker billows rose from the charcoal fires of the "smelts," where the folk of Elanus teased workable iron from treasured pellets dug from the peatlands.

I'd tended a bog-iron smelter one autumn. Hot, smoky, tedious work to keep the fires stoked and burning evenly for days on end. I'd been no good at it. The sheer ugliness of the task could not but set a man's mind wandering.

Just down the lane, a knot of shouting people broke into cheers. Peering over the bobbing heads revealed a squirming, muddy tangle of scrawny limbs and occasional glimpses of bared teeth and bloodied cheeks and noses. One of the boys, significantly smaller than the other, seemed favored by the crowd, and every twist that gave him a moment's advantage elicited a cheer and a jostle of backslapping. A stringy man with bulging eyes collected coins from the onlookers. One lad would likely get a meal for his bruises, the other naught but a boot in the backside. I'd earned my share of both. When the pop-eyed man stuck his tin cup in my face, I showed him my empty palms, bellowed an encouragement for each of the boys, and moved on.

A wedge of hammered iron dangling above a lettered signboard announced an establishment blazing with light and bursting with jolly music and fine smells. The Blade. Ah, I did love a friendly tavern, a pocket of warmth and enjoyment amidst all the cold world's ills. My spirits, far too sober with deceptions, politics, abbeys, and damnable diseases, perked up.

> *The doxy held the law at bay with tit and toe and tongue.*
> *All while the bandit stole away that night before he hung . . .*

As ever, the singing snared me like a hook trap. I joined in even before I walked through the door, and as I slammed the splintered plank behind me, a woman draped her arm about my neck and warbled the next chorus right in my ear. Laughing, I grabbed her waist from behind and whirled her about as the song required, while other men tried to pinch her tits or stomp her toe. Spoiling for action and good cheer, I let the music liven my feet to glide and pivot, heel and toe. The rhythm of the tabor took us up and down the room through the clapping crowd as I spun her dizzy and protected her from their gleeful pawing.

Well into the doxy and the bandit's fourth escapade, we collapsed over a table in breathless merriment, and I first glimpsed the woman's face. Beneath a lank cascade of mud-colored hair swelled smooth cheeks of a pleasant pink and naught else worthy of mention. My brother Max would have called her a mirror-bane.

"Two more on my coin, Holur!" she yelled over my shoulder as our pursuers abandoned us in favor of a new ale barrel being hauled in from the back room. "Though my head be swimming, my tongue is dry. And this fellow sings like a carpenter's rasp."

Coins rattled in the piper's basket, and a new dance went on without us. Still laughing, I dragged the woman up and into my arms, my hands finding a sure downward path toward the generous curves beneath her skirt. Max had always been too particular by half. Such yielding firmness demanded further explorations. My feet moved to a more languorous tempo.

She moaned softly deep in her throat, and a pleasant heat rose from her skin and through her layered clothing. I drew her closer.

"La, sir! I can't." Trapping my neck in the crook of one elbow, the woman dragged my head downward until our foreheads touched. Then she grinned wickedly, and with a deft move, stuffed her tongue in my ear, leaving my own lips and tongue poised for naught. Before I could riposte, she slipped my grasp altogether.

She didn't go far, though. A fellow with a dirty apron and skin the color and texture of oak bark held out two foaming mugs. She took one for herself and shoved the other into my empty hands, crashing her mug into mine for a toast. "To my brave defender!" she said with a smile and an ale-sodden belch. "My name's Adrianne, by the by. Though I be loath—sorely loath—to leave so game and manly a partner, my da will beat me purple if I linger one jot more."

"Alas, and I just arrived," I said, discreetly using a sleeve to blot the remains of her sloppy kiss, as I grinned back at her. "Without knowing a soul to ask where I might find the proper seasonings for my Saldon bread."

She giggled and touched my face with a plump finger. "Such a fine handsome fellow as you baking feast bread . . . it's hard to imagine."

"I've baked my own Saldon loaf since I was sixteen, even if I had to do it on a stone in a thistle fire," I said and scooped her finger into my mouth for a lick and a nip. She tasted of garlic and ale and woman. "And as I've come to Elanus in search of work and already heard the bog iron's failing, I'd best not lapse in proper honor to the Danae's feast."

"I saw a Dané once," she said, dropping her head on my chest, either because she didn't want to be heard by our rowdy companions or because she couldn't hold it up any longer. "In the bog when I was late from town and cut across close to Movre's Pool. Tall and beautiful she was. Naked, with her blue marks of magic glowing on her skin. Didn't speak, though her light guided me safe through the bog."

"More likely Iero's angel than a Dané, if your tall, beautiful creature was also kind." More likely yet another tipsy maid waked from a randy romp in a berry thicket. Legend named the Danae spiteful beings who once gave life to forests, lakes, and fields, but hated human folk. Supposedly a furious Mother Samele took the earth from the Danae's charge and gave it to the impish aingerou after Kemen lay with a Danae queen and fathered Deunor Lightbringer. Even the Sinduri Council professed that if the Danae had ever existed, they did no longer.

The girl shook her head vigorously. "Not an angel. She'd no wings. Some say Danae have wings, as they vanish right in front of you, but my grandmere told me they just turn a corner that human eyes can't follow."

"As to my baking needs . . . I've only the clove, ginger, and pennyroyal." I regretted cutting off the discussion, but the girl's time was limited, and such a companionable encounter, a staple of friendly common rooms, should yield *some* fruit.

"Ah," she said and dropped her voice to a liquid whisper. "Down Smelt Alley, third door, you'll find Gorb the seedsman. You needs must bang the door and convince the pinchfist to open his locks and trade with you, but he'll have both hazelnuts and nivat to sell. Mayhap"—she tilted her bleary gaze upward—"I should go with you. I'll bake a Saldon loaf as well and take it to the bog. Da's a smith and not got half the work he used to. Raises his yellow bile, it does. Folk pray to Iero about the war and the end times coming, or whine to Kemen and Samele about the weather, but naught's offered a pin to the Danae that I know of, asking help to replenish the bog iron here at Elanus. They're most forgotten."

Serena Fortuna's beneficence lay warm on my back. "Well, as you're late home already and risking your da's heavy hand, what if *I* were to visit this seedsman and fetch hazel and nivat for us both? I'll meet you here tomorrow eve, and we'll have a song and share it out. I'll divide my ginger with you, too. This merry meeting will infuse our bread with luck." I brushed my fingers around her cheeks and down her neck to other fetching curves, feeling her desire swell to meet my own. It had always made sense to me that magic flowed through a sorcerer's fingertips. "I'd need your coin, of course, as nivat comes so dear. But better to risk a few lunae with me than your da's bruises on these pretty cheeks, don't you think?"

Her sigh, as I bent over and kissed her on the lips to seal the bargain, came near subverting my wickedness. Willing women with even one attractive feature had the disconcerting habit of making me lose all sense. But the nivat was of first importance. I summoned up chilly thoughts of Gillarine and its confining comforts. As my rousing fever cooled again, I pulled away. Damnable necessity. I might as well be gelded.

Adrianne bade a mooning, ale-sodden farewell to our merry company, leaving me with a mug of ale, a promise of all the dancing I might desire on the following night, and three silver lunae in my pocket. A smith's daughter . . . probably the wealthiest girl in Elanus . . . a more tempting winter's companion than tidy Brother Sebastian. All sorts of schemes flourished in the flush of the moment. I wasn't greedy.

But from the talk I heard from other customers as I finished my ale, the heavy-fisted smith had only enough work to pay his debts and keep Adrianne from Tigg the Procurer's hand until the last of the bog iron was worked. An empty-pocketed son-in-law would do naught for his choler. I'd need to sell my book to make the scheme work, and in that case I could surely do better than Adrianne. Not that I was in the market for a wife. My feet were too restless for shackling.

A rattling from the corner, punctuated by challenges to manhood, prayers to Serena Fortuna, and a caller's flat tones, tempted me to a dice game. Sadly, I had never been able to summon even a glimmer of my mother's bent for divination when it came to gambling. Best not risk Adrianne's offering. Nivat was easily available throughout Navronne, being an essential ingredient for those who observed the elder gods' feasts at the change of seasons. But the native plants—a kind of pepper once grown in Morian—had failed decades ago, and as the only surviving ones were cultured by sorcery, it was always expensive. Even the mead would have to wait. I drained my mug, bade Holur and his jolly piper a mournful farewell, and stepped back into the night. Leaving a tavern for a street, no matter how busy, always put the damp on my spirits.

Chapter 10

"That should do for whatever purpose you have in mind," said Gorb as he wrapped the nivat seeds in a scrap of cloth and tied the little bundle with a thread. He stretched his tight lips into a smile no wider than the flare of his nose and dragged his dark little eyes up and down my height. "Oh, yes. Saldon Night baking, you said. As night devours the sunlight and spits it out again, you shall be well blessed."

A plaintive tale of my need for Danae help with my witch-cursed prick had induced the seedsman to unlock his door. Truly, the story itself hadn't moved him, but only my invocation of Adrianne as the proposed beneficiary of my reinvigorated better parts.

A wizened little fellow as dry and sharp-edged as his merchandise, Gorb supplied a quantity of black nivat seeds no bigger than my thumb, enough to bake three Saldon loaves or service my unfortunate craving thrice over. And for that he returned only nine citrae out of the three silver coins worth forty each. Iero bless merry Adrianne and blunt her father's fist.

I shook the copper coins in my palm. Spending one of them on hazelnuts might blunt the speculation in Gorb's hard little face. Though I hated wasting the money, nivat was used only for holy offerings like feast bread or for spellworking, and of all the spells that could be worked with nivat, only the doulon required it. I wished no rumors of tall sorcerers with unsavory habits lingering in a town the monks might visit. Fate might lead me to Elanus again.

So . . . a story . . . and how could I help but think of the cursed Boreas, the very one who had caused the need for this journey?

I leaned my head across the table and spoke softly so that Gorb's brisk fingers came to a halt. "I met a man in the wood yestereve, a rough, hairy man near tall as me and twice as broad. He was laid up with the sweats, sick and drooling, pissing himself he hurt so wicked. He showed me plate and jewels he'd stolen from a rich man's house and said if I would bring him nivat seeds, he'd trade me a jeweled dagger that would keep me and Adrianne for ten years or more."

Satisfaction blossomed on Gorb's countenance, and greed sparked his seedlike eyes.

"Iero damns those that steal," I went on as if I hadn't noticed. "But this would not be stealing to my mind, as the guilt of the theft would rest on the one who *first* took the dagger from its rightful owner. If I made the bargain honorably and filled my part as I vowed, no fault would come to me. So I said I'd find him nivat and return tonight at midnight to make the trade."

Nodding slowly, the seedsman dropped his eyes. He shoved the packet across the table and briskly brushed the table's detritus from the flowing sleeves of his green robe. "Twist-minds are an affront to the Powers. You say this depraved fellow lies close by Elanus?"

I straightened up and grinned. "I'm no fool to tell you that, Seedsman Gorb. You've a bigger supply of nivat than I can afford. But once I have my dagger, I'll tell the man where he can buy more, and Serena Fortuna bless you with whatever arrangement you can make with him."

He dipped an iron scoop into his barrel of hazelnuts and slid a few of them into my palm atop the coins. "Good fortune shared always comes back," he said. His sharp chin quivered as if he were on the verge of weeping. Or perhaps laughing.

I paused in the smoky deeps of Smelt Alley and divided my store of nivat. Half went into the green bag, which I restored beneath the false bottom of my rucksack. I tied Gorb's cloth packet, containing the remainder of the nivat, to the waist string of my braies, and tucked eight coppers into my boot. I spun the last coin in the air and caught it, already tasting mead and humming a tune to accompany its sweet fire.

But as I stopped in at the still boisterous Blade, thoughts of perfidious Boreas choked me worse than the smelters' smoke, souring my mood. That pain-racked, drooling wretch I had described would not be *him* deprived of nivat, of course, but me.

Holur's mead cask was empty. But a tankard of his best ale and a bowl of porridge soothed my ill humor, and I bawled every song and galloped the length and breadth of the Blade with every maid and matron that stepped inside—none of whom were Adrianne, all thanks to Serena Fortuna. When I tossed my fifth citré on the barman's counter, ready to buy another round of ale, the lamplight caught the polished copper and flared like a red sunburst . . . which brought to mind solicales . . . and Karish monks . . . and the life waiting for me with the coming dawn. Before Holur could clamp his sticky fingers on the coin, I snatched it back, stuffed it in my boot, and with sober regrets bade him and all the company a good night.

The crier called second hour of the night watch—one hour till midnight— as I headed out for Gillarine. Elanus showed no signs of sleep. No surprise to that. The smelters had to be kept burning through the night. As I strolled past Tigg's alley on my way to the gate, the catamite raised his head and moved a step away from the wall, beckoning me into the alley. He was alone.

I shook my head and raised two open palms in a gesture of peace—or poverty, if one interpreted gestures in marketplace dialect. The message was much the same: I couldn't afford him, but bore him no ill will.

He nodded and slumped back against the bricks.

Though my taste ran usually to women, the youth was, indeed, beautiful. A torch burned in a bracket above his head. His mellow rose-brown skin and acorn-colored hair gleamed in the firelight. The deep blue silk of his scanty tunic rippled enticingly with his movements, and the silver bracelet on his bare ankle sparkled with a gemstone of matching blue . . . a sapphire?

I halted abruptly. That a catamite in the alleys of Elanus would be wearing a sapphire bracelet did not stun me half so much as the fact that I had admired that very bracelet in a noblewoman's jewel box . . . just before I stuffed it in my rucksack and got myself an arrow in the thigh. Boreas!

My blood running hot, I beckoned the youth to the street. Down the alley, Tigg the Procurer was taking a leisurely piss.

The youth summoned a smile from some secret place and lowered his dark lashes in a way that promised to share its source. Well past its days of breaking, his voice wrapped my body like silk. "What's your pleasure, sir? Tigg has a room—"

"Shhh." I laid my arm around the youth's tight shoulders. Though he smelled exotically of cardamom and clove, his accent was directly from the riverlands of Morian, not mystical Estigure. Careful to keep him within sight of his master and myself obscured by the brick corner, I bent my head to his.

"No custom from me this night, sorry to say, but I *would* offer you a citré for a question answered."

He raised his heavy lids and buried his secrets again. "One citré buys only a small answer."

"The bracelet on your ankle. I would know where to find the person who sold it to your master. My wife—a harridan the likes of which would drive Sky Lord Kemen himself to the netherworld—would forgive me the worst of my failings if I could but take her such a trinket. And though your beauty is most worthy of much beauty in its turn, I'm thinking this little treasure was not ruinous to buy. Your master seems a . . . thrifty man."

"Your coin?" He stuck out his hand, all languorous invitation vanished.

I dug the copper from my boot and held it above his hand. "And your answer?"

A careless toss of his head threw his silken hair from his face. "Don't think to get *this* bauble. Master covets it. He said I could wear it for the street, but not when I go with aught. Big hairy fellow gave it for a night with me most of a month ago. Said he needed the blessing of lying with Karus's kin, as he was hunting a place to bed for the winter."

"That's all?"

The youth's long lashes fell toward his smooth, empty palm. "We didn't talk so much. He'd been a while without a decent lay."

Disappointed, I brushed my hand across his, releasing the coin. It vanished under the hem of his tunic, and he stepped back so that my arm dropped loose and empty. Even a touch would cost me more. I didn't begrudge him the necessities of his trade.

I eyed his slender form, neither hair nor blemish to be seen anywhere below his scalp. He brought to mind Stearc's squire Corin of the bronze braid and elegant cheekbones . . . fairer yet than this one. I felt a shifting in my braies, which circumstance startled me a bit. I was truly a pitiable case. "Fare you well this winter season, lad, with worthy companions and a light hand from those who profit from you. Indeed, you are almost enough to sway a man who finds his pleasures elsewhere."

His eyes took light from the torch as he shrugged and settled back against the wall, raising one knee to prop his foot on the bricks. "One Mistress Kellna lives out by Graver's Meadow and sells berries and rootstock here in the market. Some say she also buys and sells goods that are . . . outside the common trade. I don't care much for women, but you might find her informative. She come by new stock this month past and made profit enough selling it on to Edane Groult down near Caedmon's Bridge that she bought me two nights running for a new friend come to stay with her."

I grinned. "By Graver's Meadow, you say?"

"Aye. West on the first track outside the gates. Right fork at the old mill."

"Thank you for that," I said.

"Mayhap next time, you'll let me sway your pleasure. You're a leg up on most as come by here." The boy's gaze flicked down the alley, and his face paled. "You won't say who told you?"

"On my soul, not a word." I backed away quickly. When Tigg the Procurer stepped out of the alley and peered up and down the lane, I was well hidden behind a broken chimney.

I pulled the monk's gown from my rucksack and drew it over my head, covering rucksack and all. Then I slipped out of the ruin, clasped my hands to my chin, bowed my head and shoulders as if in prayer, and hurried toward the town gate close behind the ragged donkey boy driving his empty charcoal wagon.

The woman in the pillory spat and yelled as I passed. "Karish perversion mocks the Gehoum. The earth will bleed to cleanse itself. You'll pay, Karish! You'll pay!"

No one paid her any mind, or me, either. Not the gate guards I'd talked to earlier. Not even the short sallow newcomer riding through the gates, wearing a gray silk mask that covered half his face, a claret-colored cloak, and the black-and-yellow badge of an itinerant inspector from the Pureblood Registry. I grinned behind my folded hands, strolled across the stinking ditch, and turned westward onto the track for Graver's Meadow. Though the moon was well past full, its cold light kept me to the path.

Typical of Boreas to hole up for the winter in the first place he came to, a town small enough everyone would learn of him, and then to choose the bed of one who dealt in stolen goods. He'd never been one to think things through. And it was just like the devil to convince his *woman* to buy him a *boy*. I'd never understood what made women fawn on Boreas so—a big, hairy, unwashed brute with a gruff, foolish way about him, who definitely preferred partners with parts between their legs no female could provide. Not that he hated women. Women were his porridge, nourishing and sufficient for every day. Lads were his meat and spice.

As I walked I amused myself planning the encounter. Would it be more pleasurable to slice off the villain's balls with one of our stolen daggers or to tie him up naked in the cold and let him watch me walk away with our booty? Once I'd settled somewhere—Pontia, perhaps, a town large enough to sell one of the daggers and still keep my head down—I'd send an offering to Gillarine to thank them for their hospitality.

The track kicked up sharply. The stream, narrower here, burbled and gurgled, cutting deep into the rocky slope, creating moss-lined nooks and grottos, each with its own watery music. As a child I had imagined such a cool, mysterious nook must be a Danae sianou—the holy place where a Dané gave up its body for a season and became one with the land. Sometimes I would leave feast bread there and ask to be stolen from my family. More often I would yell, stomp the ground, and throw rocks in the water, hoping to wake the sleeping guardian. Neither activity bore fruit.

A cold gust flapped my gown around my ankles as I stepped around fresh horse droppings. And then more. I bent down and passed my hand over a mound. Still warm. Several people had ridden up this path not long before. I swore under my breath, but I'd come too far to turn back. Likely more than Mistress Kellna lived up this way.

After consideration, I removed my monk's gown and stuffed it into my rucksack. A lost monk might walk clear easier than my own self if I encountered ordinary folk, but the talk of Harrowers had unnerved me. And the captive woman had reminded me how they hated Karish.

My thigh was grateful when the path broke over the lip of the rise. The stream lay like a silver necklace across a rocky goat pasture, leading the eye toward a scant woodland and a cottage. A sweet, cozy little hideaway, cupped in the embrace of shallow chalk cliffs, easily defensible.

Unfortunately, the cottage was ablaze. A robust woman sprawled among the grazing goats with an arrow in her back, and somewhere Boreas was bellowing out agonized curses that threatened to crumble the earth beneath my feet. I would recognize his rumbling epithets anywhere.

I ran. Not back toward Elanus, which even a moron's poor sense would demand, but toward the conflagration and the screaming. Boreas had saved my life at the battle of Arin Fay, taking a deep slash on his arm while striking down the halberdier ready to remove my head. We had exchanged the favor a number of times in the long months following, so one could say I owed him nothing—less than nothing since he had abandoned me half dead. But that first time, having seen the Ferryman's hand as clearly as I would until the day I took ship with that grim spirit, I had given Boreas my oath to protect his back. I prided myself that I had never broken my sworn faith.

All too aware that the treacherous moonlight would expose any approach on the meadow track, I circled wide toward the cliffs to come up behind the house, racing as soft-footed as I could manage over the rocky ground. When I plunged gratefully into the clumped beech and oak grown up in the lee of the cliffs, the rush of the nearby flames was already waning. I crept cautiously through the snagging undergrowth of blackthorn and hazel.

The screams—hoarse now, choking grunts, wordless animal cries—did not emanate from the burning house, but from an expanse between the house and the chalk cliffs. Breaking free of the bracken, I sped through a stretch of scattered, pale-trunked beeches and caught myself just before hurtling into the open.

Beyond the bordering trees lay a rolling meadow, dotted with stands of rowan and birch. Nestled in a willow brake, a small, bean-shaped pond shimmered in the cold moonlight, its waters ruffled by the knife-edged breeze. From the pond spilled the stream that had gouged the hillside. My soul swelled at the beauty of the place; my skin flushed and quivered as if the angel choirs themselves had come to sing in Gillarine Abbey church.

But my eyes were quickly drawn to a knoll at the heart of the meadow. At the apex of the knoll, five people gathered about a splayed figure, still as death. The angled moonlight stretched their long shadows across the slope.

A howl rose in my throat. Had I a weapon . . . a bow . . . a club . . . a blade longer than my finger, I would have set upon them, never mind the odds. But as in every juncture of my life, I was inadequate. Too late. Unprepared.

A scrawny, tangle-haired man stood at the base of the knoll holding six horses. With a smothered curse at my loose-lipped folly, I recognized him as Gorb the Seedsman. He'd not worn the orange scarf about his neck three hours past.

The five were chanting a pattern of four words, one each, over and over around their circle until I could distinguish the voices—three men and two women—and the Aurellian words: *sanguiera, orongia, vazte, kevrana*. Bleed, suffer, die, purify. With every repetition, the moonlight dimmed and the weight of night and despair descended upon my shoulders like an iron yoke. After the fifth or sixth time around, a tall, pale-haired woman in an orange cloak raised her arms, holding a short staff in her two hands as if to challenge the sky. Her clear voice incised the air like a silver lancet, and every hair on my flesh rose.

> *Powers of Night and Storm and Terror, of Desert and Ice, of Death and Life,*
> *O mighty Gehoum, heed our sacrifice.*
> *Withhold our doom as we cleanse this land of decadent pleasure,*
> *Of all that distracts us mortals from our proper reverence.*
> *May this blood and fire and pain be a sweet odor to fill the long night*
>   *of thy passing*
> *And bear upon its vapors our vows renewed to purge the world of all that*
>   *stands between us and thy immortal being.*

"Heathen witch! Magrog take ye to his everlasting fire!" The raw, choking curse came from the victim at their feet . . . Boreas, no doubt of it, not so dead after all.

"Feel the cleansing fear, mortal man," said the tall woman, lowering her arms and bending over him. "Thou art a blight upon the universe, diseased, depraved, an insult to the Powers who control the world's fate. Of all thy miserable existence, only thy ending will serve a purpose. Suffer and bleed and rejoice in the terror of darkness." She plunged her staff into the ground . . . into the man . . . ripping a cry of agony from his very depths.

Horror rooted my feet as each of the five bent to touch him. Then Sila Diaglou—of course, the pale-haired woman was the priestess I'd seen at Gillarine, the warrior who could rouse people to destroy their own fields and cities in the name of repentance—led her companions down the knoll to Gorb and the horses.

The seedsman gave the priestess a leg up into her saddle. She laid a hand on his head and murmured, as if bestowing a blessing, and then she and her cohorts rode toward me. I hid myself as best I could and still be able to see them as they approached the wood. Using every skill at my command, I etched their features into my memory.

Scarce forty, Sila Diaglou was a handsome woman with a high forehead and intelligent eyes set well below thin brows. The diagonal scar that seamed each cheek tainted her beauty with cruelty. Her hair floated like beaten flax as she rode, yet her wide mouth lacked any hint of generosity or mercy. Her lips, and those of her companions, were painted black with blood.

The smaller woman followed, particolored skirts draping her mount and a fluttering orange scarf wrapped about straight black hair. No more than a doe-eyed girl, eighteen at best, she rode like a queen, soft, copper-hued features devoid of emotion. The three men, too, I memorized as they came: the one with a beardless needle chin and colorless eyes, the one with a malformed ear and oiled black curls tied into a club at his neck, the third with a dog's face, all lumps and crags, with but a fringe of hair about his round chin and a dagged cloak of purple velvet. Weedy Gorb mounted his own beast and rode after the others.

I held still until they had passed out of my hearing. Then I raced to the crest of the knoll.

Spirits of fire and darkness! Stripped to his braies, wrists and ankles stretched and bound to wooden stakes, my old comrade leaked blood from every quat of his length and breadth. Blades had shredded his flesh and punctured his eyes. The priestess had plunged her staff through his middle, not through his heart or his bowel to kill him quickly, but through his side so that every breath, every trembling shudder, tore him apart.

Swallowing my gorge, I knelt beside him and spoke softly. "Ah, Boreas, you god-cursed gatzé, I knew you'd get in trouble without me."

"Who's there?" he croaked. His battered lips scarcely moved. His head rolled side to side, as if he might be able to see, if he but turned his bloody sockets in the proper direction.

Gently I stilled him. "It's Valen, come to help you as I vowed I would."

He gasped, a whooshing stridor that only after a panicked moment did I realize was a laugh. "So I'm dead then. Of all Magrog's servants come to take me at my end, ne'er thought 'twould be you, Valen. And I ne'er thought 'twould hurt so wicked to be dead." His dreadful laughter stretched into a sob.

"Hush now." I bent over so he could feel my breath. "Neither of us is dead. The baldpates saved my leg and my life, so I've you to thank for that. I heard you were up here, and I came to— Well, that doesn't matter. Holy gods, I'm sorry I'm so late."

I could see no way to help him. Pull the stake from his middle and the splintered shaft would draw his entrails, and he'd bleed his life away in agony. Leave it and his every breath would be torment and still he would die. But only after long dreadful hours . . . or days.

"No luck today for neither of us. Threw the last of our loot into the pond, they did. After killing—" A croaking sob. "Ah, Kellna was a merry lay. I never understood when ye said the best girls danced with ye. But Kell-na . . . she danced."

"I'll pay her passage, Boreas. I promise." I ripped off my rucksack and scrabbled through the contents of the bundled rag. Nothing in the pilfered medicines would help him. Few did I even know the proper use of. But the little knife . . . "Hold still and I'll get your hands free."

With the pointed, finger-length blade of the stolen herb knife I split the ropes that bound his wrists and ankles. He could not move his tortured limbs without crying out, so I did it for him, drawing them to his sides. Then I laid my monk's gown over him. His massive body trembled.

"Somehow they knew I'd nivat. Said I was a twist-mind . . . abomination to their Gehoum . . . and I'd be better use to the world bleeding. I tried to tell 'em . . ." Growing agitation had him gasping between words. Blood welled out from around the stake. "They've left me in the dark, Valen. There's naught here. Naught. I'm fallen in a well that has no bottom. Don't leave me this way . . ."

"Hold on." I pressed my hands on his shoulders. "Let me think what we're to do."

Perhaps the stake wasn't all the way through. With one hand on his shoulder to calm him, I touched the wooden shaft. Embedded deep in the earth, the stake did not move . . .

Dread . . . terror . . . suffocation . . . I was drowning in blood. In torment. *Violated.* Soul and mind raped with fire, then immersed in a cold midnight beyond bearing. *Alone.* Sensing a desolation so profound that it seeped into the grass, the earth, the very air.

I snatched my hand away. Lifting my face to the cold air and the moonlight, breathing deep to ease my shaking, I gave guilty thanks for life and light and the broad sky above me. What rite could create this dread that crushed the heart and devoured the soul, that stole the night's glory and blighted this sweet meadow? The thought that I had brought down this vileness on my old comrade appalled me, yet plain sense said I could not have imagined such an outcome. As I could not undo my careless babbling, I saw only one way to make it up to him. No one deserved to suffer so.

"I can't undo this, Boreas. I'm sorry. If I could—"

"Didn't think so." Pain snagged his rasping voice. His forehead felt hot beneath my hand. "Ye ought to leave. Don't let the orange-heads pray over ye. Their prayin' emptied me out, till I can't think of naught but the dark—" Despair edged his words with panic.

"Hush now. You'll not be alone. I swear it. Will you trust me?"

"Ye've never broke yer word."

"Listen . . . you'll not believe my plan for winter . . ."

I told him every detail of my rescue and the abbey. Of Jullian and Sebastian, of Brother Badger and Brother Gildas, of bells and books and prayers and mysteries. Of rich smells and jewel-colored windows and rippling barley. As I talked, I drew out the little green bag and used the mirror to crush the nivat on a rock. Trying not to inhale the scent, lest it trigger my own craving, I pricked my finger and worked my perverse magic.

"Here, now, I've something will ease you a bit. Give it a try." I scooped up the bubbling black paste and poked it in his mouth.

Pain devoured him. Scoured and shook him as would a dragon lion of Syanar. I waited. When, at last, his ravaged body convulsed in ecstasy, I stabbed the sharp little knife—sure and fast and deep—into the hollow at the back of his neck. *Forgive.*

PART TWO

A Gathering of Wolves

Chapter 11

The hierarch's flat feet measured almost the same in their length and width. They pained him when he had to stand on cold hard granite slabs for long periods of time. I knew this because he crunched up his toes and splayed them out again, rocked from toe to heel, and rolled them to the side. He did not wear sandals, for, of course, he was not a vowed brother of any monastic order, but the highest-ranking clergyman in Navronne, a common practor who had achieved a rank on par with a duc. His embroidered slippers were soft purple velvet held on by white silk ribbons that crossed over his thick, stockinged ankles. Every little while he set one foot upon the other to rest it, leaving dusty smudges on the top of his fine shoes.

Feet and their various coverings and the grimy hems of gowns, robes, and other vestments were all I could see of my investiture rites. As I had for the past three hours, I lay prostrate before the high altar of Gillarine Abbey church, the unending prayers and admonitions rolling over me like the billowing incense smokes. My shoulder ached, my leg had stiffened, and my long straight pureblood nose had been rubbed raw by the same cold hard granite slabs that so tormented the hierarch's feet.

Someone sprinkled water on my head and back. Drips rolled down the shaven patch at the crown of my head. *Tonsured . . . great Kemen, Lord of Sky and Storm, what woman will ever lie with me now?* Drips spattered on my black gown, absorbed by the layers of wool. Drips rolled down my bare feet, tickling. I tried not to twitch. My trembling was due more to the marrow-deep chill creeping through me from the floor than awe of my current intimacy with the divine.

I was not wholly irreverent. I honored all gods who professed an interest in human folk, and I respected custom and rituals that evoked the great mysteries of the world: death and birth, forests, ocean, and storms, music, copulation, and fermentation. But I saw no virtue in mere endurance and had never understood why a god would wish to be so long preoccupied with any one event.

Best keep my mind somewhere close to business. News brought by the hierarch's traveling party had only confirmed my decision to stay here—plague had broken out in the Moriangi port of Haverin.

Pestilence, famine, war . . . how many times in the past few days had I heard mention of the end times? *The long darkness*, Jullian had said, as if it were a lovers' assignation for which he had been awaiting only notice of the time. Before long these doomsayers were going to have me hanging bells on my ears and painting my forehead with dung.

I dared not close my eyes. Brother Sebastian had rousted me as the bells rang for Prime, scolding me roundly for sleeping, for sleeping in the bed, for sleeping too long, and for sleeping naked. "*A monk must always lie down girded in no less than trews, shirt, and hose so he will not be late to pray the night Hours,* so spake Saint Ophir in his Rule." While I reluctantly rolled into the frigid air and drew on the clean underthings he had brought me, my mentor had tightened his lips at some additional transgression. "Are you yet a sapling like these boys who cannot yet control their fleshly dreams? Surely you did not profane your vigil night apurpose!"

It was the bed linens bothering him. I had shaken my head vigorously and shifted the treacherous appendage inside my trews, attempting to look properly humiliated while trying to remember just what had happened on my return from Elanus. Numb, exhausted, I had hidden my green pouch and the packet of knife and medicines in the garden maze outside the church and prayed that the bells I'd heard as I slogged over the last slope and down the road to the gatehouse were Matins and not Lauds.

But "fleshly thoughts" *had* dogged me all the way back through the bogs and woodlands: the taste and feel of Adrianne on my tongue and fingertips and the memory of the dusky-smooth limbs and silken hair of the catamite. Strange and perverse that such images could arouse me after I had murdered a comrade I'd sworn to defend . . . after I'd spent half the night scraping a hole in the soft black dirt of Graver's Meadow and laying Boreas and his woman there, my last coppers on their eyes and some of Brother Badger's herbs in their hands and mouths to pay their tally to the Ferryman. Somehow the simple rites in the darkening meadow had left me at peace, and then the feel of the living earth under my hands as I sought the road back to Gillarine had sent unseemly desires coursing through my flesh. Truly I was a lunatic.

The brothers were singing now. Something different this morning. From each side of the choir, right and left behind me, came a different melody—two songs twined around each other, all the beauty and simplicity of plainsong, but counterposed to make something larger and more wonderful. I had heard them practicing this work, but I hadn't known it was for this occasion. For me. Well, for Iero, of course . . . everything they did, everything they said, was to honor Iero and his saints and prophets. Nonetheless, of all the good comrades I'd encountered through the years, none had ever made a song for me. I felt like an ass, grinning into the floor.

Music infused my bones and sinews, not only my ears and soul. As a child I'd been offered no training in any instrument beyond the minimum necessary for a "cultured man's education"—*that* aborted on the day I smashed my music master's three-hundred-year-old harp into a stone pillar. Alas, my voice *did* sound like a carpenter's rasp, elsewise a bard's life might have suited me most excellently. If only I'd been born to a family of pureblood musicians, perhaps I could have put up with all the rest.

Hands touched my shoulders. "Rise up now, son of Iero and Saint Ophir, and with thy solemn avowal will thy new life begin."

Blessed gods be thanked! I tried not to appear a lumbering ox as I got to my feet.

The hierarch occupied a purple-draped chair between me and the high altar, a regal figure, though his upper lip drew up in the middle like a church spire, and the lower one, full and fleshy, drooped below it like the seedsman's iron scoop, leaving two large yellow teeth on permanent display. In droning solemnity, he intoned, "Swear thou, chosen of the One God . . ."

I knelt before Eligius and a coolly serious Abbot Luviar and swore on my hope of grace and heaven to abide by the particulars of Saint Ophir's Rule. I meant what I said, though, if anyone had listened very closely through the fits of coughing that overtook me at certain crucial moments, he might have noted that I altered a few important words, such as "for the duration of my novice vows" rather than "for the duration of my novice year."

Graver's Meadow had reminded me why I was careful about oath swearing. As the condition of the brothers' hospitality, I would do my best to obey their Rule, but I would not bind myself beyond reason. So as I knelt before the hierarch, I ensured my vows were entirely accurate. They would last only as long as they lasted.

When the swearing was done, Sebastian and Gildas dropped a voluminous garment over my head, shifting it around so that the shortest sewn seam reached halfway down my breast, leaving the black wool cape open the rest of the way down. They adjusted the cowl's soft folds about my neck and shoulders and then lifted its hood over my newly trimmed hair. The abbot himself knelt before me to slip my sandals onto my feet. And then it was done.

From the outside I must appear like these other monks, who rose from the choir stalls and followed the hierarch, abbot, and prior in orderly procession through the nave. But, as far as I could tell, my every failing and regret remained hidden under my cowl, alongside unseemly hatreds, new and old. Too bad. The morning's prayers had promised that I might leave all such burdens behind.

After we washed in the lavatorium—a capacious room in the understory of the monks' dorter where water channeled from the river ran perpetually through a waist-high stone trough—Brother Sebastian led me up the south stair to the monks' refectory for the first time. Most of the monks were already seated at the two long tables along the side walls. Facing the center of the room, backs to the walls, they arranged themselves in order of age, as it appeared, or length of time in the order, which was much the same. At the small head table the abbot and the prior sat on either side of the hierarch. Reminding me with a gesture to keep silent, Brother Sebastian hurried me past the great gap of empty places and delivered me to the table at the lower end of the rectangle. To my surprise Jullian and Gerard squeezed along the wall behind one row of monks and past the long gap of empty seats and took stools on either side of me.

The large room was spare of decoration: no paintings, statues, or carvings, no color but the burnished walnut of the floor and the palest yellow on the walls and between the stone ribs of the high, barreled ceiling. Its truer grandeur was its extravagance of windows on all four walls. Though the chilly room had no hearth, its tall windows, composed of astonishingly clear glass panes, bathed every place, even mine, with light.

Once all were seated, lay brothers carried in bowls of soup and baskets of bread. My stomach was near devouring itself after a long morning's fast on top of my night's adventure. The moment the steaming bowl was set in front of me, I snatched up my spoon and dipped, reaching for the bread basket with the alter hand. The knock of my spoon on the bowl resounded through the cavernous room like a tabor's whack. I looked up. No one else had moved.

I stuffed my hands in my lap and recalled other houses where the protocols were even less comprehensible than these. As a child, I had made an art of hiding under noblemen's tables, tormenting the dogs, tugging on the hanging edges of the table coverings, tweaking startled ladies' toes and wiping my greasy hands on their skirts, and drinking far too much wine from ewers I'd dragged along with me. I smothered a laugh, imagining the poor amusement I'd find under *these* tables.

It was a prayer we awaited, of course, intoned at length by Prior Nemesio. Once the *perficiimus* ended it, the abbot rang a small bell, and Brother Cadeus, the porter, began to read from a book sitting on the lectern. As the monks picked up their spoons and reached for bread, he announced the day's text as the writing of Juridius the Elder, a practor of Agrimo.

Gerard stuffed his mouth and frankly examined my new cowl. Then he stretched his neck and peered around behind me. As I bent over my bowl for my next bite, I tilted my head his way, exposing the bare patch Brother Sebastian's shaving knife had left, which felt roughly the size of a knight's shield. The boy's ready grin appeared around his mouthful of bread. I grinned back at him around my spoon and glanced at Jullian. The Ardran boy's attention held firmly to his bowl, his face pale and solemn. I didn't understand. He had no reason to be angry with me. Had Brother Gildas "reprimanded" him again?

I was no more than halfway through my soup when the hierarch replaced Brother Cadeus at the lectern. "Dearest Brothers, it is our delight to join you for this great occasion," said Hierarch Eligius, spreading his arms so that his wide sleeves and mantle swept in great curved folds like angels' wings. "A soul claimed for Iero's service. A voice added to the chorus that carries our petitions night and day to the halls of heaven. But as your shepherd, I must use this example for instruction as well as celebration, to chastise as well as to commend . . ."

The hierarch preached of the *ordo mundi*—clearly installing himself at the top of the fixed order of the earthly plane and relegating heathenish Harrowers to the bottom. The monks sat motionless, attentive. Gerard's mouth hung open slightly as if poised on the verge of speech. Jullian, though . . . Jullian's eyes remained fixed on his bowl.

"Rather than pronouncing faith in Iero and his anointed clergy, and fighting to enthrone our rightful king from a proven son of Eodward's body, these servants of despair preach another kind of chaos—that villeins and practors, scholars and servants must join in some whimsical preparation for an age of doom and darkness. They propound a sovereign of rumor, as if Iero might sanction a righteous claimant to Eodward's crown conjured from peasants' dreams and tavern gossip. Such deviance invites Iero's wrath and must be purged from our midst!"

Blessed saints and angels . . . *deviance!* A word to make a man look to his purse and his neck. So hopes of a Pretender and this talk of end times were named anathema . . . and poor pale Jullian looked guilty as a married man caught with his hand under a harlot's skirt. What had the boy got himself into? No more dangerous enemy exists than a holy man, especially when his writs and precepts get tangled with royal politics.

The abbot rang his bell. After more prayers, Prior Nemesio led us from the refectory. My soup remained unfinished, a casualty in a holy war.

Once down the stair, our orderly processional dissolved into quiet chaos. Many of the monks squeezed my arm or pressed my hand in companionable congratulations; others laid one open palm in the other and gestured as in offering—the monks' signing speech for a gift of Iero's blessing. As I accepted their good wishes, Brother Sebastian stood at my shoulder as proudly as if I were his own creation. For certain, the brothers were a friendly lot.

Once most of the brothers had dispersed to their afternoon's activities, a hooded monk tugged at my arm and drew me around and behind the unlit hearth of the calefactory. "The hierarch will ask you about the book," he said, his words penetrating my skull as much by virtue of their ferocity as by my hearing them. "You *will* not reveal its exact title or its history. You *will* not offer it to him. If you value the boy's safety, see that it remains here." Before I could respond, he hurried away.

I knew it was Gildas. I recognized the thatch of brown hair on the back of his hand. And who but Gildas would encourage me to lie to the authority I had just vowed to obey? He had recognized my lack of finer scruples early on. Yet it wasn't so much his particular demand that left me bristling—I'd no wish for Hierarch Eligius to get his hands on my book. But his reference to Jullian sounded very like a threat.

People had to get along as they could in this world. Gods knew I'd done my share of wickedness along the way. But when the account for a man's deeds fell due, the one to pay should be the man who made the choice to do them. Never friends . . . and never, ever, children.

"His Excellency wishes to congratulate you," Brother Sebastian said, as he bustled me down the cloister walk toward the scriptorium, where the hierarch was inspecting the monks' work. I was yet grumbling under my breath at Gildas's high-handed manner when we stepped into the cavernous, many-windowed room tucked into the understory of the library.

The place was deliciously warm, though it reeked of sour vitriol and acrid tannin—ink. Amid orderly rows of thick, unadorned columns that sprouted at their crowns into great sprays of vaulting ribs, orderly rows of copyists hunched over sloping desks, writing or painting their pages. A severely stooped monk, wisps of white hair feathering his tonsure, moved from desk to desk with a basket of small flasks, replenishing the ink horns fixed to each desk by metal hoops. Other monks sat at long tables shaving quills or stitching folded pages together. Save for the soft scratch of pens, the whisk of knives, and the rustle of pages, the place was very quiet. Holy silence was kept here as in the cloisters.

"Ah, our new novice." Hierarch Eligius's unmuffled voice resonated like a barrage of stone against a siege wall, causing heads to pop up all over. He closed the small fat book that lay on a copyist's desk, picked it up, and peered at the title. "*A Treatise on the Nature of Evil* written by Jonne of Lidowe. A truly noble work. Have you read it?" He wagged it in the air.

Uncertain whether I was expected to voice my answers or not, I shook my head.

"Do so when this copy is complete." He dropped the little volume on the desk. "Brother Fidelio, you'll see to it?"

The copyist nodded and dipped his pen again.

Brother Sebastian gave me a gentle shove, and I joined the hierarch just as he moved on to the next desk, his elaborate cloak jarring Brother Fidelio's elbow. The monk sighed silently, set down his pen, and scraped at his work with a pumice stone.

Eligius squinted at the second copyist's work. "You've a beautiful hand, Brother. Every character well formed and clear. The history of the Karish in

Navronne is an inspiring text. But I would like to see more color and variety in the capitals. You must not starve the glory of presentation in some rush to completion."

The chinless Brother Victor, my diminutive companion of Black Night, seemed to be in charge of the scriptorium activities. He flitted from one desk to another, answering unspoken questions from the copyists, fetching books from the shelves on the end wall, or using naught but his deft fingers to describe corrections to a binder's stitching.

At the next desk, a scrawny, sandy-haired younger monk held his tongue between his lips as his blackened fingers drew tiny characters in long straight lists. The blank parts of the page were marked into columns with lines of light gray.

"A fine presentation, Brother, but this—" The frowning hierarch tapped a white-gloved finger on a tattered scroll held open by lead weights. "*The Tally of Grape Harvests in Central Ardra in the Years of Aurellian Rule?* Surely more uplifting pages wait to be copied—sacred texts, sermons, or noble histories that will turn men's thoughts to Iero or his saints. Who chose this as an exemplar? Come, come, speak up."

"Brother Chancellor gives out the work, Excellency," whispered the sandy-haired monk, "and tasks us with the pages most suited to our skills. Not to set myself high, but both he and Father Abbot say I've a special touch for numbers, so perhaps—"

"I must have a word with the chancellor then, as well as with Abbot Luviar." The hierarch glared across the room at Brother Victor, who leaned over a desk heads together with a copyist.

The hierarch spoke to each of the copyists, his steepled upper lip rising high and stiff as he named more works frivolous or inappropriate. He condemned anything of mundane use: a scroll on glassmaking, a book on the building of Aurellian roads, an almanac that traced weather patterns in Morian over three centuries.

I was no judge of books and their uses. That a man could learn to make glass from another glassmaker, as I had learned to tan hides, brew ale, and cut stone from those who knew the work, made more sense to me than learning such things from blots on parchment. But then again, I could not see how a book reader would come nearer heaven by reading someone's speculations on Iero's parentage than by reading of the might of storms and sunlight over the river country.

The hierarch moved to a table where a grizzled monk traced his finger over a page in an open book while reading a set of unbound pages. The monk's glance moved from one to the other and back again.

"So, Brother Novice," said the hierarch as he peered over the shoulder of the monk and browsed through stacks that seemed to be awaiting similar examination. "Abbot Luviar has recounted how a journey of penitence brought you to this great conversion. A remarkable story."

I cleared my throat. "A wonder, truly, Excellency. I feel uplifted. Reborn, as to say."

He turned the pages of a small book, the colors of the inked patterns brighter than his ruby ring. "And you truly came upon Gillarine by chance?"

"Indeed, I wandered for days, bleeding and wounded, entirely confused as to my course. Having lived so short a time in the little village of"—I twisted my brain to come up with a name—"Thorn, and diseased with sin and violent behavior as I was, I was unfamiliar with any holy places in the countryside around. Even now, I could not tell you the location of that village or the true course of my wanderings, Excellen—"

Saints and angels! I almost swallowed my tongue. I had not noticed the man who stood stiffly in the shadow of a pillar, his hands clasped behind his back, his eyes dead with boredom. The scarlet surcoat he wore over his gray gown bore the hierarch's gold-broidered blazon of mitral hat and solicale. Of modest stature, with close-trimmed black hair, long nose, and an air of unremitting superiority, he scarcely needed the violet mask that covered half his face to proclaim him pureblood. Protocol forbade an ordinary to so much as notice him without his master's leave.

I dropped my gaze and attempted to shrink inside my cowl. "Truly, Saint . . . uh"—the name escaped me—"that is, the guardian of wanderers must have examined . . . watched . . . over me every moment of that . . . of that—"

"Yes, yes." Eligius's frizzled brown hair bobbed alongside the red cap that had replaced his mitral hat. "You carried a book of maps, did you not? Even that could not aid you?"

I dared not let the name Cartamandua arise in association with me in front of the pureblood. Why had I not thought to take a false name as long as I carried the book? It was not so long a stretch from *Valen* to *Magnus Valentia de Cartamandua-Celestine* to exposure.

"Alas, no, Excellency." *Think, fool.* I spoke slowly, so as not to stammer as I crafted my tale. "Though I valued the book because of its connection to my lord Mardane Lavorile who gave it me, I read no holy places in its maps, which were mostly common drawings of rivercourses and the old Aurellian roads that interlace Morian. Little of Ardra. Little of practical use even when I was scouting for the mardane."

"A frivolous work, then. And what has become of the book? Perhaps it is here being copied?"

"Why, I never thought of it as worthy of copying." I scratched my head, turned about, and gawked as if to review the contents of all the copyist desks. "And none of the brothers took great note of it, save that a poor wanderer had a book at all. It's certainly not one of these. I gave it up, Excellency, along with my secular garb and sinful ways. I've not even seen the thing since I determined to answer Iero's call by taking vows. I can't see how a map would guide a man's soul to heaven."

I dared not glance at the pureblood. Was he listening? Did his bent enable him to detect lies?

The hierarch pursed his odd lips for a moment and then relaxed them into a smile. "Very true. Stay faithful to true teaching, Brother Novice, and your course will be straight."

Sensing dismissal, I bowed, as I had seen the others do, and backed away carefully until my back touched the wall between two stacks of shelves. The pillar blocked my view of the pureblood and his of me. I heaved a sigh, allowing the storm of anxiety to ease.

A lay brother poked the fire and carried a lit taper to the lamps that hung from iron brackets fixed to the pillars. Outside the windows, the haze had thickened into bulging clouds, dimming the sunlight and sapping the room's warmth.

The hierarch summoned Brother Victor with a wave of his jeweled finger. "Chancellor, a word with you before I take leave."

The little monk hurried to the hierarch, his hands tucked under his black scapular, his oddly skewed features sober and attentive.

"All of you, pay heed and bear witness to my judgment of this abbey's great work of writing!" said Eligius. "A member of your fraternity has fallen into grave error . . ." He rebuked Brother Victor at great length, accusing him of supporting the deviant philosophy of those who preached coming doom by his choices of materials to copy. ". . . and so you are to immediately remove all frivolous and mundane materials from this room. Your abbot may keep or dispose of the exemplars as he sees fit. But this—"

He whipped the page of numbers right out from under the young monk's pen and threw it on the floor. A long smear of ink marred the meticulously written page.

"—and this—"

The pages on glassmaking, the Moriangi almanac, meticulous colored drawings of a millworks, and several other part-written pages joined the first one on the floor.

"—and every page copied from a profane work is to be burned in view of all residents of Gillarine as a sign of error and rededication."

Brother Victor's horror-stricken gaze leaped from the crumpled pages to the red-faced hierarch and back again. The other monks looked stunned.

Parchment to be burned? Even *I* knew how appallingly wasteful that was. Though my family's house was a wealthy one, my tutors had scraped and overwritten precious vellum time and time again. And who could measure the time and care these monks had spent on these pages?

"You, Chancellor, are to receive twenty lashes before sunset today and be confined for five days with water as your only sustenance. Set this room in order and your copyists to their tasks, and then accompany *Eqastré* Scrutari-Consil, who will carry out my judgment. He will also question each of you"—his jeweled finger denoted every one of the shocked brothers—"to ensure that you understand your duties to Iero and the *ordo mundi*."

Scrutari-Consil stepped away from the wall and bowed to Eligius, touching his fingers to his forehead. With a limp gesture of blessing, the hierarch swept out of the briskly opened door and into the rainy afternoon.

Chapter 12

"This is outrageous, Broth—"

Brother Victor silenced the sandy-haired monk with a gesture. Other monks left their desks to lay hands on his sleeves or his back, to shake their heads in silent denial, or to offer, with eloquent gestures, comfort or anger or comradeship. The chancellor briskly sent them back to work.

Hands clasped at his back, the pureblood watched impassively as Brother Victor darted about his duties. The man in red and gray needed no word or additional gesture to assert his authority over the room.

Having naught to do, I pressed my back to the wall, attempting to shrivel out of sight. I would have slipped out of the door, but Scrutari-Consil had positioned himself within view of it.

Scrutari-Consil—not a family related to mine, thanks be to all gods. The Scrutaris were known as perceptives. They were often contracted as investigators and inspectors, expected to root out lies and deceptions or to oversee town administrators. His colineal name *Consil* was unfamiliar; I could not recall the lineal bent of every pureblood family. The name's Aurellian root suggested *adjudication*, thus a bent that might lend itself to mediation, untangling puzzles, or rendering judgments. Better for my lies and deceptions if he favored the *Consil* line, though I truly would prefer the man burst into spontaneous flames like a phoenix and not regenerate until I was fifty quellae from Gillarine.

Eligius had addressed Scrutari with the pureblood honorific *eqastré*, an affectation that signified nothing. As a form of address between purebloods, *eqastré* indicated parity in rank. Between pureblood and anyone else in the world, such address had no meaning, for protocol dictated that purebloods were so far exalted by the gods that ordinaries could in no wise be compared with them. The only relationship permitted between an ordinary and a pureblood was that spelled out in a Registry contract. Sweat dribbled past my ears.

Brother Victor's silent hands were busily directing his copyists. Though I had little experience with the monks' signing speech, his instructions were easy to interpret. Those whose work had been halted were to gather their completed pages from the neat stacks on the holding tables and pile them on a long table littered with broken pens, empty ink horns, and less orderly piles of written sheets. They were to collect their exemplars, the original documents being copied, in different piles on the same table.

As each monk turned in his pages, the chancellor passed him a new book or scroll he drew from the cluttered bookshelves. Before the last had been distributed, monks had already spread new vellum on their desks and begun to measure and rule their pages with thin sticks of the same plummet stonemasons used to mark their plans. The pureblood strolled down the rows, examining the titles of the new works.

At first Brother Victor seemed inordinately calm. But as he began sorting the damaged pages and proscribed books, his hands began to shake, knocking over the heaps of pages, books, and scrolls more than once, leaving the table a heaped confusion. When he noticed me watching, a tinge of scarlet touched his pale cheeks. Abruptly, he summoned me to join him. He scooped up the piles of discard pages and dumped them into a large basket underneath the table.

When I reached the chancellor's side, his small, neat hand—steady now—pointed first to the remaining heap of books and papers and then upward. For a moment I had the notion that he was saying something about heaven. But then I realized he merely wanted me to carry the things upstairs to the library. Grateful for the excuse to leave and for the rule of silence that prevented his use of my name, I pressed my palms together in acquiescence.

The rain, now a downpour, had the gutterspouts flowing. Water had pooled in the alley and at the base of the ascending stair outside the door. Moisture spattered across the threshold as I awkwardly tried to draw my cowl over my ungainly armload of books, scrolls, and loose pages. Feeling the pureblood's eyes on my back did not steady my hands. Crinkling his red-rimmed eyes in disapproval, the stoop-shouldered monk set down his ink basket, yanked the heavy wool across the jumble, and stuffed a wad of the cloth into my already over-occupied hand to hold it there.

The open air cooled my incipient fever. The pureblood could not possibly have recognized me.

The stair was not half wide enough to carry such a load. I must either risk tumbling over the open side of the steps or scrape arms and elbows on the wall, thus smearing moss onto my new cowl. At the top of the stair I pawed at the brass latch of the library door, at the same time drawing up my knee to catch some book that was sliding out of my arms. If I took another step, some precious writing was going to drop into the chilly puddle that was seeping into my new sandals around my bare toes. By the time Jullian pulled open the library door, I was crouched in an immovable knot.

The boy gaped as if I were a lunatic. I waggled my brows and my chin toward my laden arms, hoping he or one of the monks in the room would catch my meaning before the growing heat in my thigh burst into flame.

At last understanding dawned. Jullian reached under my dripping cowl and supported the collapsing bundle as I waddled through the doorway. As the monks resumed their studies, the boy rescued the most precariously poised texts. I dumped the rest of the stack on the table beside them.

The boy and I blotted stray droplets from sheets and folios with a kerchief, stacked the books, set aside the scrolls in their cloth or leather cases, and straightened the loose pages. We had reduced the clutter by half, when one brightly colored page caught my notice. As Jullian laid another page on the pile of loose sheets, I gripped his slender wrist and pulled it away, staring at the one atop the stack. The crisply white vellum depicted a detailed diagram of mill cogs, inked in bright red and blue. A square outlined in the text gaped empty, awaiting a second drawing. I shifted several more of the loose pages and found the half-completed list of carefully drawn numbers, a streak of black ink left where the page had been whipped out from under the hand of the copyist.

What had Brother Victor sent out to be burned? Certainly *not* the pages the hierarch had selected. With so many sheets piled on the table, perhaps the chancellor had picked up the wrong ones . . . or perhaps he had assumed that I, a befuddled novice of less than a day who had never worked in his scriptorium—and thus was not subject to questioning at the hierarch's order—wouldn't notice he had switched them.

My suspicions were quickly confirmed. We had just spread out the last few pages, careful of the still damp ink, when Brother Gildas hurried through the library door. He shooed a puzzled Jullian back to his books, wax tablet, and stylus—implements of torture familiar from my own boyhood—then gestured for me to bring the stacked pages. Producing a key from under his scapular, Gildas unlocked the inner grillwork door of the last book press on the south wall and stowed the suspect pages on the shelves, slipping them between the books along with scraps of vellum he took from a basket to protect the drying ink. One would have to rifle the entire collection to discover the forbidden copies.

As Gildas locked the grate, shut the cupboard's outer door, and shot its bronze bolt back into its catch, I noted the brass solicale affixed on the door—the abbot's sign. So the contraband now lay hidden in the abbot's own book press. Astonishing.

His back to the other three monks, Gildas held a finger to his mouth, laid his clenched fist on his breast, and flicked his eyes toward Jullian. His message was quite clear: *Silence, obedience, the boy's safety*. He waited, his dark brow raised in query.

I pressed my palms together and inclined my head. As in the matter of my book, my interests coincided with his demands. I was the least likely man in the abbey to carry tales to the hierarch or his lapdog. Yet only the time and company restrained my anger and resentment.

Vowing to lie in wait for the damnable monk after supper and force an explanation from him, I started out the door to find Brother Sebastian, while Gildas smiled cheerfully, drew up a stool next to Jullian, and began to inspect the boy's work. And then the bells took up clanging. Not a call to the Hours—Nones had rung while I was with the hierarch in the scriptorium, and Vespers would not ring for at least an hour more. These bells stuttered in an unbalanced cadence that summoned the community to lay down whatever duties occupied the moment and gather at the refectory stair.

Everyone rose quickly, gathering their books and tablets and locking them away. But as Gildas and the other monks hurried out the door, I hung back. The bells would ring twice more, allowing time for scattered brethren to stopper their ink, damp cook fires, or round up sheep and goats, and I determined to take advantage of the opportunity. A matter more worrisome than frivolous copying or hidden pages preyed on my mind.

Jullian, scratching one bare, mud-spattered leg with his sandal, held the heavy door open, waiting for me. He blinked in surprise when I dragged him back into the room and pushed the door shut.

"A moment, if you would," I whispered. No finger twiddling would suffice for this. "I need to speak with you, and as you've been avoiding me so purposefully, and my life seems like to get more complicated now I'm vowed, I think this will have to do."

Pressing his back to the doorpost, the boy glanced up at me with the sidewise aspect of a thief caught. This would take some care.

I perched my backside on one of the library tables. "Tell me how you came to live in an abbey so young. Your family, I suppose. Dead, are they?" I'd wager my life on the answer to that one.

It certainly was not the question he expected. He stared for a moment, as if to read my intent. Then he shrugged. "Aye. Mam died birthing when I was six. My da was clerk to a wool factor in Pontia, or, well, he wasn't actually my da, as mine was dead. He said he'd no will left to raise a boy that wasn't his. So he gave me the choice to go on to Cradens Abbey school that's in Pontia or to apprentice to a dyer, as that fee was the best he could afford to pay. I liked schooling, so it was no hard choice. I heard he left the factor not long after that and went off to the fighting. He's likely dead now, too."

He spoke with assurance, not loud, but not whispering either, bold in his secrets and brave in his lonely confession. I knew that not every family was as easy to leave behind as mine. And the story was plausible enough.

"And does Brother Gildas always supervise your schooling?"

"For the most. Brother Fidelio used to tutor me with Gerard, who is great of heart and beloved of Iero as he saw an angel once, but who is slow of eye and head when it comes to reading. We'd work here, and Brother Fidelio would allow me to read whatever I would from the shelves while he taught Gerard. But when Father Abbot found me reading Aurellian plays by Vocaachus and Aerno . . ." His face brightened. "Do you know them?"

I shook my head.

"Well, they are very . . . worldly. Frivolous, the hierarch would call them." A trace of indignation in his posture. "But their words make music in your head and lead you to consider all manner of things. Father Abbot says they are worthy of study, but perhaps not for boys, even ones who read Aurellian fluently." His enthusiasm quickly overruled his resentments. Neither secrecy nor resentment were at all his nature.

"Ah, so you were given a new tutor to oversee your reading."

"Father Abbot said that Brother Gildas could assign my books and lessons as he did for Horach, and I am not complaining, for I am allowed to read and learn all manner of things that—" He glanced up and bit his lip. "We should go down. The bell."

The damnable bell was ringing its second course, but I could not let the moment pass. I bent over and planted my hands on my knees, which put my face something on a level with his. I hated what I would ask him. "Jullian, certain of these monks . . . Brother Gildas, say . . . they don't . . . hurt . . . you, do they? Beat you, or threaten you, or . . . press . . . you in ways you would rather they not?"

"No! Never!" His pale cheeks took on the blush of an Erdru's-month apple. "I am sent to pray without supper or to work extra hours in the pigsties or the stable when I err. No more than that."

"But you've secrets with them . . ."

He stiffened, clamping his mouth shut with the pious stubbornness I had come to recognize.

"I ask because on Black Night you said Brother Gildas had reprimanded you, and you've seemed different these days since. And because when I was not much older than you, I lived rough, and sometimes, so as to eat and stay warm, I would allow men to do things I didn't like. Some in this world, even persons who are greatly respected, will take advantage of a boy, and I would not have such things happen to one so clever as to read Voc . . . cernus and Ern—whoever they are. You are my brave rescuer, and I mislike secrets that damp your spirit."

"But those have naught to do with—" He snapped his mouth shut again and examined my face as if to judge the story of my rough living for himself. After a moment, he blew out a great puff of air and lowered his voice until I had to crane forward to hear him. "The secrets are not of beatings or unwholesome things. Brother Gildas would never! He exhorts Gerard and me to guard our virtue and says everyone should be as pure as we are."

He leaned forward, his forehead almost touching mine. For a moment a fire of excitement and conspiracy pierced his veil of caution. The child was near bursting. "The secrets are of Iero's work, most excellent and righteous that I would tell even my mother did she live and were I given leave to. But you must not *ask* me. I was rightly reprimanded for my loose tongue, and again after Black Night when I took your warning to mean you knew things . . . things you didn't know. Now I've sworn upon my mother's grave that I will *not* speak to you of these matters until Lord Stearc—" He closed his eyes and thumped his head backward against the doorpost.

I was not yet ready to exonerate Gildas. Blackguards could misuse a child's trust in many ways. If Gildas had not posed a personal threat to the boy to compel my obedience, then the danger must lie in these secret matters that linked the boy to my book and the contraband pages. So I caught the strand of Jullian's guileless exuberance and tugged on it again.

"Until Stearc . . . the Thane of Erasku . . . until he does what? Come on, lad. The One God himself arranged our meeting. He likely gave me the book of maps as well and instructed his saints to guide my feet to your abbey gates. Why else would your tongue be so eager to tell me these mysteries? I've seen Prince Osriel's vassal in your guesthouse. I've seen your abbot rally dead men to protect a prince even the sainted Gillare would abhor, and I've seen Brother Gildas cause that prince to vanish so a pureblood could not trace him. I've seen the Hierarch of Ardra nosing around your scriptorium finding *deviance* in almanacs and drawings of mill cogs, and meek brothers subject themselves to water drinking and lashes to hide those same works. And these only begin to touch the mysteries in this place. Truly, I think Iero *intends* you share the burden of your secrets with me." The god had certainly piqued my curiosity beyond common bounds.

The cursed bell ceased its clamor for the moment. Its third summoning would signal punishments for latecomers.

Inside the Ardran boy's soul there ensued such a struggle as to make the mud-soaked wrestling boys in Elanus look like pecking chickens. I thought I'd lost when he stood up straight and said, "Come on."

But he didn't set out for the cloisters. Rather, he led me through the inner doorway and down the passage toward the dorter. Only our footfalls and the spatter of rain sounded in the deserted corridor. Between the library and the monks' dorter, a daystair descended to the cloister garth. Opposite the head of the stair, the passage wall bulged outward in a bay. Each of the five window niches of the bay had its own stone seat, damp from the drizzle that blew through the window port. Jullian stepped up on the seat of the centermost niche, motioned me to crowd in behind him, and pointed a finger out the port.

Most of the world had vanished into the mist. Off to our right lay the river and the low, ghostly structures of the infirmary garth. Directly below us several steep-roofed buildings crowded together, the most prominent of them very like the guesthouse in size and grandeur—the abbot's house, I guessed. At least twenty mounted knights had mustered outside it, along with several pack animals. A liveried servant bore the red, white, and gold banner of the Hierarch of Ardra. I was amazed that no hint of such a large and well-armed escort had penetrated the cloisters when I'd climbed the stair not an hour since.

"Watch," said Jullian quietly. "I cannot tell you secrets I'm sworn to keep. But there's good reason the hierarch departs while everyone is summoned to the cloister."

Riders and servants milled about for a tedious time. The bells rang their third summons.

"His Excellency must be napping," I said. "We'd best go. You'll just have to *tell* me."

But Jullian caught my sleeve and pointed again. I leaned farther forward, allowing the damp stone seat and his muddy sandals to soak my knees so I could peer closer into the gloom.

Two men stepped from the door of the house. The one fellow was thickly draped in red, a broad-brimmed hat shielding hair and face from the rain. As he was handed up to a white palfrey from a carpet quickly spread across the mud, his sartorial splendor denoted him the Hierarch Eligius. The second man, slender and pale-haired, swung himself up with practiced ease to the back of a dappled destrier. His short cape revealed a jeweled sword hilt at his waist, fine tight-fitting boots snugged to his knees, and the purple and gold trilliot of Ardra on his surcoat.

"The hierarch came to fetch him!" I said, wishing I could disbelieve my eyes. I needed no device to identify Perryn, Duc of Ardra. "Your treacherous abbot hid the coward, and the damnable hierarch escorts him back to Palinur. Men of god! Holy men!"

"Shhh!" said Jullian.

But I was unable to keep silent. "This despicable villain dragged good men from their homes, starved them and bled them for months, promising help that never came, and then abandoned them to die. Now he sneaks away under the cloak of a traveling clergyman."

"The abbot would not have him dead," said Jullian. "Gillarine is neutral ground, holy ground. Sometimes duty and faithfulness demand unpleasant things."

The riders, scarcely visible in the rain, wound slowly out of sight behind the ramparts of the church.

"What of the men the abbot kept from sanctuary to save him? What of the men this prince will lead into another slaughter? What have your tutors said of them? Is faithfulness only for the benefit of princes?" It wasn't fair to chastise the boy, who only repeated what he'd been taught. He could not understand the world. "I suppose you pray for them, eh?"

The bells fell silent. "We've got to go now," said the boy, his thin face knotted in concern.

"We'll talk again, Archangel," I said. I yet saw no pattern that linked Jullian's safety, Cartamandua maps, and conspiracies involving abbots and hierarchs and royal dunces.

We raced down the daystair into the east cloister walk. The crack of a whip echoed from the alley between the chapter house and the library. The accompanying groan was muffled as if they'd given the little monk something to bite on. I clenched my fists and wished the man strength for this and the rest of his trial.

Prison cells were not as familiar to me as alleys and bawdy houses, but I'd experienced enough of them. Never for long, thank all gods. So close . . . unable to get out . . . no air to breathe. I'd felt lashes as well, many at the hand of purebloods who could amplify the sting with magic. But in any hour, I'd choose lashes over confinement.

Brother Sebastian glared as Jullian and I slipped into the back row of the monks gathered in the lay brother's workyard. The entire population of Gillarine encircled a bonfire blazing brightly in the afternoon's sodden gloom.

The abbot's voice, calm and precise, pierced the smoke and mist. "The Hierarch of Ardra has chastised us for failure and distraction in our work to preserve humankind's knowledge—the holy charter assigned us by King Eodward and ratified by the hierarch and his predecessors. These pages are the hierarch's evidence of our ill choices. His Excellency has left us much to consider as to the divine ordering of this world, our place in it, and our duties to our god and king. Let us pray to the One God, Creator and Preserver, to guide us onward in the path of His choosing."

A brother emptied the basket of crumpled vellum into the pit. After an initial smoky darkening, the sheets took fire with a thunderous rush, green and blue flames dancing amid the gold, illuminating the faces in the circle as the pages curled and withered. Tears dribbled down the withered cheeks of the stoop-shouldered monk from the scriptorium. No tears scored Brother Gildas's face, though. Only resolve. Jullian stood beside me looking as if he might reach into the flames and drag out the blackened pages with his teeth.

"And now, my brothers," said Luviar, "let a holy fire ignite our souls as we redouble our commitment to the work we have been given. Iero grant us wisdom and give his eternal protection to Navronne's righteous king."

Left unspoken was his opinion of the hierarch's judgment, though I'd come to think the two had concocted this event as a shield for their political chicanery. Then again, perhaps I'd best give the rumor of a Pretender more credence than I'd done before. Nothing gives a rumor foundation so much as a clergyman naming it *deviance*.

The faint honks of geese drew my eyes upward. Long, wavering black wedges arrowed southward, far too early. *Eqastré* Scrutari-Consil stood out of the rain, just inside the shadowed undercroft. He leaned his back against one of the columns, his arms folded across his chest, watching and listening.

Sleep eluded me. Despite my near sleepless vigil night, despite the exhaustion of high emotions and taut nerves—or perhaps because of them—my eyes refused to close in the quiet intervals between the night Hours. An oppressive hostility permeated the deepening night, as if the eyeless shades of Black Night's victims had gathered at my bedside. I could not silence the memory of Boreas's wails, nor of his choked ecstasy as I wrought his murder. Danger. Villainy. By Lauds, I was near sick with it. When I glimpsed Scrutari-Consil observing our procession down the nightstair into the choir, my overstrung nerves snapped.

I could not stay here. Not with a hunting pureblood in residence. No matter my missing book; no matter coming famine. Twelve years I had remained free by moving on when I needed, forgoing attachments that might tempt me to linger past safety. With silent apologies to the monks who had welcomed me so kindly, and to the god Iero who had received so little service from my vows, I slipped out of the dorter into the cold mist and drizzle in the dead hours between Lauds and Prime. By the time I reached Elanus, I'd have daylight.

Life was never so simple, of course. I retrieved my nivat bag and other contraband from the hedge garden and tucked them securely in my rucksack along with my secular clothes and the blanket from my bed. But when I emerged from the abbey gate tunnel, a near impenetrable fog had blanketed the fields. The route through the bogs remained clearly mapped in my head, but just traveling the half quellé from the abbey to the road without getting turned around would be no easy matter. I had no time to waste. Two hours more and I would be missed. And the pureblood would surely hear of it.

Damn all! I ground my walking stick into the mud. Foolish to travel in such conditions. And even the ascetic accommodation of the abbey was a prince's comfort beside what awaited me on the road. But neither argument could persuade me to risk one more day at Gillarine.

I glanced upward to the windows above the gatehouse. I would chance the main track from the gates to the road, rather than going cross-country as I had the previous night. If I was quiet, there'd be no danger of being spotted by the sanctuary watch. I poured the last dram of ale from my vigil night flask onto the path, praying holy Deunor and Saint Gillare to bless this fool's journey. Then I gripped my stick, shouldered my pack, and set out. Fifty paces and I was lost.

The short-lived battle of Black Night had churned the field that fronted the abbey into muck. Without vision beyond my outstretched fingertips, I could not distinguish the well-defined track that once crossed it. Mumbling curses at the need to spend magic—and on this field of all places in the blasted world—I knelt, marshaled what strength might shield me from the horrors wrought here, and touched the earth.

Spirits of night! How far had I wandered? I lifted my hand, shook my head to clear it, and then touched the cold mud again. The impression was the same. Bloodshed . . . yes. Seething anger . . . grief . . . the death terrors of men and beasts. A hundred quercae to my left, men had screamed out their last moments in focused torment of fire and blade. But as runners of nandia vines and sprouts of fireweed and hearts' ease recapture a blighted field in one season's turn, so had a certain sweetness veined this ground. Not a mask to hide the taint of war, but a balm to soothe its raw wounding, to quiet the din of sobs and screams, to blunt the lingering pain enough to counteract its ruinous poison. No music played here as yet. What heart that perceived such sorrow could sing? But someday . . . perhaps . . . the tread of happier lives could overlay the lingering horror. Seeds slept beneath the cold mud. Living.

Wondering, I turned my mind to business. Year upon year of crossing had created a solid track across the wounded field, easily visible to my talent. Only half a day since the hierarch's party had slunk out of here, and some monk had left traces of his sandals since then. Still wary of Moriangi watchers, I stretched my awareness all the way to the road and swept it across the foggy landscape.

Deunor's fire! Riders lurked in the wooded hollow at the joining of track and road—five . . . ten . . . I could not tell how many. I sat back on my heels and listened. Naught of man or beast scored the night this far away—which likely meant they did not wish to be heard. Wary travelers, perhaps. But the aura of villainy that had plagued me all night of a sudden had focus. Even a small party could spell danger in such times as these. They could be Harrowers. They could be Scrutari-Consil's cohorts—Registry. Before I decided whether to retreat or run, I needed to know.

I touched earth again and sought an approach from the open fields—the direction they'd least expect. Once the route felt sure, I slipped through the pale night, following the guide thread in my head. Fifty times I thought I'd gone wrong; I'd never traveled wholly blind before. But just as the guide thread gave out, my feet felt the sharp rise of the hollow's lip, and I came near breaking my fingers when my extended hands encountered the bark of a young oak.

Lamenting my bulky monk's garb, I crept from tree to tree, now following soft voices and the weak lantern light gleaming deep in the treed hollow. Somewhere beyond them, horses grazed.

"Dawn approaches. Are you prepared?" The woman's voice, cold and clear as a knife blade, chilled my soul. Only one night removed from her depraved rites, I could not mistake the priestess were a thousand other voices yammering in my ear.

The muffled answer was a man's voice, but I could not decipher his words.

"Witness this noble sacrifice, sister and brothers," said Sila Diaglou, "even as you remain vigilant. May the sweet odor of his suffering serve the Gehoum, drawing out our enemies that we might confound and crush them."

A few of them shifted position in the fog, and I used their footsteps to cover my own as I slipped closer. Embracing one tree and then another, I honed my every sense, so that I would not collide with one of the shadowed forms. Four of them besides the priestess . . . no more. Likely the same I'd seen at Graver's Meadow. Not gathered close as they'd been there. But somewhere in the center would be the priestess and the victim . . .

"*Sanguiera, orongia.* Scream, Monk. The trump of your pain shall open this battle and win the night." *Sanguiera, orongia.* Bleed. Suffer.

A whistling split of the air. A crack, as if a limb of dry oak had snapped. A heart-tearing scream told me they'd stood him upright near one of three trees, some twenty quercae from my position. I gripped the reins of my fury and held still, listening. The next lash told me which tree.

Not again. This *would* not happen again. And certainly *not* to one of the brethren . . .

Blocking out the cries ripped from a man's pain in the name of purity, I touched earth and mapped the grove, recording every tree, every shrub, every rock, stick, trench, or dip that might betray my steps or slow them. I searched out true north and etched the sense of it into my bones so that I could orient myself without thought. It took longer than I wished, knowing that the lash continued to fall, but I also knew they had no intent to be quick about their brutal game.

When my mind held as much as I could reasonably learn of the grove, I crept toward the closest of the four watchers. Only at the last step did he look my way—Boreas's needle-chinned murderer. With every minim of strength I had in me, I slammed my walking stick into the man's throat. Then I darted away. I hoped I'd killed him.

"Who's there?" As a loop snapping into a knot did Sila Diaglou's remaining henchmen gather round her, only to unravel again when one of their company did not arrive. "Radulf?"

Brisk footsteps sought the victim. "Radulf is down, lady!"

"Find the intruder!" The priestess's command slammed my gut like a fist. But I held still and did not flinch. "Falderrene, Malena, all of you, spread out. Do *not* let him escape! Hold, monk. We'll finish with you betimes."

"Quiet!" spat one of the men.

The light wavered, shifted. Another light bloomed, coloring the fog piss yellow. Close enough to hear the gasps of the injured man, the harsh breathing of their captive, and the hiss of whispered orders, I pressed my back to the slender trunk and waited for them to disperse.

The three spiraled outward from the site of their crime. Closing my eyes, I matched their movements with the map imprinted on my mind. Unable to see in the fog, they brushed stalks, snapped branches underfoot, disturbed rocks. As soon as they were spread out from their captive and the cold priestess who guarded him—not so far as I would like—I threaded my way between them. I had little confidence in my fighting ability, but I had a few other skills.

Yanking my abbey blanket from my rucksack, I returned to the downed man. He clutched his throat, wholly preoccupied with choking. I slipped his dagger from its sheath. If he died I would not grieve, but I could not shed his blood on that ground. Instead, I spread the blanket over his body, considered my intent, and constructed the most rudimentary of illusion spells—the only kind I'd ever learned to any effect. Once prepared, I stared, motionless, scarce breathing, toward the ashen cloud whence came the captive's harsh breathing. I stared until I could just make out the priestess's tall figure pacing a short path near the tree. She wielded a short blade.

"You intrude on matters you cannot comprehend, infidel," she cried. "Dare you sully a sacrifice offered to the Gehoum? I am the tool of their wrath."

You bring murder to Iero's holy ground, Harrower, I thought, snarling, *and against his might, you* shall *not* prevail.

Touching the blanket, I fed magic to my working. And waited. As the arm of a siege engine seems to crawl on its skyward journey toward release, so my spell seemed to spend eternity in its binding. My heart near stopped when I felt the blanket shift . . . and then it swelled into the very awkward likeness of a giant monk. Or a giant tent. I didn't care which way she saw it or how crude the work might be. I was already running.

"Infidel!" No coward, Sila Diaglou. She charged out of the fog, crashing through trees and scrub straight at my feeble working. "Falderrene! Morgaut! To me!"

Silently I'd circled wide of her, leaping rocks and pits, dodging saplings and branches and stones, to come up behind the tree. Before she could reach my illusion, I was fumbling at the quivering captive suspended from the thin-boled oak. I could scarce believe my luck—his luck. Two loose, twisted loops of rope were all that held his hands to the limb above his head. I slipped the loops off his wrists, grasped him in my arms, and drew him away from the tree. Though his pale skin ran dark with blood, he expelled only a faint hiss at my handling. He lifted his head—pale, too, shaven as it was, his dark eyes a stain on his white skin . . . *Gildas!*

"Valen?" Even in the wan light, I could feel his shock.

"Do I need to carry you?" I said, grinning, cheered to feel him supporting his own weight.

"No . . . no, not . . . but. . . ." He shook his head. Though his speech stumbled, he gathered up his cowl and gown that had been stripped off his shoulders and left bunched about his waist.

"Then follow me." I grasped his arm and pulled him along.

"I'll bleed you for the Gehoum, infidel!" Sila Diaglou's cry of rage followed us as I led Gildas on the shortest path out of the hollow. I didn't expect that she would follow, and she did not. As I supported the stumbling monk across the broken ground, a crash of brush and the dwindling thunder of galloping hoofbeats signaled the Harrowers' escape. As soon as I was sure, I halted.

"I think we're safe now," I said, supporting him by his arms, careful not to jar or twist his mangled back. "I'll fetch Robierre . . . the litter."

"No . . . no . . . I'll be all right. Stupid to get caught out. But, Valen"—his gaze was hot—"what, in great Iero's mercy, are you doing out here? How did you—? I don't understand."

"I could ask the same of you, Brother," I said.

"Couldn't sleep," he said, after a moment. "I needed to think, and so I played the fool, wandering about out here in the night. Walked right into their little plot."

"Exactly so," I said. "Only, *I* seem to have lost my blanket as well—hung it up in a tree to distract them. Do you think Brother Sebastian will punish me?"

He laid his blood-streaked hand on my shoulder and flashed his white teeth in a grin. "I'll see what I can do." Despite the smile, his hand quivered like a maid on her virgin night.

When we reached the gatehouse, Gildas refused my offer to accompany him to the infirmary or even to summon Brother Robierre to see to him. "No need for us both to suffer reprimands," he said, pulling his disheveled garments tight. "I'll confess my folly to Father Abbot tonight, so he'll likely not get after you until morning. Not at all, if I can manage it. I'll say only what you've told me, mention nothing of rucksacks, and bless your name eternally in their hearing. But someday, good Valen, we will speak of this night, you and me."

"I'm just happy you're living," I said. "The last fellow I rescued was dead at the end of it." As I slogged back through the hedge garden, I glimpsed Abbot Luviar racing toward the Alms Court, robes billowing. And from the direction of the guesthouse, heading in the same direction, barreled the Thane of Erasku and his secretary Gram. I had not heard that the lord had returned to the abbey. Had I not been ready to collapse as battle fever and tight-held magic drained out of me, I would have gone back to hear what drew them so urgently to the gates. But I could scarce command my feet to carry me.

I slept astonishingly well, until the bells clanged and clamored, waking me to my first day as a Gillarine's newest and only novice.

Chapter 13

The fifth day of my novitiate began as had the previous four. In the dark. After the lengthy service of Prime, we washed heads, hands, and feet in the frigid water of the lavatorium, then broke our night's fast with weak ale and bread left from the previous day. As every day, I slogged through these activities half asleep. A night of unbroken sleep had taken its place in the pantheon of unachievable delights, alongside my own private cask of mead and a Pyrrhan courtesan in my bed.

The daily chapter meeting began as usual, too. Abbot Luviar and Prior Nemesio sat beneath the grandest of the lancet windows, the one depicting Kings Eodward and Caedmon worshiping an enthroned Creator. Jullian and Gerard perched on low stools that flanked the door. In between, on crescent-shaped benches that lined the circular walls, sat the remainder of Gillarine's thirty monks, ordered from eldest to youngest. Every size and shape of man.

At my first chapter meeting, Brother Sebastian had led me around the circle to introduce me, as if he were a swineherd and I his prized sow. We had skipped no one, all the way from the eldest—straight-backed Brother Abelard, mostly blind and nearing his ninetieth year—to the youngest—walleyed Brother Simeon, eight years my junior. Birdlike Brother Nunius; the aristocratic Ardran Brother Bolene; the cottar's son Brother Adolfus, whose eyes and throat bulged like a toad's . . . My memory for names and faces had been well exercised.

Sharing this clockwork existence of prayers and work with these men was no bad life by any means. I could surely bear the monotony and excessive piety for a season. It was only when I thought of living this way unchanging until I was the age of Brother Abelard that cold sweat dribbled down my back.

I had scarce settled in my own place at the lowest end of the bench, just next to Jullian's stool and the entry, when every face turned abruptly in our direction. Brother Victor stood in the doorway, looking small and hollow-eyed and unsteady on his feet. Luviar motioned the pale little chancellor to his assigned seat without the least hint of sympathy, apology, or the conspiracy that I believed existed between them. Perhaps that was because the hierarch's pureblood followed Brother Victor into the room.

I fixed my gaze on my hands, clenched in my lap. A frigid draft more appropriate to the Frost Moon than Reaper's Moon funneled up the nightstair, swirled through the open door, and blew straight up my gown.

Scrutari-Consil had remained sequestered in the abbot's house, conducting his interviews. My heart had lurched like a besotted beggar every time a new witness was summoned. Every town of any size and every fighting legion bought pureblood contracts, so it wasn't as if I'd wholly avoided those of my own kind over the years. I told myself I just needed to keep to my usual habits . . . and pray no one spoke my name in his hearing . . . or mentioned my book.

I glanced at Brother Gildas. He appeared soberly attentive as always. To my surprise, I'd never been questioned about our encounter with the Harrowers. Prior Nemesio had cautioned everyone that Gildas had run afoul of them to the peril of his life and that I had chanced upon him and brought him back within our walls. Sometimes I wondered if it had really happened. I had collapsed that morning wrapped in my cowl, but I'd waked with a blanket thrown over me, and my well-brushed cowl hung neatly with my gown.

"Holy Father, a moment's intrusion, if you permit," said Scrutari-Consil without expression, touching his fingers to his forehead.

"Speak as you will," said the abbot coolly.

The pureblood inclined his back to acknowledge the permission. Purebloods *bowed* to no ordinary but their contracted masters and the King of Navronne. "I must commend you on your brothers' piety, Abbot Luviar, and on their . . . ardent . . . personal loyalty to you and your chancellor. My investigations of Gillarine's scribes have revealed no purpose to their work but the One God's glory. As the chancellor's confinement is ended, I deem my work here complete . . . or nearly so."

Luviar said naught.

Scrutari-Consil stepped farther into the room, his cloak billowed by the draft from the doorway. "I understand that some few members of this brotherhood labor in the scriptorium occasionally, although they are not considered scribes. I must question those persons that I may assure Hierarch Eligius I have been thorough in my obligations. And one more small matter . . ."

I tried not to fidget. I would *not* be on that list. He would have no reason to speak to me. Soon he would be gone, and perhaps I would be able to pass an hour without imagining my father's sneer as he devised a method to control me for the rest of my life.

Hands at his back, the pureblood pivoted on one fine boot, as if to take a final appraisal of our faces. ". . . I require a review of your membership list. In my general scrutiny of Gillarine and its residents, I have perceived residue of sorcery. My duty to the kingdom and its law demands that I ensure that any pureblood in your brotherhood has received the proper family dispensation. Much better that I, a Karish observant, take on this review, than a Registry inspector, likely an unbeliever, intrude upon your holy precincts."

Deunor's fire, damnation, and all cursed gatzi! Never use *magic, fool.* Never. *You know it.*

The monks Scrutari had questioned insisted that a man could hide nothing from his magical interrogations. I knew better. To deceive a pureblood perceptive you just had to present plausible, consistent testimony and obliterate any distinction in your mind between the truth and the lie—perhaps a difficult thing for holy monks. For me, the lying was easy. Unfortunately, my history, cobbled up in an instant whilst I suffered from wound fever, was as thin as these monks' finest vellum. And my name was now scribed on the abbey's roster.

"Of course you may inspect our membership roster if you deem it necessary," said the abbot, displaying no emotion the perceiver might probe. "But it would be a waste of your time. Only one of our brotherhood claims pureblood descent. His dispensation is duly recorded, and for more than twenty years he has forsworn the practice of sorcery as our Rule demands. Prior Nemesio can show you this man's credentials immediately after chapter. As for those who assist in the scriptorium, one could say that every man in the abbey does so, whether he be the lay brother who tends the fire or the boy who mixes the ink or the choir monk who petitions blessings for the generous donors of our books. I see no need for you to interview every resident of Gillarine on some arbitrary quest for completeness. The hierarch would perhaps consider it a *frivolous* use of our time and that of his valued pureblood servant."

Scrutari's nostril's flared in disbelief—as did mine, most likely. "Surely, holy fath—"

"Once you have reviewed the record Prior Nemesio will show you, your horse will be ready for your departure. Bear our prayers for good health and Iero's blessings to the hierarch. Now please excuse us. We've business to attend before the bells ring for prayers." The abbot's demeanor stood no more yielding than a granite wall.

Though I applauded his decision, Luviar's refusal made no sense, unless . . . . I glanced at the young face beside me. Jullian's eyes were fixed in the vicinity of Brother Nunius's wrinkled neck, and his fingers clenched in a knot tighter than my own. He breathed in shallow fits.

"As you say, Father Abbot. I shall pass your message—and my conclusions—to the hierarch." Stiff as Erdru's prick, the pureblood touched his forehead and withdrew. Were I Abbot Luviar, I would not request any favors from the Scrutari-Consil family before Judgment Night.

An unruffled Prior Nemesio began the day's business. Boring business. He invited Brother Nunius to speak on the fifteenth chapter of Saint Ophir's Rule—that which addressed the management of an abbey's lands and treasury and the apportioning of alms. My attention wandered.

Weak sunbeams shone through the lancet windows behind the abbot's chair, transforming the colored glass into rubies, emeralds, and sapphires. I examined King Eodward's features in the window, searching for some trace of the man I had met. He had been the exemplar of Ardran manhood—big and ruddy, beard and hair as red-gold as summer sunset, his bones sturdy and well formed, his face equally suited to laughter and sober intelligence. I glanced at Jullian—the boy was breathing again—and wondered about a rumored Pretender . . . a child . . . and an abbot who juggled hierarchs and purebloods and princes as if they were oranges. And told myself I was a lunatic.

By the time Brother Nunius's sermon had labored to its conclusion, and the prior began assigning reading tasks for the day's services and mealtimes, my eyelids were drooping. But somewhere between "Brother Aesculpius, Vespers" and "Brother Jerome, Matins," he announced, "Brother Valen, Compline."

Gods' bones! They wanted me to read! Cold dismay wafted up my gown with the draft. My conscience bloomed hotly on my cheeks. Rabbitlike thoughts of escape drew my glance to the door, where I found Jullian staring curiously at *me*.

Except on the coldest or rainiest days, I was supposed to spend the hours between Terce and dinner pursuing my studies in my carrel in the north cloister. Brother Sebastian had selected a dreadfully thick book for me to study over the next months. I didn't even know its name.

I riffled the pages of the book and contemplated the cloister garth and the shrine, mulling the problems of undead spirits and why one of them might have an interest in me, and of how I was to convince Brother Sebastian to read me the text I was supposed to proclaim at Compline.

I had already spent an hour concluding that I couldn't possibly guess which of Saint Ophir's brothers was a pureblood. My own appearance evidenced that "straight of hair, deep of color, short in stature, large in talent" was not an infallible guide to Aurellian heritage, but most purebloods *did* conform to the type. Whoever it was—and a careful recollection of every face in the chapter circle yielded no suspicion—either he was not insightful enough to connect me to the infamous Cartamandua *recondeur* or he had truly shifted his loyalties to the brotherhood and broken contact with the Registry. I was likely safe enough as long as I kept to my usual precautions. I hoped.

Inevitably, as it had all week, my mind returned to the incident in the wood. The more I recalled, the stranger it all was. The Harrowers had not been doing the same to Gildas as they had to Boreas. Sila Diaglou had said they wanted to "draw them out"—referring to her enemies. And Luviar and Thane Stearc had been running to the gates . . .

Ow! I bit my lip to keep from yelling aloud when Brother Sebastian's knucklebone rapped my skull. I stuck my books in my pockets and traipsed after his wagging finger.

Though rigorous in matters of decorum, liturgical observance, and adherence to the Rule, the tidy Sebastian had been undemanding when it came to my studies. He seemed more than willing to believe that my healing shoulder wound restricted any writing tasks and that illness still caused my eyes to tire easily, limiting my reading. In the main, he complained I talked too much, and was forever exhorting me shift my verbal excess from flesh to spirit.

"Fine mornings are too rare of late," he said as we left the cloisters for the maze of yew and hawthorn hedges in front of the church. "Let us discuss the lesson you were to master for today, and, at the same time, give praise for the sunlight. So, Brother Valen, the structure of virtue: Recite for me the seven great virtues and twelve great vices and expound upon their signs and meanings."

If he had known my answers were all guesswork, he might have admired my cleverness at getting almost half of them right. Instead, he cheerfully scolded me as a slackwit, charged me to obtain a wax tablet from Brother Victor and write out the two lists for the next morning.

"We do not expect every brother to be a scholar of Brother Gildas's level, or even Jullian's, who has as fine a mind as any student we have ever nurtured here. But you *must* master the basic precepts of divine order, be familiar with the holy writs, and the history—" The dinner bell brought a welcome reprieve from his kindly concern.

I'd grown quite fond of mealtimes, beyond the fine and plentiful sustenance. The week had taught me that the light-filled refectory was neither so serious nor so strictly quiet as the cloister or library, save during the actual reading that accompanied every meal. Which circumstance raised my hopes of garnering assistance to break the twin shackles of the Compline reading and my study text. Scrutari-Consil was gone. Gildas had shielded my abortive departure. Truly, excessive worry about the future wasted a man's life.

"Iero's grace, Brother Abelard," I shouted in the ancient monk's ear and took his arm on the refectory stair. "The sun feels a bit more seasonable today, does it not?" The crabbed old fellow frowned and shushed me, and shook off my hold. Horribly deaf, he proposed every morning in chapter to apply the rule of silence everywhere in the abbey.

Undeterred, I dropped back and offered my assistance to another of the elders. "Brother Nunius, someday perhaps you could teach me why we may give alms to ill-reputed women only in famine times. That part of the Rule left me confused." At least I could *speak* of ill-reputed women.

"Indeed, it is a strict provision," said the birdlike monk, graciously accepting my arm. "The fifteenth chapter is more important than most of us credit. Sometimes I believe I am the only one who pays it mind. You were not the only member of our family dozing this morning."

Family! By the god's toes, if I ever thought of the brothers as family, I'd bolt from here for certain. "Tell me, Brother, why does Saint Ophir forbid his brothers magic working? We're taught that pureblood sorcery is a gift of the god"—and thus we pursued *recondeurs* as doubly damned, traitors to the divine, as well as to the king—"so should not our Rule promote its use in holy works?"

"An excellent question! Sorcery is a component of the earthly sphere just as wealth and gaming and pleasures of the flesh," said the old man. "Whilst not evil in themselves, such worldly pursuits leave the soul ripe for the Adversary, who is ever seeking ways to subvert our better natures. Young fellows like you must work diligently to avoid such pitfalls as sorcery."

"And so I shall, good brother." I laughed and released his arm as we reached the refectory door. "So I shall."

"I need to speak with you, Archangel," I said quietly, when Jullian arrived with the boiled fish and stewed parsnips. "A work of mercy that will ensure your place in the heavenly choir."

He bowed his head for the prayer as the abbot rang the bell. "You should not have lied about your reading," he whispered, his lips scarcely moving. "Lies are the Adversary's tool."

The mealtime reading would begin in moments, so I had no time to question why such a minor offense caused him to sit there tight as a tabor's skin. No time to remind him that *secrets* are the closest kin to lies.

"You once offered me whatever I needed of you," I said. "Surely the god wishes you to help me become a better man."

He nodded without looking at me. "Meet me in the garden maze just after supper. Tell Brother Sebastian you need to meditate on those you've wronged in preparation for Saint Dian's Day."

His direction sounded a bit pompous coming from a boy of twelve. Of a sudden, my mad whimsy insisted on reviving itself. *An Ardran Pretender . . . here.* If such were true, the danger would be unimaginable. I buried the thought as quickly as it had arrived.

Yet as a drifting cloud grayed the light from the great windows, my spirits chilled. I could not shake the sense of unseen hands propelling me toward an unseen precipice, and even the lovely mound of parsnips touched with thyme could not disperse it.

Every day between Nones and Vespers, I reported to work in the kitchen. Though I could not seem to satisfy the meticulous Brother Jerome with my work—my chopping was uneven, my fish wastefully trimmed, and after the third time I scorched the porridge, he forbade me to come near his precious pots—I enjoyed those hours the most of all my duties. Yet on this day I fidgeted through the time as if I'd buckthorn twigs in my trews, and I came near yanking out what was left of my hair as we dragged through Vespers and supper. I couldn't have said what I was expecting.

Fog had rolled in from the river again, studding the neglected hedges of the garden maze with water droplets. Sprangling branches spattered my face as I hurried down along the graveled path toward the center of the maze and the stone bench that overlooked a green-slimed pond.

"Brother Valen!" Jullian jumped from the bench like a startled cat.

"Are you expecting other oversized supplicants this night, Archangel?" I said with a grin, hoping to put him at ease.

Unsuccessfully, it seemed. He glanced over his shoulder and gripped his arms about his slight body as if gatzi were poised to jump out of the hedges and drag him off to the netherworld. Blue-gray dusk had settled over the abbey. The days were rapidly growing shorter.

"Of course not." He bit his lip and sat on the bench again, curling his bare legs underneath him. His eyes would not meet mine. One would think it was *he* undergoing the humiliation of seeking aid from a child scarce dropped from his mother's womb.

"I thank you for not revealing my problem to the brothers," I said. "They'd pitch me over the wall did they find out. I've nowhere to go." And unholy murderers lurked beyond these walls.

When I tilted my head to glimpse his face and gauge the depth of his worry, he turned away. "I'll help you," he said. "I did say I would. But I'll not lie about it should anyone ask me."

"A fair bargain and a great kindness." I held out my psalter and my lesson book. "All I need is for you to show me which page and to read me whatever I'm supposed to say at Compline, and then to read me the passage about the great virtues and vices from the other book." I could devise some explanation for not writing the lesson.

"How will reading you the passage help you? You're required to proclaim the whole text, and Brother Abelard will complain if you get even a word of it wrong."

"I'll remember. It's just— My eyes—" Of a sudden all my usual excuses felt inadequate. "It's like a blindness in me, Jullian. I see the marks on the page, and I can tell one letter from the other if I work at it hard enough. But when I look at two or more together, they tie themselves into knots that won't unravel no matter what I do. I've tried to learn since I was a boy, but it won't come. I'm just . . . broken . . . somehow." Or lazy-minded, stubborn, demon-touched, god-cursed, soul-damaged, or willfully obtuse—all the things my tutors, parents, and siblings had named me. I must be mad. I had never told anyone what I had just exposed to a child I scarcely knew. "But I'm not stupid. Read it to me exactly, and I can remember it exactly."

Heaving a great quivering sigh, the boy laid the books in his lap and carefully smoothed the worn covers. Some fine friend I was, who had so pompously set myself to ward him from unwanted advances of the flesh, only to subvert his conscience, which he likely valued higher. As for my mad speculations, an hour's contemplation as I worked in the kitchen had already convinced me I was an idiot. Any youthful Pretender of Eodward's loins would be secured in some remote fortress under the protection of pureblood defense works, not scuffing about an abbey in sandals.

"All right, then." Jullian leafed through the psalter until settling on a page bordered with flying geese. "This is tonight's Compline—" His head jerked up at some noise from beyond the hedge.

When his gaze shifted to something over my shoulder, I was still too taken aback to ask what distracted him, for in that moment of surprise, I had glimpsed his face . . . not conscience ridden at all, but keen with excitement and anticipation.

"Brother Valen."

I jumped to my feet, enough blood rushing to my face to feed a cave of bats. "Holy father! I—We—"

Jullian stepped immediately to the abbot's side, halting my stammering with a now-obvious truth. The boy had known he was coming. *Saint Dian's Day* . . . they had conspired to get me here!

"Sit down, Valen," said Luviar. Joining me on the bench, the abbot pressed a finger to his lips and then flicked it in a quick gesture to the boy.

Jullian bowed and melted into the hedges.

"I needed to speak with you in private, Brother Novice. And as you have no doubt learned in these past weeks, privacy is not a condition of monastery life. Not physical privacy, at least, even for the abbot." His brows lifted, widening his gray eyes in an expression I would have called good humor were this anyone but Abbot Luviar.

Annoyed with the boy and the abbot—and even more with my own stupidity—I kept my jaw shut tight and dipped my head in agreement, sure I was now to hear word of my dismissal.

"Hmm. Not so forthcoming as at our first meeting?" Luviar's scrutiny felt bone-deep. "I suppose I must take responsibility for that. Though I am aware that not everything you told me of your journey here is entirely . . . accurate . . . I believe I understand at least something of your reasons for dissembling. Tell me, Brother Valen, were you a more capable man-at-arms in Ardra's service than you are a cook's helper?"

My skin heated. So he'd guessed that I was a deserter. Best not add more lies, if I could avoid it. "No, holy father."

"Your past loyalties do not concern me so much as your current loyalties, Valen, and I'll not hold you to account for choices made before you were in my charge."

The failing light made it increasingly difficult to read his face, thus I dared not feel relief.

"I've seen and heard enough of you these past weeks to believe that I can entrust you with a task I need of you tonight. Your instincts are ever generous, whether to old or young—or those in peril. You accept what is without complaint, bridling only at matters of justice. And you live your days with relish, no matter their mundanity. You have a certain honesty about you that has little to do with truth or untruth. I am not a fool. But I'm not sure if *you* trust *me*, and that is imperative, for I must insist that you keep silent about certain matters that could compromise others' safety. Matters of great importance."

" 'For Navronne'? 'For our children's children'?" Bitterness at this man welled up in me and erased every other consideration, as if the slaughtered Ardrans' blood rose from the ground beneath my sandals and their empty eye sockets glared at me.

Luviar did not flinch. His face and shaven head gleamed pale in the enveloping night. "Indeed, yes. Now, ask me the one question whose truthful answer might most influence your trust. I'll answer you—truthfully—and then we shall see if we're to proceed."

"Only one, holy father?" Again and always, my imprudent tongue.

He remained cool and sober. "For now, one question. If I cannot satisfy you enough to gain your promise of forbearance, then I must think of some other way."

So many possibilities . . . I was almost drunk with the thought of answers. Yet some of Gillarine's mysteries were but simple secrets, and simple facts would explain them. I could ask about Jullian—but a negative answer would leave me more confused than ever, and an affirmative one was so dangerous, I was not sure I wanted to know it. No, the greater challenge to trust was this man's character—which took me right back to the beginning.

"Why did you abandon Ardran soldiers to die—*encourage* them to die—for a prince you surely know is unworthy?"

He nodded, as if my question were exactly the one he expected. "We live in harsh times, Brother Valen, and as a man newly arrived here from the wide world, you know this as well as any. The lack of a righteous king speeds the ruin of our land. I speak not merely of war's grief and devastation, but of the deepest mysteries of earth and heaven, for this conflict is but one piece of a grand and terrible mosaic, with some of the other pieces named Famine, Pestilence, and Storm."

Why was it Luviar could set the hairs on my neck rising with words that would sound pretentious spoken even by a pureblood diviner? His gray eyes warmed with sympathy, as if he understood the unnerving nature of his converse and sought to soothe it even as he made it worse.

"In another age of the world, I would step not one quat in any direction to serve Perryn of Ardra's cause. But as matters stand, neither could I allow Bayard of Morian to take the final step that would assure his ascension to Eodward's throne. Not only because of his own faults, but for this: If Prince Bayard's eye is no longer fixed on his hated rival, and his hammer no longer aimed at valiant Ardra, then his attention—and that of his new allies—will turn to any who dare assert that we must deal with matters more important than the succession. Their hammer will fall on those few who fight to assure Navronne's future beyond one sovereign's reign."

"Assuring the future beyond one . . ." My mind raced, knotting and unknotting the strange events of the past weeks. "You're speaking of this end-times teaching." *The long night*, Jullian had said. *The dark times.* What the hierarch called deviance.

He propped his elbows on his knees and leaned forward to rest his chin on his folded hands, staring at the well-trodden path. "Those Ardran soldiers had pledged their loyalty and service to their prince," he continued. "I, in an arrogance of intellect and conviction, stole that devotion and transferred it to a worthier cause. To Ardra, Morian, and Evanore—to Navronne and to the mysteries that bind our land to the future of Iero's creation. Not to despair, but to hope."

He had shaped his answer with an artist's hand that took bits of colored glass and fit them together to create a portrait of kings and saints. I wondered again if Luviar had the bent—for persuasion, perhaps. For truth-telling, I hoped, for my curiosity was so inflamed, I could not have walked away had he sprouted a gatzé's barbed tail in front of me. I could not say I trusted him, but, gods preserve me, I believed him. "Father Abbot, are *you* the pureblood at Gillarine?"

His head popped up from his meditative posture, and he laughed, a full-throated burst of cheer, as robust as Ardran mead and as unexpected as an honest tinker. "Is that your measure of trust, Valen? You think I am ensorceling you? Not at all what I had hoped to accomplish. But I granted you only one answer, if you remember. More will come only if you vow your silence. If you choose not, then no burden will be held against you, nor will I look further into your past. Now tell me if I should proceed or not. Lives may depend on your declaration."

I scratched my head and tried to bury my qualms about holy men. Who was I to gainsay the abbot, after all? He had all but confessed to me that he supported what his superiors called deviance—high treason in the world of practors and hierarchs. I felt great kinship with all rebellious souls, even if they wore golden solicales. "What is it you want of me, holy father? Not a sevenday since I did swear to obey you in all things. And if you command I trust you and keep secrets, well then, who am I to say it is not holy?"

He sighed and spread his hands in acceptance. "I suppose that will have to do. Your task is simple. I wish you to meet with several others who recognize the enormity of the world's troubles. They need you to demonstrate how to use the Cartamandua maps."

My spirits, tickled with growing excitement, plunged. Of course it would be the book. Though, indeed, he had asked my aid, not for copying, but for use, which raised all manner of questions, such as where his friends wished to travel that no ordinary book of maps could take them. But this book— I was trying to avoid lies. "Father Abbot, I must tell you—"

No. I couldn't tell him I'd never used it. Once I began changing my story, the perceptive abbot would surely unravel the rest of my talespinning. Then he would be forced to choose between his life and my freedom.

I trusted no one but myself with that choice. Blood rushed to my skin with the misstep so narrowly avoided.

"The book is certainly magical, holy father, and thus appears differently to any eye that looks upon it. Its usage is likely different for any who attempt it also. I'll share what I can, but in truth, as you've clearly surmised, I've had meager success at anything in my life, thus you'd best not expect too much."

Luviar watched me silently. Waiting for me to confess more lies, I thought. I kept breathing and did not squirm.

At last he nodded. "Very well, then. All we ask is your best effort. At the opening of tonight's Compline I will assign you to keep vigil in the church through the night. When the day's-end bell rings, leave the church and return here. You'll be met. And you will not reveal this plan or what occurs to anyone, on pain of your immortal soul."

"As you say, holy father." I bowed my head, placing a clenched fist upon my breast in their sign of obedience. Then, gritting my teeth, I broached the direst topic. "I am assigned to read at Compline tonight."

"I'll have Nemesio postpone that until tomorrow." He stood and lifted his black hood, so that his body lost definition in the dusk. "Iero's grace be with you, Valen. *Teneamus.*"

"Wait! What does that—?" As he turned his back to my rising question and hurried away, I would have sworn I glimpsed a flicker of teeth that might have been a smile.

Chapter 14

The abbot had failed to mention that the "vigil" he planned to assign me was a penance for dozing in chapter. Because he announced this judgment at the opening of Compline, I was required to prostrate myself throughout the entire service, which left me in no great patience for meeting his friends. Perhaps he thought I would be grateful that he was permitting me to abandon the punishment at the day's end bell, rather than staying in place until Matins. But as the cold, unyielding granite bruised my too-prominent bones, gratitude came nowhere to mind. I could not even rejoice in the postponement of my reading.

Once the monks had snuffed the candles and retired to the dorter, a great chilly silence fell in the church. The vigil lamp gleamed emerald from the high altar. Brother Victor lay on the floor to my right. He had arrived late for Compline and reaped the same penance as mine. The chancellor had a slight whistle in his breathing that prevented any sensible thinking. Had I actually to remain in place for the full span of this vigil, the sound would surely drive me mad long before the bells rang for Matins.

When the bell tolled the day's end, the time for all activities to cease and the monks to take to their beds, I rose from the floor as quietly as I could. Brother Victor did not stir as I padded down the aisle. His presence would not be happenstance. That the chancellor would be part of the abbot's little plot did not surprise me, but it did give me pause. Luviar had not only been willing to sacrifice *strangers* to his "worthier cause," but had yielded his own partisan to lashing, imprisonment, and humiliation. Why did I not heed my own warnings about holy men?

I hurried through the hedge maze and returned to the bench by the neglected pond, vowing to detach myself from this conspiracy as quickly as possible. No good could come from mixing religion and politics. And who could be less equipped than I to get in a fight over books? Did they think to stave off some threat to Navronne with almanacs and treatises on glassmaking? Build a bulwark of books against Hansker raiders, perhaps? That might be a use for the wretched things.

Night birds twittered. The sad little scrap of moon vanished in the west. No one came. I was on the verge of giving up, when light, steady footsteps approached from the direction of the cloisters. Closer. Then heavier, louder steps came running from two other directions at once. I spun like a potter's wheel, but before I could see who was in such a hurry, some cursed villain dropped a sack over my head.

"Gatzé's whore!" I shot up from the bench, pawing at the bag. A hempen drawstring held the rough cloth tight around my neck. I dragged at the rope, but succeeded only in strangling myself. Dust clogged my nostrils. The bag scratched my face and blocked my mouth. *Hot. Close. Choking.* I could not yell. Could not breathe. Terror welled up inside me like molten lava. *No light. No air. Buried . . .*

I flailed my arms and tried to twist away. My right arm slammed into solid flesh, and my left elbow crunched bone hard enough to elicit a curse. Two outsized hands caught my wrists and pinned them hard behind me. "Here now, just be still, monk."

Jerking my shoulders and torso back and forth, I tried to use my size to some advantage, but the harder I struggled, the tighter the rope constricted my neck.

"Stop! Wait! There's no need for force," someone called. Pointlessly. No brutes would heed a man who spoke so softly.

I snarled and dragged them sideways. Feet tangled hopelessly in my gown, I toppled, dragging a heavy body down on top of me. My arms were wrenched back and up.

"Sentinels of the dark, he's broke my foot!"

"Half a madman . . . what's wrong with 'im? Hold on . . ." A heavy someone sat on me.

"Silence, all of you!" The soft voice whispered from somewhere in the spinning darkness. "Don't hurt him, Furz. Get up. What are you thinking?"

"You told us to get him to the camp without him seeing where." This from the brute who was twisting my arms from their sockets while I wriggled like a dying fish in a mudhole. His voice rumbled through my back and aching shoulders. "We heard he might be a danger."

"A danger? He's a monk! Get off him, and don't hurt him any more. We just need silence."

As the weight rolled off my back, I wrenched one hand loose and tore at the bag. Dug in my knees and scrabbled forward in the muddy grass. Tried to shake free of the hands. At any moment I was going to heave up my guts or die or both. I groaned and writhed.

"What, in all holy——? Iero's grace, just be still, Brother Valen." A new voice penetrated my skull like a bolt from a crossbow. Not loud, but very clear. "We'll take off the bag, if you'll but close your eyes and be silent. This is a terrible mistake. Do you hear me, Brother? Please, just be still, close your eyes, and we'll take it off."

Swallowing my gorge, I nodded and tried to be still. My heart galloped like a king's post messenger; blood thundered in my ears. *Just let me breathe.* Were spiders swarming over me, I would have remained still on his promise. I squeezed my eyes shut.

"Furz, get it off him," said the newcomer. "Would you, please?"

"They jumped him," said the soft-voiced one in quiet anger. "They weren't supposed to——"

The decisive man interrupted with tested patience. "You should have waited. I told you that Gildas and I would see to this."

I did not hear the response, for the bag was snatched away just then. Cool air bathed my face as I craned my neck upward, gulping great mouthfuls. Soon I was breathing normally, and sensations beyond suffocation returned. Rocks gouged my belly. My shoulders burned. My chin stung. My left foot, caught in my gown, was bent at an angle the Creator did not intend. I shifted to ease the strain, but the hands only gripped my limbs tighter, and a heavy knee crushed my chest into the ground.

Was every untoward event in all the world linked to Brother Gildas? Perhaps the whispering villain was Jullian, who seemed to be in the thick of these sordid matters as well. Instinct screamed at me to look on my attackers, so I could identify them if I lived or curse them as I died, but this mindless terror of suffocation kept my eyes tight shut and my tongue silent. I lowered my cheek to the muddy grass and inhaled the sweet scent of earth.

What foolish thoughts run through our heads in times of fear and peril. My cowl and gown were heavy with mud, clinging to my skin. Brother Sebastian would scold. I had no spare garments yet, as my height meant they had to be made new. *So rid yourself of this sodden wool and you'll get a full breath*, said my unbidden thoughts. Everywhere my bare skin touched earth—face, one knee and thigh—felt free. The earth embraced me, warm and alive and forgiving . . .

"Release him, Furz," said the decisive man, no denizen of heaven or hell, but entirely human and standing over my head. "We'll guide him to the camp ourselves."

"It's taken the two of us to hold him." The thugs growled in concert. "You're a fool to let him go. The blighting monk's got a gatzé in him."

"Did you never consider that a man attacked from behind and smothered with a grain sack might take offense—even a Karish monk? Please, do as I ask."

The weight came off my back, and thick fingers released my wrists. I rolled to my side and curled my arms in front of me, thanking every god for the gifts of air and unbroken bones, promising anew to reform my ways. Slowly I sat up on my heels, unwilling to push my luck by standing up. The two brutes hovered close enough to block the breeze, and this man, though firm and confident, was not their commander. Too much politeness from him, *asking* and saying *please*. And from the brutes mere obedience, no honorifics or respect. Obedience was sufficient, but without respect, I'd not rely on it.

As my heart slowed, my flush of gratitude yielded to the more usual mix of emotions I felt after a fight—embarrassment and anger. For all my height and natural strength, I'd never developed much technique. I'd had no combat training when I was young enough to develop true skill. Pureblood families valued physical prowess like speed and strength, and refinements such as grace and agility, but they had no use for fighting skills. Only barbarians or madmen would dare assault a pureblood. The Registry saw to that.

"We've no wish to harm you, Brother," said the man who had let me breathe, my friend forever. "Somehow these two became confused. They understood that we did not wish you to see where you were being taken and mistook our concern. I would explain why such secrecy is necessary, but that will be clear soon enough, and we need to move quickly. Someone might have heard your shout, and explanations would be awkward. So please understand this binding will be just for your eyes. *Just* your eyes."

When the cloth touched my face, I came near rising bodily off the ground. But before I could lash out, I comprehended what he'd said. Only the eyes. Not nose or mouth.

The blindfold in place, the clear-voiced man clasped arms with me and helped me to my feet. Average in height, perhaps a head shorter than me by the sound and feel of him. "We've a goodly walk ahead of us. Will your leg wound be a hindrance?"

I spat mud, wiped my mouth on my sleeve, and shook my head.

"Please believe me, Brother, we've no ill intent."

Such silliness required a response. I kept my voice as low as his. "Suffocating a fellow and twisting his limbs from their sockets is a poor introduction for those with good intents. Does the abbot know you treat his novices so?"

"Abbot Luviar will be extremely displeased"—as soon as he spoke, I felt his good humor, warm enough to dry my sodden cowl—"and I promise, we shall do our best to remedy our failing. One moment . . ."

Lighter footsteps came up on my left side—the whisperer. Their movements stirred up the faint scent of wintergreen.

"I am going to give your arm to my companion," said my friend. "He will guide you safely to our meeting place, while I dispatch these two oxen back to our camp and make sure nothing like this happens again. I'll join you before you begin."

Smaller hands took a firm hold on my elbow and forearm. "Tell me if I go too fast."

It occurred to me that I could snatch my arm from this one's grip, rip the cursed rag from my face, and run away. I could tell Abbot Luviar that his friends had dreadful manners and I would not put up with them, not even to get my questions answered. But I didn't. Once I could breathe, the whole business was altogether intriguing. Much more interesting than Compline texts or the structure of virtue.

My guide used my crooked arm as a rudder, leading me along the gravel path, northward I guessed, for the breeze which had veered southerly all week was at my back. We turned once, and then again, and the surface under my sandals became paving stone. Scents of incense and ephrain from my right and the bulk of stone told me when we passed the church. We changed direction, veering around it, and when we had gone far enough that the church no longer blocked the breeze from my cheek, the path began to rise.

The wind smelled of fish and river wrack, tinged by coming frost. My companion smelled of horses and woodsmoke and something . . .

"Careful, the pavement's broken." And then, "Left."

In the distance behind me, the abbey bell rang. One peal. The first hour past day's end.

"Steps here," said my guide, after a while. "Three downward, then stop for a moment."

Stone steps, not squared paving. Older, then. Out of the way. When I halted, my arm was released. Iron clanked softly—a latch. Oiled hinges. The hands took my arm again and guided me through the gate. We crossed flowing water on a sturdy plank bridge and then took a dirt path. The terrain leveled out, the damp tendrils of fog yielded to a cold dry breeze, and my guide picked up the pace.

Strange to experience the night as a blind man must. Birds flapping away, disturbed from a nest in the grass. Scuttering creatures. Wet grass, stagnant pools. A loon crying out the world's sorrow. The path had been well trod, a narrow trough in the turf, sticky mud in its bottom, its drier, sloping sides little wider than my big feet. So my guide's feet must tread the grass, while I walked the path. Or perhaps . . . I listened. The light footsteps squelched and scuffed much as my own steps did. Ah, a cart track, then, two troughs parallel.

Pleased with that deduction, I turned my attention to the person beside me. Listened more. Felt the hand on my arm shift to get a better hold, one finger now touching the skin of my wrist. I remembered. Inhaled. Considered. Felt my face crease into a grin. "So, Squire Corin, does the Thane of Erasku know you're a girl?"

She halted. Yanked her hands from my arm. Stepped away. Said nothing. If we hadn't already startled the moorhens, the force of her shock might have done it.

"I've not had this tonsure my whole life, you know," I said. "And the world is not kind to girls on their own, so you're not the first I've encountered in youth's attire." The world was little kinder to boys on their own.

She held silent and left me standing in the middle of a stubbled grain field blindfolded, without anything to hold on to. I didn't think I ought to reach for her. She was probably terrified enough already.

"I'll say, you had me mightily confused until today. But cutting your hair off might help. The braid leads a man's eye into thoughts of touching—

Uh . . . *my* eye, that is. Perhaps not others." I shut my mouth and held out my arm.

She grasped my wrist and elbow, more firmly than before, and strode out at a faster pace. We'd walked two hundred quercae before she spoke. "You're wearing a blindfold." Her unmuted voice was mellow and richly colored, more like a dulcian than a flute. I'd made a mistake. She was slight, certainly, but a woman grown, not a girl. "How did I give it away?"

I considered the evidence. "Well, you and your friends aren't monks. And after the abbot's talk with me, I didn't think your party belonged to any of our unsavory princes. That meant you were either someone altogether new or the thane's men . . . Well, all right, I guessed. As for you in particular . . . You *whispered* when you truly wanted to yell at those men. That was part of it. And you trusted a monk not to hurt you. Which meant you've clearly not been at the game too long—you mustn't trust *anyone*. And even when I was . . . suffocating . . . whenever you spoke, I thought Jullian was with us, though I knew at the same time he wasn't. You see, in the refectory I sit next to Jullian, whom I'll assume you know, and Gerard, the other lad. You don't—please, forgive me if I offend you—you don't smell at all the same." Excitement would have only worsened the boys' ripe stink.

"I don't smell—" She convulsed with laughter, as alive as the good earth around us. Only a moment; then she closed it all up again. "Sweet Arrosa, save me. Of all things."

"I won't tell anyone. But you should be careful. You'll give yourself away."

"Thane Stearc knows," she said. "And Abbot Luviar and Brother Gildas."

"Ah . . . and the secretary . . . Gram . . . that's who else was back there in the gardens, right? *He* knows." Brutes would care no more for the commands of sickly secretaries than for the commands of pretty youths. And I'd smelled wintergreen, a medicament used for all sorts of ailments.

"He knows," she said. Her voice was well controlled, but she really shouldn't be holding on to people's arms if she wanted to keep secrets. I'd felt far less anger from the brutes pinning my wrists than from her slender fingers touching my sleeve.

"And disapproves, I'd guess," I said.

"I cannot come to the abbey as a maiden. Saint Ophir's Rule permits only vowed celibate women or matrons in company with their husbands to stay in their guesthouse. The abbot dares not except me, lest he be called to account. So I take on this loathsome disguise. If the thane grunts and growls a bit for allowing me to play his squire, so be it. I *won't* be left out. And if Stearc and the abbot agree, the opinions of others do not matter."

I dearly wanted to ask, *Why does his opinion make you so angry, if it does not matter?* And, *Is his grunting and growling the only price the thane exacts from you?* But she was cocked like a crossbow again. Best avoid such personal matters until I knew her better.

"As you can imagine, I am afire with curiosity about what I'm doing in the middle of the night with devious monks and mysterious maidens and people who insist I cannot look upon the lands of my home abbey. But Father Abbot bade me trust him, thus I've little hope of soothing *that* curiosity. So, another question . . ."

Abbot Luviar had declared himself neutral in the royal war. I doubted that, preferring to believe in his "deviant" support of a Pretender. Yet even if the child Pretender was wholly myth and Abbot Luviar but a skillful liar manipulating me in service of one of the three princes, I could not believe his chosen lord to be Osriel the Bastard. More and more I needed to understand what I had seen and felt in that unnatural assault on Gillarine.

"As you serve the Thane of Erasku, perhaps you could tell me something of Prince Osriel and his powers."

She gasped as if I'd planted my fist in her gut. "Holy gods! How——? Why would you speak of him . . . the vile beast . . . the damned soul? Here in the night . . . when we are unprotected."

She dragged me faster. Before I could ask what *protection* we might need, the path kicked steeply upward, as if a mountain had been roaming the fields and decided to plop itself at our feet like a friendly hound. A gust of wind swirled around us, billowing my damp cowl and flapping the hood in my face. Soon rocks gouged my feet. Roots. Evergreens. Moss. Where the devil were we? I could not imagine we'd come so far as the eastern ridge.

I stumbled, flailing in the dark.

"Careful . . ." She caught me before I fell and steadied me. Then she proceeded a bit slower. "I'm sorry. I wasn't thinking. It's just that Lord Stearc is his own man. My lord bows to no master who sets himself up to rival Magrog in his cruelties."

"I didn't mean to give offense. One of the brothers told me that Lord

Stearc holds no allegiance to the Bastard Prince. I just assumed, since Erasku is an Evanori hold, you would know the truth of the cursed land and its sovereign. When he slaughtered the Moriangi at Gillarine, I saw such sights . . . faces in the night . . ."

"Even the land cannot compel loyalty to a monster like Osriel of Evanore." She spat as if the very taste of his name poisoned her. "Everything you hear of him is true. He twists magic into depravity, taints all that is good in the world. I'll not speak of him lest my tongue blacken and rot."

We talked no more for a while. She was bound up in anger and fear and purpose. I was trying not to trip and crack my head on the shin-high rocks that seemed to have sprouted from the hillside like hedge beans.

As the path leveled out, and the air spoke of damp pine, a smoky fire, and horses nearby, my guide halted. She released my arm and reached around my neck, tugging my head downward. "Let me get this off of you. We're almost there."

As she untied the cloth binding my eyes, I inhaled deeply, her hair tickling my nose. No, nothing at all like Jullian. "Thank you," I said most sincerely.

"For what? Allowing our thick-skulled bodyguards to suffocate you? Giving you a laugh at my inept playacting?"

"I had a pleasant walk in the nighttime and an interesting conversation. My head remains intact. And I smelled someone who was not Jullian."

The cloth fell away. I blinked. Her hair shone bronze in the starlight. Her pale lips curved upward. And the eyes that gazed up at me . . . great gods . . . so deep . . . reflections of heaven . . .

"Come, Brother Valen." A slight emphasis on the *Brother*.

The blood rushed from my tonsured head, and no logical thinking prevented it going where it had no place. Blessed goddess of love, what had I done to abjure such a gift, even for a season? I touched her cheek . . . cool, silken . . . and felt the heat rush to meet my finger. "Ah, mistress, you are . . ."

Her breath caught and held one moment, suspending my thought. I bent my head toward hers . . .

A distant bell chimed the half hour. She shuddered and jerked her head away. "Time runs, Brother. You must be back in the church by Matins." Her voice was hoarse. She pulled up her hood and strode away. How had I ever thought her male?

The path led between a stony bank and a forested gully, curving sharply upward. Slightly dizzy, aching with a need far deeper than lust—which great vice had most certainly tainted my soul as well—I watched her move as we walked. Had she led me into a blazing forest or a raging torrent, I would have followed.

Chapter 15

The Thane of Erasku awaited us with the impenetrable solemnity of a standing stone, the smoke of the small campfire curling about his solidity like the telltales of midsummer sacrifice. His thick arms enfolded the solid, leathery bulk of my grandfather's book. Behind him, away from the fire, a gaunt, dark-haired man tethered a horse beside two others— Gram, the lord's sickly secretary. No guards, tents, pots, or baggage were in evidence. No Brother Gildas in evidence, either, which surprised me. Likely he was yet suffering the effects of the Harrower lashes. The bruising always got worse before it got better.

"I thought you would never come." The lord was fair bursting with impatience.

"We were delayed at the abbey, sire," said the woman. "My apologies." She bowed to the thane, and then moved around the fire to join him without acknowledging the secretary.

I remained on the near side of the fire.

"I am Stearc of Erasku, Brother," said the thane. "I presume you know that. You've not endured too taxing a walk? My lad guided you properly?"

I bowed. "Indeed he kept me on the straight-and-narrow path, sir. And I managed not to plague him to distraction with my questions, though they are legion. I was too busy trying to determine where on Iero's good earth we were."

"And were you successful?" No excessive pleasantries here. The intensity that had shivered me to my boots at my first glimpse of him had not diminished. He was every quat a warlord; it was more difficult to imagine him a scholar.

"I am turned hind end first, my lord. In a thorough muddle."

"You *look* a thorough mess. Mud, scrapes. Corin, is the monk's courtesy hiding some mistake of yours? If such simple squire's duties are beyond you, I'll put you back to mucking stalls."

Woe to the man-at-arms who mistook *this* commander's orders. Why would such a man ever permit a *woman*—? Ah! A flash of inspiration struck me. A step to the side, where fire and smoke could not obscure my vision, confirmed that the lord's long braid took on a certain hint of bronze in the firelight. And the arch of their noses was identical. *Sire*, indeed.

The woman lifted her chin as if weathering a familiar gale. "I was unable—"

"My Lord Stearc, we suffered an unpleasant mishap tonight," said Gram, as he joined the other two in the firelight. No mistaking his firm, rich tone. Hard to imagine my decisive savior from the hedge garden to be the frail secretary I had glimpsed being helped onto his horse at the guesthouse. "The two guards who accompanied Corin to fetch Brother Valen set upon him as if to make him a prisoner. Something in their orders charged them wrongly. I've restricted them to camp tonight in your name and will investigate thoroughly tomorrow. Surely this good brother's generous and forgiving nature has brought him here after so rude a meeting."

I pressed a knuckle to my mouth to muffle a snicker. Generosity and forgiveness would never have brought me so far. But curiosity . . . Every moment with this odd troop—all of them angles and edges and raw passion—left me more enamored of their puzzle.

"Is Gram's assessment accurate, Brother?" *Lie at your peril*, Stearc's tone warned.

"It is more Abbot Luviar's influence that induced me to come, my lord," I said. "He intimated that your interests were of great importance to Navronne, which, of course, makes them of great importance to any loyal subject. And these two gentlemen were most sincere in their apologies."

He nodded. Not happy, but immediate fury tamed.

The secretary had a convincing way about him with lords, brutes, and novices alike. As if to cinch my good opinion, Gram offered me a skin of ale he'd brought from his saddlebags.

"Your abbot explained what we need from you?" The thane wasted no time.

I was still relishing the robust ale, wondering if Gram would notice if I drained the skin completely. Reluctantly, I replaced its plug, yielded it to the secretary with a grateful nod, and returned my attention to the lord. "Only that you wished me to demonstrate what I knew of using the Cartamandua maps, which, as I warned Father Abbot, is little enough. And that I am to keep silent about this company and its interests."

"Good. We need not waste time with discussion. Sit here." Stearc pointed to a fat log rolled near the fire and shoved the book into my arms. "Open to the marked page."

I'd not expected to be treated as a schoolboy. Hackles bristling, I sat on the log and opened the book to a place marked with a scrap of leather. The map filled the broad right leaf of the open book. Its features had been meticulously drawn in red-brown ink and delicately washed with green and rose. The emerald-green-and-black border had an exotic pattern to it.

From the time I'd left the cradle, I had been taught the rudiments of maps: the concepts of distance and proportion, the common symbols, the uses of compass rose, cartouche, and key. I had trailed about Palinur in my father's wake, marking straggling lines on tablets of wax, and pens and brushes had been stuffed in my hands as soon as I could hold them. The shapes and colors of maps had pleased my eye, and I liked to imagine that I could envision the grass and rock, cities and rivers they represented. But never was I taken on a journey of discovery beyond Palinur's walls as my brother and sisters were, because I could not master the most mundane of a cartographer's skills. I could neither write the names and distances, nor read nor write a traveler's notes. Maps spoke with shape and color and symbols, but the key to their wonder was written words. Of which I had none.

"What is it you wish to know, my lord?" I asked, suppressing long-festered bitterness. "I never used this particular map when I served Mardane Lavorile."

The thane stood over me like some oak tree out of Ardra's ancient forests, craggy and thick and overpowering. "If you have used other maps from the book, then you should be able to use this one. We have brought you to a place that appears on this map. *Here*." He placed a thick finger on an angular mark near the center of the map—a hill. "We wish to discover if you can find your way *here*." His finger skipped to another spot on the far right-hand side of the page.

I gaped up at him. "Now? At night?"

He lifted his finger to reveal the symbol—a tiny waterfall—my grandfather's common designation for a waterfall, pool, small lake, or any other watery landmark. The name lettered beside the feature would clarify which one it was.

"If you can invoke the guide spell properly, you should have no difficulty, day or night. The distance is not far. Your abbot promised you would make the attempt. So do it, or end this before we waste more time." He crossed his great arms and did not blink, his disdain as odorous as a pigsty.

Could I do what he wanted? Without knowing its bounds and scale, I could not judge distance from this map. Nor could I invoke a spell I could not read nor even discover what kind of water I was looking for without deciphering its name. But I had wits and other skills, and the lord's game posed a challenge interesting enough to overcome my distaste for the family business. For, certainly, this whole evening was a game. These fine conspirators had brought me here blindfolded, assuming I could not judge distance or direction from the abbey, believing that the moonless night would obscure paths and landmarks. I'd wager they had staged the attack, just to throw me out of sense before we began. They expected me to fail.

I touched the skin of my throat, abraded by their drawstring bag. They believed me a thick-skulled vagabond man-at-arms who had fooled a lord by pretending to use his magic book. Perhaps, with a touch of pureblood instinct and magic, I could do exactly that.

Leaning closer to the blazing firelight, I examined the map—a simple fiché—more closely. Somewhere in its tangled mysteries of words, numbers, and symbols, a fiché would reveal place names and distances, compass headings, landmarks, and obstacles to travel. This particular map detailed a countryside of forested hills, a river and its side streams, one town and three villages, a few cart roads and common walking paths. A solicale designated some Karish landmark. Other symbols I was less sure of. Each mark had a neatly lettered name that could place it in this valley or far Estigure for all I knew. Dangling from the solicale was the impish aingerou my grandfather sketched into every map.

So start with the solicale. It must certainly represent the abbey. We had walked briskly for perhaps an hour to get to this starting point. That gave me an idea of distance and proportion. And we had walked northeastward, in the main, more east than north; I closed my eyes and remembered the wind teasing my right cheek and the shaven patch on my head, a frost wind from the south. Only when we started climbing had we changed heading back and forth a number of times, but no matter, for I had but to follow the path back down to the base of the hill. The night was clear, so I could use Escalor, the guide star, to get my bearing. If the direction from the abbey to this hill was northeast, then the watery spot they wished me to find would be southeast, half again the distance we had come—leaving a conveniently short return to the abbey for a novice who must be prostrate on the church floor by Matins.

"So, can you do it?" Stearc had his hands on his hips.

"I believe I can, my lord. I suppose you would not consider telling me what I'm looking for or why this is so important?"

"You've no need to know more." For certain *this* man had not approved me for the task. Well, let him watch.

Making a great show, I placed my finger on the mark for this hill, drew it downward toward the abbey, and then across the page till I touched a walking path of the sort oxherds used to lead their beast carts to market or villeins might tread to field or woodland. Following the lines of path and road as far as they would take me, southerly through the fields and easterly into the hills of the valley wall, my finger traced a reasonably direct route to the water symbol. I noted the orange flame mark of Deunor along the way—likely a roadside shrine to the Lightbringer. Three short lines marked a dolmen, and near it lay two small arcs that told of burial mounds. That should give me enough. I closed the book.

"Will you not speak the invocation, Brother?" Stearc's skepticism rang clearly.

"When I used the book before, I always read the spell words silently, my lord. I thought to follow the same practice here . . ." I paused, all innocence, as if expecting him to contradict me.

He did not, which confirmed another suspicion. He'd had the book from the abbot—which explained its absence from the library—and he had tried to use it himself without success. Why else would he waste this time on an unlikely prospect such as me?

"We should be off then," I said, placing the book into his hands and suppressing a grin as I stood, "unless you wish me to go alone and find my way back here to report."

"No need for you to return. We'll know if you succeed." His great jaw snapped shut. I was dismissed.

I bowed. "My lord. Gentlemen."

As I walked down the path the woman and I had ascended, the three of them stood beside their fire, watching me. I assumed they would follow or

ride out to catch me near the end. Or perhaps the thane had his own pureblood or a mage to observe me from a distance or who had set some magical
beacon to announce my success. As to what waited at the end, a place no
ordinary map could take them, my curiosity outweighed my caution. The
abbot did not want me dead.

At the bottom of the hill I sought southeast, keeping the guide star on
my left, and holding a balance between winter sunrise and the mountains
of Evanore to the south. I knelt as if to relace my sandal. Touching fingertips to the earth, I spilled but a fragment of magic into the simple seeking,
hunting a route to a sheep path and a roadside shrine dedicated to Deunor
Lightbringer. A spare image resolved in my head, a simple pattern laid upon
the landscape.

Once sure of my course, I set out across the open country. Even if someone was watching me, I doubted they could hear, so I sang the fifty verses of
"The Doxy and the Bandit" as I walked, imagining clasping Corin's slender
waist as I spun her dizzy. Earth's mother, what was her true name? Why
hadn't I asked?

Deunor's shrine was little more than a chipped and gouged body, missing one arm, its head, and privy parts. The stones of the altar had been carted
away, and the astelas vines that twined every shrine of the elder gods had
been dug up. Country folk thought boiled astelas roots made a man virile.
I'd no need for that unless this pestilential drought went on too long and my
body forgot its dearest pleasures. Near three months had gone since I'd lain
with a woman, and here the night air felt like velvet on my skin. Another
brief seeking at the split of a path and I angled northerly again toward the
dolmen and burial mounds.

The table stones and barrows were only dark outlines against the stars to
the north. And just beyond them, the track branched three ways instead of
the two marked on the map—assuming I had come to the right place so far.
Instinct sent me down the southernmost, the oldest branch, judging by the
myriad layers of feet that had trod there. As the map had suggested, the path
petered out in the slopes of patchy grass and rock at the base of the craggy
ridge east of the valley.

Now came the most difficult part—to find the water source in these
trackless hills. A hint as to its nature would have been useful. With no more
paths made magic by centuries of feet, and no sure destination, this seeking
would require more power.

I scanned the horizon in a full circle. As far as starlight and good eyesight could tell me, no one watched. Kneeling on the rough ground, I closed my eyes and laid my palms on the earth. The wind blustered over and around me, scouring away the barriers of distraction and wariness, allowing my magic to flow freely. *Where is it?*

Images of pools and wells and bubbling springs passed through my mind, but none held for that one moment that proved it true. *A little more . . .*

I laid my forehead on the earth and released another fragment of power, expecting the pattern to resolve as it had earlier. My instincts would tell me the way. But before I knew it, I had pushed up my sleeves, hiked up my gown, and lay prostrate as I had been in the church a few hours earlier, bared arms spread. Instead of masonry and gilding, the dome of stars rose above my head, and beneath me lay the cool damp earth.

As I inhaled the scent of dirt and rotting grass, the boundaries of stars and flesh and earth dissolved. Worms burrowed beneath me, and ground beetles ticked their wings in their holes. A hare breathed anxiously in its den. Clouds drifted across the patterned stars above me, tickling the wool layers on my back. Far below, water trickled . . . deep . . .

Strip off these prisoning garments . . . touch skin to earth and air . . . feel the night's embrace . . . reach through the welcoming earth to find the water . . . Against the urgency of these demands—spoken in the language of mind and flesh and bone—only some remnant thread of present sense kept me clothed. But the rest . . .

Reach . . . feel . . . embrace. Open your mouth . . . taste stone and stars . . . inhale the night . . . listen . . . I plunged my hand deep . . . felt the gritty loam give way . . . dry sand and pebbles graze my knuckles . . . until I touched the sweeter moisture . . . the secret places . . . the pulsing flow of life that told of moving water, deeper yet.

A bell pealed in the distance—a sonorous touch of bronze borne on the breeze. I jerked my head off the ground and rose up on my elbows. What had happened here? My heart raced like a fox at the hunt. I shook my head. Sat back on my heels and examined one bare arm to assure myself that it was not covered with dirt or crawling with beetles and worms from plunging it through the earth. Felt a rush of heat across my skin as I realized I was more than halfway roused in altogether unlikely ways, as had happened on the journey back from Elanus. Fires of heaven . . . chastity was making a madman of me.

I forced my thoughts back to business. The bell signaled another hour gone. How many since day's end? I needed to head northeasterly again, for the water that trickled under this spot fed the abbey spring and its source lay in the ridge ahead of me. Though no overlaid image dwelt in the forefront of my mind, my body understood perfectly which way to go now, in the same way my blood knew which direction to flow in my veins. I scrambled to my feet, hurried across the barren field, and pretended I was not shaking.

The upward path was far too steep for this late of an evening. After so many days of idleness in the abbey, my body protested at the climb. My route had taken me up a treeless jumble of granite that scarred the eastern wall of the valley, a desolate crotch in the otherwise verdant ridge. No direct path. No easy ascent. I scrambled between boulders and across tilted slabs, cursing gowns and cowls and sandals. My sore feet kept skidding out from under me. Every slip meant whacked knees or elbows, abrading the skin through the woolen layers of hose and gown.

A glance over my shoulder for the tenth time in an hour and I yet spied no one following. I climbed.

At least another hour had passed, which meant perhaps one more remained until the brothers filed back into the church for Matins. I could just imagine Prior Nemesio's glee at discovering a novice so ill-behaved as to abandon a penance. Poor Brother Sebastian; my mentor would be beside himself. And even if I broke my word and told them of the evening's events, I would never be able to explain why I had taken on such a fools' errand when the simple truth could have stopped it. The puzzle was just such an intriguing exercise, and Lord Stearc had been so sure I couldn't solve it.

At the top of yet another slab, the rocks formed a wide shelf, backed up to a higher cliff. Behind me the valley of Gillarine, shaped by the sinuous hints of silver that were the looping river, stretched southward toward the mountains of Evanore and northward toward the heart of Ardra, Morian, and the distant sea. The abbey church spires rose out of the gently folded land to the southwest.

I was nearing the end of this journey. Instinct said to go south along the shelf rock and then straight east . . . which would mean directly into the cliff. I moved slowly, examining the rugged wall as I went, searching for cracks or splits or caves.

A short distance away an oddly shaped shadow detached itself from the wall. "Iero's grace, Brother Valen, how was your evening's walk? Not too troubling, I hope, despite its unsettling beginning?"

Fear burgeoned and stilled quickly. No matter that the only light was the dome of stars. I could mistake neither the pale gleam of hairless scalp nor the dark brow line nor the cool presence, spiced and warmed by good humor.

"Brother Gildas, the spider who sits in the web of all Gillarine's mysteries. Of course, you would be here." Would I ever learn to think? Of course, they'd have someone waiting at the end. They were testing me.

"I knew you would enjoy this puzzle," he said cheerfully, "being a man of puzzles as you are."

"You're all right . . . healing?" Only days had passed since his encounter with Sila Diaglou's whip.

"Thanks to you, I live. My scabs and bruises do but remind me—deservedly so—of my shame at falling victim so easily. So, can you finish this?"

I stepped toward him deliberately, continuing my examination of the wall. "Here." A darker line creased the shadowed cliff halfway between us, a seam in the rock wider than first glance showed, a high-walled passage that sliced directly into the cliff.

I led, forcing myself to keep breathing until both the slotlike passage and my search ended. The cliff walls opened into a small grotto—a well of starlight, the circle of sky above it reflected perfectly in a glass-still pool, incised in stone.

As I paused in the doorway where the walls of the notch flared into the encircling stone, a movement atop the cliffs snared my gaze. Something bright. Something blue. But staring until my eyes felt raw revealed naught but stars. Perhaps one had slipped from its place and streaked toward the earth. A warning of evil times, diviners said.

Brother Gildas had joined me and stood at my shoulder. "Powers of night, you've done it," he said softly. Wondering. "Ah, Valen, there is more to you than people think."

He stepped past me and spun in place, scanning walls and cliff tops before walking to the rim of the pool. Even as he knelt and reached out to touch the water, I wanted him to stop. No sensible argument came to my lips, only that this was no common pool to be used in common ways. Something slept here. Power? Spirit? The generous earth itself? "Brother, wait—"

Too late. The rippling rings moved outward, marring its perfection. Gildas downed the water from his cupped hands and looked up at me, smiling. "Come, have a drink. You've earned it."

Foolish. Nothing had happened. Clearly *he* sensed nothing out of the ordinary.

"I don't drink water," I said, trying to keep my voice even. He'd think me mad if I told what I felt here. "Don't trust it. And unless you can dispense me from my penance, I must get back to the church."

In fact, I could not have stepped within that grot were he fallen in the pool and drowning. Smell, taste, hearing, sight . . . my senses, of a sudden, quivered on the brink of explosion. My heart swelled with songs just beyond hearing, with words beyond knowing, with the desolation of a homely street where every door is locked to you or of winter sunset in the wild, when no hearth, no word, no welcome awaits. One step past the doorway and surely I would be flat on the granite, my skull cracked, my heart riven, as if I'd walked into the cloister garth fifty times over. Yet the sorrow that permeated these stones surpassed what a murdered youth of sixteen years could possibly know. This sleeper was not Brother Horach.

Gildas sighed and wiped his hand on his cowl. "I suppose you're right. We've a distance to go yet before we can each put our secrets to rest. But you ought to come see the water. It's so deep. So lovely. So pure."

I dragged my gaze from the pool, shivering as if I'd plunged my whole body into its frigid depths. Oh, yes, I knew that water was cold. I did not have to see the frost crystals that rimed the pool's edge to know. So little sunlight here. The encircling walls so like a prison cell.

"Are you well, Valen?"

Pressing my back and the back of my head against the wall of the passage, I closed my eyes. As if all at once, the activity of the night took its toll: scrapes and bruises, blistered feet, overstretched shoulders. The few quellae back to Gillarine might have been the road to heaven that practors and hierarchs told us was nigh impossible. And something else . . . deep inside my gut . . . a knot of fire. Blessed Deunor, no! With all that had happened . . . this new life . . . I'd scarce given it a thought. A night bird's screech near ripped my ears. "Must get back," I said. "The time . . ."

I fled, scrabbling back down the ridge, bumping, sliding, scraping on the rocks. More was wrong than mystic pools and overzealous bodyguards and wild chases through the night. The scalding in my gut did not cool. How long had it been? Five days since my investiture. Twelve . . . thirteen before that to Black Night, and one more . . . holy gods, nineteen days . . . and the last interval had been twenty-one.

The trek back to the abbey devolved into nightmare, my need quickly overshadowing the mysteries of the night. The garden maze, the green pouch tucked away under the rocks, the fragrant contents . . . *Great Iero, let no one have found it. Let the Matins bell not ring until I am whole again.* I had no idea how I was to manage it, but my growing frenzy to have the blood-spelled nivat in my hand . . . on my tongue . . . in my veins . . . permitted no logic or forethought.

Though as fit as any of the younger monks, Gildas could scarce keep up with me. "What's wrong, Brother? One would think the Adversary dogged your back. Would we all had such long legs as yours to devour a quellé so swiftly."

"I've been too long distracted from my prayers," I said. "And I'd rather not have occasion to visit the prior's prison cell. Though Father Abbot sent me on this mad venture, I've seen enough to know he'll not shield me from punishment."

I could not speak after that. My cramping legs and back threatened to seize if I slowed. By the time we reached the footbridge and the abbey wall, the threads of fire encompassed every part and portion of my body. The starlight scalded my eyes. I drew my cloak across my face, for the wind felt like a flayer's knife.

Brother Gildas unlatched the iron herdsman's gate, but laid a hand on my arm before I could rush through. It was all I could do not to cry out, for his touch felt like a gatzé's fiery kiss even through the woolen layers. "He'll not punish you, Valen. Tonight's exercise was of great importance—Iero's work. You performed better than any of us could hope. You *will* reap answers to the questions that tease you."

Sadly, his concerned kindness could not soothe me. "I must . . . clean myself . . . before going to the church. Excuse me, Brother." The mere effort of speaking caused spasms in my face and neck. I pulled away and ran across the field, past the church, and into the garden.

Where . . . where . . . ? Beside the statue of Karus as the Shepherd . . . Divine Karus . . . good Iero . . . Kemen, Lord of Sky and Storm, help me. I dropped to my knees and scrabbled in the pile of rocks beside the statue's base, frantic when I found only dirt. I had used my bent to create a void hole to hide my contraband packet here on the night I'd come from Elanus. Had I forgotten so much of magic that I had displaced or vanished them by mistake? I dug deeper until my fingers felt the cloth roll. Using my shoulder to wipe the sweat from my eyes, I rummaged inside the packet and grasped the little bag. I almost wept in thanksgiving.

I shoved dirt and rocks into some semblance of their usual aspect, tucked the green bag into my trews, and raced through the gardens past the lay brothers' reach. Though desperate, I dared not cross the cloister garth, but rather sped down the west cloister and around the south in front of the kitchen and refectory, cursing the waning hour. At every moment I expected to hear the bells.

The trough ran around three sides of the lavatorium, angled slightly so the water would flow left to right. Each of the six shallow bays on each wall formed a semicircular shelf behind the trough, and from the center of each bay protruded a lead conduit that spilled water into the trough. I chose the bay nearest the cloister to take advantage of what little light the night provided. I removed my cowl and laid it on the shelf, as if preparing to clean it. Then I fumbled the green pouch out from under my gown and spilled half my remaining nivat onto the wide outer lip of the trough.

Everything took too long. The seeds were old and tough; I chipped another shard from my precious mirror fragment, using it to crush them on the stone. My fingers were cold and clumsy. I dropped the needle and had to scrabble on the stone floor to find it. It was near impossible to grasp the linen thread, and when at last the mixture of blood and nivat sizzled, I had to fumble with the glass to find an angle where I could see the vapors.

As soon as I released magic into the brew, I knew I hadn't enough. Holy gods, what a fool I'd been. To spend my magic so recklessly on Luviar's game. To lose count of the days. Bent over the trough to hold the mirror and the thread steady, my back, leg, and shoulders cramping until I was near weeping, I squeezed the last magic from my body and let it flow down the linen thread. And still the vapors would not cease their rising and signal the doulon ready.

As if taking voice from my fears, the bell pealed. I held my breath with the first tone, yet my weariness told the lateness of the hour. The next strike came and the next, until the ten measured strikes that signaled the call to services had been completed. The noise threatened to burst my ears, as if I stood in the bell chamber itself. Then rang the triple change, double, and triple that announced the beginning of a new day. The yawning monks would be

donning gowns and cowls and sandals and starting their procession through
the passage to the nightstair. And still the pungent vapors rose from the boiling nivat. The finished paste should hold no scent.

In the dorter passage above my head, the monks began to sing, tugging
at my spirit with their music. Their music. Not mine.

I could wait no longer. I scooped the red-black droplets onto my tongue.
As I braced my hands on the trough, my head dropped to hang between my
shoulders. The first shuddering pain rolled through me . . .

Not enough. Not enough. Sobbing, I slammed my elbow into the stone
trough, hoping more pain might jolt the spell into completion. Nothing.
Again. Again . . .

As in famine times, when the crust of bread or sip of ale blunts the most
acute hunger, but leaves the want and sickness, such was the incomplete
doulon. The fire cooled; the cramps eased; the storm of my senses quieted.
But I gained no release. No rapture. Every muscle and sinew ached. My veins
felt clogged with clay. Only a few days—a fortnight at most—and I would
have to do this all again, spend my reserve of nivat because I'd been shamed
at my ignorance and determined to prove that I, the most useless of men,
could accomplish what some proud lord could not. Now I would pay.

Exhausted and sick, I splashed the cold water onto my face and head,
scrubbed at my hands and arms. *Hurry!* I packed away the needle, the mirror, and linen thread and tied the bag's drawstring to the waist string of my
trews. Then I threw on my cowl and ran for the church, brushing at the
caked mud and dirt as I ran. As the procession descended the nightstair and
entered the church, filling the vaults with songs of the Creator's glory, I flew
down the aisle and through the choir screen, and threw myself prostrate on
the cold marble. Brother Victor had not moved.

Chapter 16

A storm rolled through the valley sometime between Lauds and Prime, bringing sleet and bitter cold—a miserable morning, highly appropriate for a day that had begun so wretchedly and got only worse. A few hours' sleep had healed my bruises and blisters and soothed my torn and battered elbow, but done nothing for the doulon sickness. Plagued by both the indolence the spell always caused and the blood fever it had only dulled, I fell asleep in choir during both morning Hours.

Brother Sebastian pulled me aside after Prime to scold me for inattention, expressing shock at my bedraggled clothes. He dragged me to the lavatorium to clean them as best I could, and then sentenced me to kneel in the center aisle of the dorter clad only in shirt and trews. I was to pray and contemplate Iero's gift of clothing while the rest of the brothers ate their bread and cheese and attended morning services. By the time he permitted me to don my damp gown and cowl for chapter, my blood felt like slush.

Matters worsened. Once my mentor had chastised me in front of the entire brotherhood, Prior Nemesio offered his own scathing reprimand and decided that my punishment should continue until the day's end bell. No church services. No meals. No work or study. No gown or cowl. That this also meant no testing on the great virtues and no Compline reading was scarcely a comfort.

A somber Abbot Luviar approved the sentence. Brother Gildas raised his brows and shrugged ever so slightly. Jullian, sitting on his low stool by the door, would not look at me. I longed to strangle them all, though, in truth, anger was as difficult to muster as anything else.

The hours in the dorter passed in frigid misery. I tried to think, to make some sense of my experiences of the previous day, to sing under my breath, to plan where I would go when spring released me from this tomb. Sleep was impossible, but neither would my blood run anywhere useful like my head or my knees. So much for trust. Perhaps Luviar wanted me dead of frostbite so I could not betray his friends.

How stupid could a man get when his balls ruled his head? Why hadn't I just grabbed the book when it was in my hands and set out for Elanus? But instead I'd had to strut my manhood like a gamecock.

I shifted my knees, wincing with the ache. *Damnable baldpates.* Boreas had been right about them. *Boreas . . . by the dark spirits . . .*

Once the gruesome image of his end took hold of my head, I could not shake it. What kind of woman could do such work? What kind of perverse soul could name it holy? As the memory churned inside my head alongside the night's mad adventure and the bizarre sensations I had experienced at the pool, I could not but recall Brother Horach's equally savage murder. Could a Harrower have decided that innocents should die as well as sinners and sneaked into the abbey to work their deviltry? With orange-heads roaming the neighborhood, it could happen again.

Brother Sebastian visited me at least once an hour to counsel and preach. On the next occasion, I interrupted a sermon on rooting out the vice of carelessness and tried to explain about Boreas and Harrower rites and Brother Horach. I had scarce begun when he stopped me, insisting I must refrain from worldly thoughts for the duration of my penance. As he left me alone again, I damned him and the rest of his fraternity to their fate.

By the time the bells rang Vespers, wind raked and rattled the dorter shutters and raced through the long room. Three more hours. I feared I would be unable to move when day's end came, either from hunger or freezing. On his last visit Brother Sebastian had left a rushlight to hold off the dark. With aching knees and back, and incipient chilblains, I had no gratitude in me.

A quiet rustling at my back did not even prompt me to turn around. Probably Brother Sebastian again to tell me how sorry he was that I needed this kind of lesson. But to my surprise a mug appeared in front of my face, wreathed in steam and cupped in the small dry hand of Brother Victor. "Quickly, Brother Valen, you are wanted elsewhere for a little while."

I would like to have said that, although hell would be a pleasant change, I would prefer to freeze than dance to his abbot's command, but my lips were so numb I was saved from such an indiscretion. My trembling hands wrapped around the deliciously warm cup, and I drained the thing without taking a breath. "I don't think I can do anything quickly, Brother Chancellor."

He offered me the pile of black wool he carried over one arm. "I would suggest you try. We've only until the end of Vespers."

The still-damp wool felt marvelous. And blessed hose to cover my legs. My numb fingers fumbled with ties and laces. Soon I was following Brother Victor down the passage, shaking out my legs to get the blood flowing.

Our sandals echoed in the deserted library. I could not imagine why we'd come. "Wait here," said Brother Victor, and he disappeared into the corner beyond the last book press. The wind drove sleet against the window mullions. Ardran autumn usually waxed dry and golden. Landlords and villeins alike would be frantic to gather in what crops had ripened in this perverse season. Perhaps the bowl of the sky had slipped farther out of place.

A brief explosion of yellow light, brighter than ten lamps together, assaulted my eyes. A hiss and a snap, and the chancellor stepped into view again, little more than a shadow in my flash blindness. He beckoned me to join him. In the corner where I had ever seen blank walls—the same corner where Abbot Luviar had appeared so suddenly on my first visit—a doorway now opened onto a descending stair. From a hook on the wall, just inside it, the chancellor took a burning lamp. Or rather the implement he held appeared to be a lamp, and it appeared to be burning, though only cream-colored light, no flame, shone through its clear panes. *Blessed saints and angels* . . . Sorcery. In a house where magic working was forbidden. My feet dragged.

"Come on," said the chancellor as I hesitated, beset by visions of dungeons and flaming depths.

"This isn't where the hierarch sent you? To be punished?"

He puzzled for a moment. "Oh. The prison cell? Certainly not. Why would I take you there?"

"To improve my character?" I mumbled.

He didn't smile.

We descended two long flights of steps, which by my reckoning left us deep in the earth under the scriptorium. My throat tightened. I reminded myself of Brother Victor's *only until the end of Vespers* to convince myself that I could breathe in such a confined space. So deep.

Brother Victor halted when we reached a wide door at the bottom of the steps. Intelligent, inscrutable, he peered up at my face. "Father Abbot says he trusts you. That must certainly be true, as he commanded me to show you this without informing others of our party who have less confidence in your usefulness and character. I take no sides in that dispute as I've so little personal experience of you. I obey my abbot. But I'll warn you that no one will find the doorway or this stair were you to tell of them."

"I understand." Perhaps the opening was hidden by an illusion spell, but I'd wager that an ax applied to the library wall would find the stair.

He pushed open the door and held it to let me enter.

"Blessed saints and angels!" My feet propelled me to the center of a chamber half the size of the church. There I spun like the axis of a wheel, my neck craned so I could view the dome of light above my head. Great ribbed arches of gray stone supported curved wedges of colored mosaic—brilliant, though, as if the bits were glass. Yet I had never seen glass laid in such a shape. And though I stood deep below the earth, the mosaic of light shone as bright as if the sun lay tucked between the dome and the scriptorium floor above it, casting a gentle clarity on the marvels that lay below. For the dome was but the magical capstone on more earthly wonders.

Books, first. The walls of the rectangular chamber, three or four times my height, were lined with shelves, not full, but holding more books and scrolls than I would have believed existed in all the world. Yet this library held much more than books. Ranks of tall cabinets lined the floor with only narrow aisles between. These cabinets, faced with grillwork doors very like the cupboards in the library, held tools—here the needles, spools, thimble, and scissors of a seamstress, there the common hammers, chisels, augers, and gouges of a stonemason. An entire cabinet was filled with a carpenter's tools, another with a physician's instruments. None of the individual items seemed extraordinary. Most appeared well used, though clean or oiled and generally well cared for.

I moved faster through the array, fascinated more by the breadth of the collection than the items themselves. Two doorways opened off the great chamber, one a mere closet, lit by the spilled light of the glass dome. A rope bed, piled with a rolled palliasse and folded blankets, and an old writing desk had been shoved up against stacked barrels and crates.

But the other, much wider doorway opened into a second domed chamber as large and beautiful as the first. By this time I was scarcely surprised to see a plow, a wheel and axle from a cart, millstones, a lathe, a loom, a potter's wheel, and other, larger artifacts standing in neat rows on the floor. On the shelves that lined the walls from floor to ceiling, sat row after row of labeled sacks, earthenware pots, and glass jars. What would they hold? Food? Herbs? Potions?

No . . . the tools were for building and making and creating. The books would be for knowledge and understanding. For remembering. For beginning. The pots would hold seeds.

I turned back. From across the chamber by the outer door, Brother Victor watched with sober interest, his hands loosely folded at his waist.

Some of the pieces came together then. Luviar's grand mosaic of war and famine and storm. The books on glassmaking, and drawings of millworks, and records of vineyards that no longer produced grapes. Were cuttings of grapevines preserved in these bags or jars? Surely those who could create domes of light and a door that opened with magic so powerful it stood my hair on end could preserve a living vine. *Teneamus*—we preserve. For the dark times. For the long night.

I gazed up at the shining dome, majestic in its beauty and magic. A promise of hope. "You call this the lighthouse," I said.

The chancellor dipped his head in acknowledgment.

What was happening to the world? How did they know? What was the connection with my book of maps? I could not even choose where to begin.

"Come. Vespers will be ending soon."

"But I've so much to ask."

"In time, Brother Novice. Should you prove faithful, you'll be told all. For now, I pray you be worthy of Father Abbot's trust."

"Of course. Certainly. I won't say anything. Not to a soul." Who would believe me?

Before I knew it, I was kneeling in the dorter again, shivering in shirt and trews. Save for the taste of leek broth in my mouth and the vision of light in my head, I might have thought the grand library a dream brought on by hunger and cold and a broken doulon. Nothing in my experience or imagination could have conjured such a place.

I dismissed my pique at the monks' annoying discipline and spent the next two hours formulating questions to ask were I given the opportunity. I speculated on how the magic of the lighthouse was done and who in this place might have done it—the mysterious pureblood monk?—and I considered what I would have chosen to preserve were I stocking a magical lighthouse to sustain me beyond the end of the world.

I was almost sorry when the day's end bell rang and good Brother Sebastian laid a blessing of forgiveness on my head and a blanket on my shoulders. Almost. As I hobbled off to bed, I thought my knees might gleam blue and purple in the dark—as tales described the enchanted sigils of the Danae when they walked the wild places of the world.

"All right, it was *Father Abbot's* little surprise got me near dead from suffocation, not yours. But my skull will surely crack if you don't relieve some of my curiosity."

Jullian and I had met in the hedge garden after supper on the day following my long punishment. Though the maze still had me twitching at every noise, expecting grain sacks to be dropped on my head, it was the only place we could talk for any length of time. My Compline reading had been reset for this night, and gods bless the boy forever, he had fulfilled his promise to read it to me. Now, as we lingered in the gathering dark, I was trying to nudge the boy into some further revelation of Luviar's conspiracy without breaking my promise. My immortal soul could not afford the burden of an abbot's wrath. Sadly, I was having no luck at all.

"I'm sworn, Brother. Please, don't ask me. I can say only that the abbey is neutral ground."

So earnest in his honor. If he knew that I'd spent the time before his arrival stuffing my last supply of nivat into the parcel under Karus's statue, he would run from me like one of these plaguey rabbits. Had these conspirators stored nivat in their lighthouse? The sudden thought cheered me past the point of sense. If I could only ensure a supply, I could stop thinking about this damnable curse altogether. I'd just have to discover how to get into the place.

"Tell me more of Palinur," said Jullian, reverting to his favorite topic of conversation. "I can't imagine such a grand city. Are there truly statues of every one of the Hundred Heroes set before the king's palace? Though I know Grossartius is but legend, because Iero sends our souls to heaven or hell and not back to mortal bodies, he is my favorite of the Hundred. Is he quite large and well muscled? I've always imagined him bigger than Brother Robierre and taller even than you."

A west wind had brushed away the previous day's storm and left the evening astonishingly pleasant. Time yet remained before Compline, and I wasn't ready to go indoors.

"I'd much rather talk of why, in all that's holy, this flock of mad monks and gruff lords shares their secrets with a talkative boy of twelve-almost-thirteen." While babbling freely of his studies and abbey life, the stubborn little donkey would speak nothing of his raising beyond what he'd told me in the library. "It speaks highly of your character. And, of course, Brother Sebastian says you are the brightest scholar ever to study here. You've much to be proud of—"

"You've heard it wrong! I'm not half the scholar Brother Gildas is. And Gerard is far more holy, for I'm so easily distracted when I think of what I've read and the adventure tales you've told us. I *do* talk too much, and I'm wholly untrustworthy, for I've told you more than I should already. The moment I'm sixteen, I'm going to take a vow of silence!"

So soon after our study of the great vices, I should have known better than to use the word *proud*. Truly, if he were Eodward's child, I didn't think he knew it.

I ceased probing and soothed his worries about excess pride and boyish sins with a lurid saga about Grossartius the Revenant's return from the dead to serve King Caedmon. The bells began to strike. He jumped up as if a gatzé's tail poked him from underneath. "We need to go."

I sighed and unfolded myself from the bench. "Indeed. Brother Sebastian will have my skin if I'm late. My knees won't survive more penance."

The boy giggled. "I heard you made a sight, kneeling there in just shirt and trews all day. Brother Jerome said you were as blue as a jay and looked as if you might eat your sandals."

I stuck my foot and its unchewed sandal out before us. "Thanks to holy Iero, no need for that."

My Compline reading went very well, though I realized afterward that I had opened the page for two days previous—the page with the geese—and not the one I was reciting. Fortunately no one looked over my shoulder. Several of the brothers offered congratulations and kind words as we left the church. Brother Gildas stood last in the short line.

"You did very well for your first service reading," he said, as we strolled companionably through the upper passage toward the dorter, anticipating the day's end bell. "A bit stiff, perhaps, but practice should improve you. You are a man of many talents, Valen."

Why did he keep saying that? It bothered me that he might be one of those who had less confidence in my "usefulness and character," as Brother Victor had put it.

"So are you going to tell me what I was punished for?" I said softly enough that no one else could possibly hear. "My knees would very much like to know."

"Soiling your clothes? Sleeping at services?" The good brother grinned cheerfully.

Such a friend could drive a saint to drink. "The grain sack was *your* idea, wasn't it? To get me thoroughly muddled before your test."

"I'm truly sorry for that," he murmured, clasping his hands piously at his breast, looking straight ahead, and picking up the pace. "I had no idea it would distress you so."

"Thus you owe me an apology—a favor." I ducked my head lower and scarcely moved my lips. "And you know what I want: What does that puddle in the hills have to do with preserving knowledge and Evanori warlords and three—or is it *four*—royal princelings?"

"We cannot discuss such things here. Father Abbot warned you. I understand you've been given some *enlightenment*." His lips hinted the beginnings of a smile.

I wanted to kick him.

"Father Prior will surely assign you more readings after tonight, Brother Valen." He spoke more boldly as we neared the library door. "As you succeed in your assigned tasks, you earn more trust . . . and more tasks. As it happens, Brother Chancellor has received word of a book of Aurellian poetry that might be available to borrow from a lord down near Caedmon's Bridge. Brother Adolfus is to travel there tomorrow. Father Abbot says that, as a man so recently of the world, you might be of use in the negotiation."

Oh, no. No more traveling with the abbot's friends. No more of this conspiracy business. I hated being their ignorant pawn.

"As much as I appreciate our brothers' *trust*, the god teaches me constantly of humility," I said. "I've never been particularly successful at any single occupation, perhaps because my true calling is this quiet, retiring monastery life of simple prayer and simple service. I intend to devote my best efforts to making myself worthy of that calling, avoiding all things grand or mysterious . . . or dangerous . . . or *deviant*. Besides, my leg would never bear me so far."

Surely it would be better to live out the season quietly and escape with my skin intact to enjoy what I could of the world before it ended. The doulon had me in its stranglehold, and were I ever so blessed as to survive its shedding, my diseased senses and explosive restlessness would leave me as mad as my grandfather. Not even such a wonder as the lighthouse would tempt me to use the bent for aught but my own need. Look where such had got me.

Gildas laughed in that way he had, encompassing his entire being. Then he laid an arm around my shoulder and pulled me close, heads together. "Grand and mysterious events have a way of catching up to us even when we have no such course in mind. Someday I will share my own story with you. Good night, Brother. Safe journey."

He was still chuckling as he disappeared through the library door. I walked on toward the dorter, grumbling under my breath, yet unable to be truly angry with him. If only I had displayed my ignorance about the book. One would think I would have outgrown pride after so many years of stumbling so ineptly about the world. Seven-and-twenty years and I'd shed not a single one of the great vices.

The infirmarian had assured Father Abbot that exercise would be good for my healing thigh, thus Brother Adolfus and I were dispatched on our errand as the bells rang for Prime. The west wind's respite had been too brief. Purple-gray clouds hung low over the mountains, threatening a miserable day.

The road cut south through the abbey grain fields, where a few lay brothers were reaping barley that stood astonishingly undamaged despite the storm. Abbot Luviar had charged Brother Adolfus to summon the local villagers along our way. Though bound in service to the abbey, they had not yet come to aid the harvest.

The toad-faced Adolfus made it clear from the beginning that he would likely not speak to me beyond our business. "Journeys are excellent occasions for contemplation of our life's road through the vales of doubt, the fens of sin, and the occasional mountain peak of divine inspiration. Silence will be our guidepost."

As this was the lengthiest statement I had ever heard from the man, I'd borne no great expectation of conversation. But I had hoped he might be one of the "cabal," as Jullian referred to the abbot's little group of conspirators, and thus be willing to enlighten me on our mission. I had no illusion that we were truly off to negotiate use of a poetry book.

Drawing up my hood and tucking my hands up my sleeves against the cold, I wondered how I might divert my "life's road" to some nearby town where there might be a seedsman or herbary. To that end I had brought

along the gold button and silver spoon. Though I'd likely not get the trin-
kets' full worth, I might get enough to buy nivat for a doulon or two. Only
enough seeds for one use remained in my pouch, and possessing even a
small supplement might soothe this anxiety that dogged me. The disease
lurked in my bone and sinews alongside the craving for its remedy, both
waiting to take fire.

Shrines dotted the roadside. A patch of wildflowers drooped beside a
wooden representation of Karus. Rotting travelers' staves had been stuck
in the ground about a painted statue of Saint Gillare. An older stone figure, halfway devoured by orange and red lichen, represented Erdru bearing
his uplifted platter of grapes. A statue of Arrosa, her hand about a naked
mortal's member, had toppled over, leaving her poor lover separated from
his better parts.

Beyond Gillarine's fields and pastures, the landscape changed abruptly
to rolling meadows of yellowed grass and ankle-high briar tangles, dotted
with stands of scrawny trees. In one of these meadows, half a quellé past
the abbey's boundary fence, stood a ring of aspen trees. Legends called such
rings holy to the Danae, who were said to especially love to dance there in
autumn when the leaves turned gold. This dreary, precipitous autumn had
tainted the leaves black, and they'd fallen before ever they were gold. What
if they never gleamed gold again?

Fool, I thought, shoving away the dismal speculation. *These monks will have
you believing their end-times nonsense.* Yet such belief as could create the marvelous lighthouse could not be so easily dismissed. The unseasonable cold
and gloom seeped into my every pore.

Five quellae past the aspen grove, the cart track rose steeply for a short
way, leveled out and traversed a meadow, then rose again, the terrain like
a series of giant's steps toward the southern mountains. The river was no
longer a lazy looping band of silver, but a younger stream that plunged from
the mountains and raced through a gorge off to our left. To our right a gray-
green forest of spruce and silver birches mantled the rising hills, occasionally
dipping its folds into the sweeping meadows.

We met neither seedsmen nor herb sellers nor indeed any people at all
along the way. The first village we came to was well overgrown, red plague
circles fading on its crumbling houses. We did not dawdle there. A second
settlement showed signs of more recent disaster—tools and carts bearing
but early signs of rust, painted sigils of ward and welcome still bright on

the lintels. But a heap of decaying sheep fouled the nearby pastureland, and perhaps other creatures lay unburied, as well. We covered our noses with our cowls and hurried past.

As soon as we could breathe, a shocked Brother Adolfus fell to his knees and prayed for the missing villagers of Acceri, who usually worked Gillar- ine's planting and harvest. Evidently the abbey had received no word of their distress.

He should have waited a quellé more for his prayers. A third village, Vinera, had burned mere days ago. The sharp wind off the mountains shifted a blackened shutter and ruffled a length of frayed, muddy cloth tangled in a smashed loom. No corpses were visible, but I could see what had happened. One of the stone hovels had been made into a charnel furnace.

"Who could commit such sin?" Brother Adolfus's voice shook, as I showed him how the doors and windows had been blocked to prevent escape.

"Harrowers," I said, snatching the fluttering orange rag from a charred post and grinding it under my foot. "They take the folk who'll agree to fol- low them and send back raiders to slaughter the rest."

We did not linger. Though I pulled my hood lower, so that I could see nothing but the muddy ruts and Brother Adolfus's hem, the odor of burning lingered in my nostrils. Perhaps the world had already ended.

By late morning, we had completely lost sight of the river as we climbed a long series of switchbacks. Horses had traveled this road in the past day. A great rushing noise as of wind or water grew louder as we pushed on.

No gentle meadow awaited us beyond the crest of the climb, but a broad, treeless hillside, creased with a succession of low scarps. Beyond these alter- nating strips of vertical rock and grassy terraces, the land broke sharply up- ward into a formidable cap of barren rock. A blocklike fortress perched atop the crags, the grim ramparts more a part of the rock than distinct from it.

The road wound back and forth in deep bends to circumvent the scarps and traverse the broad terraces. Midway across the expanse, a waist-high cairn marked a branching of the track. The left fork arrowed across the slope toward the river gorge. The right snaked westward for half a quellé before beginning the ascent of the breathtakingly steep shelf road to the fortress.

"These mountain lords all think they are eagles," said Brother Adolfus, gawking at the forbidding road we'd yet to climb.

As we slogged toward the cairn, backs bent and heads ducked into the wind that flapped our cowls and gowns, a simple arch of dressed stone came into view in the distance, spanning the gorge. Caedmon's Bridge. Two broken columns marked the bridge approach, and a small mounted party, too distant to make out numbers, waited beside them. One rider galloped in our direction.

"Are these the ones who burned Vinera?" Brother Adolfus sounded ready to charge.

"I'd say not. Were they hostile they'd not be sending only one to greet us."

My eyes did not linger on the bridge or the people, but rather scoured the rugged land beyond the chasm. Caedmon's Bridge marked the boundary of Evanore, the land of trackless forests where the sun never penetrated, of rivers of flowing ice, of forbidden mountains where gods had made it impossible to breathe—the land of Prince Osriel and his terrible warlords and mages who served Magrog, lord of the netherworld. To cross Caedmon's Bridge placed a man's soul in mortal peril, so stories said, and would boil a pureblood's brains.

Though wary of the Bastard Prince and his perverse magics, I had borne no fear of Evanore itself—until I looked upon it. Indeed the land seemed grayer than where we stood, as if the clouds that muted the sun were thicker there. Unreasoning emotion swelled in my blood. Not the sense-blinding assault I'd felt in the cloister garth or at the pool. Not pain or terror at all. More a directionless anger and a sorrow so deep as to make a stone weep. A fearsome thing, that looking upon a landscape could so wrench a man's spirit.

Hoofbeats pounded the track from the bridge. The horseman drew rein at the cairn and waited there, patting the neck of his sidestepping bay as we approached. "Good morning, Brother Adolfus and Brother . . . Valen, is it?"

The dulcian voice erased all thought of the horrors behind us and the brooding land to the south. I yanked off my hood and looked up. She had cut her hair. The wind flicked the chin-length strands of bronze about her eyes and her cheeks, where a smile threatened to break through her sober courtesy.

"Master Corin," I said, bowing to cover my own foolish grin. "A great pleasure to see you again. Brother Adolfus, this gentle youth is the Thane of Erasku's squire."

I tried not to drool or sigh or otherwise make a fool of myself. I even forgave her greeting me from horseback, the beast so close to me I could feel its exquisite temper expelled in hay-scented snorts and blows. The woman's posture astride the beast presented me a full view of a shapely leg clad in scarlet hose—not peg scrawny as with so many of her noble sisters, but rather looking as if she ran and danced and lived with all of herself. Oh, dear goddess Arrosa, what I would not have given to run my hand upward along that red-clad limb.

Harness chinked and jangled in the distance as two other riders approached more slowly, leading a riderless mule. While I gripped my cowl tight against the wind, and my desires against even stronger natural forces, the woman turned to my companion. "Edane Groult is laid up with gout this morning, Brother Adolfus, so he asks if you would be so kind as to attend him in his hall. He has sent down two escorts and a mule to bring you up. Unfortunately, he did not expect two of you. My master was just departing on his way back to his hold and offered my services to greet you and convey the edane's message."

Brother Adolfus was nonplussed. "Of course I will ride up. Brother Valen *could* walk, but his leg is just now healing from a dreadful wound. I don't know . . . to leave a novice behind . . ."

"The edane's men will return for him, Brother. Meanwhile, my own lord is willing to delay his journey and provide Brother Valen company and refreshment for his wait."

"Well then, that will do very nicely." Brother Adolfus's conscience seemed much eased at the thought of me being provisioned. I was less sanguine, seeing now how matters were to work out. No second mule would be sent. Some excuse would be given when I did not appear in the edane's hall, while I would be dispatched on some ghost hunt with the Thane of Erasku. How much finer if I could wait here alone with Corin.

The mule arrived; Brother Adolfus mounted. As the monk and the nobleman's two servants moved away, the woman extended her hand to me, allowing a smile to break through. "Would you accept a ride to the bridge, Brother? Blackmane will certainly carry us both."

"Ah, mistress . . ."

Could she have presented any choice more painful? Saint Ophir had definite opinions on his followers having physical contact with women—a matter I had conveniently failed to recall as she'd led me blindfolded about the valley of Gillarine. I could have conveniently forgotten it again, save the horse appeared much more disturbed by the idea than her kind invitation would attest. He sidled and jinked so anxiously that a determined frown supplanted the woman's smile.

"Alas, I am not permitted." I stepped back to give the demon-cursed animal a bit more room. "And I don't think your beast likes me all that much."

"Nonsense. He's as placid as a cow." She said this with conviction, though, indeed, my distancing might have been a handful of sugar in the devil equine's mouth. "Come along, then. As you answered our first question so well, we've another puzzle for you."

She held to a slow walk, slower than necessary. I did not protest, and walked as close to her as the beast and I could bear. "I don't suppose you might give me a hint about the purpose of these exercises with the book of maps. I've received no reward for my first success but chilblains, bruised knees, and a reputation for slovenliness."

"I'm truly sorry for your trouble. The purposes of the cabal are not mine to reveal, but I vow they are of critical—"

"—importance to Navronne. To our children's children. So I've been told. Lives depend on secrecy, thus a novice's knees and unbridled curiosity are of poor account."

"Many lives. You must believe that. Those who hold this responsibility have yielded everything in their lives to serve this need." Her bitter argument took no heed of my teasing. And surely the horse was not responsible for the hard look she cast toward the bridge. Such an expression did not belong on such a face.

"One answer, then, and I'll pry no more for the moment," I said.

"Good Brother, I cannot—

"I would know your true name, mistress. And don't say 'Mag' or 'Popsy,' for you are no more a villein girl than you are a lad. My mind finds a great void in its constant untanglings and unwindings of these dire mysteries, for I cannot set a proper name to one certain face. Perhaps if I could bound that face with a name and set it in a proper sequence with Thane Stearc the Formidable, Gram the Sickly, and Brother Gildas of the Mysteries, as for labeled jars on a shelf, it would not persist in distracting me from more serious thoughts. Elsewise I must strive to deserve more punishments just to give me more time for contemplating the question, and what would Iero and his saints think of such a sacrilege?"

Ah, Deunor's fire, her laugh resonated in my bones as if I were a harp and she the player filled with passionate music. I would have babbled my nonsense the night through to hear such tunes as she could pluck on me.

"Elene, good brother. My true name is Elene, but I would advise you not to use it in front of my father. For the time, my own folly has made me none but Corin, his less-than-satisfactory squire." She kicked the bay into a gallop, and they raced through the hazy morning toward the bridge. I could not take my eyes from her.

Elene . . . The name, the flesh, the laugh played out the sweetest harmony of creation.

Chapter 17

"I suppose you wish to rest," said the Thane of Erasku when I joined him, his daughter, and his secretary by the bridge.

"Good morning, my lord," I said. "Indeed my feet are more bruised than a drunkard's liver."

Brother Adolfus's mule had reached only half the distance to the fortress hill. As the goddess of love had produced no chain of circumstances that might leave me alone and naked with a similarly unclothed Elene, I was feeling a bit mulish as well.

"You're most kind to offer to wait with me for Edane Groult's transport, Lord Stearc, but please do not feel it necessary to delay your journey. Surely those clouds will split at any time and beset us with rain. Be on your way and godspeed!"

The three of them stood between the crumbling columns. Shards of white marble, stained and streaked with black, littered the flat muddy ground. What forces had shattered pillars as broad as my armspan? Even broken, they rose to twice my height. Lightning, perhaps, or siege engines, used in some long-ago attempt to destroy Ardra's only link with Evanore for a hundred quellae in either direction.

Elene stood at her father's side, one step behind his massive shoulder. The gray daylight revealed even more likeness between them, if any personage so ferocious and intimidating as Stearc of Erasku could be said to resemble a graceful woman. Their noses were blunt, cheekbones prominent, and jawlines square—hers formed in ivory, his in granite. The air around them seemed to quiver like heat rising from paving stones in deep summer.

The thane snorted. "You're not such a fool as to think this meeting is by chance, are you, monk? We've—"

"Excuse me, my lord." Gram stepped out from behind Stearc, slightly stooped, black hair whipping in the wind. The secretary looked younger in the daylight, though even more wan and weak beside such exuberance of life as this father and daughter. "I've the provisions you required me to pack for the good brother." Head inclined in deference, the gaunt secretary proffered a wineskin and a canvas provision bag. "I'll bring the book, and we can discuss our needs as Brother Valen takes a moment to catch his breath."

"If he can do this at all, he should be able to do it quickly," grumbled Stearc. "He can fill his belly as we wait for sunset—assuming the damnable sun still exists behind these clouds."

Thanks be, Gram's good sense prevailed. I sat on a round of marble and made sure Stearc's impatience did not worsen from waiting for me to devour the barley bread, soft cheese, and good ale. A fire would have been pleasant, but I'd no mind to delay my refreshment until I'd given the lord my answer to today's puzzle. He'd likely throw me from the bridge when I refused to help. I could not waste more magic on their ventures. Only a few days and I'd need everything I could muster.

"My lord, if you've brought me here to question me further about the maps," I said, when I was well through the little feast, "I'm afraid I've no more to tell you. I demonstrated everything I know in your first test. Any man with the knowledge you hold could have done the same."

"Evidently not," snapped Stearc, clasping his broad hands behind his back as if to keep from throttling me. His leather jaque strained with the display of his chest. "Others attempted to use the spell and trace the exact route you took. But they experienced no extraordinary guidance from the map. In hours of searching, they never came nearer the Well than the cliff. What caused your attempt to succeed where others failed?"

He leaned toward me, the pressure of his interest weighing like an iron yoke. Mouth stuffed with bread, I shrugged. But in truth I was not so nonchalant. So the eerie little pool Gildas and I had found . . . the Well, they called it . . . was indeed one of the hidden places that only my grandfather's maps could reveal. The wind poked its chilly fingers under my gown.

I'd not used the guide spell of the map, only my bent and my instincts. What did that mean? I was not familiar enough with the more obscure pureblood arcana to know. My father could not find such places without using the enchantments of my grandfather's maps—one of the matters that embittered him so sorely, I'd always thought. Max had always been more adept at tracking than at route finding. But then, I had been adept at nothing.

"Perhaps someone told you how to find the Well." Stearc might have been a magistrate. "Or you ran across some mention of it in documents at the abbey."

I came near choking. "No, my lord, I certainly did not read of the place. And I doubt—"

"Show him, Gram."

The secretary sank to the grass just in front of me, sat back on his heels, and opened the book on his knees, searching for the page he wanted.

"Here, Brother." He turned the book to face me.

I wiped my hands on the empty provision bag and tossed it aside, then took the book. The open page contained two small maps. The secretary pointed to a grousherre, painted in bright reds and yellows. The map was too small to have a cartouche. The tiny words embedded in twisting vines and leaves that filled the narrow borders of the little map would hold the spell.

The characters flowed together like a river of ink as soon as I looked on them, of course, but I needed neither cartouche nor border to tell me what this map depicted. The meticulous drawings of fortress, bridge, columns, river, and branching path were enough to identify the very place where we sat. Interesting that the twin columns were shown whole, each of them bearing a capital in the shape of a trilliot. King Caedmon had been the first to order the wild lily of Navronne sewn onto his cape and his banner and emblazoned on his armor.

My gaze swept the grass between us and the gorge. Among the shards of marble tumbled around us might be those very capitals. Such an odd sensation for that moment, as if I lived in both times at once and might soon see Caedmon himself defending the bridge, as his warlords retreated into Evanore to hold its mountains and gold against the invading Aurellians. The black-haired invaders from the east—my ancestors—had turned their acquisitive eyes upon Navronne when they discovered that the minor sorceries they could accomplish in their own land were not only easier to work, but took fire with power here. They called Navronne the Heart of the World.

And then, of a sudden, I envisioned my grandfather, a scrawny, squinting old man, his lean shoulders hunched, his thick hair gone white, beard yellowed around his mouth, sitting alone by a campfire on this hillside, his

long fingers like spiders' legs sketching this scene in his worn leather traveling book. Alongside the delicate pen strokes that represented the objects in
the map, he would scribe a column of inked letters and numbers, noting
the measures and proportions, names, and colors he would use to bring
out the message he wanted to convey with this grousherre. He had chosen
to show the fortress much smaller than the columns, had decided to depict
the thrashing river of less moment than the bridge that crossed it or the
overgrown paving stones of the approaches. Grousherres were about relative
significance rather than accurate measure.

"Brother?" Gram remained sitting on his heels, facing me across the
book.

Fire washed my cheeks. I shook off the cascading visions and the hostility
and resentment that inevitably accompanied thoughts of my family. "Sorry.
What is it you wish me to find?"

The secretary laid his slender finger on the largest object on the map.
"This."

"Oh!" I had assumed the great tree that spread its ghostly branches across
the entire page was but part of the book's decoration. Naught but straggling
grass grew anywhere on this hillside. Certainly no tree stood where the map
suggested, at the cairn where the path from the valley divided into two.
"These maps were drawn years ago," I said. "If the tree was ever here, it must
have been cut down."

"Perhaps the tree is only hidden," said the secretary, softly encouraging.
"Try it."

"Try what?" I said, blank for the moment.

"Invoke the spell of the map!" bellowed Stearc, throwing up his hands.
"What do you think? Spirits of night, must we be forever plagued with idiots
and fools?"

"Give me a little time with the brother, my lord, and I'll explain what
we seek . . . as we agreed."

Gram's quiet insistence held sway. The thane betook himself to the brink
of the river chasm. Elene's glance wavered, but after a moment, she followed
dutifully after him. They strolled onto the bridge—a fearsome thing to my
mind, no more than one horseman wide and lacking parapet or railing. There
they sat, legs dangling over the unseen void.

Gram blew out a great puff of air as if he did the same, though his precarious state seemed more related to his testy lord. "Please excuse my mas-

ter, Brother. He is in a most difficult position, his life forever balanced on a knife edge. Those things he would do to right matters—deeds he has trained for his entire life—slide ever farther out of his reach."

"Because he conspires against his own lord, the Bastard Prince?"

No matter whether Osriel himself came to power—Kemen Sky Lord protect us from such a pass—whichever of the other two brothers became king would need to make alliance with the Bastard Prince to prevent his rival doing the same. Evanori lords who had failed in fealty to Osriel would be safe nowhere.

Gram's gaunt features twisted into a wry mask. "Indeed, that's a part of it."

He tapped the page again. "So, to our problem: We have learned that this particular map will lead us to a location of great importance, a place where we can leave a message. Those who must receive the message live nearby, but we aren't sure exactly where. And we need their help. But we've had no more luck with this map than with the one to Clyste's Well. And so, again we ask your assistance."

"But if they live nearby, surely this Edane Groult—"

"Edane Groult has no dealings with these neighbors," said the secretary dryly. "He would not recognize them were they to sit on his shoes. Or if he did, then his aged heart would stop."

My skin began to creep. How far did Abbot Luviar's arrogance of intellect take him? If he could redirect a man's loyalty to his prince, what could he do with a man's loyalty to his god?

"What neighbors might these be, living so close to the cursed land?" I said, sounding bolder than I felt. "I am pledged to holy Iero's service . . ."

. . . and to Kemen's and Samele's and that of all and any gods and goddesses who allowed men to keep their skin and balls and fingernails and enjoy life without excessive torment. Unlike Magrog the Tormentor. The Adversary.

Gram lowered his head for a moment, as if in prayer, then lifted it again and glanced at me, though not so far lifting or so long glancing as to confront me as an honest man. "Good Brother Valen, we propose to deal with neither the Bastard Prince nor the Adversary nor their demonic lackeys, I promise you. Tell me, have you not read the inscription carved above your abbey's gates?"

"When I entered the gates of Gillarine, I was in no state to be *reading* anything, Master Gram," I snapped. I had the sense he was patronizing me behind his quiet manner, so like a monk himself. I didn't like it.

"The inscription says, *The earth is God's holy book.*" He said this softly and with sincere reverence. Without hint of superior laughter.

"I've heard the abbot say that," I said. In point of fact, out of all the prayers and mumblings I'd heard throughout my stay at Gillarine, it had been one phrase that made sense to me. It spoke of worth in common things where others saw naught. And it recalled the words of the sanctuary blessing: *by Iero's grace . . . by gift of earth . . . by King Eodward's grant . . .* And now these men spoke of holy wells. Of hidden trees. Of unseen neighbors whose presence might stop a man's heart. Of my grandfather's maps that could guide men to—

I stared at Gram. His dark head was bent over the book, only a swath of his wide forehead visible. A lock of dark hair had fallen forward, but surely underneath it, his eyes would be wild and fervent. Holy men. Madmen. I fought to keep sober. "By my soul, you're hunting angels!"

He was too intent upon his folly even to blush. "Not precisely. We believe there's been some confusion through the years. Your god may send angel messengers to tend our souls and guard us from temptation, but care of the earth is charged to other beings. Their stories have been told for as long as men have sat around fires under the stars. They live in realms of earth, not heaven, protecting and enriching the land they walk—that *we* walk—yet ordinary men cannot find the way to their dwelling places, save by luck or magic. Somehow, the pureblood cartographer who drew these maps could discover them whenever he chose, using only his pureblood bent. And now, using one of his maps, *you* have opened the way to one of their most hallowed places."

Struggling to keep from laughing at his sincerity, I touched the naked figures that supported the ribbonlike borders at the map's four corners. One was the aingerou my grandfather had stuck into every drawing in the book, claiming he did so because I was so fond of them. But the other three figures, two male, one female, poised on toes, legs stretched and bent as if dancing on the page, were no round-bellied imps, but tall and graceful with perfect bodies and flowing red curls. Angels, one might say, though they had no wings. This all began to make some sort of perverse sense. "You speak of the Danae."

Gram stood up, pulling his billowing cloak tight. "The long-lived have retreated far from humankind. They may be extinct, as reports claim. But a reliable source tells us that if we leave an offering at this tree before the sun reaches the zenith, a Dané will surely come at nightfall to fetch it, if even one yet exists. Then we could present our petition."

A surge of good humor threatened to plaster a grin on my face. I brought my hand up as if to mask a cough. "An offering . . . so you've brought *nivat seeds* to buy a parley." For if the Danae loved feast bread flavored with nivat, lore said they would bargain gems to obtain a quantity of the seeds. Nivat no longer grew in the wild.

"Yes. But first we must find the tree."

I breathed gratitude to Serena Fortuna and controlled my excitement, bending my head over the map again lest he mark my improved humor. "A marvel that would be, Gram, to discover the Danae after so long. I've doubts I can help you, but with Iero's grace, I'll see what I can do."

The wind blustered, snatching at our hair and cloaks and the fine vellum. I smoothed the page and held it to prevent its tearing or wrinkling. My fingers tingled and pricked as I brushed over the inked drawings. Spellcraft, certainly, as much a part of this book as compass roses.

I rotated the book to the left and then to the right, allowing my eyes to travel the lettered border and my lips to move slightly—Gram was watching very closely. Then I laid a finger on the bridge approach and dragged it to the branch point of the path whence the roots of the great tree spread like a spider's web across the painted hillside. All the while my mind was racing, sorting through the magical tricks that pureblood children learn as they learn to breathe and walk. If only I had listened better to my despised tutors.

"I don't think we can find this tree where it is not," I said. "But when I touch the roots on this page . . . perhaps . . ." Leaving the prospect dangling, I shut the book and gave it back to Gram.

I would need a few things to make this work. When I stood up and stepped a few quattae to my left, I made sure Gram could not see what my foot encountered. "Do *you* accompany me this time?"

He bowed in acknowledgment. "One moment, if you would. Lord Stearc would join us as well."

While he hurried off to fetch the thane, I reached down and grabbed the wadded canvas provision bag underneath my foot and stuffed it up my sleeve. Then I began to prepare a small voiding spell, the finest boon for a boy who wished to hide purloined items—wine, coins from his father's purse, his mother's divining cards, his man-smitten sister's love philtres, or his brother's prized knife. Strolling through the clutter of broken marble, I also sought a plant of some kind . . . Ah, there! Tucked up beside a boulder-sized chunk grew a scrabbling astelas vine. Astelas had nice spreading, hairy roots.

The others were returning from the bridge. Cupping my hands to my breast, I dropped to my knees, bent forward, and touched my forehead to the earth. Thanks to the summer's incessant rains, which had left the ground damp and pliable, I was able to pull up the astelas, roots intact. Before rising from my prayerful posture, I stuffed the plant up my sleeve alongside the bag.

At a respectful distance, my companions waited for me to complete my devotions. The first spell structured and waiting, I closed my eyes long enough to prepare a second—this one an inflation, the simplest kind of illusion. When it was ready, I rose and joined the others.

"One thing before we go," I said. "As I prayed Iero to guide our steps, I recalled that each time I've used the book, neither human nor beast has accompanied me. Perhaps that circumstance has somehow contributed to the successful outcome."

"The book says nothing of such a practice," said Gram, "but we can certainly lag behind, if you believe it might help. It's almost midday. If our first attempt should fail, we've no time for another today."

"Exactly my thought," I said, delighted at his practical reasoning.

"Just get on with it," said Stearc. Was the man ever other than angry and snappish? "We can walk. Corin can bring up the horses. We're no womenfolk needing to be coddled."

I refrained from smiling or glancing at Elene, who had drawn up her hood. "All right then."

As I strode briskly across the hillside, I honed my spells, straining to recall the nuances of skills so long unused. I could afford no explosions or sparks this time. I also plucked the leaves and stem from the astelas, scattering the bits and pieces of greenery by dropping them between my cowl and gown so they drifted to the ground as I walked. By the time I reached the cairn, only a thick clump of roots remained of the plant inside my sleeve.

As I knelt beside the pile of stones, I quickly traced an arc on the lichen-covered stone from the earth to a point a handsbreadth above the ground and back down again, allowing magic to flow through my hands into the voiding spell. The substance of the stone retracted—squeezed aside, as to say—to create the void hole, a gap in the side of the cairn. I reached in and scrabbled in the earth, spreading and burying the astelas roots as best I could.

Now the second spell—the inflation. Magic swelled and passed through my tingling fingers into the buried roots. Trusting that I had remembered enough, I unraveled the voiding spell to close the gaping hole. A gamble, this. To use the bent as I'd sworn not to do. To spend power that I would need within days. But to throw such an opportunity back into Serena Fortuna's face was surely more risky yet. I rose and waited for the others to arrive.

"I see no tree," said Stearc, planting his hands on his waist, uncomfortably near his weapons. Gram and Elene flanked him, the secretary paler than ever, the woman flushed and rosy after tethering their horses a few hundred quercae up the hill, then running to rejoin us.

"Though the cairn is not shown on the map, the map spell led me straight to it," I said, feigning puzzlement. "Each step away from it jibes wrong."

"The tree should be here," said Gram, crouching low to examine the cairn. "We should be able to see and touch it as Gildas saw and touched Clyste's Well. The journal speaks of the Sentinel Oak as a meeting place of the two planes."

The cairn bore no markings. The rocks had likely been piled up to mark the path when snows lay deep. The secretary's long thin fingers brushed the stone and earth around the cairn. He looked up. "My lord, come. There's something here . . ."

I stepped back, allowing Stearc a place to kneel beside his secretary. "Take down the stones," he said. "Corin, come. Lay to it."

Elene and the two men dismantled the cairn before I could breathe another prayer. And there, protruding from the ground, was the rough-hewn stump of a modest-sized tree. Its dead roots, a nice thick, woody spread modeled from the astelas roots, poked from the earth here and there. I felt as proud as a father must upon viewing a new-birthed son.

The thane folded his arms and regarded the stump. "It seems smaller than the description of the tree would warrant."

I wanted to mount a defense of my progeny: *Too large and it would have disrupted the cairn. Smaller and you'd not believe. It is so nice and woody, well aged in its appearance. And I've not created so substantial an inflation in twelve years, at the least, so credit me a bit, fearsome lord!* The stump should last a month or more if no one worked a spell of unraveling on it. Unraveling spells—the bane of a boy's illusions—had been as common in my family's house as arguments.

"The map brought you here, Brother Valen?" said Gram, frowning. "You're sure?"

"Nowhere else. The guide thread I feel as I follow the map's course fades even these few steps away." I returned to the secretary's side and knelt beside him. Spits of rain struck my face and pocked the disturbed earth about my lovely stump.

"Nothing for it but to make the attempt," said Stearc. "If the monk is wrong—of which I have little doubt—we've lost nothing but a day already wasted. The morning has almost run."

Gram, still troubled, nodded. He shifted one of the smaller stones left tumbled about from the destroyed cairn and laid it at the base of the stump carefully, as if judging a precise orientation. Elene watched him, and I watched her, wondering at her pinched lips and stormy brow. Some enmity ran deep between these two—both of them people I would be pleased to account my friends.

I kept my preoccupation with Elene's expressive face well hidden beneath the shelter of my hood, shifting my attention only when Gram pulled a small bag from the pocket of his cloak and set it on the stone. A distinctive scent, of pepper and almond, of dust and mushrooms, flooded the air. Blessed Samele, I could have picked the man's pocket twenty times over!

I touched the little bag. Oiled canvas. Common brown. Very like the provision bag hidden in my sleeve. Slightly smaller, closed with a black silk cord instead of a leather tie. Surely enough nivat for a year or more. It was all I could do to refrain from snatching it up and racing the coming storm back the way we'd come, past Gillarine and all the way to Palinur. Sell half the seeds and I would be set for half a year.

But I'd never get away. These three rode horses and carried swords and smoldered with passion about their madness. Deception was a healthier course. Patience. Depending on how the next few hours went, I should be able to take what I wanted with none the wiser.

I withdrew my hand and stood up. "Great Iero, shed your blessings here."

Gram held an open hand out to Elene. "Do you have the box, Corin?"

From the pocket of her jupon, she drew a small tin box that she handed to Gram. He sprinkled some of the contents on the stone and shifted the bag of nivat to cover what he had just put down.

"Salt," he said, as if sensing my question. "To hold the Dané here while we speak."

"Why would you do that?" I said, aghast. No matter that I did not believe anything would come of his offering or his message. Some things were so wrong that it was better not even to mime them. "Fetter a Dané? Bind it? When you've come begging their favor?"

"It's only to stay the sentinel long enough for us to speak. We'd never force them. But we *must* be heard. If we knew another way, we'd use it."

"They'll never forgive you. Of all things, Danae are free." My grandfather's stories came back to me. None could bind the Danae to field or forest or bog. "They choose their own places, Gram. That's why you give them feast bread . . . to induce them to stay. That's why you leave an undisturbed plot when you plow a new field or set aside a wild garden when you build a new house, so the Dané who tends that plot of ground can yet come and go at will. Elsewise he might leave to find another place, or she might be trapped amid the human works and die. Bind them, and you'll lose everything before you speak one word of your message."

"This whole scheme is madness," said Stearc. "We must proceed as we decided. This fool of a monk doesn't know what he's doing. Nor do we. Come, Corin, we need to set up a shelter before this everlasting rain washes us into the river."

"We try as we can, lord," said Gram, more to himself than anyone.

The thane strode off toward the horses, and his daughter followed. Gram shook his head and started up the hill after his master. A few steps and he paused, waiting for me to join him.

The clouds had closed in over the southern mountains, and veils of rain and fog drifted over the river and the bridge. The fortress had vanished into the murk. Confused, unreasonably disturbed, praying their oiled bag would protect the nivat seeds from the wet, I joined the secretary, and we trailed after Stearc and Elene.

Gram walked more slowly than Stearc and his daughter. Though he seemed at the verge of speaking several times, he never did. Perhaps I had offended him with my blunt speech—silly, as I thought about it, to argue over legends. He could do as he liked with his foolery.

"So am I to wait here, too, and help you pursue some other plan should this one fail, or is someone from the fortress truly bringing a mule to fetch me?" I said after a while. "I'd rather see the outcome of this venture. To see a Dané . . . blessed saints, it would be a miracle. But if I'm to go up to the fortress, I'd as soon leave before the rain worsens."

Gram lifted his head, roused from his thoughts. "The edane *will* send his mule for you eventually. We were able to arrange a delay, but only until midafternoon." A few more steps and he stopped to rest. He glanced up at me, a thoughtful expression on his face. "I've already revealed more than Thane Stearc would approve, and he'll not wish you to remain. However, I could argue it with him . . ."

"No, no. He seems a difficult enough master. I'd not put you more in the way of his wrath."

Gram chuckled and glanced out from under the soggy locks of dark hair now dribbling water down his deep-carved cheeks. "That is a kindness, Brother. I could wish you were around us more often. Perhaps we would stay civil. Though our goals are like, our opinions diverge mightily, and to argue with anyone of the house of Erasku is a futile exercise. They are the harder rock from which the mountains of Evanore have sprouted."

Stearc and Elene had moved the horses into the lee of a low scarp that split the hillside. They were already unloading packs and satchels.

"I've sensed that," I said, relishing my view of Elene's delicious body as she went about her work. "And the squire demonstrates as virulent opinions as the lord. At our first meeting, after that unfortunate encounter with a grain sack, I made the mistake of asking Corin about Prince Osriel."

"Indeed?" We plodded uphill again. "And you lived to tell about it? The house of Erasku has no use for the Bastard."

"Corin's vehemence was reassuring. When Prince Osriel attacked the Moriangi at Gillarine—" Of a sudden, the memory laid a blight on my fey mood. "I just wanted to make certain your little test was not enlisting me in the Bastard's legion."

"Ah. I've heard fearful stories of that raid—apparitions, a cloud of midnight, the mutilation of the dead. You do well to keep cautious of the Bastard's poisonous madness. Thane Stearc walks a difficult path, unable to side with any of the three. We had a narrow escape from the abbey that night."

"So who *does* he favor for the throne? Who do you favor, for that matter?"

Gram shook his head in the same hopelessness I felt. "Both Perryn and Bayard have young children. If the brothers maintain a stalemate, Lord Stearc believes we may be forced into some sort of cousinly union and a regency. Not a happy prospect when spring brings Hansker raids."

We had reached a level with Stearc's camp. The secretary rested his back against the scarp, expelling a relieved sigh. He cocked his head. "Tell me, Brother Valen, if we fail tonight—and I am no more sanguine than my master—and we arrive at some new insight that invites your participation, may we call upon you again? I do value your aid . . . and your advice."

"I don't seem to have much choice in the matter. This is all a great mystery, and I'm thinking my head will burst soon with wondering." Indeed my mind was hopelessly jumbled as I tried to link the Danae to the lighthouse and the end times. What interest had Danae in books or looms?

Gram's wry, twisting smile granted a moment's grace to his stark face. "Your abbot must enlighten you further, Brother. Tell him what you've learned this day, and he will likely supply the rest . . . in far more civil terms than Lord Stearc would do. We need men and women of courage, goodwill, and varied gifts. Clearly *you* have a gift where this strange book is concerned."

"Well, we'll discover the truth of that at sunset, I suppose." I returned his smile, regretting the need to deceive the mournful fellow.

Indeed, I felt privileged to be allowed such glimpses of Gram's private self. Servants of volatile lords had to control themselves quite strictly. The secretary had been forthcoming to a degree others had not, and I held no prejudice against madmen. The armies, the alleys, and the finest pureblood houses of Navronne were filled with them.

I offered him my hand. "For now, farewell, sir. I must hike up this monstrous hill before I am soaked through. You'll convey my respects to the thane and his man?"

He nodded graciously and took my hand, showing no surprise at the unclerical gesture. The fingers that circled my wrist were firm, but cold, and his own wrist hammered with a blood pulse that spoke of more excitement than his quiet manner displayed. Or perhaps it was merely the racing heart of an unwell man who had pushed too hard to climb a hill.

I did not take to the fortress road, but hiked only as far as the next scarp that banded the hillside. Though Stearc's party lay hidden behind their own step of rock just below me, the dark ribbon of the cart track was clearly visible down the hill from them. The darker smudge and scattered rocks marked the fine stump where my year's salvation lay waiting. I huddled against the short wall of rock, sinking into its shadow, drawing my cowl and hood close to shield me from the rain. Anyone coming down from the fortress to fetch me would see no one on the road or in the fields. Come dusk, I would put the last step of my plan into action.

The hours passed slowly. Sleep crept over me like the clouds and fog drifting across the gray-green landscape. Yet whenever I started, from grazing my cheek on the rock as I slumped or from the cold drizzle on my hairless patch of scalp when a gust of wind lifted my hood, the light seemed unchanged from my last waking. I was only wetter and colder. I settled deeper against the rock wall. *Pretend you're warm; you've done that often enough. Just stay awake . . .*

Yawning, I played out the plan over and over again. *As soon as the light fades enough to leave shapes and landscape indistinct, slip down toward the stump. Pray the rain continues. They'll never see you. Empower the illusion. Replace the bag of seeds with the empty provision bag that will now appear exactly the same.* To empty the nivat into the provision bag and leave the empty one behind would take too much time. *One last touch of magic . . . a flash of blue light as the night closes in . . . easy, as you creep away unseen. Then the long trudge up the hill to the fortress. I'll think of a story for Brother Adolfus . . . for the edane whose mule driver won't have found me . . . Sympathize with Gram and Elene that their Dané eluded them . . . sympathize tenderly with Elene . . .*

My eyelids weighed like lead . . . and still the game played out . . . over and over . . .

Trigger the spell . . . creep silently . . . careful . . . timing . . . all was timing . . . switch the bags . . . slog upward . . . a story . . . one more lie . . . a flash of spiraling sapphire in the night . . .

I sat bolt upright. Deunor's fire, it was almost dark. The wind had died. The rain had stopped. Banners of fog lay in every hollow and niche, the world now colored with charcoal and ash. I shook off the dregs of sleep, cursing my everlasting carelessness. How long would Stearc wait to scoop up his bag of nivat and yell at Gram to devise him another plan? Impossible . . . unbearable . . . that my scheme or my magic should go to waste. Scooping up a fistful of earth, I recklessly poured magic into seeking a route through the twilight.

Once sure I would not tumble over the scarp into Stearc's lap, I sped downhill. But I had not traveled half the distance when I glimpsed lights of deep and varied blue moving through the fog. A few steps closer, until the scene halted my feet and left me gaping. Exactly as I'd seen in the fog of my dreaming, the light was drawn into long coils and spirals . . . into delicate vines and leaves that hung in the thick air . . . living artworks as bright and rich-hued as the windows of Gillarine Abbey church. They drifted in sinuous unison away from the demolished cairn. Away from the tree—an oak of such a girth its bole could house a family and of such expansive foliage it could shelter a village beneath its limbs.

"Wait!" Gram's cry bounced off the rocks and fell dead in the thick air. "Please! Hear our message . . . for any who dance in Aeginea. We need your help. *Envisia seru, Dané.*"

The blue lights paused and shifted, turning . . . the movement revealing the canvas for the artist's magical pen . . . long bare limbs entwined by sapphire snakes, and flat breasts traced with azure moth wings, half hidden by a cascade of curling red hair . . . a pale cold face upon which a glowing lizard coiled its tail about a fathomless eye, while the reptile's scaled body drawn in the color of lapis stretched across an alabaster cheek. So beautiful . . . so marvelous.

"Human voices are thorns in our ears." The voice of the wind could be no more soulless. She was already moving away.

"Our estrangement shadows our hearts." The speaker's dark shape— Gram's shape—moved between me and the apparition. "Meanwhile, the world suffers, and we seek to understand it. Can we bargain? Will you convey our request to Stian Archon or Kol Stian-son?"

I wanted to scream at Gram to move out of the way so I could see more, yet I could not accomplish even that. My limbs were frozen in place, stricken powerless with wonder. But I smelled her . . . wood rush and willow and the rich mold of old leaves and shaded gullies . . . she came from the fen country.

Everything of my own life—past, present, thought, sense—paled and thinned, having no more substance than smoke alongside the substance of her. I felt starved, fading.

Standing beneath the spreading branches, the Dané paused and cocked her head to one side, raising her brow so that the lizard's tail twitched. "Bargain . . . and forget betrayal? Forget violation and poison? Forget thievery?" She breathed deep of the night air. Her nostrils flared. Her lip curled. "Thou canst not claim ignorance, human, for thy very blood bears the taint of betrayal and thy flesh stinks of thievery. The long-lived do not forget. Offer recompense for betrayal; uncorrupt that which thy poison has corrupted; return what was stolen, and we might consider a hearing."

"Theft? Poison? I know naught of—"

No need for Gram to finish his claims of ignorance. She had vanished in a rush of air, as if she had wings to bear her back to heaven. And no spreading oak stood at the cairn. Only my ugly stump.

Sodden, chilled to the marrow, I sank to my knees and tasted all that remained of the night—charcoal and ash, empty of magic. I pressed my forehead to the cold earth and wept.

Chapter 18

"Brother Valen! Are you injured? We heard a cry."

Bobbing lantern light announced Elene well before she knelt beside me and brought her face down near my own. Even without sight I would have known her. She smelled of fennel soap and horse, damp leather and wet pine smoke, of a warm human woman, not the woodrush scent of the cold Dané.

"My lord, over here!" she yelled. And then quieter, "Brother?"

"I sprained . . . fell . . . I was on the way . . . the fortress . . ." My lies limped into nothingness. I inhaled and began again. "I stayed back to watch. Waited up the hill. Saw her."

That was all I could muster. I could no more explain the fullness of grief that had overwhelmed me than I could explain my pain in the cloister garth, my dread at the pool in the hills, or why in the name of heaven a Dané had come to a tree stump made from a weed. I knew only that when the blue sigils vanished, I felt as if some great door had opened in the world and all joy had rushed out. Were the king's own minstrels surrounding me, I could not have sung with them or danced to their music.

"So it was not just the three of us who saw and heard. Lord Stearc and I each thought we were dreaming. Gram even spoke to the creature! But you look dreadful, Brother. Are you sure you're not hurt?" Elene laid a hand on my shoulder, and the sheer kindness of it came near setting me weeping again.

"I've not been myself of late," I mumbled. "Ill. No sleep. So much praying. A different life." I tried to sort myself out, dragging a sleeve across my face as I sat up. How long had I knelt here weeping like a babe bereft of its mother's tit? My reaction made no sense at all. I hated feeling so helpless, so at the mercy of emotions without cause. "It's nothing."

I'd wasted the day. Wasted my bent. Of course, the Dané had taken the nivat. She would not have come at all if not for the seeds. So beautiful . . . so strange and majestic and proud . . . such magic . . .

Ah, stars of night, that was what hurt so dreadfully. To look upon such power that dwelt so near us, in tree or pond or meadow, and yet so vastly distant. Never had dirt and ignorance and uselessness weighed on me so. The damp, heavy wool of my drab monk's garb itched and choked me. Stories said the Danae danced to the music of the stars. Easy to see how people might mistake such a being for a messenger of heaven.

"Brother Valen! What are you doing here?" Stearc's sudden presence assaulted my spirit like a cadre of Moriangi foot soldiers.

I shook my head. I was doing well to sit up, trying not to feel anything, terrified that my next move would ignite the fire in my belly. My waste of magic likely meant that the next doulon would be no more successful than the last. And then my nivat supply would be gone. *Ass! Ignorant, blind, rock-headed ass!* I wanted to slam my head on the rocky ground. All the images I kept at bay descended on me at once: the pain-frenzied youth in the Palinur alley, thrashing in his own filth and vomit, the whore in Avenus whose eyes screamed when you touched her hot, rigid limbs, paralyzed with cramps and seizures. Better to slice my own throat than end like that.

"He stayed to watch, sire. He says he's not injured. We should tell him—" After a sharp gesture from her father, Elene bit off whatever else she wanted to say.

"I'll vow I believed you a charlatan, monk," said the thane. "That a nobody, a cowardly hireling bowman with no family of consequence and an arrow wound in his back, could interpret the book when better men could not seemed unrighteous and impossible. But it seems I erred."

I did not even bristle.

The thane crouched beside me, his oiled leather jaque gleaming in the lantern light, his hawkish bearded face flushed with zeal and thirsty with curiosity. "Sword of the archangel, I cannot comprehend what we just saw. I've never believed any of these legends. How did you do it? What key have we missed in this confounded book?"

"I don't know." Luck? Fate? How could anyone believe that I—a man of so little skill that I never had and never would accomplish a single thing of worth in my life, so blindly thick skulled that I could not untangle the meanings of the simplest markings on a page, and so weak of will that I had enslaved myself to the doulon—had done anything to summon such a being? "I did only what I've done before." Exactly nothing. I could not explain it.

Gram arrived shortly after the thane, moving slowly. The secretary was stretched tight. His black cloak and the sharp light on his deep-etched features made him look like death itself.

"We should get back to our blankets," said the thane when he spied Gram. "Foolish to stand here in the cold. Come on."

Before I could resist, Stearc grabbed my elbow and hauled me up as if I were no larger than Elene. No threads of fire shot through my limbs, demanding the doulon's solace. Thank the gods for that.

Stearc grunted an order at Elene, and father and daughter hurried off. Gram and I trailed behind as if drawn along in their wake.

"You removed the salt," I said.

Gram nodded as he muffled a bout of harsh coughing.

"I'm sorry."

"You were right," he said, and absently pushed damp hair from his face. It promptly fell down again. "It wouldn't have made any difference to bind her. She wasn't going to do what we asked in any case."

We found no more to say on the short walk down the hill.

A sullen Elene thrust a blanket into my arms when we reached their camp, and then retreated to a spot well away from us. Stearc removed his swordbelt and tossed it on the ground beside her. Her mouth tight, she rummaged in one of the saddle packs, set out stone, rag, and oil flask, and set to cleaning and polishing his long-sword. Her silence bulged and stretched near bursting.

They had pegged a canvas awning to the stone and supported it with three hinged poles and a tangle of rope. The ground underneath was damp but not soggy. Bundled in cloaks and blankets, Gram and I squatted beside the lantern, as if the weak yellow light might warm us.

The thane pulled out a wineskin, took a few swallows, and tossed it at Gram. "Now we know the nivat works, we should try again. Perhaps a different creature would be more accepting."

Gram took a long pull at the wineskin. "She is a sentinel," he said, rubbing his forehead tiredly. "One charged to watch the boundaries between human and Danae. She would most likely respond to any advance here. Her own sianou is probably somewhere nearby. But after hearing her, I believe that other Danae would reject us as well. Her dislike was not some private matter."

"But it was aimed directly at you." Elene made no attempt to mute her voice or her hostility. "Have you done something without telling the others?"

"Hold your tongue, squire, or be sent home. I warned you." Stearc jerked his head. "Go see that the horses have not pulled their tethers. Now."

Though Elene clenched her jaw in the very image of her father, she slammed the sword back into its sheath, jumped to her feet, and snatched up the lantern.

"Hear me, Corin." Gram rushed into the angry silence as the woman strode into the night. "The only betrayal I know of is Eodward's failure to abide by their terms and return to them. Perhaps they've come to think of that as stealing what 'belonged' to them. Their help. Their care. No theft is mentioned in the journal."

Their family quarrel could not hold my attention this night. The mention of King Eodward's name sparked in me like flint on steel. Eodward who was said to have lived with "angels" for a hundred and forty-seven years. Eodward who had asked a saucy-tongued man-at-arms to take a message—

"Aeginea." The word spilled from my lips.

"What's that, Brother?" Stearc and Gram said it together, as if they had forgotten I was there.

"When you spoke to the Dané, you mentioned a place called Aeginea. What is it?"

Though I addressed Gram, another bout of coughing rattled the secretary's chest. The answer came from Stearc instead. "Aeginea is the Danae's own name for the lands where their archon holds sway, where they celebrate the turning of the seasons and dance the pattern of the world they call the Canon. Though we don't see the name on any of Cartamandua's maps, we believe it exists both within and apart from our own land."

"It is Navronne," said Gram, hoarse from his cough. "The Heart of the World."

"And King Eodward . . . what does he have to do with all this?" I was half afraid to ask, sensing a tether of obligation reaching out from the past to bind my choices. Somehow doubly bitter after having seen a Dané.

"That is a very long story," said Stearc. He stretched out on the bare ground, wadded a blanket under his head, and pulled his cloak around him.

His hand moved out and touched the swordbelt, loosening his knife in its sheath. "Too long for tonight. We should sleep now."

I was as wakeful as if my wastrel drowsing up the hill had been a night's unbroken sleep. Even after the thane began snoring, my thoughts would not keep still.

Though Elene's departure with her lantern left us in the dark, I heard Gram rustling about in the packs, unstoppering a flask, drinking something that seemed to soothe his cough better than the wine had done. He must have sensed my wakefulness, as well, for he began to speak softly, as if not to wake his master.

"Almost seventy years ago, a young Janus de Cartamandua-Magistoria first found his way into Aeginea. I don't know how he accomplished it. Who truly understands pureblood sorcery? But while traveling there, he encountered a human man of some eighteen years. The Danae called the youth Caedmon-son, and said his father was a man they honored as a friend of the Danae and the one human who was ever true to his word. History tells us that Caedmon's four elder children were slain as the Aurellians drove through Morian and into Ardra. The Danae told Cartamandua that Caedmon had begged them to foster one remaining child—an infant son. The Danae archon, one named Stian, agreed to take in the child and a tutor sent by Caedmon to see to the boy's education.

"Writings and papers in the tutor's possession, as well as the tutor's testimony, corroborated the story. Though fascinated by Cartamandua and his tales of Navronne's struggles with the Aurellians and the Hansker, the young man had no interest in returning here. Life . . . time . . . runs differently in Aeginea. Though their seasons follow one upon the other at the same pace as ours, their days can seem like a year or an hour—much as a river spans only the distance from Elanus to Palinur, yet meanders faster and slower through straights and eddies on its way. And a human's life spends more slowly there—we calculate seven of our years to every one of theirs."

"Eodward," I said. Of a sudden, dry history took on new life and meaning. Like Stearc, I had never truly believed in the legend, only in the man. One hundred and forty-seven years would translate to one-and-twenty—the age of Eodward when he appeared from nowhere to reclaim Caedmon's throne. "How do you know all this?"

"Lord Stearc has come into possession of a journal relating to those days. Its accuracy is unimpeachable." Clothing rustled in the dark. Gram's hunched silhouette blocked out the stars in the clearing sky. "The Danae insisted Cartamandua swear to keep the secret of Eodward's existence."

"But he didn't." No one in my family would have kept such a secret. Not if the telling could enhance their prestige among the other purebloods.

"For a while, he did. But twenty-one years later, when all realized that Aurellia had become a fragile, decadent shell, Cartamandua told a friend about the young man—Caedmon's living heir. This friend, Sinduré Tobrecan, was the high priest of Kemen, and it happened that Tobrecan's closest boyhood friend Angnecy had just been anointed Hierarch of Ardra, the followers of the elder gods and those of Iero and divine Karus linked by this strange mechanism of fate. Seeing hope for the future in their own friendship and in the miracle of Eodward's life, they convinced Cartamandua to lead them to Aeginea, using his book of maps. There they beseeched Eodward, who had aged little in all that time, to return to Navronne and take up his rightful throne, lest chaos descend upon the kingdom with the fall of Aurellia. The Hansker longships were poised to attack and drive us into barbarism and savagery."

"And this time, he came," I said, wondering. "He was one-and-twenty."

"It was not an easy choice. Eodward loved and honored his Danae family, and considered himself one of them. His Danae mother guided his training, as is their custom, and he rode, danced, and hunted with his Danae father, brother, and sister. But from Cartamandua's first visit, Eodward had dreamed increasingly of Navronne—a land he lived in, but had never really experienced, for as you have noted, the Danae realms are our own realms. We but tread different paths. When Eodward decided to come here, he vowed to return to Aeginea before they danced the Winter Canon thrice more."

"But he didn't," I said, remembering the words he'd spoken to me on that long-ago battle's eve. *Tell them I don't think I'll get back . . .*

"He could not. He had children of his own and a thriving, glorious kingdom that needed him desperately. The Danae, still bitter at Cartamandua for breaking his vow, and unhappy with Eodward for his leaving, named Eodward's failure to return as betrayal, compounding their own long grievances with humans. After a time, the king began to age as humans do, yet he fully intended to return to Aeginea as soon as his children were strong enough to carry on his work. He died still believing the Danae would forgive him and that he could live out his days among them."

I shook my head. "He knew he would never go back," I said. "His children were never worthy to succeed him."

"Clearly not." Gram sighed and hunched his blanket around his shoulders. "And other things have happened in the years since that caused the Danae additional grievance—perhaps this violation and the thievery she spoke of—and they've forsaken all human contact. Now we need their help again, and I don't know how we're to get it."

"But you won't tell me why. It's this business of the lighthouse and the end times."

"I am but one player in a very large game. You should sleep now, Brother. Tomorrow we'll decide what to do next."

While Gram was speaking, quiet movements in the dark on the far side of the snoring Thane of Erasku told me Elene had returned. "Tell me about Corin," I said on a whim. "I sense a restless spirit there. Is he reliable? Trustworthy?"

"Reliable?" Gram laughed bitterly. "If the world could take shape from one will alone, then it would surely match young Corin's vision of how things ought to be. And it would be a world so just and fair . . . so glorious and compassionate . . . your Karish angels would choose to live here in Navronne instead of heaven. Do not doubt. Should every man of this cabal fail, Corin will carry it ahead alone come heaven or hell, victory or ruin."

I smiled as I pulled up my blankets, a moment's respite from a pervasive despondency. All through that long night, I heard restless movements from two pallets besides my own. Only the Thane of Erasku slept much that night.

"Unable to read while you are walking?" said a disbelieving Brother Sebastian.

I stood before him in the monks' parlor outside the dorter, damp, dirty, and exhausted, more from the night without sleep than the few quellae of the journey. After a predawn breakfast of cold cheese, Stearc had ordered Elene up to Fortress Groult to inform the edane that Brother Valen had wandered into their camp after getting lost in the rain and fog. Brother Adolfus returned with her, as it transpired that the poetry book was one that the abbey had already copied. That fact hardly surprised me. We had arrived at the abbey shortly before midday, and I prayed my mentor's annoyance would not forbid me dinner.

"After vowing to improve your attentiveness, you get yourself lost. And atop this foolery and despite all your promises of obedience, you refuse to honor your elder's wish to join him in your avowed duty of prayer along the route."

"I *am* sorry, Brother. The jarring of walking, especially with my limp, makes the words on the page run together. I'll strive to improve this weakness in the future as the Blessed Gillare heals this lingering mortification of my flesh." Even lies came hard today.

"Clean yourself and fetch your new spare gown and cowl from Brother Tailor," said Brother Sebastian. "Report to Brother Jerome for the rest of the afternoon. After Vespers we shall sit down and work out your reading syllabus and examination schedule for the next month. We must pay more rigorous attention to your studies and deportment."

I bowed and thanked him, dreading the unhappy exposure sure to come very soon now. I would suffer yelling, admonitions, and penances until my hair turned white. But at least I had achieved one of my aims. Luviar would surely not dismiss me after my unlikely successes with the book of maps, whether I could read or not. Somehow, even that small accomplishment could not cheer me. The world felt old. Broken.

Of course, Brother Jerome would be out of sorts that afternoon. He complained of having only barley vinegar to use for his pickling, as the grape harvest had failed, and that salt had grown so dear he had to be a pinchfist with it just when he needed it most. Brother Sebastian must have sent word of my transgressions. Instead of allowing me to sit in the warm kitchen and chop turnips or carrots to go into his crocks of vinegar and salt, Brother Refectorian had sent me to the cold, stinking butcher house to bleed and strip a pig.

As I wrestled the massive carcass in a vat of steaming water to scrub off its hair and buried my hands in its stomach cavity to sever and draw out its entrails, I imagined the scene in the guesthouse. Stearc, Gram, and Elene were likely head to nose with the abbot, the chancellor, and Brother Gildas—probably Jullian, as well—all of them bathed, dry, and drinking hot cider, talking of magical libraries, beings of legend, and the end of the world, while I was rendering a sow.

Sullen and resentful, I sorted all the nasty bits. White, lacy caul fat into the bowl for present use. Bung and rectum onto the waste heap. Emptied guts, destined to hold Brother Jerome's fine sausage, into the brine crock along with the emptied bladder and stomach. My new spare gown was clean no longer, and my sandals and feet were splashed with blood and filth. Brother Sebastian would have no mercy.

The heart and liver had just gone into a bowl for the kitchen, and my sore hands had just plunged another length of gut into the cold running water of the butcher house conduit to scrape it clean, when I glimpsed a brick-red cloak in the vicinity of Brother Butcher. The two of them stood outside the doorway of the wooden building. Though my hands were freezing, my face grew hot enough to cook the damnable pig. Was I to be forever splattered, filthy, or slug-witted in front of Elene? Bad enough that half my skull was bald and I stank worse than Jullian.

"Brother Valen!" Brother Butcher, a lay brother with a neck as wide as his head, also possessed a bellow worthy of his victims. "The squire says you're summoned to the abbot."

Blessed release! "Of course, Brother. I'll stop off at the lavatorium to wash, and then—"

"Not so, Brother Novice. Brother Sebastian has sent out word to all that you're to hop to your duties with no dawdling or digression. They wouldn't have sent for you *now* did they want you to come *later*. So be off with you. I'll take on your pig."

Sighing, I dropped the gut back into the crock, plunged my arms into the conduit flow, and scrubbed at them with my numb fingers. After a handful of icy water to my face and a swipe with the only clean spot on my gown, I hurried through the butcher house, and bowed to the thick-necked lay brother. Though wet and freezing from fingertip to armpit, blood and offal still grimed nails and pores and the cracks in my skin. I grabbed my cowl from the hook by the door and threw it on.

Elene's hood covered her hair, and she did not speak as she marched away. Brother Butcher watched from the doorway as I followed meekly after her.

"Good day, Squire Corin," I whispered from under my own hood as we hurried past sheep pens and pig wallows. "I certainly hope your return to Gillarine was more fragrant than mine."

"The abbot is always welcoming, though we don't come here for the hospitality." Her tone smacked far too much of serious affairs.

"Well, of course, you don't. Though I don't see that purposeful misery will solve any of the world's problems, either. Which leads me to ask . . ."

She tripped briskly up the steps that crossed the low wall that divided the abbey's outer and inner courts, and rather than take the eight steps down, she jumped straight to the ground, as nimble as a cat. I jumped as well, which left me feeling something like a mast with billowing sails, as my gown caught the air. My thigh did not even twinge when I landed.

I paused for a moment and watched her walk ahead toward the lay brothers' yard and the brewhouse, the sight of her an antidote to my dogging melancholy. She moved like a dancer or a juggler, not frail or bony, but well muscled, her back as solid and well formed as her front. A most pleasing view, though truly it seemed very odd to have the luxury of examining a woman in breeches and jupon while I traipsed behind her in skirts.

She peered over her shoulder. Best get my mind back to business. We would soon be in the inner precincts where even quiet conversation could be noticed and overheard. Two full strides and I caught up with her.

"... which leads me to ask, Is someone ever going to tell me what is coming, so I can decide whether to keep watch upward to see the bolt of fire from heaven or downward to see the ground open underneath me? Will the world end in fire or ice, Squire Corin? Though I have my own guess as to that." I shivered as the damp wind blew off the river, smelling of dead fish.

She slowed just a bit. "I told them they ought to be honest with you. But my father won't hear of it, because—"

"—because he heard I had an arrow wound in the back. He despises me as a coward, and thus believes me incapable of keeping secrets."

"For Abbot Luviar to be dismissed for sheltering a deserter would be disastrous to our cause. But you've proven yourself, so you deserve to hear the truth." She planted herself in front of me, hands on her hips. "The earth itself will not end, only the life we know—cities and towns and villages, plowing and planting. Herds are dying. Famine and disease will bring barbarians, not just Hansker, who will surely come first, but wilder folk from the north and west. Yet they, too, will lose all they have. Summer will vanish, and, in the struggle to survive, men will forget books and tools and art and all the things we've learned in centuries. The Harrowers will get what they want. We will see the end times, but with no blessed ending in heaven."

She believed this quite sincerely. I could tease no further. "How do you know? How do *they* know? Yes, the weather is foul, the war cruel, sickness rampant, yet we survive. Navronne has suffered before. Nobles are always underestimating the strength of common folk. What's different this time?"

"Where are the monks, Brother? Where are the students who once came to Gillarine for schooling—fifty in my father's time, with more hoping to come? How many villages lie ruined like those between here and Caedmon's

Bridge? Where are the grapes of Ardra or the summer fruits of the river country or Evanore's wild boar that sustained my ancestors when the Aurellians forced them to live in caves like beasts? People abandon faith and paint their foreheads with dung. We don't know why our downfall will happen. Everyone has a theory. Brother Victor thinks our present cycle of history just happens to be worse than similar ones of the past. Abbot Luviar believes that some dread event has caused a rip in the binding of earth and heaven. But those of the cabal are men and women of intelligence, wisdom, and a vision that is broader than one abbey or one kingdom or one faith. Besides, it has all been seen by a friend of my father's. Now, come. They're waiting for you."

"Thank you for telling me," I said, as I caught up to her. "I won't betray you—any of you. I'm actually quite proficient at keeping secrets."

She didn't respond. As I considered all she'd told me, one word rose from her tale like a youthful blotch on a girl's clear skin.

"Elene . . ."

She picked up the pace through the passage between the granary and the brewhouse, where the cloying smell of roasting barley was so thick it could choke a man.

"Corin . . ."

We strode across the guesthouse yard where I had first glimpsed her face. An exposed place. Three men in green livery approached the guesthouse from the direction of the stables. Anyone could pop out of the door or the five different passages that opened on the yard or could peer out of the myriad windows of the house.

But the blemish had swelled into a boil, and despite the risk of being overheard, I laid a hand on Elene's shoulder as she grasped the brass door handle. "*Seen* . . . you mean *foreseen,* as by a pureblood diviner?"

She dragged the heavy door open and slipped out from under my hand before she answered, else I might not have barged into the columned atrium after her in full view of the group in the guesthouse parlor. By the time she said, "Yes," it was too late.

As Brother Victor passed around a tray of steaming cups, and Gram worked at a writing table, a short, robust woman robed in mauve and blue silk stood talking with Abbot Luviar, Brother Gildas, and Thane Stearc. Her heavy black hair had been twisted and wound into a great loop, fixed to the back of her head with a gold fan, spread like a peacock's tail. The blue, green, and gold sprawl of interlocking beads on her ample breast proclaimed her a

Sinduria—a high priestess of the elder gods. The thick stripes of kohl outlining her eyes and the eyes graven on her silver bracelets, set with pupils of opal and lapis, proclaimed her a pureblood diviner. And her shock when she saw me, quickly followed by amusement, quickly followed by triumph and contempt, proclaimed her my elder sister.

She raised her finger and pointed through the parlor doorway straight at me.

"Oh, Deunor's fire, Lassa, don't. Please don't." My voice echoed like frogs rasping in the fine antechamber.

But she was a Cartamandua, and so did my twelve years of freedom end with her one contemptuous word. "*Recondeur.*"

Chapter 19

"**M**agnus Valentia de Cartamandua-Celestine . . . a Karish monk. What divination could have prepared me for this?" Thalassa's laughter left her breathless. "Have you been driven out of every other house in Navronne in only twelve years, little brother? Or have you conquered every woman's heart with your everlasting charm, so that the only ones left to share your bed are celibate old men and guileless boys? Do these monks know what you are?"

The others had come out of the parlor and now stood in an awkward half circle ten paces from me, gawking.

"I have lived a life of my own choosing," I said, closing my eyes so I could no longer see Elene, clapping a hand to her mouth, or Brother Victor, his odd features so eloquent in condemnation, or Gram, peering at me curiously, as if I were something not quite human. "I have bound myself where I would and walked away when I would—"

"—and great rewards it has brought you. I can see and smell. But I'll not believe you are here because you have chosen a life of purity and service. Even this corrupt and failing world has not changed so much. I'd advise you to check your valuables, Luviar. And look to your daughter, Lord Stearc. Valen bedded every serving girl and lad in Palinur before he was fifteen. Evidently he can breathe on a woman and set her fawning—maybe men, too. We were never able to *prove* he does it with magic."

Thalassa had ever been adept at making her point. Sorcerous seduction was one of the few crimes for which a pureblood could be arrested. As with everything forbidden, I'd tried it. But I left it behind when I learned of pleasuring.

"I knew it," said Stearc, growling. "By rock and stone, a pureblood renegade . . . he endangers us all with every breath. We should kill him——"

"My lord!" said Abbot Luviar, moving slightly to the front of them all, his pock-grooved face unsettlingly flushed. "We do not speak of murder in Iero's house! Whatever his status in the secular world, Brother Valen is a vowed novice of Saint Ophir, my responsibility and my charge."

"Father Abbot," said Brother Victor, "the law is clear. If we do not turn him over and even the remotest hint of his status as *recondeur* becomes known, the consequences could ruin us. We don't know if the lighthouse can survive the destruction of the abbey. Whatever else, *you* and *Gillarine* will be lost to our cause, and the stocking of the lighthouse will surely come to a halt. With the royal succession near settled, our position is precarious enough. Yet, if we give him up, he knows enough to bring us to ruin."

Brother Victor's emotionless logic was far more terrifying than Stearc's outburst. But then again, naught should terrify a dead man, and I *was* dead, no matter whether or not these people allowed me to keep breathing.

"The hierarch will welcome his information about our plans and use it. The lighthouse is compromised, as are the identities of those in this room——"

"Of course," I said. My skin burned. My soul burned. "Because I refuse to live as a slave to my family and the Pureblood Registry—allowing them to tell me whom I may speak to, what profession I must follow, whom I will marry, and what children I will or will not breed, allowing them to sell my life to the highest bidder—then I must necessarily be untrustworthy."

"It is not merely your refusal to submit, Valen," said Thalassa. "It is that your refusal to submit is the key to your nature—wholly and entirely a servant of your own pleasure. I would not trust you with my dog lest you have discovered some amusement in tormenting dogs. I cannot and will not stand idle and allow you to escape the consequences of a lifetime's self-indulgence."

"You know *nothing* of my life," I said.

She broke from the circle and walked slightly behind me, so that I would have to turn away from the others in order to face her. I refused to turn, though I felt her examination taking in my filthy habit and offal-stained feet and the sweating, blood-grimed hands I clenched at my back.

Every bone and sinew demanded I run. But I was not so naive as I had been at eight, when Thalassa had taunted me into my first break for freedom, only to stand smirking as my father hauled me home by my hair. The liveried

men outside would be Thalassa's escort—pureblood warriors with magically tuned senses. She could summon them with a thought.

"You even foul your monk's costume, Valen," she said.

I held my tongue and my position, trapping the familiar hatred inside
until my skin stretched with the size of it.

After a moment, she drifted back toward her fellows. Only thirty, she
moved with the imperious gravity of a lifelong queen. Though her temple position left her exempt from the mask and cloak required of purebloods when
mingling with ordinaries, her gown and jewels certainly met the Registry stan-
dards of conservative elegance. A Sinduri high priestess, one of the five highest-
ranking servants of the elder gods. Our father must be preening.

"Abbot Luviar, I must and will report my brother to the Registry. Our
family has endured twelve years of disgrace that will be relieved only when
he is returned to our discipline. I am, as ever, wholly committed to our task,
but we must find other means to accomplish our goals. Valen is mentally
unstable and entirely untrustworthy, and I'll vow that any help he has given
you has been purest chicanery. You needn't fear for our secrets. I've ways to
ensure his silence before he is remanded into Registry custody."

And *that* chilled me to the marrow. The Sinduri were known to have
potions, spells to alter the mind. My bravado crumbled in an instant. "Holy
father, please, don't let her—"

Luviar's hand stopped my begging before I completely abased myself.
"Sinduria, Lord Stearc, friends and brothers, before we undertake some
drastic course, we must proceed with our conclave. Rightly or wrongly, I
took it upon myself to bring Valen into our circle. And despite his regrettable
lack of . . . candor . . . he has been of great assistance. We cannot separate
our needs and his abilities from his fate. So let us sit and consider both issues
together."

The abbot swept through the door and into the parlor, Brother Victor on
his heels. A seething Thalassa followed. Lord Stearc waved Gram and Elene
into the room ahead of him. He himself remained near the door, as if prepared to rush back through and prevent my escape. Only Gildas was left
with me.

He shook his head and grinned. "I thought I had guessed your secrets,
Brother, but I will say you have confounded me. A pureblood sorcerer. And
Janus de Cartamandua's grandson on top of it. I shall surely wake up tomor-
row living on the moon."

He took my arm, and we strolled across the atrium as if going into supper in a nobleman's hall. As we stepped onto the plum-colored carpet of the parlor, he leaned close and whispered, "Be patient, friend. We'll not abandon you."

"I'm sorry," I whispered, bolstered by his friendship. "I needed a refuge. I never intended—" But, of course, intention had naught to do with anything. I had knowingly put them at risk. Only now did the callousness of that choice hit home.

Six straight-backed chairs formed a circle next the hearth. Gildas joined the abbot, Brother Victor, Stearc, and Thalassa, who were already in place. Luviar waved me to the last unoccupied chair of the inner circle, between Gildas and Brother Victor. Gram humbly pulled up a stool just behind Thane Stearc. Elene, a proper squire, remained standing beside the door to the atrium, her hands clasped at her back, eyes straight ahead, her face a mask.

"I cannot credit that you would admit Valen to our deliberations, Luviar," said my sister, her bead collar clicking as she shifted in her seat. "He should be confined. He *will* try to run away. It is his lifelong habit. The sooner I blind his knowledge of our secrets the better."

"I appreciate your sentiments, lady," said Luviar. "Yet the tale of our experiments with your grandfather's book might give you a new perspective. Of course, we must evaluate Brother Valen's contributions differently in the light of this new information about his lineage. Gram, would you please report on the events of these past few days?"

The secretary stood, bowed respectfully to the abbot, Lord Stearc, and Thalassa, and began a detailed, well-structured, and as far as he was capable, accurate account of our search for the pool known as Clyste's Well. Nauseated, my throat parched, I slumped in my chair as he recited. The knowledge that Thalassa's accusations were substantially true did not improve my disposition in the least. The room felt unbearably hot. I wished I dared throw off my cowl or open a window.

Gram paused his recitation to ask Brother Gildas to confirm our discovery of the Well. Brother Gildas stated soberly that to his fullest belief, the pool was the one for which they had been searching. ". . .though I saw no evidence of a Dané guardian there."

Before the secretary could move on to the tale of the tree and the encounter with the Dané, Thalassa leaned forward. Her painted eyes, already larger than life, widened into great dark windows. "So you believe that *Va-*

len read our grandfather's book of maps, recited the guide spell under his breath, and led you unerringly to a Dané sianou?"

The abbot looked puzzled. "Yes."

"Go on. Tell me the rest." Rouged mouth fixed in judgment, she folded her arms and sat back, biding her time, poised like a cat on the brink of a grand leap.

I closed my eyes and sank lower in the chair. I tried to bury my head in my hands, but I could not bear the stink and had to stuff my hands up my sleeves instead. My sister was going to tell them I could not read. Then she would relate how I had made an art form of lies since I was out of the crèche, how I had preferred to steal what I wanted rather than be given the very same thing by people I loathed, how I had destroyed everything of value I had ever touched, that I had spent three-quarters of my life from age five through fifteen besotted with drink, and had broken every rule of civilized society as if it were my sworn duty.

The wretched part was that, once she had told them those truths, they would believe everything she said of me, true or not. I hated that thought more than I had hated anything in a very long while. I hated what I had seen on Elene's face. On Brother Victor's. On Gram's. At least I'd not had to witness Jullian's reaction. *Recondeur*—traitor to family, king, and gods, one who spits on the power to work magic, the greatest gift given to humankind. And the boy already thought he knew the worst of me.

I pondered how I could possibly wrest some shred of dignity from this day. Stripping a pig now sounded like an afternoon's delight. Meanwhile, Gram took up the story from our meeting on the hillside below Fortress Groult, ending with the Dané vanishing into the night.

"You actually saw one of them . . . spoke to a Dané?" For the first time, Thalassa's attention was diverted from scorn and anger, her expression open in sincere astonishment.

"*She* spoke to *us* is more like it," said Stearc. "She certainly did not listen . . ." He assessed the encounter as he had before—wondrous, but accomplishing nothing of substance.

"Have you anything to add, Brother Valen?" asked the abbot, startling me out of my gloom. "Anything that you observed that Gram has left out? Lord Stearc says you seemed . . . caught up . . . in the incident. And we need to know exactly what you did to invoke the power of the map on both occasions. Did you bring some pureblood sorcery to bear beyond that held in the book?"

They were all staring at me again. Luviar's inquiry had reminded Thalassa of her day's pleasure—righteous duty and personal entertainment entwined. She was near bursting, her heavy loop of hair quivering, her full red lips ready to spew condemnation for years of my petty insults and my not-so-petty offenses against her and the rest of our kin.

Well, nothing for it. I sat up straight.

"I was indeed overcome with the sight of the Dané," I said, feeling lingering echoes of my strange grief even as I spoke of it at such a distance. If I was to attempt honesty for a change, I could not ignore the experience. "I've seen naught in all my life . . . in all my travels . . . in all my dreams . . . so fearsome and, at the same time, so marvelous. I felt this . . . immeasurable grace . . . that they yet live. Someone once told me that the Danae were the living finger of the god in this world. Perhaps that's what I felt . . . that I was unworthy to see such a wonder."

Though I had begun my confession hoping to garner sympathy—any advantage that might help mitigate a dismal future—somehow I had wandered very close to emotions I had never thought to share with anyone, especially one of my family. Profoundly unsettled, I continued. "I cannot tell you how I found the correct place to leave the nivat or even how I was able to locate the Well, except that it was some odd mixture of luck and ordinary experience at finding my way about the world and, yes, inherited talents. But it is impossible that I invoked the power of the maps."

Puzzlement and disbelief had them shifting in their chairs, but I allowed no interruption. If I dared so much as look at them, I'd never go through with this.

"As my sister is yearning to reveal, I am afflicted with a disorder of the mind, a blindness that leaves me incapable of deciphering written words. At a more appropriate time and place, I will beg forgiveness for this and all my deceptions, holy father and good brothers, hoping that you will understand my fear in the face of your great kindness when I came here wounded and desperate. My experience of family is difficult—the details best left unspoken—but I assure you that I professed my vows with sincerity, if not . . . without reservation. As to how my disorder affects my use of my grandfather's book—*my* book, as it happens, not my family's, as he gave it to me on my seventh birthday—it means I cannot read place-names or written spells, and so must rely on my instincts, inborn talents, my knowledge of maps, and my spellmaking skill to interpret the drawings."

I resisted the urge to add more. No need to humiliate myself further. If I was to be shipped off to Palinur to the gentle discipline of my family and the Pureblood Registry, I would get my fill of humiliation.

Stearc mumbled oaths. Brother Gildas masked a grin with curled fingers. Gram looked thoughtful and, for once, did not drop his eyes when they met mine. Unfortunately he was too far away for me to read anything in them—not that I was likely to see anything at all rewarding. Elene remained in the doorway, but now her back was to me. Probably for the best.

"Do *not* allow him to get away with this," said Thalassa, tight as a moneylender's fist. "Were Valen standing at Mother Samele's right hand and suggesting I ascend her holy mount, I would not move one step forward, lest I fall into Magrog's pit. He is a consummate liar—"

"Sinduria, if you please." Gram's quiet insistence drew their attention away from me, for which I was grateful. "Lady, the last time we spoke of Janus de Cartamandua, you indicated that he was very ill. Does he yet live?"

Not shifting her glare one quat, Thalassa jerked her head in the affirmative.

"Impossible!" The old man had been half in his grave before I'd run away—past seventy years old and addled beyond use. And gods knew I'd wished him dead often enough before and since. How could he not be dead?

"Brother Valen, did your grandfather know of your difficulty with reading?" Gram pursued whatever mad line of reasoning he had begun without altering his tone.

"Everyone in the house knew of his willful ignorance," Thalassa snapped before I recovered wit enough to answer. "Valen's only *disorder* is his despicable, intransigent soul. Surely you cannot swallow this playacting?"

"Please, Sinduria, hear me out." Gram raised his hand but not his voice. "The causes of your brother's condition are not relevant here. Only whether Janus de Cartamandua knew of the problem, which you have confirmed that he did. So, Brother Valen, your grandfather gave you the book on your birthday. Do you believe that he intended you to use it? Or was his intent merely to give you something of value to cherish or to sell?"

"To *cherish*? Hardly. Every time Capatronn—my grandfather Janus—returned to that house, he tried to teach me of the book. I hated it. I hated him. I did everything I could think of to be free of his lessons. But he insisted, saying that I must use the book to follow in his footsteps, and that our family would come to be the most powerful in the world. He was crazed with the idea and made me swear over and over, on holy writs, on shrines, on my life, and always, always with my blood, that I would use the book when I was old enough. When I was 'free to do as I pleased,' he put it. He stank——"

Gods, I could still smell his sour body, the stench of urine and ale and his rotting teeth when I saw him last. And I could see him on so many occasions before that, his black eyes bulging as he made me prick my finger yet again and slap the aingerou that supported the mantel over his hearth, leaving a bloody smear.

I reined in my disgust. "He was . . . is . . . mad. It was unpleasant."

Gram nodded as if I had just given a recitation of the great vices and virtues or an accounting of the abbey grain stores. "So I would guess that reading is not essential to your use of the book. That would explain your success. And if you, as a . . . an ill-mannered, rebellious boy . . . refused your grandfather's tutelage, that would explain your uncertainty as to how that success was accomplished."

A nice hypothesis, but I didn't see what difference it made. If I didn't know what I had done, then I could scarcely repeat my "success." But the gaunt secretary had tangled the others in his thread of reasoning. When he leaned forward on his stool, scarcely visible around his lord's thick shoulder, they leaned forward to listen.

"Two matters require we consult the Danae. We must discover if they can shed light on this upheaval in the natural world, and we must present our request with regard to the Scholar. My Lord Stearc sees no hope in further approaches through the Danae sentinels. Danae have ever distrusted humans, and now, it seems, they despise us. Which means we must travel farther into Aeginea and directly approach those among the long-lived who might yet retain some fondness for Eodward. Stian and Kol are our only hope to be heard."

Brother Victor had been rubbing his lip thoughtfully as Gram spoke. Now he dropped his hand to his lap and crinkled his brow even more. "Rightly spoken, Gram, yet the Dané's reference to thievery and violation is worrisome—clearly obstacles in our path, though we've no idea what they mean."

Good to hear of crimes they could not lay at my feet; I had never stolen from the Danae. Though the consideration of how close I'd come to stealing the offering of nivat gave me a sudden shiver. The damnable, cursed doulon.

The chancellor turned to Thalassa. "Lady, have you had any success in learning more of the Danae's withdrawal from human intercourse?"

"No. The old man is confined to his room and speaks nothing of sense to anyone."

"You have mentioned in the past that his ramblings include frequent references to . . . a person you cared not to name. Is it possible . . . ?" Brother Victor was surely a master of diplomacy. His gaze flicked to me, and my sister did not whisk his head off with some priestess's spell.

"Yes," she said, twisting her mouth in distaste. "Valen was ever his favorite. No one could understand it. When he gave that vile, undisciplined child the last extant copy of the most precious book in the world, our parents—"

Thank all gods, she stopped, perhaps realizing that the seamier aspects of the Cartamandua-Celestine household were perhaps not the proper topic for a serious group of monks and lords come to discuss the end of the world. I had arrived at the same conclusion in my own rant.

Gram was standing now, his sober tunic hanging loose on his thin body. "Abbot Luviar, it seems to me that the god has brought us at least a slim hope of answers," he said. Bathed in the smoky light from the tall windows at his back, less stooped, he took on a certain dignity. "Brother Victor is correct. Before we can approach the Danae, we must understand these grievances that have caused them to retreat from human contact. And we must learn how to use the maps to travel in Aeginea beyond the sentinels, for that is where we'll find Stian and Kol if they yet live. Gildas has found no way to move past the Well, yet we know that Eodward visited the Well and walked as far as the 'valley beyond it to the east,' implying that he traveled from the west as from the abbey. So we are clearly missing something. As Brother Valen is the only person who has taken us even so far as this, I believe he holds the key both to these answers and to our interaction with the Danae."

"Pssh!" Stearc regarded me with a look appropriate to rotting meat. "How do you propose for him to discover these answers that even you have failed to unlock? The man cannot even read his own book of maps. I say the danger a *recondeur* poses far outweighs any service he can offer."

I stopped listening. Were they ever going to ask my opinion? Such an odd group of people. The enigmatic abbot. Brother Victor, whose unflappable, relentless reason was more unnerving than Stearc's contempt. The Evanori warlord, himself a cipher—a scholar and warrior, a man who treated his secretary with a remarkably even hand while bullying his own daughter. Stearc seemed genuinely caught up in this mad venture. Worried. They were all worried, even Thalassa. It was easy to imagine my sister had come here solely to bait me, but she was a member of this group. *Intelligence, wisdom, and a vision that is broader than one abbey or one kingdom or one faith*, so Elene had said, referring, among others, to a member of my family. Truly a wonder of wonders.

". . . see your reasoning. You think to have him question his grandfather." Brother Victor's quiet conclusion stung me awake like a stealthy wasp, as if Brother Infirmarian's lancet pricked a mortified wound.

"No!" I yelled, on my feet before his last word had faded. Pain and hatred and crippling memory exploded from that incision like pus and septic blood. "You cannot force me to do that! I have naught to say to any of them. The old man is mad. You heard her say it. I won't."

"Brother Valen . . ." Several of them said it. They were all standing now.

"I cannot," I said, fighting to hold back the onslaught of the past. "You don't understand. Tell them, Thalassa. Tell them what happened every time Capatronn left to go adventuring." The only person my father loathed more than me was Janus de Cartamandua, but pureblood discipline forbade him touching his own father.

I was already halfway to the door . . . shaking . . . furious . . . when I realized I had nowhere to go. Turning my back on them, I retreated toward the window, where I clutched the iron frame and stared into the yard. I tried to recapture my wonder at what I had seen at Caedmon's Bridge—a living magic in the universe. Such a sight should leave all other events trivial. But all I could see, all I could feel, all I could hear were my grandfather's conspiratorial whispers and his robust chortling as he rode away on his great horse, leaving me alone to face my father's strap. Even my hatred for the man who beat me until my bowels released and confined me hungry and bleeding in my spell-darkened room could not match my hatred for the man who kept promising to set me free of it and never did. I had sworn I would never look at my grandfather again. Never speak to him. Never listen to him. He should be dead.

"Destroy my mind with Sinduri magic if you wish," I said through gritted teeth. "Send me back to pureblood slavery if you wish, or throw me in the river with a stone hung round my throat. But do not ask me to sit in a room and have a civilized conversation with my grandfather."

I did not hear their hasty deliberations as I pressed my forehead against the cold glass, raging and swearing—at myself more than anyone else. What use to be so angry over past misery? I had set myself free of that house, and if

I had found only fleeting enjoyments and unsavory habits to soothe my restless nature, well then that was unfortunate. But at least I had made my own choices, whether to tan hides or steal a dagger or soldier for a king, whether to bed a woman or winter in an abbey or expend my magic on the doulon. At least I had lived.

When Brother Gildas broke away from Abbot Luviar, took my arm, and led me from the guesthouse and into the garden, I did not speak to him. I would waste no words on them ever again. I would lift not one finger to conspire in their madness.

The evening was still, a pale silver sheen of flagging sunlight behind wads of gray wool clouds. For once, the only storm raged inside me. Back in the guesthouse Thalassa was surely recounting the wicked tales I had so cleverly diverted earlier. Even worse, she could be telling them the whole sordid story of my childhood. Gods, how I hated the thought of that. But I would not waste any more time trying to explain.

Gildas held silent as we strode between the hedges, past the scummy pond, past the statue of Karus and uncountable images of saints put there as reminders of how we ought to live. I soon realized the monk was not leading me anywhere in particular. Only walking. Thalassa's two guards followed at a discreet distance, ready to pounce should I breathe wrong.

Rabbits sat paralyzed in the center of the path as we approached, darting out of our way just before we stepped on them. Two magpies screeched at us and then at each other and at the squirrels chasing through the hedges. Thunder rumbled from beyond the mountains.

I stared numbly at the path, my steps gradually losing their initial frantic pace. Eventually the bells for Vespers rang, and as the last tones drifted into silence and birdsong, my most acute fury seeped away. Still, Gildas waited.

"Don't you need to be back at the guesthouse deciding what to do with me?" I said at last. "I'm not going to run off—not with those two brawny goslings prancing after me as if I were their dame. They'd have no second thoughts about violating the cloisters to chase me down, if that's what concerns you."

"I belong with the cabalists little more than you," said Gildas. "I've been involved with them only three years. I help where I can, but my primary role is different from that of the others. They've not even told me how to open the lighthouse as yet. Only Victor, Luviar, and Stearc know that."

"They're all mad. Gods . . . Books and plows and Danae. Monks and princes, warlords and my sister the high priestess. An abbot who plays them all like strings on a vielle."

"The ever-sensible Gram has not told you the connection between all these things?"

"It makes no difference. I'll not dance to their music no matter what." I shook my head. "And they're not likely to tell me any more now, are they? Just more of my mind for my sister to obliterate lest I spew my guts to the hierarch and betray you all."

We strolled through the hedge maze, a flock of sparrows twittering as they pecked at the worms the week's rains had washed onto the path. Plainsong wafted faintly from the church, the pure melody twining itself around my anger, soothing my aching head.

"You must confess you are an enigma. What are they to think of you—a pureblood who throws away his position . . . his magic . . . to chop vegetables in a monastery? A man who could vie for power with princes, yet who has not bothered to learn to read?"

"Tell me of *your* vocation, Gildas," I snapped. "Was it your mother's prayers brought you here? *My* mother used predictions of my tormented demise to amuse her friends."

"You don't want to hear of my mother. She forbade us to eat berries on the last day of the week, for all know that the seeds would sprout vines in our bellies to grow out our ears if swallowed on Samele's day. My mother believed that if she left a trail of blood between her door and the town well, a gatzé would come and grant her three wishes. Every child in Pontia would follow her to the well each day, taunting, asking what was her wish. She died with her veins flat from bleeding them. She— Well, you are not the only man with difficult family." He barked a laugh.

I stopped in midstride. Harsh, lonely . . . of a sudden Gildas reminded me of a Pyrrhan exile I'd once met. Pyrrhans believed the world beyond their land's borders existed only in their imaginations, and thus every day spent outside Pyrrha felt askew—outside of time, in the wrong place. A blessed grace that Gildas had found a place he valued so deeply as Gillarine. "Ah, fires of heaven, Gildas . . . I'm sorry."

Flushed from chin to the crown of his shaven head, he averted his face and nudged me forward again. "You'd no way to know, unless thought reading is a Cartamandua bent."

"I've always imagined you at the very least some noble's younger son, done out of inheritance by an elder brother or sister and sent off here unwilling. Perhaps even our rumored Pretender."

His smile tightened. "Not in the remotest instance. My family had nothing. Certainly nothing I wanted. They were not . . . scholarly . . . and my mind hungered for more stimulation than stitching leather to fit other men's feet. Pride of intellect led me astray for many years—until I began to look beyond the material world for answers. Humility is a difficult lesson."

No one had ever shared such a clean and honest piece of himself with me, especially on so private a matter. In my first days at the abbey he had offered me his friendship, and caution had made me refuse him. Too late now. I regretted that as much as any consequence of this wretched day. "At least you've a mind for lessons. Some skulls are too thick."

He grinned and shook his head. "Come now, we have no time to recount our mournful pasts. You need to decide what to do next. Right now they're debating whether to send you to Palinur as a novice of Saint Ophir, as Abbot Luviar wishes, or as a recaptured *recondeur* in the high priestess's custody." He cocked his head in inquiry. "Truly you have a right to know why the abbot wants to keep you on his leash. Shall I tell you?"

"Do as you like."

"Gram could recite it better, I suppose, with his tallyman's mind. But here's what I know . . . Twenty years ago, Brother Victor and Brother Luviar, scholars and visionaries of extraordinary perceptions, came to believe that certain changes they saw in the world were serious enough that they needed to prepare. Their studies and calculations intimated that some twenty-five or thirty years might pass from the depth of crisis until men and women were ready to hear again of books and plows. They recruited a few people to help them build the lighthouse to survive the worst. Being of middle years themselves, they decided they needed a younger man to stand with the lighthouse, a Scholar who knew both the content of the books and how to use the tools they had chosen to preserve. Even in so short a span, much knowledge could be lost. If those who know how to warp a loom are dead, who will prevent others from burning the loom to stay warm?"

I said nothing. I preferred to forget these people and their plotting. They needed no vagabond jackleg to help them.

My lack of response did not deter Gildas. "And what if we were to lose all those who can read? City dwellers are most susceptible to plague. To ravagers. If the cities die, if learning dies, we are sent back to the land, to nights in the wild forest with spirits we can no longer tame with words, to awe of these Gehoum—the Powers who make the sky grow light or dark, whose righteous wrath is fire and storm . . ." His words trailed off.

An icy breath traced my spine, very like the night Sila Diaglou plunged her stake into a bleeding Boreas. I shuddered. "If I didn't know better, I'd say *you* were the diviner in this cabal," I said.

He laughed away the mystical fog that had settled over him like the haze cloaking the river in the night. "I've no magic. I only read the sayings of diviners and heed them." He waved for me to keep walking as he talked. "Luviar and Brother Victor chose one of their finest and most versatile students at Gillarine's school to be their Scholar, a young warlord of Evanore."

"Not Stearc!" I said, not believing it even as I said it.

Gildas nodded, tucked his hands up his sleeves, and rounded a corner between the straggling yews. "Stearc applied himself to read every volume as they stored it away and to learn the working of every tool. But when blight hit the vineyards, and King Eodward had still not named a successor, Luviar and Victor began to believe that the dark time could last longer and lie deeper than they'd thought. The lack of a strong and righteous king makes the coming decline far more severe, you see. Stearc agreed that they needed to prepare someone younger to become the Scholar."

I halted again and stared at his hairless skull and well-hewn face, at the clear, unmarked skin, at the brown eyes never lacking in irony, tucked under the line of his dark brow. "You."

No wonder he forever smelled of sheep or smithing or yeast and barley. No wonder he was forever reading. He was the one chosen to survive and remember and, when the time was right, teach. The keeper of the lighthouse. The memory of a bed crammed up against stacked barrels aroused a dreadful understanding.

"Great holy Iero, they're going to shut you in there, aren't they? Seal you in the lighthouse. So you'll survive the worst. Alone . . . for years . . . alone . . ."

"That was the original intent. Don't look so horrified! I thrive on solitude and silence. It is the only peace we're given in this world. And consider, I would have infinite occupation and no interruptions. However, a few months ago, we received new information that threw our whole plan into doubt."

He moved on. I followed, unable to ignore the story. A rabbit sat chewing in the middle of an intersecting path, scampering away only when we were close enough to step on it.

"Stearc brought your sister into the cabal. He knew and respected her from other dealings with the Sinduri. She worked a grand divination, a whole day of incantations, burning herbs, and magical water basins, a marvel such as those of us raised outside pureblood halls had never seen before. And what she augured confounded the cabal. Two hundred and ten years until the dawn. A very long night indeed. Too much solitude, even for me! Somewhere along the way, Stearc had come by the private journal of Eodward's tutor—a Moriangi monk named Picus, sent by Caedmon to accompany and educate his son in his exile. And so, thoughts turned to the Danae."

Lost in imagining the dreadful destiny they had planned for Gildas, I failed to grasp the connection. "I don't understand."

As joyful evensong floated from the church, Gildas laughed again, not so merrily this time. "It seems we are both condemned to a life we would not choose. Instead of granting me a few decades of peace, solitude, and study, they wish me to go live with beings who despise humans, disdain scholarship, and who fight among themselves over which tree belongs to whom. If it can be arranged, I am to live in Aeginea."

"Live with the Danae? Seven years for one . . . thirty years. So you would be . . . what?"

"According to this fey reasoning, when the madness fades and men realize they need what I can teach, I shall be but nine years past my fiftieth birthday—no older than Abbot Luviar, a hale and vigorous man. And perhaps not even so advanced as that in terms of health and strength, for once back here Eodward remained a man in his prime until well into middle age."

"Deunor's fire!"

And as I contemplated this mad scheme, the most personal of Gillarine's recent mysteries unraveled as well. No more wondering why the abbot had allowed an unsavory vagabond to join his holy brotherhood. He must have thought my grandfather's book a gift from Iero himself. Had I not told him that I had successfully made use of the book, he would likely have kept only the book and sent me away. And I would still be free. After twelve years evading the prison of my birth, my lies had caught me up at last.

"Ah." Gildas halted in midstride and pointed down the path. "It appears as if the decision has been made."

Thalassa's two liveried guards hurried toward us. I imagined shackles tightening about my wrists. My gorge rose.

"Strike me," said Gildas, grasping my shoulders and spinning me about to confront him. Fiery excitement bloomed in his face.

"What?"

"Strike me and run. Through the cloisters to the bridge behind the infirmary. Wait at the dolmen in the grain fields south of the river. I'll tell them a shortcut—misdirect them. As soon as I can, I'll bring food and coin, whatever you need. But wait for me. Promise." He grinned and let his grip slide down my arms, shaking me out of my astonishment. "The cabal will find a road that is not built on the backs of dead men."

"Ah, Brother, you must not—"

"Strike! Go!"

A hopeless scheme. But life's breath to one suffocating.

I drove my fist into his smiling face. His smooth skin broke and the fine bones shifted as I summoned the pent fury of the day to fuel the blow. My aim was not merely to play the necessary part, but to keep him blameless, for his gift was not only the strike, but the suspicion that must inevitably surround it, and I knew well which injury could harm him more. Make one worse, and the other might be eased. They'd blame his misdirection on his muddled head.

"Iero's grace, Brother," I said, as he crumpled into the yew hedge. And then I ran.

Chapter 20

"I should just go," I said, as I blotted stray water droplets from my neck.

A storm had blown in soon after I reached the ancient stones of the dolmen, and the broad lintel stone, though something like a roof, did little to shield a man from wind-driven rain. The worst of the storm had passed somewhere between the ringing of Compline and the day's end bell, but by the time Gildas at last popped out of the fog, I was thoroughly soaked and incomparably edgy. I had waited more than four hours, telling myself every moment that I was a madman to do so.

"No! You must not stir from here," said Gildas softly, crouched close enough I could make out his face. Voices carried in the fog. "Your sister insists that you'll run fast and far. They're scouring the countryside, the river, and the woodland tracks. They've alerted the watch in Elanus. They'll never imagine you've remained so near the abbey and in a barley field to boot. Even the purebloods— You're one of them, Valen. Surely you've spells to conceal your path, spells to confuse them."

"I'm not at all good at spellcasting," I said. "*Obscuré* spells are unreliable at best, and I've never made one work. I cannot just sit here."

"Be patient. They'll soon tire of useless searching in the dark. And the moment they decide to wait for dawn, you're free of them."

Gildas's eyes flashed in his pale face, blotched and swollen from encountering my fist. Though breathless from his hurried journey, his voice was tight with excitement. I had been on the run too often for excitement, and I was much too close to the abbey to feel free.

"I'm sorry I had to come here with so little. But I didn't want you to wait any longer without word. I hadn't counted on you putting me in the infirmary!"

"Yet you've brought me Iero's own gift." Upon his arrival, my wet, bat-tered, and bedraggled friend had shoved a fat wineskin into my hands. "And I do thank you for it and for this chance, but I daren't wait longer."

"You need your secular clothes; they'll be watching for the cowl. And if you're going to avoid towns until you're well away, you need food. Give me another hour."

I turned his head so I could see his swollen jaw. "Holy Mother, I *am* sorry for this. You oughtn't be trotting around with a bruised head. You'll get dizzy and fall in the river. And you *must* not be caught helping me. Do you even understand what they'll do to you?" He'd be god-blessed to see daylight ever again.

His teeth flashed in the rainy darkness. "Your sister's purebloods ques-tioned me before Compline and now think I'm asleep. I can get into the dorter and the kitchen without anyone the wiser. But they'll certainly be back to question me, so I'll send one of the boys with your things. The abbey will be in such an uproar, they'll be able to slip in and out easier than any of us. And they admire you so."

"No!" I said, sharper than I intended. "Not the boys. Of course they'd do anything you ask them. But no, please. I'd rather do without."

I had no reason to believe Jullian or Gerard would still "admire" me in any way, assuming they ever had. Even so, I refused to put them in jeopardy. At least Gildas was a man and had some idea of the world and its horrors, but those boys . . . they would die in prison.

"They're very careful and I'm sure they'd not betray you, but if you prefer, I'll come myself during Matins. Promise you'll not leave before that. I'm quite recovered." His hands squeezed my shoulders, solid and reassuring. "You saved me from Sila Diaglou's whip, Valen. Did you think I'd forget?"

I wrestled with fear and need and the desire to be gone. I could likely survive the next few days with no money, no food, no secular clothes. But of course I had a far more urgent lack. Four days gone since my incomplete doulon. Saints and angels, how I hated this. "Brother, if you can . . . I've left a packet hidden in the garden all these months, a few things I'd not like to abandon. A knife. Some extra medicine for my leg."

One look inside the bundle and he would know. By sight or scent, nivat was unmistakable. If Gildas had risked so much to get me this far, then per-haps he could even forgive a bit of perversion.

"I'll bring whatever you like." After I described how to find my bundle, he gripped my shoulders. "An hour. You are in the god's hand, Valen."

"And you, good friend," I said, as he sped through the stubbled field, vanishing almost before I could blink. "Be very careful."

You're a fool to wait, Valen. Better to be caught running than squatting like a toad. It was the same argument I'd had with myself all evening. But for twelve years, doing the unexpected had kept me free. Gildas would do as I asked. A fascination had captured him since the moment he'd learned I was pureblood, driving him to help beyond reasoned friendship. If we were successful, perhaps he'd have a chance to tell me why.

Pulling up my hood, I settled back against the cold stone and took a long pull at the wineskin. Though I expected ale, the essence of grape and oak warmed my gullet. *Oh, friend Gildas, blessed be your name. And mighty Erdru, holy lord of grape and harvest, how could you have so cruelly abandoned your worshipers?* I took a second drink, feeling the wine scald the hollows in my belly. With every swallow, I named Gildas holy.

I ought to sleep. The coming days would be long and difficult, and sleeping bodies were harder to locate with magic. But the events of the past weeks roiled in my head like cream in a churn, and strangeness hung about me like a fever. Through the hours of waiting, I had imagined I was hearing things through the drumming rain . . . sounds like sighs and breathing, like worms gnawing their way through dead flesh, like heartbeats and green shoots struggling to break through the mud and rock. I kept my hands clasped tightly in my lap, remembering the earth breathing under my hand as I searched out the route to Elanus. If I laid my palms down tonight, I felt the eerie certainty that I'd detect a heartbeat.

Holy ground. Of course, the world was infused with divine mystery. Everyone felt such things on occasion—saw faces in the clouds, experienced a day in the midst of winter when it felt as if spring had leaked through the boundaries of seasons, felt prickles when walking through a darkening wood. But I had never thought myself closer to such mystery than the next man. Signs and portents had never shaken me, never driven me to any action beyond kissing the nearest aingerou or pouring a libation for the appropriate deity. But here in this valley . . . in the cloisters, on the road, in the hills. What was happening to me?

Likely what I felt tonight was nothing save these ancient rocks. Simple and stark, dolmens were scattered in the open country throughout Ardra. No one knew what purposes they had served—burials, ceremonies, boundaries, markers. Yet anyone with even a touch of magical sensibility recognized the power that lingered about them.

And I had seen a Dané. Only now as the rain spattered on the stone and showered softly on the barley could I recapture the wonder of it. They lived . . . beings that could dissolve into earth or water or tree. Beings that could hear the music of the stars and weave life into the fields with their dancing. Knowing the legends were true . . . the world could never look the same to me.

A breath of wind swirled the mist, bearing the powerful sweet scent of rotting grain. I pulled my hood lower, huddled the wineskin closer, and drank again, closing my eyes. I didn't want to see what beings might live in a place so ancient. I didn't want to hear the creaking as the stones shifted with the breathing of the earth. I shuddered. What had Gildas said? *If the cities die, if learning dies, we are sent back to the land, to nights in the wild forest with spirits we can no longer tame with words, to awe of these Gehoum . . .*

"Brother Valen?"

The soft voice sent me to my feet with my stomach in my throat. Giddy with the wine and foolish musings, I imagined all sorts of things before I associated the voice with the human shape standing near a mound of musty grain stalks ten paces away. "Mistress Elene?"

"Yes."

I pressed my back to the stone, peering into the darkness, trying to glimpse other movement. "Have they sent you to drag me back? I warn you I won't go other than feet before, and I don't think you're capable of overpowering me on your own. Or perhaps you've brought comrades?"

"I'm quite alone." She stepped under the lintel rock, water cascading from her cloak. Her wet hair curled about her face. "I spied on you and Brother Gildas in the maze and followed you out here, determined to bring you back. When you stopped so close, I believed you were having second thoughts. So, like a moonstruck chit, I've hidden behind that pile of sour barley all this time debating whether to speak with you or just to pray you would go back on your own."

I did not mistake her reference to "moonstruck chit" for any more than description. Nor did I tease her about it. Her face, so pale in the night, was tied into much too sober a knot.

I sank to the ground again, leaning against one upright stone. My feet and my back reminded me of two exhausting days, a sleepless night, and a butchered pig. "I'm always glad for company, mistress. But I can't believe your father would approve." Certainly not after Thalassa's jibes.

"He won't." She matched my position against the other upright. "My father would prefer having a son and flies into a rage when I show any independence of mind. Even when he can't find reason to refuse a request, he seeks a way to make his acquiescence unpleasant. If I'm to be chastised anyway, I might as well do as I please now and then."

"Thus your cheerful life as Corin the Squire."

"He calls me Corin even when we're alone."

This confession was couched in such rueful exasperation that I laughed in sympathy and tossed her the wineskin. "So we have both cursed our families with unfulfilled expectations. At least you bear no fault for your father's disappointment, as I'm sure a scholarly man such as Stearc will recognize eventually. My family has no such consolation. I was a dreadful, obstreperous child, who set out from the crèche to turn their well-ordered household bottom side up and who maliciously tormented every unfortunate who stepped within my view. My sister's reports of that are perfectly true."

Elene took a single swallow of wine and slowly replaced the plug. Earning my eternal gratitude, she tossed it back to me. "I think your sister does not know you as you are now."

I took a very long swallow. Perhaps the wine would blunt the whispering seduction of the night. The mist curled around my cheeks and tickled my ears like a woman's tongue. The earth pulsed beneath my legs and backside. The richness of Elene's voice drew soft fingers up my thighs. To keep talking was an effort.

"Nor do you know me, good Corin. If you're feeling guilty for leading me into that little mess this afternoon, don't. I am quite good at embroiling myself in messes on my own." I shifted position, moving close enough to offer the wineskin again.

She shook her head and leaned forward, her knees drawn up, her hands clasped firmly in front of her legs. I could feel her breath on my face. I could smell the barley on her. The layers of damp leather. The woman underneath. Foolish to allow such distraction . . .

"If I'm to feel guilty, then I'd rather more fault than an accidental meeting to justify it." Her voice played like music in the night. "I came here to ask you— No, to plead with you. The cabal needs you, Brother Valen. I'm surprised at Brother Gildas helping you escape. I never judged him a man to care about anyone's personal safety. He is quite single-minded. But he is a fool if he thinks the lighthouse cabal can succeed without your assistance.

Your sister has tried everything to glean the information we need from your grandfather with no result. And since the day the gods brought you to Gillarine, each of us has tried to unravel the book of maps and got no farther than a bare cliff and a crossroads cairn."

"And how do you propose I assist you? Do you understand the somewhat limited prospects for a recaptured *recondeur*? Until the day I die I'll not be allowed to piss without three guards watching me. You're all mad anyway." Her choice of conversational topic cooled my rising fever.

"The life of a pureblood . . . I'd always thought it holy. Your people live hidden, so honored, valued, protected, elevated beyond all of us who must struggle with everyday life, as if you spend half your days in heaven, returning only long enough to produce wonders. I thought a *recondeur* must be soul-dead to leave such a noble gift as sorcery behind. Yet I cannot believe that of you."

How could I explain that the favor of kings and a life of luxury, ever shielded from want and war, was not worth the price? What ordinary would ever believe it? Few purebloods besides my own mad self had ever believed it. Everyone who'd ever known me swore that I spoke such heresy to excuse poor skills and willful ignorance, or to service childish whim made stubborn by "unfortunate conflict" with my father. All agreed my nature insupportably perverse. Yet my belief was rooted as deep as any knowledge or understanding I possessed.

The night hid her expression, leaving us a certain intimacy, like comfortable bed partners after the frenzy is past. "Mistress, when your men threw that grain sack over my head, I was convinced I would die from it. No matter that the bag was loosely woven. No matter that your intent to let me live was soon clear, and that the restriction of my sight was part of a well-considered plan. Had the sack been woven of spider's silk wound with gossamer, the cord about my neck softer than angel's wings, and your bodyguards' hands as gentle as your own, it would have made no difference to my horror and dread. I could not breathe. Pureblood life was very like that for me. Now it will be worse."

"Surely, whatever your problems in the past, your family will see you've changed." She was truly naive.

"Ah, lady, you don't know my family." I touched her face, so pale in the fog, cool and damp. And my hand slid around the back of her neck, pulling her gently toward me while stroking the downy hair and soft skin, feeling the strength and pride of her. So alive . . .

Her breath caught, but she yielded, warmth flooding her skin under my fingers. Imminent danger . . . escape . . . caution . . . vows . . . all slipped away, the pulse of the night driving me where I'd no intent to go. It had been so long. The ache within me grew, trapping breath in my lungs, obliterating thought as my lips touched hers . . .

Torches flared from the direction of the abbey. Shouts accompanied them and were answered from the mist on our flanks. Blessed saints and angels, how stupid, how inexcusably weak, lust-blinded, and incautious, could a man get? She *wanted* me taken.

"Magrog have you, woman!"

Elene shot up from the ground in the same moment I did. "Brother Valen, wait! I didn't—"

I didn't dally to hear her excuses, but sped southward into the fog, stumbling blindly until I stopped cursing perfidious women and threw every sense I possessed into the race. *Feel the thicker mist hanging over the river on your left . . . smell the wrack and weed . . . hear the whisper of water in its deep channel. Feel the road on the right . . . the tread of feet . . . of wheels . . . of hooves and paws for a thousand years . . . the restless horses patrolling there . . . waiting for you to stumble. And the earth underfoot . . .*

I stopped and tore at the laces of my sandals. Throwing them off, I ran barefoot, feeling the prickling stubble of the barley field and the cold, sodden earth. Instinct warned me of holes, channels, and rocks and guided me southward, upward, away from the abbey.

The fog swallowed the torchlight and voices, and my bare feet were light, little more than a mouse's tread through the fields. I slowed a bit and controlled my breathing so as not to give away by gasps and gulps what I gained by speed.

A pale line emerged from the fog—a rampart of stone—the abbey boundary, a waist-high rubble wall out here in the fields, not the smooth-dressed ashlar of the abbey's public face. I slapped my hands on the top and leaped over the wall, trying to remember the terrain to the south, the route Brother Adolfus and I had traveled toward Caedmon's Bridge. Broad meadows between the road and the river, broken by swaths of trees, and then the short steep climb toward the higher meadows, the giant's steps toward the mountains.

Chest heaving, I knelt and pressed hands and forehead to the earth. Stretched my mind forward. Swept it across the landscape. *Safety . . . ha-*

ven . . . guide me . . . The night shifted a little. *Left. A path limned with moonlight.* I popped up and ran.

The breeze swelled, swirling the fog, thinning it here and there. Patches of stars appeared and were as quickly obscured. Angle right and around to avoid a spring and a thicket. Foolish as it was to hope, I began to think I had eluded them. My destination—the refuge—felt near.

Hoofbeats to my right. On the road, much too close. Torches again. Damnable beasts to bring pursuit so fast.

I burst through the edge of the fog. The night was clear; the stars gleamed above a lush meadow, broken only by a ring of trees with smooth white trunks and bright gold leaves. I'd thought these aspens were already bare . . .

"Ho there! Get him!" The hoofbeats dulled when they left the road for the grass of the meadow. Or perhaps my heart thudded so ferociously it drowned out the sounds of pursuit.

A searing finger touched the back of my neck. Of a sudden my feet felt shod in iron. Stumbling, I dragged them onward, unwilling to concede the race. Another bolt touched my back—no mundane weapon, but sorcery, a brutal binding of limbs and will.

I was so close to the ring of aspens. What safety might lie there when I had already been spotted, I could not imagine. Yet I believed that to reach it must yield victory. Only a little farther . . . a few steps . . .

A third bolt took my knees, and I crumpled a mere ten paces from the rustling trees. The stink of horses and diseased leaves gagged me as I fell.

Until the end of days I would swear that a naked man, a dragon traced in blue fire upon his face and limbs, reached out to me from the grove. But it was too far, and the fourth bolt of fire made the night go black.

They rolled me onto a palliasse thinner than the one in the monks' dorter, and with only hard floor, no sling of ropes underneath it.

"Can he breathe properly? Swallow?"

No, I wanted to say. *He cannot breathe, not if you've put him in a cell.* The place smelled of rusted iron and musty stone, fresh straw and old piss. Prisons were prisons, even in an abbey.

"Indeed, sir abbot, all those things. We are not permitted to injure him." The perfumed man who had hauled me up from the ground and thrown me over his saddle sounded as if he'd a broom up his backside. His scent was cheap; his contract with Thalassa must not pay well. "The spell merely prevents voluntary movement. He is probably awake even now."

Fingers shoved my eyelids open and I stared directly into the yellow glare of a lamp. My eyes blinked and watered. From behind the glare two shadowy faces looked down at me.

"There, you see, sir abbot. He hears us. The *recondeur* seems a bit unhappy at his state."

Trapped within the bonds of my flesh, I struggled to strike . . . to scream . . . to move . . . half crazed already.

A cool hand rested on my forehead. "I regret you could not trust me, Valen," said Luviar. "I would have protected you. Trust breeds faith. And faith, honesty, and compassion are the roots of honor. With your gifts and a smattering of honor, you might have done great good for the world. May Iero transform your intransigent heart."

The blurred faces moved out of view. The lamp was taken away. My skin shrank as the yellow light wavered, latches rattled, and a door was opened, stirring the musty air, causing wild shadows to dance about the low, mold-patched ceiling.

Please don't leave me here!

The door slammed shut. The locks clicked. The darkness and the walls closed in.

Chapter 21

Voices, light, and cheap scent yanked me into full awareness. This event was not a waking. I had not slept. But at sometime in the long frigid night of suffocation and terror, I had clawed open a hole in my mind, a deeper darkness void of thought, a place to huddle and stay sane. Now, unrelieved by sleep's murky unwinding, I could remember exactly the events of day and night that had led to my current position flat on my back, eyes open, in the abbey's prison cell.

Thalassa's kohl-lined eyes and her long straight nose hovered above me. She laid a finger in the center of my forehead, whispered a word, and an invisible whip stroke tore through me from head to toes. A mighty unraveling.

I curled up in a knot and rolled to the side, muting my cry in a fit of coughing, my gritty eyes squeezed shut. My spine stung.

A hand closed over my mouth and pressed tightly, as if to silence my cough, even while another pressed from the back of my head. The hands—Thalassa's, surely—were quickly removed, and I felt a void at my side as she moved away.

"Silos, inform me at once if you sense one scrap of magic from this cell," she commanded. "We'll silkbind his hands at the first hint of it. And tell the monk he may bring something for Valen to drink. But no ale or spirits. And nothing to eat for today. I wish the *recondeur* to remain sober, and a hungry day will remind him of his manners. We leave for Palinur in an hour."

"Yes, Sinduria," said the scented lackey.

Had anyone ever suffered such a sister? Between Thalassa and Elene, I vowed to swear off women altogether. Would Elene have let me take her body just to fulfill her holy purpose?

A swish of silk on stone and the door slammed shut behind Thalassa. I remained huddled on the palliasse, trying to summon the resilience that had sustained me as a child, trying to convince myself that I would not bend to their will just to avoid another night like the one I had just endured. The deepening cold bruised body and spirit, weighing as iron-linked mail on my limbs. I could not stop shaking.

The door opened and closed again. Light danced at the edges of my eyelids. Someone wearing sandals walked the five steps from the door and crouched beside me, smelling of damp wool and the boiling herbs of the infirmary, overlaid with traces of mud and grain fields.

"Sit up, Brother Valen. I've brought you water. You need to drink and change clothes, and then we must pray for your true repentance and a safe journey."

"I don't drink water, Brother Gildas," I said, my voice as rough as if my night's screams had been aloud instead of trapped within my skull.

"They're not going to give you anything else for a while, and if you fail to cooperate, they'll force it down you. You are no longer a child to take petty victories from stubbornness. Now, sit up."

Men of insight. If my childhood had been lived out among ones like these, I might have turned out differently. I rolled onto all fours and sat back on my heels, cramming my frozen hands into my sleeves. Gildas sat cross-legged on the floor in front of me, holding a green pottery flask. Beside him sat a small brass lamp and a pile of clothing that could be none but my own stained jaque, braies, and boots.

"How is it *you* are here?" I wiped my eyes with the back of my hand. "Are you a pris—?"

He pressed a finger to his mouth and jerked his head slightly backward toward the iron-clad door at his back. Its upper half was a thick grate. Anyone in the darkness outside the door could see and hear what went on in the cell.

"Father Abbot sent me," he said. "I told him I bore no grudge for the bruises, and assured him that my incompetence could not set you free again. Your guards—*both* of them—are purebloods."

So they did not suspect his complicity in my escape. A touch of resentment cooled my good feelings. I supposed Elene thought Gildas too valuable to their little cabal to reveal his role in the night's fiasco. At least he had tried to help.

"Drink this, and dress yourself in your secular clothing."

I unstoppered the flask he gave me, sniffed at it, and stuffed the stopper back in again, pretending my throat did not feel like gravel. Water—my foretold doom. My mother might be a wretched parent, but she was a talented diviner. "So my novice year is at an end, is it?"

"For now. The Sinduria and Abbot Luviar have agreed that you will not be permitted to hide behind the cowl as you face the consequences of your transgressions. However, the abbot wishes me to remind you that you are not released from your vows. You remain sworn in obedience to him and to the Rule of Saint Ophir and are not to speak of certain events. Can you tell me which ones?"

I shoved the water flask back into his hand. "Despite what everyone believes, I'm not stupid."

"Come now, tell me. I'm required to hear your recitation."

"I'll not reveal any of his—" My tongue balked at the word *secrets*. I began again. "He assumes I'll tell of the—" I tried to say *lighthouse* but was unable to speak the word.

Again, and then again, I attempted to speak of the abbot and Gillarine and the conspiracy. I pressed my hands to my head as if to trap the words that kept escaping somewhere between my mind and my mouth, but concentration seemed to make no difference. *Danae, lighthouse, conspiracy* . . . I could not voice them.

"What have they done?" I tugged at my hair until my scalp burned. I was awake. In control of my body. Surely I could command my own speech. Surely . . . As I spewed half sentences and fragments, I remembered Thalassa's hands squeezing my mouth and head and began to understand. "Is that why you're here? Did they send you to test her damnable spell?"

Frantically, I sped through thoughts and memories in search of holes or gaps. Nothing of current or past events seemed to be missing, but then, how would I know?

"Valen . . ." Gildas laid his hands on my shoulders, but I knocked him backward.

"Listen to me! Listen!" Gildas got back to his knees and reached for me again. I twisted and shoved him away, but I could not both concentrate on the gaps in my speech and grapple with a man so determined and so surprisingly strong. Eventually he caught my upper arms and squeezed them tight to my body, shaking me until I met his gaze. "Be easy, Brother. This is well done. They've put a simple binder on your tongue with regard to these matters. Nothing more. I promise you. Father Abbot would allow nothing of a permanent nature. Yes, they wished me to test you. As the restriction is now proved, nothing further should be needed."

"Am I to thank Luviar for that?" I said. I thrust my forearms between Gildas's and slammed them outward to break his grip. He winced and rubbed his arms, and I was glad of it.

He did not touch me again but crinkled his brow earnestly. "You ran, Valen. Blame the one responsible"—his face was all apology—"and forgive him. Now we need to move on. They'll be coming for you soon. The Sinduria wishes to leave for Palinur before Prime."

He picked up my old clothes and held them out to me. "Though you must relinquish the cowl and gown, Father Abbot says you may keep the shirt. A biting cold has settled in since the storm."

Stiff with anger at Gildas, at the monks, at myself and everyone else within Gillarine's walls, I made no move to take the stack. What had come over me in this place? I knew better than to trust anyone.

His eyes flicked quite obviously from me to the bundle. And then again. The third time he did so, I held out my hands. As he laid the neatly folded clothing on my open palms, his warm fingers grasped one of my hands and guided it to the middle of the stack. And there I felt a small wad of tallow-stiffened canvas, drawn closed with a leather thong.

I glanced up quickly, my heart galloping.

Raising his thick brows and smiling ruefully, he released the bundle and stood up. "You are a man of many virtues, Valen. Be *very* careful as you don these worldly garments again, lest you be snared from the path of right . . . or reason. There are always choices to be made, even in the life you were born to."

Hot blood flooded my skin until I felt as if I must glow brighter than the lantern. I hated that he knew. What was wrong with me of late, worrying so much about what people thought of me? Gildas was but an overzealous monk. Gram a meek secretary. Jullian a smooth-chinned whelp. I could always find new friends.

Laying the stack beside me on the palliasse, I stripped off my cowl and gown. The stiff jaque bound tight over the thick, loose wool shirt. As I pulled on the braies, I quickly tucked the bag of nivat away and tied it safely to the waist string.

"And now drink the water—yes, you must. Then we'll pray." Gildas held out the flask.

My mouth felt like a nest of thorns. I had to drink something. He observed me closely as I drained the tasteless contents of the flask. *Ugh . . . a drink for cows . . .*

My stomach roiled at the first sip. Then a cramp twisted my gut, and my overheated skin blossomed into a cold sweat, as if my mother's divination had truly come to pass.

"Valen, what do you feel? It's only water." Gildas might have been shouting down a well.

"I don't usually drink—" The word *poison* came to mind as I hurriedly found the rusty pail in the corner of the cell, ripped off its cover, and vomited up every drop of the foul stuff. Even when it seemed everything must be out of me, I could not stop heaving.

Gildas knelt beside me as I huddled over the bucket. His hands felt like ice on my blistering forehead. "Come, lie down. I'll tell Father Abbot and the Sinduria you'd best not travel today. Ah, friend . . . what strange miracles happen in this world. Nothing is out of the realm of possibility."

He half carried, half dragged me to the palliasse, and threw the thin blanket over me, then grabbed his lamp and hurried out the door. Before his footsteps died away, I had fumbled my way back across the floor to the bucket, retching.

The rest of the day flowed together like wet ink on a page. As feeble daylight waxed and waned through a slot high on one cell wall, a string of visitors paraded through my cell—the abbot, Thalassa, Gildas, Thane Stearc, one at a time and then all together, talking and arguing too softly for me to hear. I could pay them no mind anyway. I was on my knees in the corner hunched over the fouled bucket, trying not to vomit up the entire contents of my skin. Brother Robierre questioned me between spasms, examining my tongue and fingernails, eyes and throat.

Even Gram came. He stood in the corner for a while, arms crossed, watching the others as they watched me. After a while he stepped close, laid his hand on my shoulder, and mumbled some incomprehensible sympathy.

As the Compline bell rang, I crawled back to my palliasse. Brother Robierre returned soon after. "The worst seems past," he said, once he had verified that I was alive. "Were you trustworthy, we could have made you more comfortable in the infirmary." I had never heard the kind infirmarian so frosty.

"No matter." My raw throat made everything sound harsh.

He wiped my face with a damp rag and laid yet another blanket over me. "The abbot charged me to inform you of my findings. You were not poisoned. Anselm found naught in your spew or your blood. Your body tells me that you are entirely healthy. So this must be some condition of your blood. Perhaps sorcerers cannot tolerate blessed water. I've not treated your kind . . . purebloods . . . before."

I shook my head and laughed. "Purebloods were never my kind."

He did not see the humor. "Then perhaps it is the soul-poison of a man who would so betray the gifts of the good god and so endanger those who welcomed him as a brother. I will petition Iero to break your sinful spirit, Valen. Here—" With deft hands, he raised my head and emptied a vial of something strong and sweet down my gullet before I could protest. "Now you've settled a bit, this should ease your stomach."

"I'm sorry, Brother," I mumbled, dropping my head to the palliasse, feeling his draught sapping my remaining strength. "But you cannot possibly understand."

He stood to go. "One more thing . . . Young Gerard was supposed to serve in the infirmary this evening, but the lad has not been seen all day. You ever took an interest in the boys, and someone told me you might know where he was off to."

"No . . . sorry. Truly."

The iron door clanged shut behind Robierre.

The day's end bell had rung at least two hours since. That had been the last time I heard movement in the dark stairwell outside the door. Only two pureblood guards, Gildas had told me, and even purebloods had to sleep. Head pounding from holding off the effects of Brother Badger's draught, I crept across the floor and touched my finger to the bottom of the door. Despite the doulon looming ever closer, I could not afford to hoard my magic. Flooding power into the spell, I drew my finger up and around in a sweeping arc on the stone beside the door, and back to the floor again. Then I grabbed my boots and crawled through the void into the stairwell. Still no sound.

The touch of open air on my cheek guided me up one narrow stair. I avoided brushing the wall. Hopes rising, I turned and slipped up the second course, bare feet soundless. One more turn, one more climb. I glimpsed a rectangular opening filled with stars . . . and then a squat silhouette blocked the opening.

"Do you think us fools, *recondeur?*"

I charged upward, barreling into the man, but at least three more bodies flung themselves on top of me as I tried to choke the life out of the one under my chest. It took them little time to wrestle me off their comrade, back down the stair, and into the cell. While two men held me down, two more folded my hands, fingertips interlocked and tucked inward, and bound them with silken cord, effectively precluding any application of magic. By the time they had unraveled my voiding spell and slammed the iron door behind them, the bells rang Matins.

Once I stopped fighting, Brother Robierre's draught drugged me out of thought. The image of a gawky youth with a slow head and a ready grin quickly became tangled with that of riders in wine-colored cloaks and a naked man glowing with blue dragon sigils . . .

When the bells rang for Prime, the two purebloods arrived to release my hands and bring me a cup of small beer. They found me awake already, sitting on my palliasse, attempting to formulate some grand speech to throw at my captors or some scheme to get free. But thoughts of a dutiful boy who was not where he was expected had distracted me. Which made no kind of sense. Gerard had likely had enough of bells and prayers and righteousness.

The window slot yet gleamed gray when Thalassa swept into the cell impeccably coifed and gowned—today in vermillion that set off her black hair and acorn-colored skin. Gold disks at her temples held back her veil and accented the thick black lines curving about her eyes. She dismissed her men to wait outside and close the door behind them. "Stand up."

Sadly, my morning's meditations had revealed naught to say worth the effort of irritating my throat and naught to do worth the trouble of remaining seated. As a boy I had fought until they forced me—to eat, to dress, to stand, to yield—the forcing far more horrid than whatever submission I had refused. Somehow I had lost that kind of resilience. I could not bear the thought of my sister's pureblood lackeys laying hands on me again. I stood.

"A few rules before we go," she said, nodding in approval at my wordless acquiescence. "No matter how you have abased yourself in these past years, you are pureblood, and you will remember your manners and discipline on this journey. The majority of our escort will be ordinaries, and you will maintain distance and detachment as you were taught. I see no need for you to speak at all, in fact, but I will leave you capable lest you fall ill again. I expect no repetition of your foolish escapade of last night. I would prefer to have left you unrestrained for the journey, but that is clearly impossible. Until you give me your word that you will not attempt escape, and convince me that you mean it, your hands will remain silk-bound and your feet shackled."

She paused, chin lifted, as if waiting for me to lash out. But this was not the day to fight. My knees felt like mud. I needed to eat. I closed my eyes, longing for her to vanish.

She didn't, of course. "Punishment and restriction await you in Palinur, as you well know, but your behavior in the next days will influence my recommendations as to their severity and extent. And despite what you would prefer to believe, my opinion *will* carry weight with both the Registry and Patronn."

"I have no doubt of that, *Sinduria serena*." I bowed from the hip and touched my forehead with my fingertips, as was proper to a pureblood of superior rank—which was any one of them at present.

Clearly my intonation of her title and the proper female honorific struck her as insufficiently reverent. When I straightened up again, her full lips were tight, and her dark eyes sparked like struck flint. "You *will* submit, little brother. You have squandered your life and your talents. The time has come for you to focus your attention on something beyond your own pleasure. And we will begin that return to discipline now," she said, and handed me a small piece of embroidered white silk.

I unfolded the fabric and stared at it for a moment, my fingers tingling with the minor magics woven into it. One edge straight and slightly stiffened, the rest irregularly shaped. One oval opening for the eye, its borders elaborately embroidered in white thread. Neatly sewn tucks to shape it around nose, mouth, and chin. A mask, or rather a half mask, for purebloods covered only one side of the face when appearing among ordinaries. The half mask was a symbol of our second self, the sorcerer within us that "ordinary" eyes could not see. The mask set us apart, enhanced our mystery, and gave us a certain anonymity among those we did not care to have know us. Only ones like Thalassa or the Gillarine pureblood, whose positions mandated other facial decoration or required family dispensation, were exempt from the discipline of the mask.

"It won't fit as your own should and will. But Silos had an extra and was willing to loan it until we get to Palinur."

No restraint they would use to bind me would be so loathsome, as she was well aware.

"You believe you know me, Lassa, and in some things"—I flipped the mask between my fingers—"your judgment is correct. But I will *never* be like you or the rest of our kin. I have walked free in this world, and I won't forget it."

But this was not the day to fight. So I lifted the scrap of silk to my face and aligned the stiffened edge down the center of my forehead, nose, and mouth, feeling the spider-thin fabric tighten across my left cheek and brow. Its spelled weaving caused it to adhere along its borders and around my eye and hairline and lips, imperfectly in this case. Silos's face was clearly wider than mine; the thing reached halfway across my left ear. The silk smelled of his cheap perfume.

Thalassa cocked her head to one side as I lowered my hands. "Not comely, especially with your ridiculous hair, but sufficient to remind you of who you are. Perhaps, with a return to discipline and some time for thought, you will come to appreciate your position."

She summoned her two guards, short, sturdy men with the straight black hair and deep skin color typical of purebloods. They wore green half masks trimmed in purple to match their livery and wine-colored cloaks. They silkbound my palms together, fingertips tucked in, as they had in the night. Then they affixed a lightweight shackle to my left ankle, draped the dangling end of the chain over my wrists so I would not trip on it, and led me up the prison stair.

We emerged in the yard between the library and the abbot's house whence Prince Perryn had ridden out with the Hierarch of Ardra. A party of horses and ten leather-clad men-at-arms waited near the front door. What appeared to be the entire complement of the abbey—monks and lay brothers— filled the rest of the yard. Many somber. Most gawking. Neither Stearc nor his daughter nor his secretary was present.

A new storm was upon us. The sharp wind tore the layers of scud that fronted massive gray clouds. Cloaks and gowns flapped like pennons.

Abbot Luviar and Prior Nemesio stepped from the front rank, exchanging farewells with Thalassa. From their exchanges, I gathered that my sister's public business at Gillarine had something to do with sheep breeding contracts for her temple's flocks.

Jullian stood alone between the lay brothers and the monks, staring at me in shocked disbelief. His eyes traveled from the mask to my bound hands to the loop of metal about my ankle and the slender chain draped over my wrists. I tried to catch his eye . . . winked at him . . . but it was as if he could not recognize me behind the mask.

The face that had drifted in and out of my troubled dreams all night was nowhere to be seen. Young Gerard, great of heart, but slow of eye and head when it came to reading, was not there.

I turned to the abbot, interrupting the inane formalities. "Is Gerard not found yet?"

Thalassa stiffened and raised a warning finger. "Silence, *recondeur*."

"Please, he is a friend . . . a good boy. Father Abbot—"

"We have a party searching," said Luviar. "You indicated you had not seen him."

"Not since dinner on the day I returned from Caedmon's Bridge. If I could help . . . Lassa . . . *Sinduria serena* . . . perhaps my skills could—"

"You might possess the skills to search for the boy, Valen," said Thalassa. "But you have long since squandered trust. I cannot permit it."

"But—"

"Silos, see the *recondeur* onto his mount. Bind his wrists to the saddle, his foot to the stirrup, and his horse to mine. Then you may aid Abbot Luviar in his search as we discussed."

The abbot said nothing.

Hatred flooded my veins in that moment. I hated Thalassa and her purebloods and their smug righteousness. I hated the abbot and his single-minded passion. I hated past, present, and future with equal bitterness, and I hated the estrangement I saw in Jullian's eye. I hated that they would not allow me to help one of the few people in the world I'd give a pin for, and I hated that my sister's warning stayed my feet—if I misbehaved again, the future could be even worse. The desire to run was an arrow piercing my lungs. Most of all I hated that after twelve years of running, I could think of nowhere to go but away.

The perfumed man in the green mask and wine-colored cloak took my arm, but I shook off his gloved hands for one moment. For these past weeks, the men of Gillarine had given me a place, and I could not depart without acknowledging their kindness. Touching my bound hands to my forehead, I faced the brothers of Saint Ophir and bowed from the hip. Then I allowed Silos to lead me away.

PART THREE

Bitter Blue Days

Chapter 22

Lukas, the sallow valet, scraped the last hair from my chin and dabbed at my face with a damp rag long gone cold. It was tempting, as always, to poke him in the ribs or let fly a particularly foul obscenity, just to see if he would flinch. He wouldn't. Of years somewhere between forty and fifty, the dried-up little ordinary had likely come into pureblood service when he was twelve. He knew very well that his position and livelihood depended on absolute discretion and perfect deportment in the face of temperamental fits, sorcery, and even forced service to a creature of such reprehensible character as a *recondeur*.

Released from his unwelcome ministrations for the moment, I drifted over to the window, rubbing my head that still felt itchy and odd. Almost three weeks had passed since leaving Gillarine, and my hair was at last the same length all over. Scarcely a knucklebone long, of course. Lukas had trimmed all of it to match my regrowing tonsure. Neat. Seemly. Like my shaven chin, clean, trimmed fingernails, and the plum-colored silk shirt and unadorned pourpoint of sober gray velvet Lukas laid out on my bed. Like my temporary accommodation here in the Registry palace—a small, barren chamber, high above the unhealthy airs of the streets, its window discreetly barred, its door firmly locked, and its walls wrapped in spells that made it impossible I work any of my own. The molds of pureblood custom and protocol were squeezing me back into the shape laid out for me before my birth. No blood, no mess. No breath. No life.

I pressed my forehead to the glass. Snow again today. Frosty Palinur sprawled down the hill toward the river, the unfinished towers of the cathedral protruding like bony arms reaching for heaven's mercy—only too late.

The groves and vineyards that blanketed the gentle hills, rolling toward the horizon and beyond, were buried in killing frost. Sky, cloud, and horizon formed one chilling mass of gray, a pure reflection of my spirits.

"Your shirt, *plebeiu*." If such a stick could be said to enjoy anything, Lukas enjoyed addressing me by the low title, reserved for purebloods in disgrace. He assumed I cared.

Lukas dangled the silk shirt from his bony hands, playing another of his games by remaining stolidly beside the bed, so that I must walk over to him to be dressed. If I stood my ground, I would be late. Yet to dress myself in the presence of a servant was a breach of pureblood protocol. Either offense would reap punishment: a meal withheld or reduced to bread alone, an extra hour added to my day's humiliation, or my lamps extinguished an hour early. Every infraction, no matter how small, earned its consequence. Brother Sebastian would approve.

I crossed the room. As I stuck my arms in the soft sleeves of the shirt, the locks on the door snapped open, and a chill draft blew in a thickset man muffled in a claret-hued pelisse. He whipped off his mask, and snowflakes flurried from his hair and shoulders onto the polished wood floor.

"Magrog's prick!" The oath burst out of me like an untimely belch. Though I was working with great diligence at discipline, I was not yet ready to face more of my family than my excessively prim, excessively hostile elder sister. Besides, I had last seen my brother, Max, on Black Night, attending Bayard the Smith. "What the devil are *you* doing in Palinur . . . here?"

Lukas scurried to take Max's things and hang them on the brass wall hooks. With a drawn-out sigh, Max pulled my one chair out of the corner and sat down, raising his thick, bristly eyebrows. "Manners, little brother?"

Blast him to the fiery pits! To abase myself to my brother soured my stomach. But Lukas would relish reporting any lapse in protocol. Gathering up the personal opinions I'd strewn about for public viewing, I clenched my teeth, touched my fingertips to my forehead, and bowed deeply from the hip. Purebloods did not reveal emotions. Purebloods did not develop friendships. Purebloods must remain detached from other people so that their magic, which belonged to their family or contracted masters, would not be tainted. Every human relationship must be rigorously shaped and strictly constrained by manners, protocol, and titles awarded according to rank, gender, and kinship.

"Greetings, *ancieno*. Please forgive my humble welcome after so many years. Alas, I've no refreshment to offer, no gossip to share, and you have already found the only seat in my apartments save the bed. And having no idea of your current title, I can add no more honor to the greeting. Are you as elevated as our sister?"

I chose not to mention I'd seen him with Prince Bayard. I was falling easily into pureblood habits. Secret knowledge was liquor in our veins.

"You tread a bridge of sand with speech like that, *plebeiu*. Did they permit such impertinence in the Karish monk-house?" Max grinned and propped his muddy boots on the bedcovers, just missing the gray velvet garment. "Damn, I wish I'd seen you gowned and shorn! The mere consideration of our wild, truculent Valen all prim and prayerful has me thinking gatzi have turned the world backside before."

"*Willing* submission comes easier, *ancieno*. Would you mind very much if I continued to dress? I am required to be ready at Terce—third watch." He'd likely not know the Karish term that came so naturally to me now.

He waved his hand, weighted heavily with a ruby and sapphire ring. "Wouldn't think of interfering with your duties. Pardon me if I enjoy the sight overmuch. I certainly don't want to be seen out there in the streets gawking at you, but it quite thrills me to watch you brought to heel. You've caused us all inordinate trouble."

I motioned Lukas to continue. He dropped a second shirt of fine wool over my head and then added the pourpoint with its interminable buttons down front and sleeves.

"I arrived in the city late last night and heard the news," Max continued. "The infamous Cartamandua *recondeur* brought to heel at last. Our family disgrace—well, not lifted, but relieved. Nothing can erase what you did. Did you know you cost Patronn his royal appointment? Twelve years he's lived now without a contract of his own. If you thought he detested you before . . . well, you surely know more than I about that. Do you think he still has the strap?"

Clearly my sins had not taxed Max's humor as sorely as they had my elder sister's; he had always enjoyed my punishments and humiliations inordinately. Yet I could not help but feel his excessive good cheer rooted in some circumstance beyond my capture. "You appear to have prospered despite my transgressions. What kind of contract do you serve? Lassa's given me no news of the family."

In fact, my sister had hardly spoken to me in our eight miserable days on the road. And though she had hovered about me like a bee on clover during my two days' testimony before the Registry, taking every opportunity to warn me against demonstrating my tongue-block in front of my questioners, she had not visited me since the judgment.

"I've a respectable contract, though it's paid less than half what a Cartamandua of my skill should command." Max pulled off his gloves one finger at a time. He fondled his grand ring, turning it to catch the light. "At least it's active scouting and advance work, not scrawling maps. Bia's taken the Cartamandua bent as well and is working for Patronn, inking his revisions or some such tedious task. Nilla has entered the eerie realms of divination. Two and two . . . so the family balance is left to you. Or do you still resist the call of your blood and the demands of discipline, presuming to some profession beyond the family bent? You've skills in so *many* areas, as I recall. Perhaps you've developed healing powers, or you've chosen to teach fertile young minds to read . . ."

As he rattled off a list of scholarly and magical pursuits, I stood mute. Every response that leaped to mind would reap more punishments.

He shoved the jeweled ring onto his thick finger and raised his eyes to meet my own, his smile as gleeful as that of a huntsman who bends his bow at a hobbled buck. "Come, tell me. What are you, Valen? You've surely not taken the bent for divination, else you'd hardly have let yourself be captured. But then again, why would I expect you might be competent at anything?"

His were but a child's barbs, no matter that they stung a nerve grown raw. If I refused to let him see more, perhaps he would win only a child's pleasure from them. So I changed the subject. "I can't imagine the twins grown enough to choose their bent. They were what . . . eleven last time I saw them . . . twelve? All ribbons and sulks."

Lips pursed in discontent, he settled back in his chair. "Our little sisters have grown up. Nilla is the beauty, as you might guess. Her looks got her a decent match—Luc de Galeno-Mercanti, a physician thrice her age who is contracted to the Duc of Avenus. Her divinations focus on her husband's patients—a bit unsettling for them, I think. Perhaps now you're back under discipline, the Registry will allow her to birth a child before her husband is wholly incapable. Bia's minor rebellions ceased when she saw what happened to you—or perhaps when Matronn locked her in her room for half a year lest she follow your course. Patronn has not yet found a husband for her. Neither girl is happy with you. I'd recommend you stay out of their way. Easier in Nilla's case, off in the damp of Morian as she is. But Bia—"

"I'll watch my back."

Lukas knelt to tie up my hose and lace my boots. I scarcely knew my younger sisters, Petronilla and Phoebia. They had been but wasps in the garden of family. Max and Thalassa had been the snake and the shrew. So what was the snake doing here?

"Who is it holds your leash, Max? Your master must be headquartered in Palinur. Or has he loosed your golden chains so far as to permit random family visits?"

"My master's business has brought me to the city," said Max. "Business of critical importance to Navronne's future. I've no leave to discuss it—or him—with anyone save family. Yet I doubt such exceptions should be extended to *you*. You might be tempted to use the information to buy your way out of your unhappy lot. Only a sadist or a halfwit is going to consider a contract for a twelve-year *recondeur*. You know nothing of leashes, little brother. Not yet."

My brother rocked the chair back on its rear legs, his bulk overflowing it. From the time I shot past his height at age ten or so, Max had always managed to be sitting when we were together. And he had always enjoyed taunting me with the privileges he earned from being the dutiful elder, while I suffered the consequences of my errant nature. Evidently, nothing had changed.

"Keep your secrets, *ancieno*," I said. "I am, as ever, hopelessly unreliable when it comes to family loyalties."

Having finished with my boots, Lukas picked up a hinged contraption of delicately engraved silver from the small table beside my bed. With perfect patience he waited for me to kneel before him so he could slip it over my head. He could not completely hide his delight in this particular duty.

"You must excuse me from any further conversation," I said, as I dropped to my knees. I thought I had managed the encounter well, but it was impossible to hide bitterness at this point. Not with Max here.

My brother lowered his chair legs to the floor with a jolt, watching goggle-eyed. "Ah, fires of Deunor, they have done you proud, Valen," he whispered. "You, the lad who threw fits when locked in his bedchamber ten times the size of this room."

A delicate silver band three fingers wide encircled my throat. From it graceful silver coils stretched up my neck to support a mask that covered the left half of my face. This mask was not smooth, accommodating silk, but rigid silver that sealed my lips closed, blocked one nostril and one ear, and obscured one eye. Lukas latched the cursed thing at the back of my neck and fastened the thin metal strap that held it over my head. The Registry judge who had insisted on the mask had been most annoyed that in all my tedious accounting of my twelve uncontrolled years, I'd not implicated any ordinary he could hang.

A grin materialized on Max's broad face. "Does it close in on you, little brother? Does the world appear warped, with only one eye to observe it? Can you feel the restraint, the control? Spirits of night, how you must loathe this."

I ignored his baiting as I rose from the floor, fighting the urge to ram my head into the wall, practicing Brother Sebastian's lessons to shift words from tongue to spirit and allow them to float, discorporate, into the ether. Lukas settled a garish yellow cape lined with ermine about my shoulders, adjusted its drape, and pinned it to the left with an amber brooch just as the cathedral bells struck nine.

The key snicked in the door lock again. Two snow-dusted men in wine-colored cloaks and silk half masks entered, carrying deceptively plain bronze staves. Without meeting my brother's eyes, I touched my fingertips to my forehead—half flesh, half metal—and bowed to Max and then to my jailers. The Registry men quickly silkbound my clenched hands—we were all quite experienced at this now—and I followed the two down six flights of stairs and out into the street.

Our boots crunched in the frozen muck. On this, the tenth day of my punishment, our route led to the Stonemasons' District, a familiar haunt from my days working on the cathedral. There I was to spend the hours until sunset exhibited on a public platform, my foot shackled to a loop of iron.

Ten days, ten districts. Two more days to complete the round of the twelve districts of Palinur, and two additional days in the Council District after that. I had reaped the two extra days for a breach of discipline—attempting to throttle my guards the first time they approached me with the silver mask. Since then, I had been a model of submission; the consideration of wearing the silver mask for one extra turn of the glass made me physically ill.

The frost bit at my exposed skin, and I hunched my shoulders, trying to induce the folds of the ugly yellow cape to cover my hands. The cold would be wicked on my immobilized fingers this morning. If only the wind would die down, my layers of fine clothes would keep the rest of me warm enough. Better than most of the poor devils in the streets.

My daily excursions through Palinur—the city I knew best in all the kingdom, a city of culture, beauty, and friendly, expansive people—had shocked me. Filth piled up in the streets. The residents' faces gaunt and frightened. Diseased. Once-prosperous avenues were scarcely more than rubble, wooden houses burnt, stone ones picked apart. At least half of the great statues of the Hundred Heroes that ringed the palace precincts had been toppled and no one had bothered to set them upright. So many stones had been stolen from the low wall that joined the statues that it had the look of a snaggle-toothed jawbone. The richest city in the kingdom was no longer any different from the rest of Navronne.

As we hurried across the expanse of the central market, it seemed even smaller than yesterday. Seedy and grim, the *pocardon* or "little city" of shops and carts took up less than a quarter the area it had when I had first left home. Though a piper's mournful tunes still quickened the air, the denizens of the market, who long ago would snatch an awestruck runaway from the street and lead him in a merry reel through the market stalls for the sheer joy of it, had vanished. And on this morning, the shoppers who had once laughed and made way for those dancers snarled at each other over blighted turnips and tufts of mud-caked wool—or glared at a tall freakish sorcerer in an ermine-lined cloak and silver half mask being herded through the lanes by two pureblood guards, and cursed him for squandering privileges they could never aspire to.

On this tenth morning the gaunt face of the royal city had taken on a more immediate tension—beyond the matter of starvation and hopelessness and unseasonable winter. From the moment we left the Registry tower, I had the same eerie sense as in the hours before a battle—the uneasy quiet, the fingers of fear reaching through skin and bone to grip the soul, the blur-ring of boundaries between earth and sky, between past and future. I could not shake the sense that Palinur, hitherto untouched by the war, was soon to bleed as well as starve.

Above the citadel that crowned the hilltop, Prince Perryn's gold and purple pennant whipped and snapped in the sharp breeze alongside the white trilliot of Navronne. But Max was here on his contracted master's business—the business of our prince's mortal enemy.

The earth itself will not end, only the life we know—cities and towns and villages, plowing and planting. I had not believed in the lighthouse cabal and their talk of end times. But my days in the royal city had given me pause. We were not yet to the solstice—only days past the equinox—and ever-temperate Palinur was buried in snow and ice. The arrow of war was aimed at the heart of Navronne, which was the Heart of the World. What if Luviar was right?

Though it was an ordinary day for working, hardly anyone was abroad amid the mills and tool shops of the Stonemasons' District. Small groups of men huddled together in alleyways, halting their conversations to stare as we passed. Grinding wheels and grimsaws stood idle in the workyards, winches and chains snared in unbroken ice beside piles of old scaffolding, rotted and tangled with dead weeds. Even the crowd of ragged boys who capered alongside us each morning, hurling taunts and frozen mud clots, numbered but twenty or so, less than half the size of the previous days. Only the pigeons seemed lighthearted, making free of the stoops, benches, and rooftops, fluttering upward in great swarms as our little procession marched through the gray morning.

We turned a corner into an open square, where all the streets of the Stonemasons' District came together. Here, as in every district square, Aurellian pipes and conduits fed the district well—this one topped by a pyramid of rose marble. And here, as in every district square, a pillory and flogging post stood on a raised platform. In front of the empty pillory, the Registry had installed a stone block and surrounded it with a ring of iron stanchions linked by silken ropes.

Caphur, one of the pureblood attendants appointed by the Registry to oversee my punishment, jerked his head for me to climb the platform and mount the block. Though a youngish man of modest size, he had inordinately heavy jowls that grew prodigious crops of hair. When I was in place, he attached the shackle about my ankle to the iron loop affixed to the block. Then he and his partner, whose name I didn't know, took their places outside the circle of stanchions.

The two purebloods would prevent curious ordinaries from touching me. As my Registry judges had emphasized so tediously, the purpose of this exercise was not physical harm, but "education by way of unseemly exposure to the common population." That is, a reminder that the "simple" demand of submission to my family and the Registry protected me from such filth, ignorance, and drudgery as existed among ordinaries. That is, shame and humiliation. They had neither understood nor appreciated my laughter at this pomposity.

All in all, this aspect of my punishment could have been far worse. To stand outdoors was cold and uncomfortable, but far less painful than a lashing and, for one with my peculiarities, infinitely preferable to close confinement. A smirking Caphur had told me that the Sinduria had particularly recommended this exhibition as the best way to teach me the lessons I required. I needed to consider that. My sister knew very well of my particular terrors.

Across the square a pyramid-shaped block of granite marked a frowzy lane. Allowing my eyelid to sag, I imagined I could hear Frop the Fiddler sawing on his vielle at the Plug and Feathers, situated halfway down that lane, and feel the music that always set my feet dancing as I downed the taverner's strong mead. A little farther down the lane and around the corner, squeezed between a tool grinder's shed and a smithy, a man could indulge in a hot bath and a friendly whore at the Bucket Knot, my favorite sop-house, a warm and welcoming place.

Smiling to myself, I installed Elene's face and lush figure in my imagining, whirling her to Frop's music and hearing her laugh as she had on that morning at Caedmon's Bridge. Ah, gods, what pleasure to touch her . . . to feel her naked warmth beneath me, her heart racing from the dance . . .

A stinging blow to my frozen flesh shattered my vision. The wind had whipped the hem of my heavy cape into my face. Elene had betrayed me. So no warmth to be had in visions either.

Unlike the first nine days, it took an hour for more than urchins and beggars to gather. But the chance to gape at a pureblood eventually overcame even the mysterious anxieties of the day. The yellow cape announced my offense. Scarred laborers hefting buckets or tool satchels, hollow-cheeked matrons clutching ragged children with haunted eyes, and shopkeepers wearing dirty aprons and furrowed brows drifted into the square like autumn leaves collecting under a maple, speculating aloud as to my identity, my history, my magical talents, and my future, knowing they would never be told such mysteries. They were likely wondering if the silent guards were going to do anything more with me. Likely hoping for something interesting, such as a nice flogging or maiming.

I kept my back straight and my unblocked eye open and focused forward as was required of me. My exposed right cheek stung with the cold. Though the mask shielded the left cheek from the wind, the silver chilled quickly, cooling the sweat that had formed beneath it as we walked. Soon the masked half of my face grew colder than the other, as if encased in ice that penetrated my flesh and froze my bones, as if knives mounted on the inside of the metal half face lacerated my cheek and brow.

As the ragamuffins spat and lobbed mud balls at my back without interference from the masked guards, the people grew bold with their comments: *Soul-dead . . . demon-cursed . . . real silver . . . Has he flesh under the metal, Mam? That fur's no sheep's coat nor rabbit's . . . Don't have to work . . . Don't even have to fight, they don't . . . Everything's given . . . god-given . . . while we starve. Never saw one of 'em so tall. He vomited his gift right back at the Sky Lord's feet . . . their cocks metal, too? Cover a pureblood female and their Registry'll cut off your cock. Spat on the Gehoum . . . Should burn all them as betray the Powers . . . Throw 'im in the river with that mask and he'll sink . . . meet the gods he's cursed . . . recondeur . . . traitor . . .* As if I could not hear them. As if I stood somewhere far distant behind a barricade of silver.

Afternoon brought more snow and new waves of muted gossip that rippled through the assembly. Forbidden to turn my head so my exposed ear might hear better, I heard naught of the reports.

As evening approached, my neck and shoulders ached miserably. My fingers felt dead. My nose ran unceasingly, stimulating a subtle panic that I would soon be unable to breathe. Despite my layers, I could not control my shivering. My exposed eye welled with tears from the bitter wind, and no amount of blinking could clear it, threatening my sole occupation. I derived some amusement from observing the odd folk who came to gawk at me, those like the tall, slender man in a sky-blue tunic who stood apart at the back of the crowd, his long hair plaited with green ribbons. He must enjoy spectacles; he had come every day.

A small, purposeful shift in the increasingly restive crowd signaled a new arrival making his way to the front. He soon stood immediately in front of me, a small person cloaked in black. Holy mother . . . I blinked rapidly and risked a reprimand by swiping my upper arm across my eye. The man wore a cowl! He lifted his hood just enough that he could see as high as my face, allowing me to glimpse his own odd features that looked as if they were ready to slide off his chin. Brother Victor.

Great merciful Iero, they'd come to rescue me! Somewhere under his scapular would be an ax to hack the chains away. I strained to see through the flurries and gloom. Perhaps Gildas was here . . . or Stearc. The Evanori war-rior could take on Caphur and his friend. Surely . . . My hands trembled in their unyielding wrappings. My blind eye leaked tears unrelated to the cold. *Buck up, you great ox!* Why just now at the verge of freedom did the loathsome horror of this captivity threaten to undo me?

After only a moment, the chancellor dropped his hood and raised his palm, five fingers spread wide in Iero's blessing. But as he lowered his hand, he briefly held it vertically, fingertips heavenward, at his breast—the broth-ers' signing language for the abbot—and then clenched his fist and pressed it to his heart. *Obedience.* And then . . . nothing. Gods. Nothing.

Anger flooded from my hollow breast to my frost-nipped cheek. How dare they lay their pious obligations on me?

Discipline forbade communication with an onlooker, but surely the little monk must see the flush of fury heating my face. He stood there for a while longer, his small hands folded piously. The milling crowd gradually swallowed him, and I could not judge when it was he left the square.

Gildas had said Luviar would not release me from his tether as long as he had use for me. What did he think I could do for him, trussed up like a string doll forced to perform for laughing children? *Damnable holy men!* I hated them all.

Chapter 23

On the eleventh morning of my exhibition, as we marched into the Temple District, we passed no more than ten people. Though I remained maddeningly unenlightened about events in Palinur, I judged the situation had gotten worse. Five temples faced the great circle—those of Kemen, Samele, Erdru, Deunor, and Arrosa. Throughout the day, liveried servants bore every size and shape of burden up the broad steps of the brightly painted buildings: calyxes and caskets small and large, crates of statuary and rare fruit, wine casks, grain sacks, urns, and caged birds. Someone even led a matched pair of white oxen into Kemen's gold-columned temple. Offerings to placate the gods. The wealthy people of the city were worried. I imagined I could smell the nivat. Some of the boxes surely contained that most favored offering.

Though I tried to banish the thought of nivat as soon as it arose, my mind would not let go of it, and I found myself plotting ridiculous ventures to slough off my bonds and snatch the most likely containers. Whatever would I do when I needed it again?

I had used my last supply on the journey to Palinur. After three days on the road, Thalassa had accepted my word that I would attempt no magic and allowed me to travel with unbound hands—my salvation two nights later when my disease struck and I was forced to pay the price of my incomplete doulon. That her aide Silos—he of the cheap scent and well-aimed firebolts—had eventually detected my spellworking, and that she had angrily bound my hands and shackled my feet for the rest of the journey, did not matter. Neither of them had found the mirror or the needle or discovered the truth. I owned one secret for a while longer, from all but Brother Gildas.

The worst part of this whole disgusting mess was that these unpredictable intervals between attacks of my disease had fueled a subtle anxiety that never left me.

Thoughts of Gildas led inevitably to thoughts of Brother Victor and what he could be doing in Palinur. I scanned today's crowd. He wasn't here. Surely he would not have come all this way to deliver one more warning to keep me mute. If the cabal no longer needed my help, then how, in Magrog's fancy, were they planning to contact the Danae? *Bah,* I thought, *let the pious pricks flounder.*

Reminded of the wonders I had seen at Caedmon's Bridge, I let my imagination stray. I imagined the Dané woman dancing in the moonlit fields beyond the abbey, joined by the man with the dragon sigils. The Danae twined the lives of trees and lakes, rocks and stream into their dances, so stories said, joining the elements of the world in a great pattern, so that a vine in Ardra and a river of Morian and a rocky pinnacle of Evanore became part of one great whole. What magic, what vigor, would enliven such a dance. Under my breath I hummed the harper's song I'd heard on the road to Elanus; the Danae would dance to such music as that. I could almost feel them leaping and whirling . . . caught up in the moment as I had been in the Elanus tavern . . . stretching, driving, pounding their feet—

"Attention, *plebeiu,*" snapped the voice in my ear. Caphur's fingers dug into my arm and jostled me. "Open your eye and look upon the ugliness of the ordinary world. You are forbidden to escape your punishment in sleep."

The squalor of Temple Square and the gawking crowd scrubbed away the glorious image, and the howling wind deafened me to the music of memory, leaving only a starved ache in my chest. Legends and stories . . . the Danae might live, but no pattern existed in this ugly world. In all my years of running, I had never felt so alone.

As the day waned, the torments of flesh obscured those of spirit. The snow turned to sleet. My face felt stripped raw from peppering ice and the abrasion of freezing metal. The wind drove ice-bladed knives through clothing and flesh and bone. Every part and portion of me was frozen. I could scarcely see, and my clogged nose forced me to breathe through my mouth—the pinched half of it outside the mask. I struggled to remain calm. Only the approach of evening held off despair.

"Harrow! Purify!" A scuffle broke out in the back of the twenty or thirty remaining gawkers—a mix of elaborately gowned temple aides, beggars, and idle drovers, and the tall, odd man in the sky-blue tunic.

I pressed my snow-crusted arm across my eyes, trying to blot the tears and drips. A bony youth, wearing a Harrowers orange rag tied around his head, had pushed to the front ranks, supporting himself on a crutch. Half of one of his legs was missing. He waved a clenched fist at me. "Them as flout the gods cause these evil days. Them as serve the Snake of Ardra or the Bastard of Evanore, them as worship in corrupted temples or Karish halls . . . they bring forth the pestilence. Only Prince Bayard sees the truth. But the drums ye hear be not the valiant Smith's drums but the drums of doom. The Gehoum howl on the wind! The earth cries out for harrowing! Make it level. Make it smooth! Purify!"

He raised his hand . . .

His missile glanced off the silver mask just over my cheekbone. Pain lanced through my skull. Eyes watering, I staggered backward.

Caphur jumped down from the platform and briskly kicked the offender's crutch out from under him. The youth crashed to the pavement, and the masked guard touched his bronze staff to the fallen lad's back. The tip of the staff glowed red. Smoke curled upward from the ragged cloak and burst into flame. The boy wailed . . .

Great Iero's hand! Though the mask trapped my bellowing curses in my throat, I lunged at Caphur, swinging my bound fists at his bristly jowl like a bludgeon. But my shackled ankle brought me up short, and I crashed into an awkward heap, one foot on the platform, the other foot and knee twisted behind me, still on the block. The Registry man dodged my blow without a glance.

The Harrower youth flailed and screamed. A few onlookers rolled him in the snow and beat at him with hands and cloaks to smother the fire. Others ran away. Caphur stepped back and waved his staff, pointing at one and then another of the murmuring crowd until they backed away from the platform.

Caphur's partner dragged me to my feet and motioned me back on the block. I wrenched my shoulders from his grasp. He raised one finger in warning and motioned again.

There's nothing to be done, I thought. *Not today. You'll only make things worse.* Grinding my teeth, I stepped up and dropped my arms, straightening my back and head as was required. My overseers faced the crowd, staves gripped firmly in their hands, prepared to defend me. I could not stop shaking.

A tall woman bundled in ragged cloak and orange scarf pushed to the front and pointed a long finger at the fallen youth. "Heed the work of arrogant princes! Their pet sorcerers, abominations to the Gehoum, can slay us at their will. Noble and pureblood live in corrupted luxury and praise imaginary gods, whilst we burn, our children starve, our grapes fail.".

Her voice seared the gloomy afternoon with lightning—blazing far beyond the group in front of me, reaching into alleys and byways, shops and taverns. "Tell your brothers and sisters. Fetch your cousins and uncles and friends to lay hand to the Harrow. Not until the false princes and false teachers have been purified will the Gehoum set the seasons right again."

The last of the temple aides scurried away toward the green-and-red painted temple of Samele. A sudden bluster of wind raised whorls of snow and then died as quickly as it came. As two ragged citizens piled snow on his blistered back, the crippled youth began to whisper between his sobs, "Harrow. Purify."

The woman in the orange scarf took up the chant, tended and nurtured it as if it were a budding flame, moving through the crowd and touching one person and then another on the shoulder. Though only a few in the crowd wore orange rags, many joined her in the chant. More and more, until the words pulsed like a soft heartbeat. "Harrow. Purify . . ."

At the boundaries of the square in every direction, torches winked out of the gloom and flowed toward the center like fiery streamlets emptying into a lake. The Harrowers' chants echoed from the painted facades around the square, the pulse become war drums.

Sleet clicked on my half-metal face. The wind whipped my cloak as if it were tissue. Had the cursed sun not yet set behind the blackening clouds? Shackled to the damnable block, I had no pleasant thoughts about being the center of a riot.

The urchins and beggars scattered like dry leaves in the wind. The remaining drovers ran for their rigs. The man in the sky-blue tunic had vanished. My guards hefted their staves higher, and for once I rejoiced that they were sorcerers. The flood of fire swept toward us.

A shouting arose among the chanters. They pointed toward the golden-domed Temple of Samele, where a short robust woman, wearing the green and gold robes of Samele's priestess, stood on the broad steps between the green and red columns. Torchbearers stood to either side of her, and their light glinted in the gold fan rising from her long black hair. Even from such a distance I could see the dark lines about her eyes like a mask. Thalassa.

The streamlets of fire curved toward the temple, as if they had encountered logjams in their course. When the chanters in front of me hurried off to join their fellows, the rabble-rousing woman hurried away into the dark streets, her evening's work done. The burned youth lay abandoned, already half buried in snow. Melting gobs slid from his blackened flesh.

Two ranks of green-liveried guards poured from the temple and fanned out on either side of Thalassa as she began to exhort the mob. Half deaf as I was, I could not understand her proclamation, but only the hisses and jeers that punctuated it. Flaming torches arced through the night, thrown toward the temple. Thalassa raised her hands and the torches shattered into showers of sparks that fell back on the crowd. Did Mother Samele appreciate the advantages of a pureblood Sinduria?

Mesmerized, I scarcely noticed as Caphur unlocked my ankle. But he tugged at my arm and I half stepped, half stumbled from the block and the platform. As my shepherds marched me away, I twisted my head to see over my shoulder. A green veil of light now hung over the surging throng. The line of temple guards, wielding clubs and staves, had surrounded the mob. Screams and curses rose louder.

The lurid scene was soon lost to view. With grim urgency, the guards rushed me through rapidly darkening streets, winding ever upward toward the Registry tower that sat near the lower walls of the citadel. As we crossed the deserted marketplace, a large troop of horsemen—perhaps seventy men with no visible colors—galloped toward the broad causeway that led to the palace gates. The pennants billowed heavy and listless on the battlements, only half visible in the swirling snow and sleet. I halted in my tracks.

Caphur growled impatiently. "Keep moving."

When I shook my head and raised my bound hands in the direction of the banners, he lowered his staff and stared, as well, touching the shoulder of his partner and pointing where we looked. The trilliot—the white lily of Navronne—still flew on the castle of Caedmon and Eodward, but the purple and gold banner of Perryn of Ardra was nowhere to be seen.

Yet, even as the world shifted, mystery took a stranglehold on my spirit. From across the empty expanse of trampled snow, the tall man in the sky-blue tunic and green ribbons stood watching us. I blinked and squinted. His feet were bare. On such a day. Wondering, I raised my bleary eye, met his gaze, and knew him. He had once reached out to me from an aspen grove, his bare skin glowing with sigils of blue fire.

Caphur snatched my arm and dragged me stumbling from the square.

I paced my tower room in the dark. Though shed of my frozen finery, I was not yet warm. Once free of the hateful mask, I had dared denounce Caphur as an arrogant coward for burning a cripple. That outburst and my violent behavior in the Temple District had cost me food, light, and warmth. Lukas had provided me one flask of watered ale for my supper and dressed me in dry layers of cambric and plain, padded wool, but had left my little brazier unlit and taken away my lamp. Tomorrow would likely bring more extensive penalties. I grabbed a blanket from the bed and wrapped it about my shoulders. So be it.

My pacing took me to the window again, back to matters of far more import than impotent *recondeurs* or even scorched madmen. Frost rimed the corners of the panes. After three years of war, could Palinur have been taken without a fight? Certainly Ardra's prince had fallen. The missing banner was no mischance, no oversight. Not in these times. Yet Bayard's banner had not been raised. I saw no evidence of battle in the night and storm beyond the tower, only scattered fires in the lower city. Thank the gods for the snow and damp that would check the spread of flames.

And then there was the matter of the barefoot man. Here in my tower room, it was easy to blame my nonsensical conclusion on cold, hunger, and a yearning to see something of hope in a world disintegrating before my eyes. He'd had no dragon wings scribed on his face or on the bare legs that poked out from under his pale tunic, yet I felt a certainty that stripped of his odd attire he would display the dragon marks. A Dané here in the city. A Dané I had seen before. Stories said Danae died if they remained too long in cities or man-made dwellings.

Locks rattled and the door slammed open. "Magnus Valentia de Cartamandua-Celestine, stand forward."

I spun away from the window and backed into the shadows. Perhaps my penalties had come earlier than expected. A midnight visitation was every prisoner's nightmare.

The lantern dangling from a fleshy hand illuminated a thickset man with a fat black braid and a drooping mustache. He wore his black silk mask in the horizontal fashion, covering only his eyes and brow as some pureblood families prescribed. Caphur and his partner stood behind the newcomer.

Stepping out of the shadow, I dropped the blanket and bowed to my principal Registry overseer, Sestius de Rhom-Magistoria, some colineal relation of my grandfather's family. "*Domé*."

"Prepare to go out."

"Of course, *domé*. If I might inquire—"

"You may not."

Of course he would answer no question of mine. I could imagine the instructions of the Registry judges. *Keep the prisoner ignorant. Keep the prisoner frustrated, isolated, and on edge, not knowing what humiliation will befall him next. Prove to him that he has no control over his life.*

Suppressing pointless fury, I laced up my damp boots, snatched the yellow cloak from the hook, and fastened its clasp at my shoulder. Then I turned to Sestius, the silver mask in my one hand, a silk one in the other, and the inquiry posed on my face.

"Use the silk. We're in a hurry. But bring the other. You are not finished with it yet. More insolence and you will be wearing it for a year."

I bowed and slipped on the silk mask. It felt like a second skin compared to the silver. But I did not escape every discomfort. Caphur brought out his roll of silk cord and bound my hands. Tighter than other days. Showing his teeth, he also made sure that the silver mask came with us. Bristly hair poked through the silk of his own mask around his bulbous chin. Likely his family discipline mandated a clean-shaven face, else Caphur could have grown a beard the size of a hedgehog in three days' time.

They whisked me down the stairs, where a party of two torch boys and eight or ten armed ordinaries waited. Only an extraordinarily dangerous night would occasion purebloods to call in extra escorts.

We hiked briskly through the deserted city, skirting the main streets and marketplaces. Ice coated every blade, twig, gutter, and cornice. I shivered in my ermine-lined cloak and thanked the Lord of Sea and Sky that the wind had abated.

I could not imagine where we were off to so late, until we climbed a long flight of worn steps to a crossing lane that bordered an ancient wall. The otherwise straight bulwark of stone, the remnant of some early defense work, had been designed to circumvent a notched pyramid of native rock. In the notch, water bubbled from moss-lined cracks and dribbled into a pool the size of a wide-brimmed hat. The pool, called the Aingerou's Font, never dried up and never froze, and every spring a different variety of flower grew out of the cracks in the rock. Even lacking the Cartamandua bent, I could have found my way to this lane from the depths of the netherworld. For fifteen wretched years I had resided not half a quellé from the Aingerou's Font.

The tree-shrouded lane followed the ancient bulwark past the Font to a walled stone house built in the grand Aurellian style. Large airy rooms enclosed inner courtyards, the sprawling structure ornamented with pedimented windows, meticulously designed gardens, fluted pillars, and brightly painted arches. A bronze gryphon, grasping a rolled map in its claws, loomed above us from the iron gate. As Sestius rang the bell, my entire being felt as hollow as my growling stomach. I was home.

The gate swung open before the echoes of the bell faded. A man in green livery motioned us into the snow-draped courtyard. Caphur dismissed our escorts, dropping a small pouch in their gawking leader's outstretched hand, while the man in green exchanged a private word with Sestius.

I stood stiffly by, my mind skipping from one thing to another, unwilling to acknowledge the arrival of a moment I had dreaded for so many years. Three lamps hanging from iron posts lit the path to the front door. Lights shone from a few rooms: my father's study to the left of the entry door, the reception room to the right, my mother's bedchamber around the corner on the right. Horses had been here before us. Four or five. They'd been led around to the stables. The hedges had grown tall. The ancient lime tree had lost a limb; it would never survive this kind of cold. The green livery . . . one of Thalassa's men from the temple then . . . Was she here?

Focus, Valen. You must keep your wits. Keep your temper. Control your tongue. Submit. I had to convince them that I was chastened, else I would spend the rest of my life in silken hand bindings and silver masks and ankle shackles.

I gazed longingly through the gate that was closing behind me, back down the lane where the Font bubbled quietly in its niche. Someone now sat in the niche beside the mumbling spring. Startled, I squinted down the dark lane. *Holy gods!*

The gate clanged shut, closing off my view.

"Move along, Magnus Valentia," said Sestius, opening his hand toward the front door in invitation.

The overseer trudged through ankle-deep snow toward the skewed

rectangle of light that streamed from the now open door. I followed dutifully behind him. But somewhere deep inside me rose a tickling sensation
that quickly spread to my chest and throat and mouth. My cheeks quivered.
Droplets pricked my eye. I pressed my lips together, but to no avail. At last
I slammed my fists to my mouth, attempting to muzzle the laughter I could
not stop. How foolish . . . how wondrous was life.

Sestius halted and narrowed his eyes. He laid a hand on my arm. "What
is it, lad?" His testy authority yielded to a gruff sympathy. "No need to be
afraid."

No need . . . Another quake of hopeless hilarity shook me and I tried to
wipe my eyes with my wrist. Sestius appeared confused.

"What has possessed you, *plebeiu?*"

"Ah, *domé*, pardon . . . please. It's just"—I pressed my wrist hard against
my mouth—"no one ever calls me *Magnus Valentia*. Any more than they call
my brother *Maximus Goratia*, or my elder sister *Thalassa Minora*, or my younger sisters *Phoebia Terrae* or *Petronilla Terrae*. You see, my father named us all
after geographical features, and it was left to us to dig around in them for
names that didn't sound ridiculous. And you tell me not to be afraid . . . so
kindly . . . and here I am coming home after twelve years away, looking like
some gangle-limbed canary and with my hands—"

He did not understand in the least. How could he? He had not seen what
I had.

"Please forgive me, *domé*. I am just inexcusably ill-mannered, and light-
headed as I've not eaten since morning and these days have been exhausting,
as is only right, of course."

I needed to stop babbling. And I should very likely beg some god or
other to remove the grin that would not leave my face. Life was as sublimely
absurd as my name—some barren little island off the coast of Aurellia, inhabited entirely by great gawky birds. Why else would I imagine that I had
seen the intricate outlines of a brilliant blue dragon coiling down the bare
limbs of the man sitting beside the Aingerou's Font? Or that I would swear
that he wore green ribbons plaited in his curling red hair and had met my
gaze with eyes the color of aspen leaves in autumn? I had not been mistaken.
I was being followed by a Dané.

Bowing respectfully to Sestius, in whose word lay the power to extend
my unfortunate exhibition in the city, I waved my bundled hands toward the
door. He huffed a bit, and looked at me as if I were a lunatic. Which I sup-

posed I was. But perhaps, if the world was going to end sometime soon, it didn't really matter.

We walked down a short brick passage, Caphur and his shadow trailing behind us. I was still smiling when I stepped into a vine-hung courtyard with a giant lily-shaped brazier blazing in the center. My father was waiting.

Chapter 24

The little courtyard had only a latticework roof of scrolled iron, yet the colored flames that danced in the lily-shaped brazier left the enclosure excessively warm. Appropriate, I supposed, as the courtyard was dedicated to Deunor Lightbringer. Lamps hung from iron posts, adding yellowish light to the orange and red firelight.

My first glimpse of my father sobered me quickly, causing a certain constriction in my chest I had experienced since I could remember. In the view of the world and more particularly, the Pureblood Registry, the powerfully compact man standing beside the flaming brazier held my life in his hands.

Oh, he could not kill me without consequence. A pureblood, even a *recondeur*, was too valuable an asset to dispose of without extreme justification. But pureblood heads of family, male or female as lineal customs or contracts dictated, wielded the power of a despot over their offspring by way of the entitlement to negotiate unbreakable contracts for those children's professional services, marriages, and rights of procreation. They could even sell their services to a murderer, as long as that murderer agreed to abide by the terms. Unless one became the head of family or achieved extraordinary rank in the ordinary world, as Thalassa had done, a pureblood never lived other than as a bound servant—a cosseted slave.

My father's appearance had changed very little in twelve years. Though he must be approaching sixty, he was as broad through the shoulders and as tightly built as Max. His wide hands and short thick fingers that could wield pens and brushes with elegance and precision had once choked the life out of three Hansker raiders . . . as he had reminded me on many unpleasant occasions. His long straight hair, gathered into a thick horsetail in the back, remained solidly black, though his forehead, always high, now extended halfway across the top of his head—a tonsure of a kind, to be sure.

I pressed my wrist to my mouth. The fey humor had not deserted me entirely. *Concentrate, Valen. Manners.*

"Patronn." I dropped to one knee on the brick paving and touched my bound hands to my forehead.

Though I knelt to acknowledge my father as head of our family, my resolution to mind my manners did *not* extend to the words of honor and respect a son would normally offer at such a time. He would not believe them anyway. Neither did I wait for his permission to rise. He was not a king.

"It seems the gods have granted you good health," I said, once on my feet again. I kept my tone neutral. "I presume Matronn fares well also."

My father perched half sitting on a stone altar where the household left platters of bread and pots of honey as feast gifts for the god. His dangerous, well-groomed hands were loosely clasped at his firm waist, where a belt of gold shells draped handsomely across a tight-fitting pourpoint of purple and gold brocade. The hands and posture were deceptive. He was not at all relaxed. His dusky complexion, typical of purebloods, had taken on a ruddy cast, and his full lips, so like Thalassa's, formed a thin straight line. No mistaking his state of mind.

"Your mother has no desire to see you."

Not surprising. Seeing me, she might be forced to acknowledge my troublesome existence, a task she had avoided diligently since my earliest memory. "That's unfortunate. Please convey my salutation."

Petty as it was, I could not subdue the satisfaction that coursed through me as I stood before the man I had once named Magrog the Tormentor's twin. I now stood a full quercé—four hands—taller than he. His seed might have grown me, but I liked to think I had taken naught of my parents but the black color of hair and eyes, the straight nose, and the magic of their blood.

A fidgeting Sestius, having removed his mask and retrieved a roll of vellum and the silver mask from Caphur, interrupted this tender reconciliation. "*Eqastré* Cartamandua-Celestine, we must complete the prisoner transfer. I cannot comprehend why the *recondeur*'s punishment has been interrupted . . . and at such an hour . . ."

My father snorted contemptuously. "It was certainly not my doing. Evidently someone in the Registry, higher placed than you, *Eqastré* Rhom-

Magistoria, felt it risky to have any one of us exposed to the rabble during this unsettled time."

He motioned Sestius to the table beside him. As the administrator unrolled his scroll, my father's cold gaze traveled over me. His nostrils flared as his eyes fixed on my silkbound hands. "No surprise to hear that Valen has shown himself insolent and violent," he said to Sestius. "But I'm surprised you found it necessary to curtail his use of magic. He was never competent."

"We've witnesses that he cast spells to aid his escape from the Karish abbey and attempted more on the journey to Palinur. He is completely untrustworthy. Here——" Sestius tapped a spot on one of his pages. "You must acknowledge the transfer of custody, though, as you were informed, we will keep our men here."

"I don't like strangers in my house. My daughter, the Sinduria, has insisted on providing Temple guards as well." My father pressed his thumb on the page, triggering a spell that would identify him to the Registry. I felt very like a hanging goose at the poulterer's.

"Though I am sure the Sinduria's attendants are well qualified, the Registry must supervise the *recondeur*'s restriction until his sentence is completed." Sestius rolled his papers back together so tightly he could have used the roll as a cane. "Your son has three days' punishment to fulfill, at the least. And as he physically assaulted and verbally abused one of his overseers today—a man protecting him from harm from a rapacious mob—I intend to see him flogged before we're done. I advise you keep him on a short leash." Sestius never allowed sympathy to interfere with discipline.

My father brushed his wide fingers over the silver mask that lay on the table. "Valen will not escape his duty again. If I have to pry up every rock in this kingdom, I will secure him a contract with a master who can control him."

Of course, Patronn would wish to remind me. The Registry inserted certain standard clauses into pureblood contracts. Clauses requiring adherence to Registry breeding rules. Clauses requiring recognition of the Registry as arbiter of all contract disputes. And protective clauses ensuring we were maintained in safety, dignity, and luxurious accommodation appropriate to "extraordinary beings of proven magical lineage." In running away, I had forfeited my rights to those protective restrictions. Whatever master he selected for me would be permitted to ensure my faithful service in any way he chose—confinement, whips, isolation, starvation . . .

Sestius took his leave, ordering Caphur to cooperate with Thalassa's temple attendants and to report any conflicts. I remained standing near the brazier, sweating beneath my fur-lined cloak, my face itching beneath the silk mask. My good humor had completely faded.

As the outer door closed behind Sestius, two men in green livery appeared at the inner door. A whiff of cheap perfume identified one of them as Thalassa's temple attendant Silos, the observant fellow whose hands wielded paralyzing firebolts and whose nose sniffed out spellmaking. Worse and worse.

"You may escort the *recondeur* to his quarters," said my father, walking past me as if I did not exist. "I've no need and no wish to see him any more than necessary. He is not to wander the house or grounds unaccompanied. His meals will be taken in his quarters unless I specifically summon him to dine. Work out your guard schedule with these Registry people." He waved at Caphur to join the two in green and then flicked a wrist to dismiss us all.

A hundred retorts popped to mind as my father left the courtyard. At fifteen I would have spat them at his back, sauced them with curses and obscenities, and forced the guards to drag me to my bedchamber. But I held my tongue. I had tasted freedom, and until the day I lay rotting in my grave, I would not give up hope of regaining it. If yielding present satisfaction to lull my captors was the price required, I would pay it.

The east wing was the oldest of the sprawling house, little more than low, musty chambers with small windows huddled along two sides of an overgrown court, on that night draped in snow. The walls were thicker there, and consisted of irregular, alternating layers of brick and rock that gave them a rough appearance. I remembered the rooms as being filled with broken furniture, old carpets, spiderwebs, and beetle husks.

Most of the windows gaped darkly. The low-pitched wavering mewling of a cat in heat came from one dark corner of the square. Silos dispatched his companion to show Caphur his quarters and the facilities of the house and then motioned me toward a section where light gleamed through thick shutters. I had to duck my head to enter.

Despite the rough exterior, a habitable apartment awaited me—two connecting rooms, a bedchamber and a sitting room, cleaned and furnished. Though not the broken sticks I remembered, its accoutrements contrasted starkly with those of the main house. A plaited wool rug on bare stone instead of thick carpets on mosaic and tile floors. An earthenware basin for washing instead of Syan porcelain. A hard chair instead of velvet lounges. A small eating table with two backless stools beside it. A coal scuttle beside the hearth. No hanging maps or exotic artifacts to remind visitors of the Carta-mandua talents. No magical cards or bronze water bowls left easily available for Celestine divinations.

Coals blazed in the sitting-room hearth. A kettle hung over the fire, and a bathing tub sat beside it. A shirt of fine linen lay neatly over the chair back. My sour-faced Registry valet stood beside the hearth, eyes unfocused, hands clasped properly behind his back.

"You must be Lukas," said Silos, latching the door behind us. "Assigned for personal service by the Registry."

The valet bowed stiffly.

"As I am sure the Registry overseers have informed you, the Sinduria Cartamandua-Celestine has arranged for me to supervise the *recondeur*'s confinement while in this house," said Silos.

"Yes, *domé*."

"Overseer Caphur will be taking his orders from me as well."

"I understand, sir. I was told to see to the *plebeiu*'s bathing upon his arrival. Do you approve?" I enjoyed seeing Lukas's face darken and shrivel like an old grape at Silos's assumption of command. My valet clearly did not believe a Registry employee, even an ordinary, should be taking orders from a temple attendant, even a pureblood.

Silos was unfazed. "Proceed with your duties. Unfortunately this wing has no piped water, but you'll find the household staff efficient and accommodating. You've been shown the kitchen?"

The valet nodded, bowed, and departed through the courtyard door. A soft whining and a skin-prickling heat burst infused the room as he passed through the door. They hadn't bothered to mute the door ward, designed to alert my guards that someone had left the room.

Fine as a hot bath sounded, I wasn't sure I could bear another hour with Lukas. At least the rules of household privacy would keep both Registry and temple guards at bay while I bathed.

"I'll take those off now," said Silos softly, pointing at my hands, startling me out of my murky deliberations.

The temple guard had slipped off his mask and hung it over his belt. Large ears poked through his dark straight hair. Though his address was proper as always, his wide face expressed neither gloating nor severity. Perhaps forty, he seemed a bit soft around the edges for a Sinduria's bodyguard. But our confrontations at the abbey and on the journey to Palinur had taught me not to take him lightly, despite the unprepossessing body and his fondness for flowery scent.

"I'd be grateful," I said, extending my arms. "I hope you've less constricting means to ensure my good behavior while I'm here."

As Silos unwrapped the silk-clad lump joining my arms—I could no longer swear the bloodless bundle was hands—one side of his mouth curved upward. "You wouldn't be imagining I'm going to tell you about our precautions, would you? I've not forgot you had the better of me on the road."

"I didn't escape," I said. Happily for me, Silos's skill at spell detection lagged his skill at hurling paralyzing firebolts, else I would be a madman already. On that night of my last doulon, somewhere between Gillarine and Palinur, my spellworking had not waked him. He'd only detected the magical residue in the morning. For the rest of the journey, he had mumbled curses at himself.

"I was too slow picking up on what you were about. That won't happen again." He slipped off the cords and tossed them on the table. Then, kindly, he peeled off my mask and threw it down beside the bindings. "Tell me what spell you worked that night, and I might tell you some of the ways we have to keep you from running away from this house."

"Ach . . ." The cords had left deep grooves in my flesh. I fumbled to unfasten the clasp on my horrid cloak, but my fingers felt like clubs. I shook them vigorously and moved closer to the fire. As my fingers throbbed, I shot him a halfhearted grin. "Tell me what protections you've set up here, and I might tell you what I was doing that night."

He shrugged in mock apology as he unhooked the clasp for me and threw the yellow cape over a chair. "I'll say only this. There's only the one passage out of this courtyard, and you will be sure to meet either me or my partner, Herat, or this Registry man, Caphur, if you should venture it. This door will remain locked—only a formality, as your father requests it—but we will know of any comings or goings. You may walk in the yard in company with one of us. Your needs will be taken care of. The Sinduria sent a personal attendant for you . . . an ordinary . . . but this Registry fellow, Lukas, was here already."

His equitable manner emboldened me. "Can you tell me, good Silos, what news in the realm? I've heard naught of the world since we left the abbey. But Prince Perryn's banner no longer flies above the citadel."

Silos went to one of the windows and ran his fingers along the iron frames—checking the locks, I assumed, or installing wards. Though common wards could prevent spellworking, they could not disrupt a pureblood's bent. Unfortunately, tracking and route finding in this chamber would lead me nowhere but to the door.

"I'm sorry, *plebeiu*," said Silos. "You remain under Registry censure, thus are not privy to news. Your sole task is to attend your own behavior and submission to your family."

Ludicrous. The world was crumbling and I was supposed to be concerned with masks and manners. "Of course, that's true," I said, straining to remain civil. "And you are pureblood and must serve the Registry's wishes, as well as my sister's. But even the Registry does not interfere with a man's duty to the gods. So surely then, as a servant of the goddess Samele and her high priestess, duty-bound to reclaim a soul who has been dabbling with Karish ways, you are permitted to discuss matters of worship . . . of the temple. Such as the rioters today . . . some of them Harrowers . . . so many . . ."

"Once Sila Diaglou declared for Prince Bayard, Prince Perryn gave her Harrowers the run of the city to appease them. But they've no loyalty to buy. Instead they've put themselves on every district council. They run out the magistrates and judges with fearmongering and threats of burning, then name their own to fill the places. And they're doing the same in the temples."

He moved to the door and ran his fingers about the perimeter. "Three months ago, Jemacus, second to the high priest of Erdru, burnt his temple in Trimori and declared himself a Harrower. We've heard he's on his way here and that half the priests in Erdru's temple are his men. Every temple staff is eating itself with suspicions and examinations. Chaos, that's what the Harrowers want. All of us eating roots and cowering in caves. What 'purity' lies in chaos and ruin?"

I shook my head, trying to recapture a memory as fleeting as starfall. Jullian had once said something . . . that someone had told him everyone should be made pure like him and Gerard.

A sudden anxiety stabbed through every other concern. How could I have forgotten? "Silos, did you find Gerard—the boy at the abbey?"

"Is *this* a matter of your soul as well, *plebeiu*?"

"Yes. Well, of course it is. He was . . . is . . . my vowed brother."

He raised his eyebrows, but did not argue. "The boy was not within the abbey precincts. We found his footsteps mingled with many others outside the walls, but could discover no definite direction to them. We've no reason to believe he's harmed."

Likely the boy was tucked safely in his own bed back home, having decided that girls were more fun than celibate monks or studious Jullian. Likely. So why couldn't I believe it? Ready to be done with this wretched day, anxious for Silos to depart, I squatted and held my hands closer to the little brazier.

The temple aide brushed the dust from his hands and jupon. "I'm off now. Behave yourself, *plebeiu*. I don't like you twisting words and dealing lightly with the gods to get your way." He remained stiffly by the door, his lips set in a prim line, waiting.

Of course. Manners. I stood up, touched my still-tingling fingers to my forehead, and bowed. Every pureblood was my superior. "Good night, *Domé* Silos."

As soon as he was out the door, I hurried to the bedchamber window. The cold night air took my breath as I yanked the balky casement inward and peered into the night. A quivering energy about the window indicated more magical alarms to warn of my escape. My poor skills gave me no hope of shaping an unraveling spell. Thus, for the moment, I let my eyes adjust to the dark sloping lawn and the thin line of beech trees and low wall that separated this wing of the house from the lane and the Aingerou's Font.

No movement was visible through the leafless branches. No dark blur against the night or the embankment. No blue dragons scribed in light on muscular limbs.

I gripped the casement and stared into the empty night until I was so cold I could scarcely move. *Dealing lightly with the gods* . . . perhaps I had been. A catch in my throat threatened to unleash emotions I had no use for. Somewhere the lonely cat was still wailing.

When Lukas returned to undress me for bath and bed, he snorted and slammed shut the casement. Thank all gods he was not pureblood. They would hang me before I bowed to him.

"I cannot sit in that room all day and pick at my scabs," I said as I strode down the cobbled paths of the knot garden. "My father said I was not to roam unaccompanied, so accompany me or explain it to him, whichever you choose. He very much outranks you, *domé*, and is not happily thwarted."

Caphur, the Registry overseer with the hairy chin and short legs, dodged snow-laden branches and tripped over broken paving, struggling to keep up as I sweated out the frustration of a long night of little sleep and an entire morning of doing nothing. I felt ready to tear down the garden walls with my teeth.

The squalling I had thought was a cat had broken into cackling and screams early that morning. Only one explanation had come to mind: They housed mad cartographers as well as *recondeurs* in the east wing. My grandfather was confined not a hundred quercae from my apartment. By midday, I was half crazed with the racket . . . and the thought of its source. When Lukas arrived with my dinner, I bolted through the door into the open air. Though only one alarm had triggered, not two, prickly Caphur had spotted me instantly and latched on to me like a wasp.

The din from the corner apartment quickly drove me out of the overgrown courtyard, through the brick arch, and around the washhouse. I remembered this garden as the sunniest of the little patches of nature sprinkled about my family's rambling house. Not that there was much sun in evidence this day. Moisture-filled clouds bulged and sagged onto the roof tiles.

The meticulous plantings of the knot garden appeared flat and soggy under the patchy snow, blackened leaves and dead stems instead of colorful swaths that shifted hue and pattern through the year as the various plants bloomed and faded. Silos and the second temple guard posted themselves at the outer wall, lest I take the wild notion to fling myself at the piled stones and skitter over them like the lizards that lived there in true summer. Tempting to try it anyway. Caphur alone, I might challenge. The bristle-faced Registry man was strong, but not particularly quick. Burning the Harrower youth had shown him unimaginative and brutish. But Silos . . . My body well remembered his precise and paralyzing sorcery as I ran from Gillarine.

No, escape would be impossible as long as my guards were so edgy. I had to wait. I had to behave myself, to lull them into belief in my compliance. Stupid to have walked out like this.

When I tired of circling the same half quellé of path and the same gnarled blockage of grievances, I returned to my chambers, bearing some faint hope that Lukas had not disposed of my meal in his haste to report my ill behavior. To my dismay and astonishment, I found my father seated beside my brazier.

"Patronn," I said, genuflecting.

He flicked his hand in a gesture that I interpreted as "continue with what you should be doing, if you can possibly complete it before I get too impatient." So I sat on one of the stools while Lukas, wearing no expression but smug superiority, deftly removed my muddy boots, replaced them with gray slippers, and blotted the damp from my shoulders, back, and head with a soft towel. Unable to stomach the yellow cape, I had worn no outer garment, despite the chill.

Protocol forced my valet to withdraw to the bedchamber and close the door once his sartorial duties were completed. Poor nasty, spying Lukas. I rose and awaited the reprimand to come.

"You didn't run." Less anger than I expected. Suspicious, though, and a bit off-balance. Almost tentative. I had never seen my father this way.

"You did not forbid me to breathe, Patronn. Only to intrude on your sight. I've never seen you in the knot garden." I *would* keep my temper. Or, at the least, I would force him to lose his first. "Did you *wish* me to run? Silos's firebolts are impressive and quite debilitating."

"I've had an inquiry about a contract."

Bravado drained into the region of my great toe. Max had been right; anyone interested in the contract of a *recondeur* was more likely brute than saint. No point in asking the identity of the inquirer. My father would tell me or not at his pleasure. Why had he come here—to watch me tremble? Did he imagine that terror at a perilous future would make me beg him for a lifetime's forgiveness?

"That must be gratifying," I said at last, clasping my hands at my back. At the least, I would give him no leverage.

He leaned forward, his dark eyes blazing of a sudden. "If you had ever shown just one minim of appreciation . . . of . . . of . . . loyalty . . ."

"Appreciation? Loyalty? For what?" I gaped at him. What skewed perception had him using such words with me in such aggrieved fashion? "Lord of Sea and Sky, I was your *child*! I never asked to be some weapon of war between you and the cursed gatzé who fathered you."

I would not accept assignment of blame for our difficult past. After twelve years of drowning all serious thoughts in mead and dancing and the requirements of survival, I'd had far too much time to think these past weeks.

"I know not why I am as I am, or why you have loathed me since my earliest memory, but you tried to beat it out of me because you hated *him*. You *made* me, Patronn. You birthed me with your cock, and you formed me with your strap and your hatred. Now, unfortunately for both of us, you must deal with me. So do as you have ever done . . . as you damnably well please."

So much for keeping my temper.

Livid and shaking, he shot from the chair, pointing one finger as if to loose lightning at me. "How dare you speak to me in such fashion? You are no child of mine."

His declaration—the foulest, the most dreadful condemnation that could be spoken from a pureblood father to his offspring—fell between us with the impact of an iron gauntlet thudding to the floor. Something—those irretrievable words or the sight of his trembling hand—infused me with inordinate calm. I pulled up to my full height and enjoyed looking down at him. "Then let me go."

"Oh, no," he said, moving to the door, his rage held dangerously tight. "I have responsibilities to this family—something your unnatural soul will never understand. This contract will remove your face from my sight, your foul speech from my hearing, and the burden of your existence from my shoulders. Every pureblood will see the sweetness of this resolution and marvel at the ways of fate. Command your valet to dress you appropriately, Valen. Tonight our family will celebrate a sealing feast, and by tomorrow the unseemly past will at last be put to rest."

He slammed the door before I could answer. I lifted the chair where he'd sat and threw it at the door. Dust and cushions and splinters of wood and stone rained down on the woven rug, but the chair came to rest on its side. Intact.

I bellowed and laughed at the same time, as this rebellion came to the same pitiful ending as every other. Was my life to be the very archetype of futility? Nothing changed. Nothing settled. Nothing accomplished. Every day I'd lived under his roof I had prayed to hear that I was not Claudio de Cartamandua's child. Now, even if I could believe it true, I knew it made no real difference.

I clamped my hands at the back of my neck and squeezed my head between my forearms, trying to crush the useless rage and nonsensical terror that had set me on this course of madness so many years ago. For it was not just the enmity between me and my father and my grandfather—the anger, spite, and bitterness that had forever plagued this house—that had me ready to slam my head into the stone. The flaw was in me. Somewhere I was broken, not just in my ability to decipher words on paper, but in my ability to live in this world.

One of my childhood tutors, the first and last who had ever bothered to listen to my rants, had argued that the duties and restrictions of pureblood life were no more demanding than those of any privileged family. One had to pay for the position one inhabited in this world, he'd told me, and I should be grateful for what I was given. In a frenzy I had shoved him into a brick wall and ransacked his study, pawning two of his precious books for the money to get myself royally drunk. I was eleven. In the years since, logic nagged that his arguments had merit. But my body and spirit yet refused to accept them.

Somewhere in my gut grew this septic knot, this disease that made me lash out in madness at the merest hint of constricting walls, that imbued me with unnamable fears and cravings that tormented my body, savaged my senses, and sent me crawling to the doulon. I had thought I would grow past it, that my disease was an artifact of an unfortunate childhood and that making my own choices would reduce its power. The days at Gillarine had fooled me into thinking I might win. Though I'd known full well that I—an unscholarly man of scattered beliefs and feeble principle—did not belong in Ophir's brotherhood, I had managed to accommodate the abbey's discipline without going mad from it. But now my problem was worse than ever. This sense of entrapment, loss, waste, and emptiness threatened to undo me. I had never felt so hollow, so helpless, or so afraid.

The door to the bedchamber opened softly behind me. A few tiptoed steps. A breath of air as the door to the courtyard opened and closed. Cowardly Lukas. He likely thought I would kill him. He didn't realize that I was no good at that either.

I slept most of the afternoon. Rain hammered on the slate roof and dripped and pooled in the courtyard, making freezing soup of the snow. As the charcoal-colored daylight gave way to darkness, Lukas braved the bedchamber to light the lamps. I felt him creep to my bedside.

"No need to wake me," I said. "And I'll not break your arm. You're not worth the punishment I'd reap."

He jumped back as I swung my feet to the floor and ground the heels of my hands into my eyes. When I at last looked up, he was pouring steaming water from a pitcher into the earthenware basin. Behind him, hanging from hooks on the wall, were such an array of brocades, velvets, and furs as could finance a small army for a year—my assigned costume for the evening.

The signing of a contract outranked any celebration of god or saint in a pureblood household. With the exception of my grandfather, who had not been allowed at table since I was thirteen, everyone would be at the sealing feast: my mother, Thalassa, Max, if he remained in Palinur, Bia or Nilla, whichever of the twins Max had said was still living in this house. It would be unthinkable for them to miss such an occasion, no matter their duties or preferences.

I considered refusing to change out of the rumpled gray pourpoint I'd slept in, but only briefly. Might as well maintain a little dignity. If I behaved, perhaps they would not bind my hands. That one circumstance might yield a sliver of an opening for the flimsy scheme I'd come up with as I had moped and drowsed and toyed with a spider I'd found crawling across my nose.

Might . . . perhaps . . . a sliver . . . The best plan I could come up with was idiocy. But I could not sit placidly and allow them to enslave me. As for the consequence of failure, I could see nothing worse than what I faced already. I'd escaped this house before and had been sure I'd find a way to do so again, given time. But I'd not expected a contract offer so soon.

Two hours later, I was washed, shaved, trimmed, and buttoned and laced into my finery. I wore no jewels; my father would not trust me so far as that. His tailor must have hired half a village to come up with such elaborate garments reasonably fitted to my measure in so short a time. Even so, Lukas had to stitch up my undersleeves of red and gold striped silk to show through the slashed sleeves of the green velvet pourpoint, and take hurried tucks in the rear of my black silk breeches. The tailor must have assumed anyone with so long a leg must also be broad abeam. At least no mask was required. Sealing feasts were not public spectacles; the only ordinaries present would be household servants.

If I was successful in my attempt, perhaps I could draw out the gold thread that picked the borders and seams of my green velvet and sell it for enough to eat. I laughed aloud at the image of my unsewn finery flapping loose as I raced through Palinur's sordid alleyways.

My despairing humor elicited a shocked expression from Lukas, who had spoken not a word since my waking. He pinned the yellow cloak at my shoulder. A ratcheting of the door lock and a blast of winter air brought Silos and Caphur . . . and their ball of gray silk cord.

"By the Creator, *Domé* Silos, am I not to eat or drink at my own sealing feast?" I said, facing the open door squarely as they moved one to either side of me. I clamped my hands tight under my arms, fingering a small porcelain cup I'd kept from breakfast.

"Fold your hands, fingers in, *recondeur*," ordered Caphur.

"*Domé* Cartamandua would not have you run tonight, *plebeiu*," said Silos quietly. "The stakes are greater now, as you well know, and your history speaks against you."

Stupid to run, after all. Thalassa's man had done his work well. The outer walls of my apartments had proved impervious to spells. Guards would surely be standing in the arched passage—the only exit from the courtyard—and every step of the way into the main house would be watched. Only the overgrown wall of the courtyard was left as an escape route. And the voiding spell I had prepared to tunnel through it could not be quickened until I touched the wall—a very long way across the yard.

But when had futility ever slowed me? This house felt like a tomb, the masks and cloaks my grave wraps, this contract the seal that would close the stone behind me. Despite my rage-fed swearing and mindless vows, I did not want to die. So I ran.

The moment I broke the plane of the door, I released the spider I had so carefully nurtured in the little cup, pouring magic into the illusion that would make him seem the size of a cotter's hut. Caphur screamed, which pleased me. Then *I* screamed and pitched forward into the muddy garden, my back burning as if set afire like that of the Harrower youth in the Temple District.

Icy slush seeped around the edges of the yellow cloak and slowly penetrated my layers of silk and velvet. Beneath my face and chest, my voiding spell left a rapidly filling mudhole where daylilies had once grown. I could not move.

"I'm sorry, *plebeiu*. We can't have that. Not tonight." Silos's voice remained quiet and unruffled as his firm, yet not ungentle, hands dragged me up and brushed the dead leaves and crusts of ice from my clothes. The remnants of my spider rained down over the courtyard like flakes of black snow. I had never even touched the wall.

"Magrog's fiends, that's wicked," I croaked. My throat felt scorched. "Where did you learn to do that?"

Silos clapped me on the shoulder, grasped me securely by the arm, and guided me back to my apartments, where a smirking Lukas wiped my face and sponged my velvets. A red-faced Caphur hobbled my ankles with shackles and a very short chain and proceeded to incapacitate my hands. At least the yellow cloak was sodden, filthy, and totally unsuitable. To wear a cloak between the east wing and the main house was a bit excessive anyway. I wasn't even late for the festivities.

Chapter 25

Candlelight splashed over the grand oval table from two long candlebeams of polished ebony, suspended from the coffered ceiling by silver-braided ropes. Reflections of the hundred tiny flames gleamed in silver spoons and sparked and shimmered in gold-rimmed platters, green enameled bowls, and etched glass goblets. The members of my family gleamed and sparkled, too, as they gathered about the knee-high stone table that stood at the heart of any pureblood household—whether or not that household had a heart.

Silos had bade me pause just outside the dining room as he locked an inner door behind us, thus cutting off one possible escape route should some miracle free me from my shackles. So I waited in a small arch, hidden by the shadows that pooled in the corners of the dining room, masking the sideboards and servers' tables. I fervently wished I could remain there unnoticed and unremembered.

My father, resplendent in a stiff pourpoint of red brocade, a heavy pectoral chain banded with rubies and emeralds, and a red mantle worked in gold-embroidered gryphons and lined with white fur, stood at one end of the oval table. He watched with folded arms as Max settled my mother onto her pile of cushions.

My mother's sculpted cheeks looked peaked. The heavy kohl diviner's lines about her eyes appeared more ghastly than I remembered, as her thick black hair was now streaked with white. But her well-filled white bodice glittered with diamonds; her black mantle was lined with the long silvery fur of the Denab fox; and her diamond-ringed fingers still leaked power enough to make the light around her shiver. My mother was a formidable enchantress. And a drunkard. When the doors to the main courtyard opened just behind her, the scent of wine wafted across the vast room to my niche, though the shimmering carafes on the table had not yet been broached.

Thalassa, her green cloak glittering with raindrops and her hood draped gracefully about her neck and shoulders, swept through the gilded doors and hurried toward the outsized hearth. The marble mantel was supported by twin carved gryphons, each taller than two men of my height. There she embraced a thick-waisted young woman in dark blue silk, my younger sister Phoebia.

Bia had grown slightly taller than Lassa, though her body had failed to develop the curves of our robustly female mother and elder sister. Long black braids, plaited with pearls and silver cord, wound thick and shining about her head, and her skin had developed a deep coppery hue, which I thought quite pretty, and an immense grace, considering the dreadful bout of girlish pustules that had afflicted her as a child. She had always resented her twin sister's more fortunate complexion. Mine, too, though my pale coloring, so different from other purebloods', had earned me a full measure of her ridicule. Bia looked tight and anxious tonight, her gaze darting about the room until it settled on me.

"Here he is!" Phoebia's exclamation echoed sharply through the room, causing Thalassa to jerk her head around and hushing the quiet talk among the three at the head of the table. "Samele's night, he is so tall!"

Duty done, Silos motioned me farther into the room. I moved slowly, so that the humiliating clatter of the chains against the floor tiles might sound less like a millworks. We halted at the edge of the thick rugs and the jumble of embroidered seat cushions that bordered the table.

Five pairs of eyes stared at me, seven if you counted the "second eyes" drawn about those of my diviner mother and sister.

"Manners," whispered Silos.

Though tempted to throttle him, I settled for a glare. Who likes to be reminded of irksome duties they are resigned to fulfill?

Taking a knee was, of course, impossible with my ankles hobbled. "Patronn," I said, touching my bound hands to my forehead. "Greetings of evening and feasting." Neither his rigid posture nor unblinking glare relaxed in the slightest. But then again, protocol mandated only some acknowledgment on the part of the superior, not anything of graciousness or welcome. I rose when I spied his fist clench.

A second bow, this to my mother. "Matronn, the years have not dimmed your presence."

A spasm in her shoulders might have been a response. Her painted eyes never left her cup.

And one for Lassa: "*Sinduria serena,* your goddess must be grateful indeed for your courageous defense of her temple yesterday."

I almost added my own thanks. Whether or not she had intended it so, her appearance on the steps of Samele's temple had diverted much ugly attention from me. But then again, I would not have been exposed but for her self-righteous meddling. So, no exceptional greeting for Thalassa. She, at least, opened her palms in my direction, before turning away to speak to my mother.

Though Max was elder, Thalassa's rank had trumped his place in the order of greeting. My brother looked dashing in his knee-high boots of pale calfskin, studded and buckled with gold, and a handsome topaz-and-copper-colored doublet that set off his dusky skin. Though the plain gold band about his forehead caught the light, his eyes sparked far brighter. His business in Palinur must be going well. He grinned at me as I bowed.

"*Ancieno,* to see you twice in two days after so long away staggers the mind . . ." . . . *and I would quite like to know what causes your smug cheer.*

And finally Bia: "*Serena pauli,* you have grown fairly. I promise not to set your braids afire tonight."

Her lip curled and nostrils flared. I half expected flame and smoke.

Max's report that Bia had dabbled in her own rebellion had been interesting. I could well imagine my parents' harsh reaction to the least hint that she might follow my lead. Any sympathy she may have had for my cause had likely withered under their heavy hands. But as I lowered my wrapped hands from my forehead, I extended them toward her and shrugged in what semblance of humor I could manage on a night when my soul languished in a pit from which it might never emerge.

"*Vyrsté.*"

Bia whispered the nasty word across the table, but my father heard it. Faster than an angel flies to heaven, he stepped around the table to her side and whipped a palm across her cheek. The slap echoed sharply in the silence. "*Never* in my house."

To impugn a sibling's blood purity was to impugn the family's blood purity—an unconscionable slander. My sister glared at me unchastened, the mark of Patronn's hand deepening the rich color of her cheek. What would she say if she'd heard my father's outburst of the afternoon?

I bowed to Bia again, pressing my hands to my breast in sincere apology. How awful that my presence made her willing to suffer Patronn's wrath. Awful to see that nothing had changed in this house. Awful that her rebellion had not taken her away from it even for a few years. She likely assumed I was mocking her. In truth, my stomach gnawed itself as it ever had when my father struck any of us.

"You may take your accustomed place, Valen," said my father, affable again as he sat on the piled cushions beside my mother. "Despite your lack of apology for your misdeeds, I'll not insist you sit at a separate table tonight. As the terms of this contract offer specify a lifetime extent, and I am unlikely to summon you back for any reason, this evening will be the last time your presence or absence at this table need be remarked. The rest of you, be seated so we may begin our celebration."

A hollow welcome, to be sure. The uneasiness that had festered through the afternoon at the abrupt and unlikely offer for my contract flared anew, an unformed anxiety lodged near my breastbone. A lifetime contract—not unheard of. But such an agreement would most often occur after several shorter successful ventures or with exceptional recommendation. What made unskilled magic in an undisciplined package worth gold enough to please my father? I could think of no reassuring aspect of a blind offer for my entire life.

"Are you reciting your Karish prayers, Valen? Take your place." My father's eyes smoldered behind his ungracious humor.

My "accustomed place" was halfway down one side of the table, between Lassa and the empty place that was Nilla's. As her home in Avenus lay too far distant for her to attend on such short notice, her place was marked by a porcelain bowl filled with rosebuds. How had they marked my empty place all these years? A tin plate of thorns?

The ornate gold cup of the head of family sat at the vacant end of the table opposite my parents—a concession to my mad grandfather's continuing existence. My father had assumed the duties of head of family sometime near my fourteenth birthday, after presenting evidence to the Registry of my grandfather's worsening mania and need for confinement. It must gall Patronn sorely that the old gatzé yet lived.

Bia lowered herself to her cushions gracefully. She sneered as my attempt to do the same came near toppling me into the long, shallow libation bowl that adorned the center of the table. Silos caught my elbow and helped me down, preventing the unseemly disaster. After politely assisting Lassa to her cushions as well, he withdrew to the shadowed arch. Max coiled easily into the place between my mother and Bia, kissing our younger sister's hand with a rakish grin and whispers that prompted girlish tittering.

Once we were in place and a steward had poured the wine, my father raised his crystal goblet. A skull-like grimace masqueraded as a smile. "So many of us together again . . . it does my heart good to see it. Though our *recondeur* remains lamentably unchastened, we receive him back into our embrace tonight, while at the same time celebrating an exceptional opportunity for him to do his duty by the family. Amid the vagaries of political change—the rise and fall of princes and kings—the Cartamandua name yet soars. The blood that fills our veins makes even our dregs prized. Let us offer proper reverence to Kemen, Lord of Sea and Sky, to Samele, Lady of Earth and Wind, and to our family's especial patron, Deunor Lightbringer, Lord of Fire and Hearth, for this restoration of our honor."

With each invocation he raised his cup higher. Then he poured half of his wine into the bronze libation bowl and drank the rest in one swallow. The steward had to refill my mother's cup before she could do the same. My father's face flamed scarlet at this slight delay in ceremony. Once my mother had tipped a paltry spoonful of her wine into the bowl and drained the rest, my three siblings poured and drank in their turn.

Truly we were a sorry excuse for a family. No matter the future, the prospect of a curtailed stay in their bosom did not grieve me.

My own crystal cup sat gleaming like a great ruby of temptation, within easy reach for one with usable hands. The smell of the potent vintage came as near anything to driving me into groveling submission. *Ah, gracious Erdru, Lord of Grape and Harvest, if I must be shuffled off to some grim lot, could I not at least be drunk?*

I leaned toward my elder sister. "Will your goddess overlook my failure to join in this pious practice?" I said in a mock whisper. "Perhaps you could hold my cup for me . . ."

Lassa ignored my irreverence. Instead, she raised her refilled glass toward my scowling father. "Patronn, my mistress, divine Samele, surely guided me to the *recondeur*'s hiding place among the Karish. I offer the goddess the entirety of my evening's refreshment and advise the rest of you to do the same. With the realm so unsettled, we must not take our debts to the divine lightly."

My elder sister had never shied from conflict with my father, but was far more diplomatic than I had ever been. She had not defied, but certainly displeased, Patronn by leaving his control for temple service when she was sixteen. She proceeded to empty her entire cup of wine into the libation bowl and prevented the steward refilling it. Bia hurriedly did the same. I came near moaning at the scent.

When it became clear that no one else was going to give up their wine to the gods, my father signaled the servants to begin serving the meal. "It matters naught who sits Caedmon's throne," he said. "Our interests will be well served with any outcome."

"Not so, Patronn," said Max, whipping out a jeweled eating knife. "Navronne needs strength on the throne. The Hansker grow bolder every day that Perryn and Osriel refuse to recognize Prince Bayard's legitimate claim. Traders tell us that the Velyar and the Sydonians have sucked all use from their own lands and will be on the rampage by spring, as if they can smell our weakness. Prince Bayard is the only one of the three who knows how to fight barbarians."

"Bayard *is* a barbarian," said Thalassa. "Who else would make a pact with Sila Diaglou? The Harrowers will bring him down in his turn, Max. Did you know they consider purebloods as blasphemous aberrations in need of 'cleansing' the same as Karish priests or Sinduri? At least Perryn could have—"

"Never fear, sister," said Max. "My prince can control a few ragtag fanatics. Perryn of Ardra is a weakling dandy who tried to cheat his way onto the throne. He couldn't even hire a competent forger. Now that Perryn's cowardly ass is bared for all to see, Osriel will have no choice but to heel as well. He hasn't mages enough or warriors enough to challenge Bayard on his own. Evanore's gold can rebuild whatever these mangy Harrowers tear down better than it was before. Let the storms of purification rage their little while . . . and rid us of a few laggards and slums . . ."

Bia laughed uneasily. My mother drained another cup. Max raised his wine cup with one hand, and with a motion of the other drew from it a burst of colored sparks, swirling the flying particles into a glittering ring that hovered over his head.

". . . and if the fanatics win the day and chaos reigns"—with a quick spread of all five digits, he dispersed his crown into a shower of color that tickled my nose—"then who is more likely to survive than a pureblood, who can terrify the fearful masses with a twiddle of his fingers?"

Fool, I thought. *What do you know of survival?* Unless he had learned to conjure food from grass or wine from bare vines, neither finger tricks nor Cartamandua magic would fill his belly if these end times came to pass. He had seen war, but his royal contract would have assured that he had never gone hungry, never slept but coddled in furs, never lacked for clothes, servants, or gold enough to buy whatever he lacked. I looked around the table at my family, entrenched in this strange world I had so long refused, and of a sudden, felt older than all of them. They had no idea what they faced if the Harrowers had their way.

As if summoned by Max's cheerful bloodthirst, servants descended on us like a plague of silent gnats, carrying platters of roast duck that I knew would have skin like crisp bits of heaven, delicate fish sprinkled with rosemary and nuts, and plump vegetables golden with saffron.

Unable to partake, I closed my eyes and imagined myself away from this table. How fine it would be to be sitting in the light-bathed Gillarine refectory eating stewed parsnips, stolid Brother Cadeus scratching his nose as he droned some interminable lesson at the lectern, Brother Robierre kindly buttering old Abelard's bread, and Jullian and Gerard sitting on either side of me, grinning at each other around their soup spoons. Such a room needed no marble hearth to warm it. I had not thought I would ever miss the abbey so.

Which thoughts, of course, led me back to the nagging worry about Gerard. Had the boy ever been found? He'd not seemed at all a rebellious sort, but always performed his duties cheerfully. What would lure him from the security of Gillarine? Gildas had thought to send him to the dolmen with my provisions, but I'd told him not to. Deunor's fire . . . had he done it anyway? What if the boy had gotten lost or tripped and cracked his head on a stone in the night? No, no. Gildas would say something if he'd sent the boy into danger. And then my thoughts slipped further afield. How much more interesting this dinner would be were the members of the lighthouse cabal our guests—enigmatic Luviar, incisive Brother Gildas, the scholar-warrior Lord Stearc and his intelligent secretary Gram, and Elene . . . Elene in a woman's gown that clung to her ripe figure . . .

". . . but I was surprised to hear of the Karish hierarch's move. After so many years of loyalty to Perryn, to turn on him so abruptly."

Thalassa's comment snagged my attention. My eyes snapped open.

"The hierarch saw which way the wind was blowing," said Max, gesturing to a serving girl to sauce his meat with more fruit conserve from a red enamelware dish. "*Providential* that he would find the long-lost writ so soon after Prince Bayard trounced Perryn at Wroling, don't you think?"

Deunor's fire! Eodward's writ of succession . . .

Thalassa waved away the servant trying to install frosted grapes on her plate. "The Sinduri meet at dawn to discuss the implications. Bayard's debt to this hierarch could alter the balance in favor of the Karish apostates. Though we've tried to remain neutral throughout—"

"You're saying Hierarch Eligius found Eodward's will?" I burst in, unable to withhold longer. All eyes turned to me.

"This Karish priest claims he's found Hierarch Angnecy's copy of the missing writ and that it names Bayard king," said Thalassa, her tone unemotional. "Even if the document is authentic, one wonders at the timing."

Tales said Eodward had made three copies of his will. One he had hidden in some place of safety where it would be revealed at his death. The other two he had entrusted to the two clergymen who had brought him back to Navronne, Sinduré Tobrecan and Hierarch Angnecy. But no verified copy had ever been brought forward. Angnecy had preceded Eodward in death and his successors as Hierarch of Ardra had long professed ignorance of any such document. Tobrecan had died in Evanore in the same month as Eodward, and his copy had never surfaced. In the early days of the war, Prince Perryn had produced a writ that cited his own name as heir—purportedly Angnecy's copy. But the paper had been declared a forgery by three witnesses out of five. In any case, no one would accept it as valid without the confirmation of either of the other two copies.

Thalassa's ringed eyes, smoky and shadowed, met mine for the first time that evening. I'd have sworn I felt their heat drill through my skull. "As a result of the 'astounding revelations' contained in this newfound writ, Hierarch Eligius has withdrawn his support for Perryn and turned him over to the Smith." Her voice took on a more sober cast. "The implications are profound . . . as even you can well imagine."

I recalled the abbot's warning: Once the succession was settled, Bayard's hammer would fall swiftly on those who had not supported him wholeheartedly. And Thalassa, who had tied herself to conspirators who insisted that the world's survival trumped the rivalries of princes or clergy, sat directly in that hammer's path. By allowing me to hear this news, she had—knowingly and deliberately—laid a weapon in my hand. Were I ever to find a way around her tongue-block, I might sell her secret, perhaps buy myself some consideration in royal circles. Was she so confident in her spellmaking? Or did she believe my new master would assure I had no such opportunity? Or was she telling me something altogether different?

Max brandished a fist-sized portion of duck on his knife. "Are you surprised at your Karish friends' perfidy, Valen?" He grinned at me. "Perhaps your sojourn in the abbey gave you a taste for adult intrigue instead of childish tantrums."

"Valen remains eternally self-absorbed," said Thalassa, reverting to her lighter tone, as if I were not present. "His head is empty, his most important concerns his belly and his male endowments." She nodded to my mother as if to apologize for so indelicate a reference. "I doubt he holds to a single monkish virtue. Even if he knew aught of serious matters of the world, he'd not lift a finger to involve himself."

Why was it that my sister's unrelenting barbs brought to mind the Abbot of Gillarine and his admonitions to obedience, his lessons about honor and the need to divert personal interest and loyalty to higher purpose? She might have been a painter who washed her artwork in tones of poisonous sepia, yet rendered a most familiar subject.

Lassa was a member of Luviar's circle—those who had committed their lives to the purpose that gods worth our honoring did not mandate terror or ignorance or unthinking subservience. I watched my elder sister as she picked at her meal and sparred with Max, and confessed that I did not know her as well as I thought I did.

"Never saw anyone so sly as that abbot." Max devoured another bite of duck and distracted me from rethinking Thalassa's motives. "Luviar, is that his name? Prince Bayard was dreadfully unhappy to learn the fellow allowed Perryn to sneak off with the hierarch. The Karish eunuch will pay for that bit of chicanery. I'm not so happy with him either. Sullied my reputation with that little vanishing trick, he did. I'll find out how he hid the simpering snake in that monk-house if I must strip off his holy robes and dangle him over a bonfire to do it. If you know the secret, Valen, I might find it in my heart to pour that cup of wine down your throat! Tell me, little brother, have you ever had such a sober month since you gave up Matronn's tit?"

I shrugged. As Max leaned over and smacked a great kiss on Matronn's hollow cheek, I glanced at Thalassa to see her reaction to Max's talk of the abbot. Even considering Max's penchant for exaggeration, I found his words disturbing. But my sister ignored us all as she spooned honey from a dish and dribbled it on a piece of bread. She handed it across to my mother, who had eaten nothing all evening.

Bia whined at Max to tell his story of the abbot and the vanishing prince. My brother was always ready to take the stage. I wondered if he would tell of the wall of midnight that sent him and his master and the Harrower priestess into abject flight from Gillarine. A fleeting vision of the eyeless dead laid out on the field sent a shudder through my limbs.

While Max preened and related grand tales of the victory at Wroling, I closed my eyes and tried to plan my next move. Which was, of course, entirely impossible. Every scheme died with the same thought: a lifetime contract with a stranger who could restrain me as he saw fit, who could decree that I would never again see the light of day, who could prevent me ever speaking to another human being if I did not track his enemies or poison his wife or work whatever other magic he required of me. I would live without recourse. Without protection. Bound. *Saints and angels, preserve me.* I dragged my ragged thoughts back to the present before I vomited in my empty plate.

". . . and that was the very same Karish house where Valen was hiding?" said Bia when Max concluded. "What strange fortune!"

"If I'd only known," said Max, cocking his head thoughtfully and narrowing his eyes at me. "I could have dragged him back here weeks ago. Were it anyone but Valen, I might wonder whether he was caught up with Luviar's treasonous games. But Valen would more likely bed a monk than involve himself in serious doings."

"I've heard Bayard will take control of Palinur before morning," said my father. "The Registry has advised us all to strengthen our house wards to fend off this Harrower rabble. Prince Osriel is expected in the city as well." He tore at a dried fig with his teeth. He was relishing this occasion.

Max licked his fingers, smirking. "Did I mention Evanori gold? The Bastard Prince cannot squat atop such treasure any longer, playing his nasty little games and scaring children. He must acknowledge Bayard as his king or prepare to face his wrath."

"Osriel is an abomination," said Thalassa with disgust.

My mother, who had been emptying her wineglass with regularity and trying unsuccessfully to avoid looking at me, shuddered and drew her mantle close. Her dull gaze flicked to me again. "Claudio," she whispered, tilting her head toward my father, her kohl-ringed eyes sunken, her hollow cheeks paler than ever, "I've Seen this Osriel, who steals the souls of the dead. He craves the life of angels, but is forever barred from their realm."

As happened every time my mother spoke the words "I've Seen" in just that way, the room took on a certain tomblike staleness, and the candle flames dimmed as though viewed through smoked glass. Creeping fingers tickled my spine, as they did whenever events recalled the doom of blood and water and ice she had once spoken for me.

Lassa laid down her knife and stared at my mother, as if to glean the wholeness of the vision with her own talent. Max shuddered and tossed another cup of wine down his gullet, averting his eyes.

My father alone remained exempt from the effects of my mother's pronouncements. Only in front of guests did he do aught but dismiss her. Dabbing at his mouth with a square of linen, he savored Max's and Thalassa's reactions with the same gusto he chewed his meat. "Let Thalassa worry about the Bastard's soul," he said. "Think. Osriel surely wishes to examine this purported writ of Eodward's will. Perhaps even challenge it. I've heard he possesses Tobrecan's copy, though he has never produced it. No wonder that, if Bayard's name is cited. It's likely long burned." Patronn smiled with bloodless lips. "If Bayard can persuade Osriel the writ is sound and that alliance is in his best interest, the war is over. We shall all prosper, even—"

"Valen?" The throaty whisper came from the direction of the kitchen door, along with a sneaking giggle. "My boy come home? My good lad grown? Why hast thou kept this news from me, Claudio?"

"Raphus! Petro! Where are you?" bellowed my father, jumping to his feet. "Get the madman out of here!"

My grandfather hobbled quickly across the tile floor, astonishingly spry for a man of more than eighty summers. A green-and-yellow patterned robe flapped over stained tunic and loose trousers. Food was the most pleasant of the likely substances clotting his matted white hair and beard. A fetid stench preceded him.

My mother recoiled and clapped a lace handkerchief across her mouth and nose as he planted a kiss on her cheek. Max wrinkled his nose and sucked at his wine cup when my grandfather grabbed a wad of his hair and jiggled his head affectionately. Bia, rigid, stared down at her plate as if to pretend a madman wasn't patting her coiled braids. But even as he touched the others, his bright mad eyes fixed on me.

"Where hast thou been, boy? Hiding, I think. Good. Good. How old be thou, Valen? How old? Come now, tell me. Thou shouldst be close to the day."

"Seven-and-twenty, Capatronn," I said, bile in my mouth. "And how old are you? Too old to be living, I think. Too wicked to be living, certainly."

He chortled gleefully and clapped his hands as he rounded the end of the table, his bare feet attempting a dance step. I stared at the libation bowl, the etched bronze glinting sharply in the candlelight. I sought the scent of wine instead of my grandfather's reek and tried to imagine it was dulling my senses . . . dulling memory, hatred, and revulsion.

"Wicked certainly. Yes. But I've told no secrets, and they've not found thee, have they, boy?"

My father charged through the door to the kitchen, still shouting for my grandfather's pureblood caretakers. The other servants who cowered in the shadows—ordinaries—were not permitted "adversarial contact" with any pureblood. Thus they could not wrestle my grandfather back to his room. Silos was nowhere to be seen.

Meanwhile my grandfather crept up behind me and whispered in my ear as he had always done, lapsing in and out of Aurellian and Navron. "We'll show them, boy. *Prasima*—how long till thy birthday? Claudio keeps me shut away, so I know not the day or season. Tell me. *Prasima coteré*—how long till thou'rt free forever?"

"You're too late, Capatronn," I said. I did not whisper, but held up my silkbound hands so he could see. "They found me. And I doubt I'll ever be free again." But I would. I would, else I'd be dead or as mad as he was.

"Shhh . . ." He pawed at my shoulders, stroked my arms, and pried at my chin, trying to turn my face toward his. "All grown up now. Tall, aren't thou? Not like these dull fools. I knew it. Tall and beautiful . . . so far above. Stand up and show me. But how long till eight-and-twenty? On that day thou shalt be free of them forever. Tell me." He hammered his fist on my shoulder. "Tell me, Valen. I've kept thee free. Given everything for thee alone. How long?"

I stifled my annoyance. Somehow, seeing him in the flesh sapped my fury. However hateful and cruel the old gatzé had once been, he was only mad now, echoing this old nonsense in my ear. His dementia had ever been fixed on my birthdays. "Ten . . . twelve . . . weeks until my birthday, I think."

He wrapped his arms around me from the back as if to heave me up. He was still strong. "Stand up, boy. Stand up and let me see. So cruel . . . so cold . . . they despise any who are not like them in all ways. But they'll never break thee. I saw to it."

"Leave me be, Capatronn," I said in exasperation more than anger. "Live or die as you will, old man, but just leave me be. You never took me away. You never set me free. I had to do it all myself, but I failed."

I shifted around to face him as a tired man instead of a defiant child, so that this once in all my life he might believe what I said. "I don't want your—"

My mouth hung open, paralyzed in the moment. The insult I was poised to throw died unspoken.

My grandfather's face was a landscape of suffering, creased with pain and scarred with madness, his skin rough and tattered like leather left to rot. He had chewed his lips raw. And his eyes . . . Lord of the Sky, I had never looked so close . . . so deep . . . coal black and searingly hot, a damned soul gazing out from the maw of hell, begging for one word of consolation . . . filling with tears even as he bobbed his head like a mad gypsy's puppet.

"Ah, Clyste," he whispered, touching my cheek with a dry trembling finger. "Not even for thee could I allow it."

Two brawny men dragged him away before I could react, before I could ask what he meant or why he invoked that name, a name perched on the edge of memory and mystery.

"Wait!" I said. But too late. The caretakers were already bustling him out the door.

"What was all that?" asked Max. "He wants to throw another party for your birthday?"

"Yes," I said, struggling not to reveal that I was as bewildered as I had ever been in my life. "Perhaps he thinks I'll turn into something useful when my years are eight-and-twenty—the perfection of seven times the magical balance of four."

My livid father straightened his fur-trimmed mantle and stood at his end of the table. "Despite this unseemly interruption, our feast is not yet done," he said, his voice quivering with anger.

It would not have surprised me to see his leather strap appear in his hand. But it was merely a scroll of parchment that he snatched from a silver tray a servant set beside his plate. The scent of hot beeswax drifted on the warm air. "This night we seal the first and last contract of our *recondeur*. When the opportunity arose this morning, I felt Serena Fortuna's blessing enfold our house once more. Valen needs a strong hand, a master who can control his violence and deceit and bend him to his duty. And yet our family will never stoop to unworthy contracts, even to salvage what we may of Valen's honor."

"Perhaps you would like to review the document, Valen?" He brought the scroll around to my place and unrolled it on the table in front of me. "Tell me, do you find any terms you would like to change? I can have pen and ink brought."

Cheeks on fire, I squinted and strained to make out the letters that might hint at whose name was listed on the contract. But of course the sun still rose and set, and the earth still plowed its course through the stars, thus the blotches mixed and mingled on the page like swarming bees, defying my comprehension. Sweat rolled down my neck. I wanted to scream at him to tell me who my master was to be. But without hope of altering his gleeful course, I would not give my father the satisfaction of begging for an answer I would learn soon enough.

"No objection or qualification?" He snatched the page away and returned to his place, pleased with his little joke. "So we can proceed, then."

My mother unsnapped a gold disk from her neck. She turned it over and over in her hand as my father positioned the ends of a red silk ribbon looped through the tail of the page and dripped a puddle of wax from a small pewter ladle onto the joining.

"Who is this master, Patronn?" said Thalassa. "Should we not be told before the papers are sealed? Of course it is entirely your and Matronn's decision, but my position makes certain demands." I was amazed to hear she didn't know.

"No one in the temple will question my choice, Thalassa," said my father, frosty and imperious.

He jerked his head at my mother. My mother pressed her disk to the wax and held it. After a moment, she lifted the slip of gold, threw it on the table, and reached for her wine.

My father affixed his seal beside my mother's. "Who but royalty deserves the service of a Cartamandua-Celestine? The Duc of Evanore will send his man to retrieve Valen tomorrow morning."

My flesh went cold as a widow in winter, and the bottom fell out of my stomach. The Duc of Evanore . . . My father had contracted me to Osriel the Bastard.

"Patronn!" Thalassa jumped to her feet. "What are you thinking? Valen is your son!"

Phoebia gaped at me as if I were already some flesh-eating monster. Max clapped his hands to his head and collapsed backward onto his dinner cushions, roaring with laughter. My mother emptied her glass and waved for more wine.

"Mind your manners, Sinduria," snapped my father. "You are still my daughter, and you sit in my house."

Thalassa snapped her fingers at a servant who scurried away to retrieve her cloak. "Never again, Patronn. Not as your daughter, at the least. You have disdained my path since I first submitted to the temple, and you have scorned my position that brings honor and respect to all purebloods. I will apply to the Registry for independent status, and I do not think they will refuse me. Not after this madness."

In a swirl of silk, my sister crouched beside me. "Forgive me, Valen," she said softly. "I've never understood this bloody war between you and Patronn. I still don't. But I'll do what I can."

I stared up at her, numb, scarcely comprehending what she was saying. What uses would the Bastard have for me? Tracking down corpses and gouging their eyes? Seeking the path to the netherworld? Mapping the realms of the dead? Weaving magics to snare the unwary? I'd heard that his mages tried to keep a victim living while they took his organs for their dark workings. Perhaps they needed more power. Perhaps I was to hang in their web while they stole my magic . . . my blood.

My sister pressed a cold hand firmly to my forehead for a moment, and then swept from the room, leaving me with naught but a sensation like an arrow piercing my skull and a deadness in my soul.

Bia wailed at my mother, horrified at the thought that the Bastard Prince himself might walk through our door.

My father bellowed at Silos. "Set extra guards about the western walls tonight and lock the courtyard gate. Reinforce the wards on Valen's door. The man who lets him escape will never see daylight again."

Max was still chortling as Caphur and Silos led me out of the noisy brilliance of the dining room and into the quiet night. I hobbled through the ice-skimmed slush, my thoughts as frostbit as the night.

"Your Registry valet has returned to the city, *plebeiu*," said Silos after a while, as we threaded the courtyards and brick passages. "I think he was afraid of you."

The pain in my head had dulled. I allowed myself to see nothing, feel nothing. This night's events could not possibly pertain to me. My father could not have bound me to the monster of Evanore for the rest of my life. My grandfather could not be something other than I had always believed. His words . . . the same words he had babbled in my ears for as long as I could remember . . . could not be demanding new interpretation now I was old enough to hear them. And the name he had invoked . . . Clyste . . . *Clyste's Well*, they had called the walled pool beyond Gillarine's valley, a Danae holy place. I could do nothing about any of it. Osriel . . . holy gods . . . for the rest of my life.

"The bodyservant sent by the Sinduria will attend you tonight," Silos continued, as if I might care.

Even when we stepped into my warm apartments and he began to unbind my hands, my trembling did not cease. Caphur poked up the coals in the brazier and left. Silos bundled the silken cord into a ball and unshackled my ankles. I did not move except to wrap my arms about my churning belly. Probably a good thing I had eaten nothing.

"The Sinduria will do what she can, *plebeiu*." Only then, as he raised his eyebrows and nodded a good night, did I heed him. "But do not try to escape again. More than me will be watching the walls tonight, and they'll not hold back as I do." He closed the door softly behind him.

Someone appeared in the doorway of my bedchamber, but I could not be bothered to look. I had to decide what to do. My head felt like porridge. My gut ached.

"I've been sent to attend you, Broth—*plebeiu*." The youthful voice cracked like a donkey's bray.

Purest disbelief spun me about. "Jullian!"

Chapter 26

The boy must have grown three quattae in the weeks since I'd left Gillarine. Whether it was the green temple livery or the grim circumstances, he looked older as well. And though forthcoming with news of Gillarine, he no longer babbled with the tongue of innocence. Resentment and withholding laced his every politeness.

"I'm truly sorry to hear Gerard's not found," I said, forcing my thoughts to focus as we sat close to the little brazier, devouring the cold roast duck and soggy bread he'd brought from the kitchen. "He didn't take anything with him at all? Has he family?"

"Not even his cloak. And he has only his gram in Elanus; she hasn't seen him. Father Abbot fears he is harmed and that's why he brought me away from Gillarine, besides to come here and take your messages and pass on his. I ought to be back there searching for him, not—" He pressed his lips together.

"Not playing servant to a *recondeur*."

His downy cheeks flushed. "The lady—the Sinduria—believes I'll be allowed to stay with you wherever they send you next. She'll set up some way for me to get messages back and forth."

My head swam with heat and fear. Thalassa had sworn to help. Gods, she had asked my forgiveness and threatened to break with my father, and I'd scarcely given her a thought. But she would have sent Jullian before she knew where I was going. "No. You cannot stay. It would be a comfort . . . more than you know . . . but after tomorrow, they won't allow it. *I* won't allow it."

But tonight . . . Somehow Jullian's presence moved me to decision. To action, however useless.

"Who has come with you to Palinur? Brother Victor, I know, and you said the abbot . . ."

"Father Abbot and Brother Victor have been summoned to appear before the hierarch tomorrow at Terce. Brother Gildas and I accompanied them. We're staying at a priory here in the city. When he left Gillarine, Father Abbot spoke to the brothers as if he weren't coming back. He gave the care of the lighthouse to Father Prior—"

"Nemesio? Is he mad?" I threw the bone onto my half-filled plate, the last bites of meat still attached. "Nemesio likely betrayed him to the hierarch!"

"Prior Nemesio helped build the lighthouse with his own hands." Though he kept his voice low, the boy could have cracked nuts in his jaw. "His father and brother are carpenters, villeins of an edane with great landholdings in Morian. We'd not have half the tools and seeds were it not for him. He would never betray the abbot. Never. You don't know us at all."

Clearly not. How easy it was to look backward and see myself as young and stupid and unforgivably self-absorbed. Had *I* aged so much these few weeks? The boy's deepest grievance sat before me as bald as a monk.

"And *you* don't know *me*, either, do you?" I said, wiping my greasy fingers on the table linen. "A traitor to god and king, you think. Not the wounded soul you rescued at the sanctuary gate."

"Aye. I don't know why Father Abbot thinks one like you could help us." He began twiddling his eating knife. "He said I was to obey you on my soul's life."

His chin jutted bravely, but his eyes flicked from his knife to my hands as if hell's fire might come shooting from my fingers. Best he never see Silos's tricks.

I sighed and reached for his wrist, stilling the dangerous play of the knife. If I were to trust him at my back, I preferred him to think me a man and not a monster. "Listen to me, Jullian. Surely some men must come to Gillarine with all sincerity, believing Iero has called them to your life . . . your good and holy life . . . and then chafe at the rules and break them and not understand why. Eventually they realize that they are meant for other things—to marry and have children, perhaps, or to farm their own ground, or to soldier for their king. All good and holy things, too. It just takes them some time and grief to discover the truth of what the god intended. That could happen, could it not? That has happened at Gillarine, I'm sure."

"But you never intended to be our brother—"

I held up my hand to hush him. Why was it this boy demanded such painful honesty? I had lived my whole life believing what others said of me, while screaming to the world and to myself that I didn't care. Now a half-grown innocent forced me to seek explanations I had never bothered to unravel. Here at the end of everything, in some small way, I was beginning to understand.

"I'm not speaking of my stay at Gillarine. You're right about that. I was hungry, cold, and wounded, and I needed sanctuary, which you and your kind brothers gave me. But this other matter . . . I did not come to pureblood life of my own choice, but was born to it, and so one could say the god meant me for that life. Yet from my earliest days, before I could even consider such things, I chafed . . . sorely . . . at our rules and did not understand why. For good or ill, I've broken every one of them, much as a failed monk might do while wrestling with his destiny. Many of my deeds are simply my own wickedness, and people are right . . . you are right . . . to condemn me for them. But my choice to be a *recondeur* . . . Jullian, the belief is so strong in me—just as fierce as your belief in the abbot and his lighthouse—that the gods or fate or destiny must surely intend me for other things than this. Likely not the monastery either, to be sure . . . but something . . . and I have to keep searching for it, else I must admit I'm mad as well as sinful and deem my whole life a waste. I am not ready to do that. Not yet." Though the glass was rapidly emptying.

He held quiet and stared at his greasy plate, littered with bones and scraps. Then, abruptly, he jumped up from his stool and vanished into the bedchamber. When he came out again, he carried a large canvas bag.

"Jullian, please don't leave. I need your help to—"

He plopped the heavy bag into my lap. "Are you to ask your grandfather our questions tonight?" he said, still resentful. "Father Abbot said that's what you would do."

The surety of this assertion confounded me, for only as I sat here talking to the boy had I accepted that I must speak to the madman before I left this house. "I wasn't— Not exactly. I—"

"Father Abbot said I was to tell you that he trusts you. Open it."

Skeptical, I drew open the bag. In my lap lay my grandfather's book of maps. I was dumbfounded. Luviar believed these pages held the key to preserving the knowledge of the world through two centuries of darkness, and he had just entrusted them to the hands of a liar and a thief, a traitor to god and king, a prisoner incapable of escaping his own house.

I felt Luviar's cool gray eyes on me, as if he stood beside Jullian, and I imagined the arch of his brow and the hint of a smile at the corner of his mouth. What kind of magic did a man wield to unravel men's souls and mold them to his bidding? Here at the nadir of fortune, the abbot had granted me a moment of profound grace. In thanks, I would have done whatever he bade me.

Wrestling with time and possibility, I smoothed the leather binding and reshaped my plan. "Before I leave this house tomorrow, I must speak with my grandfather. If you'll help me get out of this apartment for a little while tonight so I can do that, I'll take this with me. I can't promise. But I'll try to get Father Abbot's answers as well as my own."

Though he did not smile, Jullian jerked his head. His mortal judgment had been stayed, but I was not sure for how long. He put his hands on his slender hips. "So tell me what to do . . ."

Protocol granted even a *recondeur* bound to the Monster of Evanore privacy for anything involving bodily intimacy. Thus, if someone in my father's house took the wild notion to visit a violent renegade in the middle of the night, he or she would hold off long enough for me to finish bathing. Jullian was smaller than Lukas, so it was only natural that it would take him longer than Lukas to haul enough hot water from the kitchen. I would have perhaps an hour.

". . . so if anyone comes, just say I'm unclothed and you'll bring word when you have me dressed again. You must be firm and sure. No wavering. No apology. You must think like a servant of Samele's Temple. Though not a pureblood like my guards, you would consider yourself above the house servants. Can you do that?"

"I think so."

"Be sure, Jullian, for if you're caught . . ."

"The Sinduria told me the consequences if I'm caught helping you. And I told her that I would do whatever was needed for *Iero's* work." His thin shoulders were stiff and square.

I had not thought I had a smile left in me, but the image of this Karish aspirant with a cracking voice and downy lip saying such a thing to a high priestess of Samele could not but make my face twitch. "And my sister truly arranged this . . . approved of your helping me?"

"Aye. She said she wasn't sure you'd be willing to speak to the old man, but I was to tell you that you're the only hope for getting sense out of him.

And that she was glad she was there to keep the Harrowers off you. I wasn't sure what that meant."

"Yes . . . well . . . that's another story. But if the occasion should arise . . . when you see her again . . . tell her *I'm* glad of it, too." My sister baffled me.

We pulled the tub from the corner to the rug before the brazier. Then I sent the boy off to the kitchen for the first pail of water, describing how he could take a slightly longer route and verify that no guards were posted at the corner apartment or inside the courtyard.

A purple and black tunic, black breeches, hose, and boots had been laid out in my bedchamber. My garb for entering my new life, I supposed. The silver mask had been laid beside the clothes. I swallowed hard and vowed not to think again of tomorrow, but only of tonight, and how in the name of all gods I might get sensible answers from my grandfather.

I changed out of my fine clothes and into the plainer garb more suited to sneaking about in the night and stuffed the book of maps back into its bag.

The locks rattled, and the door flew open. Jullian lugged in a heavy pail of steaming water. I took it from him and dumped it in the tub. "Only one man inside the courtyard," he said, breathless. "He's standing in the corner at the outer wall, where there are no rooms. It's too dark to see your door from there, but he came running the instant I stepped out. They've closed the archway gate to the rest of the house, and he must unlock its magic to let me through each trip. There's two more fellows in pureblood cloaks posted just beyond the gate, so only a step will bring them into the yard. I heard more voices outside the walls. Lots of them."

"You told the fellow you were coming out again?"

"Aye, but he went back to his post in the corner."

"Good enough. It means they trust my door wards to warn them if I step out. Take a bit more time on your next trip. Tell the kitchen maids the bucket was too heavy, and you'll need to fill it more times with less in it. Tell them I'm demanding the water be hotter. Blame me. They'll understand that."

"Very well."

"If someone seems suspicious, and you think I need to get back here, or if you need me for any reason, drop your pail outside the corner apartment. I'll hear it. But do not—now, listen to me—do *not* lie to the two at the gate or to any other pureblood. You've no experience at lying, and as sure as fleas bite, they will detect it in you. If they ask you if I'm out of my room, tell them the truth. Tell them what you think of me. Tell them I'm a servant of

Magrog half again your height and could break you over my knee—which is entirely true, and I'll do it if you try making up stories. Keep your abbot's secrets as you've ever done, but blame me for this whole mess. Do you understand?"

He hesitated.

"Blame me, Jullian. They cannot do worse to me than they've already done, unless it is to hurt you or the brothers of Gillarine. I'll sit right here with this book all night if you don't promise."

"Very well. I won't lie to them if they should ask."

I grabbed the book and a shielded lamp and slipped through the door alongside him, so the ward would be triggered only the once. Flattening myself against the wall, I listened as he met the guard and they walked toward the gate. Then I crept across the courtyard to my grandfather's door.

The windows of the corner apartment were dark. From inside came a soft, low droning, as if a dulcian player had got stuck on one mournful note, and no matter how he wrenched and blew, he could not change it. The absence of charged heat about the locked door meant I had only a lock to break, not magical wards. I dared not use a voiding spell—it was too "loud," too different and would surely be detected by those guarding this courtyard. Rather I touched my fingers to the lock and assembled an unlocking spell, hoping to have better luck than I'd had in Gillarine's library. Trying not to rush, I loosed a bit of magic to flow into the spell and through it into the old bronze pins, shifting them ever so slightly, feeling my way. Such a slow dribble of magic would not be noticeable in the midst of the heavy wards elsewhere in the courtyard. As long as I didn't get impatient . . . or run out of time . . .

By the time the last pin released and I pushed open the door, my teeth were vibrating and Jullian had taken a third trip to the kitchen. At least my eyes had adjusted to the dark. I stepped in, closed the door behind me . . . and almost retreated immediately. The stench was near unbearable—every foulness a confined human could produce.

A couple of low stools and an unlit brazier took form in the shadows. There was little else to be seen in that barren darkness but a clutter of clothes and blankets on the floor. The droning note came from the far left corner of the room, a mournful song of mind-death and despair.

"Capatronn," I said softly. "Are you awake?"

I picked my way through the clutter. Not all clothes on the floor, no . . .

parchment . . . pages and pages spread out, crumpled, folded, stacked. And amid the various stinks hung the familiar mix of tannin and vitriol—ink.

"It's Valen, Capatronn. I've come to talk."

He was huddled in the corner, eyes open, staring into nothing. I set the lamp on the floor, far enough away he could not kick it over, and tilted the cover open slightly. He clutched a wad of vellum sheets, and a string of drool sagged from his mouth and pooled on the crumpled pages. Those who label madness as release from pain and worry have never encountered such a sight. In that moment pain and worry entirely comprised my grandfather's existence.

"Capatronn, can you hear me?"

As if I'd struck him, his head jerked, and his hands flailed wildly, his pages flying everywhere. "Valen! My good boy . . . I feared they'd taken thee!"

"Shhh . . . we must be quiet." I sat down in front of him, leaving the bag containing the book in my lap. To settle him I had to catch his flying hands and hold them tight.

He bobbed his head, chewed his raw lips, and snatched his hands from mine. "Yes, quiet and careful. They're close tonight . . . I feel them close. They *touch* me." He shuddered and tapped his bony fingers on his skull. "Careful, lad. Careful. 'Tis no life for thee."

My skin prickled. "No one's close. I need you to tell me some things I've never understood. Secrets, I think."

He pressed his knuckles to his mouth, his gaze darting anxiously around the dark, filthy room. "Secrets. Bargains. Promises. Contracts. Everything is secrets and contracts. For thee. To be safe. To be free."

I hardly knew where to begin. But the chill beneath my layered clothing and the memory of the watcher at the Aingerou's Font set my course. "Capatronn, who is Clyste?"

"Cannot tell that. The contract . . . thou canst not know." He gnawed on his bleeding knuckles.

"She's a Dané, isn't she? Her sianou—her place of guarding—is a pool in the south of Ardra, only a few quellae from Caedmon's Bridge near Gillarine Abbey. Clyste's Well, they call it."

"Ahh . . ." He put his hands over his ears. "Thou canst not *know*. Don't say it. He'll think I told thee and put me in the daylight dark."

"Who'll think it? Patronn?" Why would my father care if my grandfather told me one more story about a Dané? And what did pureblood contracts have to do with beings of legend?

"Daylight dark and nighttime dark . . . no light ever. No drawing then. No painting. No scribing. Then I'll go mad!" As if he realized the absurdity of this statement, he planted his hands atop his head and cackled as he let it fall back against the wall. When the manic laughter shifted into shuddering sobs, I came near giving up hope of any sense. But after a moment, he leaned forward, tears glinting on his cheeks, and whispered, "Too late for Clyste anyway . . . too late."

"Why too late?"

"She told them naught of our secret. So the others locked her away to punish her. Chained her with myrtle and hyssop so she could not take bodily form. She told them naught of our bargain. So they bound her to slow fading. So young . . ."

The others. Other Danae. She was one of them.

I tried to ask more about the Danae, but every question became a knife thrust, wrenching sobs from his bony body. I had to try something else.

"Look, Capatronn, I've brought my book." I pulled it out of its bag and eased around beside him. "I thought you might look at it with me as we did when I was a boy."

His spasms waned as I allowed the weight of it to rest on his knees and opened it, ready to snatch it away if he tried to harm it. But his finger hovered over the title and then glided, not quite touching, over the glorious elaboration of gryphons and angels wrought in emerald green, scarlet, and gold that glinted in the lamplight. "I made this. I. When my head was right. The finest maps ever in the world. Mine."

"Yes, indeed." Madness had clearly not dimmed his self-admiration. "Remember, you gave it to me when I was seven. Patronn was furious."

"Spited Claudio with the giving. He exacted such a price . . . keeping me from thee. Beastly. Shamed me to bargain with my own blood. So it pleased me to spite him. But my mind was forfeit . . . failing . . . and I had to give the book early."

"And I was a wild, horrid child who never appreciated the gift. You made me swear to use—"

"Only after eight-and-twenty!" He snatched my hands away from the book and crushed them in his bony fingers, still incredibly strong. "Go not into their lands until thou art free. Only then. Thou gave me thy promise. Swore on the aingerou with thy blood. Thou must be careful with the book . . . Wait until the time is right and thou canst walk every corner of the world without bond or bowing to any. Thou'lt remain as thou art. Promise, Valen. Promise! I betrayed her so thou couldst be free." His eyes and hands and head twitched.

"I always thought you meant I'd be free of Patronn, free of this house. But you didn't, did you?" I eased my hands from his grip. He clenched his gnarled fingers to his breast and I enfolded them in my palms. "You meant something else altogether."

"Free of *them*. Free of their Law, free of their dread summoning. Thou shalt be the greatest of the Cartamandua line. Our family will be powerful beyond dreaming. Thou shalt map the whirlpools of time, the vales of memory, perhaps even the very bounds of heaven and hell. But I cannot *tell* thee. Forbidden. Punished. Mad . . ." His eyes flared hot and wild in the dim light.

"It's all right, Capatronn. I'm here and safe." I changed course again to soothe his rising agitation, tacking toward answers like a sailing ship against the wind.

I turned a few pages of the book. "Let's look at the maps—tell me again how their magic works so I can use them *after* I turn eight-and-twenty." Time was running, and I had to calm my own frenzy. "Anyone else must read the spell in the cartouche or the border, but I— You knew I could not read words and might never learn. So how could I ever use the maps?"

"Foolish boy. I *taught* thee." He shuffled through the pages to the first map and tapped his finger on a tiny mark at one corner. "I opened this book to thee, who art without words, yet complete. For thee only, every map has one. Feed it magic . . . trace thy path and feed it, too . . . and the land will open its arms to thy skills. Not yet though . . . not yet."

I nudged his dirty finger aside and uncovered a grinning aingerou. He had put one on every page. "So I touch the aingerou and release magic into the page. Then I trace the route, feed it magic as well, and I can find my way without reading. Is that right?"

He clapped his hands and chuckled. "Clever, is it not? And thine own power will take thee farther yet, for thou art of my blood, thy bent incomparably strong."

It was all I could do to hold back my finger from the page, but I dared not work spells here.

"Earth and air and sky are one whole," he said. "At the boundaries of thy knowledge—the boundaries of the world's map—walk and listen and feel the joining of earth, air, and sky, seeking thy desire. Take up thy pen. Thy blood—Cartamandua blood—bears the magic; thy fingers will funnel it through pen to page and the way will be clear. Travel the way thou hast scribed, and begin again."

"But I don't use—" No. No need to confuse him. I had never needed pen or ink to envision a route. When he had enjoined me to "feel the earth" back when I was a child, I hadn't understood that he meant some abstract "sensing" of the universe that would only take shape when marked on paper. I had believed he meant for me to lay hands on the dirt as we did when tracking footsteps.

"Claudio never could do it. He draws only what he sees, for his mind is clay. Thou, lad . . . thou art quicksilver." His trembling fingers turned the leaves, one by one, touching, but not quite touching, the inked features, the bright drawings on the grousherres, the elaborate designs of frames and cartouches. "Thou shalt find the places even I could not."

But unless I could get free of Osriel, I would have no opportunity. Someone other than me would have to lead the cabal into Aeginea. "Tell me, must others use the aingerou as well—before they can use the written spells?"

"No. The book is thine *alone*—not for Claudio, not for Josefina, not Max or the rest. With the gryphon charm canst thou permit others to use it as it was made. *Thy* choice."

The gryphon charm . . . great gods . . . no wonder he'd had me recite that bit of doggerel until my head split. "So I touch the gryphon—this one"—I pointed to the gilded beast on the front cover—"work the charm with a person's name, and that person can use the book. My choice."

He bobbed his head happily. "Thy choice. Thine own book forever."

"Tell me, Capatronn, do any of these maps show a way into Aeginea?"

His fingers paused in their explorations, and he raised his face, stricken. "Go not to this place where I am, Valen . . . to this dark place . . . this mad place."

"No, no. I just want to see the map you used to find Eodward. It must be very fine. Beautiful. Showing the power of your blood, of your art and magic. Then I'll know which map not to follow until I'm eight-and-twenty."

He leafed through more pages until he reached the very heart of the book. The open page displayed a wholly unremarkable fiché, little more than a line

drawing without colors or gold leaf or any other elaboration. Very little lettering. One might have thought it a preliminary sketch bound into the book by
mistake. The landform outlined so vaguely was certainly Navronne.

"No map can show the way," he said. "Aeginea is everywhere. Nowhere.
But this"—his tremulous finger drifted across the page from small notations
of a tree and an arch to five rosettes scattered here and there in no particular
pattern—"depicts its heart and its mystery."

His chewed and broken nail touched a rosette, causing another symbol
to appear beside it like a shadow, only to fade as he moved on to the next.
I glimpsed the symbol for a mountain and another for the sea. A third, located beside the rosette at the top of the map, I didn't know, but the fourth
showed the same waterfall symbol he had used for Clyste's Well. If that one
did indeed depict the Well, then the tree and the arch must certainly be
Caedmon's Bridge and the Sentinel Oak.

"This is the Center," he said, reverently, as he touched the fifth rosette,
which was nowhere near to being the accurate center of the other symbols
or the page itself. If the arch was Caedmon's Bridge, then it lay well south
in Evanore. Its shadow symbol was a bolt of lightning, a notation I had never
learned. "Here is where the Chosen dances to bring all life to joining."

His grizzled mouth and chin worked in tight spasms, as he gently
smoothed the worn edges of the page. His eyes filled with tears.

"Saved only this one map of them all. Promised Clyste to destroy them,
so no human could travel there. The long-lived had grown to despise and fear
us. Clyste said I could keep my promises without the maps. But this is my
life's greatest work. Our family's glory."

Thus we reached the heart of the matter. "Why, Capatronn? Why do the
Danae despise us so?"

He shuddered and jerked, and I was afraid he would retreat again. But he
took a quivering breath and gathered his spasming limbs. Summoning control, I thought. Every emotion, every physical expression required constant
mastery to prevent it running wild. His head jerked and his eyes squinted
and blinked as if someone was striking him.

"We lie," he said at last. "We betray. They cannot grasp our nature and
dance it into their patterns. Sometimes our needs make demands of us they
cannot understand."

"As with Eodward who did not return to the Danae, though he had
promised he would."

My grandfather bobbed his head. "That was but one of so many. They did not blame me for that one. Nor for the Scourge."

"The Scourge?"

"Some humans *want* to drive them away. They foul groves and springs, trees and fields. Sometimes"—he leaned close and dropped his voice—"they damage the Canon itself. The long-lived never speak of it lest we learn the power we have over them. It is their direst secret: that they cannot cross the barriers of tormented spirits. If the guardian is not joined with the tainted sianou when it is poisoned, she cannot return to it. The Canon is corrupted, and the guardian wastes with grieving. If joined, the guardian is trapped—ah, holy ones—trapped inside the sianou. Chained as if with myrtle and hyssop, but chained with poison, and so he does not fade, but dies there. Both land and guardian lost forever. Forgotten. And so is the Canon broken."

"Tormented spirits?" I said, wrestling with the ideas of dancing that could be broken and Danae who could be murdered while outside their bodies.

"Violent death. Corrupt blood." My grandfather's face crumpled. "They did not blame me for those crimes—nor any human save madmen. They could not believe that any reasoning creature would purposely break the Canon. And they knew I loved the dance. Ah"—he clutched his heart—"to see the dancing in Aeginea again. But never will I. Never. I am lost until the last ages of the world. They do not forgive."

As fog lifts from the mountains, revealing a new world of snow-draped crags and sunlit pinnacles, so understanding grew in me. Not only about the world and coming chaos, not only about the savage rituals of Harrowers and royal bastards, but about what I saw in front of me. I took his chin and drew his face around so I could look on his pain-racked visage. Every word of sense, every moment of stillness, cost him.

"Capatronn, what did you do that the Danae have punished you so terribly? That they have broken their last ties with humans? You must tell me, Grandfather."

"I"—his brow creased; his lips twisted and fought to shape the words—"*stole* from them. A treasure they did not value. I had the right, but they could not forgive the loss of it. And then I failed her. Ahh . . ." He gasped and gripped his head in his hands, drew up his knees, and curled into a knot. The book slipped off his lap.

I laid my hand on his trembling shoulder. "What treasure? What was worth all this?"

His fingers curled and he drew his fists to his head as he began to rock. "Cannot tell. Cannot. Secret . . . secret . . . secret." Though he was trying not to, he moaned . . . louder by the moment.

"Can I help you? I could stay a while."

"Naught." He shook his head wildly, even as he clamped his jaw over a scream, and wrenched his shoulder from my hand. "Naught can be done. Go."

I quickly gathered up the book, stuffed it in the bag, and snuffed the lamp. As I crept through the darkness toward the door, my grandfather began retching violently. The stench of vomit and loosened bowels followed me to the door.

"Go!"

"For the book . . . Grandfather . . . thank you." I pulled the door closed behind me. Breathing deep of the clean, wintry air, I leaned on the thick oak that muffled his rising screams and wished that most futile of all wishes: that I could begin again and weave the knowledge I had just gleaned through the days of my life.

Swallowing hard, I crept silently through the frozen courtyard. I stopped in the rose arbor, brushed the snow from the stone bench, and sat, pulling the book from its bag again. The book must go back to Luviar, and if it was ever to be of any use to the cabal, I had to open it to them. Tonight, for I might never have the chance again. I had to trust that they would use it wisely, accounting for the information I would send them. And so, accompanied by the unholy melody of my grandfather's screams, I touched the golden gryphon and recited the bit of verse he had pounded into me years ago.

> With mighty sinew, beak and claw,
> Feathered wings and eagle's eyes,
> The gryphon guards its nest of gold.
> Ripping, flaying sinew raw,
> Crushing rib and limb and jaw
> Of all who seek its agate prize,
> Save for the . . . wily . . . hunter . . . Luviar . . . bold.

I fed magic into the charm, which was supposed to impart whatever virtue you named to whomever you identified as the *hunter bold*. As a boy I had always inserted my own name as the hunter, wishing for strength to fight off my father's next beating or cleverness to elude recapture when I ran away. I had hoped to use the golden nest and agate eggs to pay for my own house or buy my own contract, before I knew such possibilities were as much myth as the gryphon itself. I'd not even known how to quicken a spell in those days.

The golden gryphon pulsed with warmth and light, and I considered whether to give access to anyone else. To leave it with only one seemed risky. So Gildas. He was younger, less prominent, and the Scholar, who needed to find the Danae. And one more? I considered Stearc, but settled on Gram, the secretary, instead. Clearly the conspirators relied on Gram's intelligence. And he understood the Danae better than any of the others.

Once done, I packed the book away and peered around the edge of the arbor to watch for Jullian. When the slight figure trudged down the path from the kitchen, lugging a heavy pail, I followed and slipped through the doorway behind him into the warm and comfortable apartment. The bathing tub was filled to its brim.

The boy about jumped out of his skin when I grabbed the door from his hand and closed it softly behind us. "Did you see him? Did you learn anything about the book? Is he truly mad?"

"Yes to all three. But first, did *you* have any trouble? Any suspicions?"

"The pureblood—not the one in these green clothes, but the other one in black and yellow—stopped me on the last trip and asked if I liked serving you. His hand was on my head as I answered, and I felt . . . unclean." The boy averted his eyes.

"That was Caphur," I said. "An overseer from the Pureblood Registry. Very skilled at his work, and he doesn't like me very much. I hope you told him the truth."

He nodded. I surmised that Caphur had approved his answer. I did not press to hear it.

I sat on the chair and summoned him close, lowering my voice even more. "So tell me, how did the abbot and my sister plan for you to send them information?"

"The false priestess said I should tell the people here that she had thought-summoned me back to her temple," he said. "Or I could ask for Silos and tell him a particular word she gave me, but to do that only if things were very bad. Elsewise, I'm to wait until she sends for me."

I kneaded my scalp. The plan was much too obvious. No one would believe Thalassa summoning the boy in the middle of the night so soon after getting him assigned here. Having grown up with a brother like me, she didn't understand what trouble Jullian would have with lies. I could not risk his safety by having him sneaking about with secret passwords.

"We're going to do things a bit differently. In a little while, I am going to start yelling at you and throwing some things. I want you to run both to Silos, the fine-scented temple guard, and to Caphur, the one in black and yellow, and tell them that I've frightened you. Tell them you want to return to the temple and that, of course, the Sinduria will allow it. Only that."

"But—"

"You can't take the book. You might be searched. I'll hide it here under my palliasse, and the Sinduria can retrieve it. Here's what you need to report to her . . ."

They weren't going to like what I told them—that my grandfather had stolen some treasure from the Danae but refused to name it, and that they should look to Prince Osriel, who mutilated the dead, or these Harrowers, who sacrificed violated bodies to their Gehoum, as the root of Danae hatred for humans. He had even claimed such rites *broke the Canon*. What did that mean? Was it possible that some ritual dance could determine the fate of the world? Now I had seen a Dané, anything seemed possible.

Perhaps the conspirators could use this new knowledge to strike some bargain with the Danae and find out. And any stolen treasure of my grandfather's was likely to be in this house. If they could persuade the Danae to say what he'd taken, Thalassa could likely find it. Three of the cabal should be able to use the book, at least, leaving them with no need for a Cartamandua to guide them. Whether these things fulfilled their need, I couldn't say. I had no more leisure to think.

". . . and lastly, I need you to tell Brother Gildas . . . only him, please, no one else, for I am sorely shamed by it . . . that I desperately need to see him. Tell him that I am . . . beset by my old sins . . . and need Iero's grace that only he can bring before I go to my new life. Can you remember all that?"

The boy rolled his eyes, a portrait of pained tolerance.

Despite my guilt at burdening a child and a holy monk with my perversions, I could not restrain a smile. "Well, of course, you can. The brightest scholar ever come to Gillarine. And the bravest. And the kindest. A light worthy of a holy lighthouse. Tell me one thing, lad; you've never— No one's ever said aught to you of your real father, that he was . . . special . . . in some way?"

He shrugged. "Mam told me he was a scribe who drank so much his liver rotted. She showed me his portrait that his sister drew on a bit of bark, so I could know him. But she said good riddance to him and that my new da was the better man."

So much for legends, rumor, and Valen's clever insights. I squeezed the boy's thin shoulder. "Godspeed, Jullian. You make *me* wish to be a better man."

This time, when I picked up the padded chair and threw it into the wall, two legs broke off. The stools, the upended table, and all the scraps from our dinner splashed into the overfull bathing tub, inundating the rugs. While making silly faces at Jullian to soothe his fear, I yelled and cursed and threw myself at the door until the hinges snapped. As soon as the door crashed into the courtyard, he ran. When Caphur and Silos found me, I was ripping up my fine clothes and dropping the silks, brocades, and fur-lined cloak into the greasy water. A knot burned in my gut.

Thoughts and plans roiled in my head all through that long night as I lay tied to my bed, feeling my disease and my craving devour me and praying for Gildas to come. My grandfather had been trying to protect me, not from my family, but from the Danae. He had violated their trust . . . a man who had traveled their lands for years . . . who had guided a high priest and a hierarch to Eodward and brought them safely back to Navronne. Janus de Cartamandua had turned thief, and in retribution for his crime, the Danae had severed their last ties with untrustworthy humans and threatened the grandson whom, for whatever inexplicable reason, he favored. To shield me from their vengeance he had let them take away his control of his mind and body. Great gods, what had I ever done to deserve such a sacrifice? What secret bargain had he made with this Clyste? And why would one more birthday set me free of their threat?

The Dané at Caedmon's Bridge had confirmed his story, speaking of thievery and treachery, of poison and bargains broken, and she'd said that we must return what was stolen before they would deal with us. What treasure had he stolen that could exact such a dreadful price? A "treasure they did not value," but were determined to have back. Something he believed he had a right to.

The knot in my belly drew tighter, shooting bolts through my limbs, setting off firestorms of cramps in my calves, back, and biceps. Warnings. All my life I had ignored warnings, putting them out of my mind as fast as they were issued, for I believed them but more shackles on my freedom.

I could not imagine what significance my grandfather attached to the age of eight-and-twenty. Yet, while lacking weeks until that mystical occasion, I *had* used the book in some fashion to intrude on a Danae holy place and to summon one of them to an unwanted meeting. Now Danae followed me through fields and town. And even before I'd used the book, the earth that was their domain had pulsed under my body as if it were alive, and their holy places—the cloister garth and the pool in the hills—had barraged my senses like siege weapons. What did my grandfather fear might happen to me? Perhaps I had worse things to dread than a lifetime of bound service to Osriel the Bastard.

Amid these fearsome questions rose wonders, too. My sister's help . . . the abbot's faith . . . and one phrase that hung vivid and poignant in the cold night, like the last, lingering tone of plainsong. Unimportant to any but me. My grandfather had altered his book for me . . . *who art without words, yet complete*. What did that mean? Why did those words from a madman soothe a hurt so deep and so raw? Another mystery to occupy my mind in the bleak days to come.

As the hours crawled by, cramps, sweats, and insidious craving claimed one part and then another of my body. Events and words, hopes and beliefs blurred together, impossible to sort. By morning, I could not think at all.

Chapter 27

"Brother Valen." The voice sliced through the pain like a steel claw through skin. "I've come to give you counsel."

"Gildas?" I whispered harshly. *Lord of Earth and Sky, let this be Gildas.* I could not open my eyes to confirm it, lest my head fall apart, lest my teeth crack and fall out. The disease had come full upon me in the night. And the hunger.

"Yes. Iero's blessings be upon you this morning, Brother. I understand this fear that sets you trembling. And you are right to seek the Lord Iero's grace before embarking on this voyage of duty. I wish I could change what is, but I've brought at least temporary comfort. You must seek the ultimate solution for yourself."

Praise all saints if *temporary comfort* meant nivat. "Iero's grace, Brother Gildas."

"Sirs, I presume you will leave us some privacy to speak of a man's immortal soul."

A wave of flowery scent had me gagging, and the fingers that tugged at the ropes about my chest and legs might have been a gatzé's flaming tongue. "He looks ill. Perhaps he needs a physician, not a practor."

"Would not the prospect of bondage in Evanore give you pause for your soul's health, sir?" Ever-calm Gildas.

"Bound service, monk, not bondage. Purebloods have duties that ordinaries cannot comprehend." Ever-prim Silos.

Go away, I thought.

"Vowed initiates of Saint Ophir have duties that heathens cannot comprehend. But we shall not argue those things here. I am this man's mentor and confessor, and merest decency demands your tolerance. Please step out whilst I pray with Brother Valen."

Pounding footsteps, crashing doors, slamming shutters. One might think a herd of cattle had stampeded through the cold room. Silos and his scent vanished. Then I felt the scrape of razor knives that was but soft breath on my face. I dragged my eyelids open.

"I don't know precisely what I'm doing here," he said quietly, his eyes remarkably unworried under his dark brow. "To encourage such perversion of the body is a great sin. Brother, you must give up this horror."

"I'm like . . . to give it up in the coming m-months," I said, my teeth clattering with chills, not fear. "It's a sickness drove me to it. Please believe me." Stupid to care what he believed.

"A sickness?"

"Never had a name for it, and now it's so tangled with this cursed spell . . ." The spell that had me yearning for boiling oil to scald my feet or a hook blade to tear my skin. "Please, Brother, I beg you tell me you've brought it."

"I found a bit in the priory kitchen. Not much. I didn't know how much you needed. What must I do?"

To hear that Gildas was willing to help had me sniffling like a maiden. I'd not been able to think beyond the possibility of obtaining the nivat. I'd known naught of how I would manage the using, bound as I was. I tried to concentrate on the task. "At my waist . . . the green bag."

Gildas dug through the layers of blankets and clothing. "The Sinduria said you hold the book of maps. I should take it out when I go."

"You can't. Caphur . . . the Registry man . . . he'll sense its magic. Think you're stealing. He'll take it. Lassa must retrieve it. I can't— Sorry I can't help more. Tell Luviar I would if I could. Willing." I could not examine my growing resolve to aid the cabal, only regret that my damnable weakness and blighted future left me useless to them. Beyond such fleeting concerns lay only pain and need.

"I'm glad to hear you're willing. This devil prince must not have you." I fought not to scream as his fingers fumbled at my waist. "I know people of influence in this city. We'll see you safe with us by midday."

Even as I despaired of its fulfillment, his ferocious declaration warmed me beyond measure.

He drew out the little green bag I had so painstakingly kept hidden through the past weeks. "Now tell me what to do."

"How much did you bring?"

He unwrapped a scrap of cloth and showed me a generous mound of seeds, enough for at least three or four doulons. Amid mumbled prayers and thanksgiving, I told him how to crush the seeds and that he must free two of my fingers so I could work the magic. ". . . only twenty seeds. No more." Only enough to ease my sickness.

As a youth, I'd seen the doulon-mad wallowing in refuse heaps and filthy hovels, scarred, starved, and forever shaking, tongues thick, unable to articulate a clear thought. One old man had scratched his skin off, trying to rid himself of invading "beetles." Even enduring the pain of giving up the doulon would not have healed his broken mind at that late stage. I'd always been careful.

"And the rest of the seeds?"

"Into the green bag."

"Are you sure you don't want me to free your hands entirely?" he said, a few moments later, looking dubiously at the two fingers of my right hand he'd wrestled out of the tight silk bindings. "We could rewrap them after."

"Too slow. Won't take long for Silos to detect spellmaking." I would not have my savior compromised. "Now, p-prick my finger. Draw blood."

He jabbed the silver needle into my fingertip, and I managed not to scream. He had to grip my bundled hands and hold them over the crushed nivat so the blood could drip, as I was too unsteady and too awkwardly positioned to do it.

"D-don't t-touch the stuff," I said, as he squeezed my two trembling fingers together to hold the thread steady. "The instant the fumes stop rising, when the scent fades, help me get it to my mouth. Then get out."

He nodded, his expression curious, but not disgusted as I'd feared.

"Bless you forever, Brother," I whispered, as I released magic to flow through my fingertips and bind the nivat to my blood.

Gildas fixed his gaze to the mirror fragment. I could see neither mirror nor fumes nor even the mound, but only glimpse a distorted reflection of the bubbling mess in his clear eyes. It looked huge and evil. I closed my eyes, ground my wrists against the rope to sharpen the pain, and tried not to vomit into my friend's lap as he crouched beside my bed.

"Now," he said, in what could have only been moments. Or perhaps I merely lost sense in the meantime. "It looks black and thick, as you said. No fumes rising in the reflection. Shall we?"

I nodded, unable to speak. He used my own fingers to scoop up the reeking glob and put it to my mouth.

I convulsed. Howled. Drowned in fens of pain and pleasure . . . of guilt and shame and joyless rapture.

"What have you been up to?" The flower-scented Silos burst through the murk of my perceptions. He tugged at the ropes. Spent an inordinate time checking my hand bindings and fussing over the bloody marks about my wrists.

I raised my leaden eyelids to a glare of cloudy midmorning streaming through the open door. Gildas was nowhere in sight. I hadn't noticed his going. Neither had I felt him tuck my fingers back into their shroud nor seen him pack away the guilty evidence that now poked reassuringly into my hip.

"Nightmares," I said, my tongue thick. Had the world burst into endtimes flames before my eyes, I would yet sink into blessed sleep, burying the remnants of my shame. I had never felt so drained. So heavy.

"You work spells in your dreams?" Silos dropped my limp appendages heavily onto my belly. "A good thing *I* came and not Caphur. Your clerical friend did not tuck the extra cord about your fingers. What has he done with you? He looked smug as an adder as he left."

I closed my eyes and smiled. "Brother Gildas cleansed my soul. When the Bastard Prince eats it, he will suffer a flux." As I'd learned on the journey to Palinur, Silos's skills at detection were less impressive than his lightning bolts.

"You are a fool, *plebeiu*. And the Sinduria is a greater one to indulge you. Perhaps when I tell her you're working magic with the Karish, she'll reconsider. Last night she petitioned the Registry for your transfer to her custody, saying this contract your father has arranged is evidence of madness in the Cartamandua line. Her petition was refused." He sniffed the air and poked about the bedcovers.

Shadows chilled my comfortable warmth at his mention of the future. "She's wrong"—my father was not mad, only soul-dead—"but I'll not tell anyone that. Tell her I can keep secrets."

Secrets. Only as I said the word did it penetrate my iron skull that Thalassa had unraveled her tongue-block. I had talked with Jullian and my grand-father of Danae, even speaking the word *lighthouse* to the boy. I dragged my heavy arms across my face and whispered the word into my sleeve just to make sure.

Surely this meant my sister trusted me; Abbot Luviar trusted me. Blessed Jullian had sent Gildas to succor me. And Gildas had promised they'd come to my rescue. Perhaps they *did* need me for their plan. In a wash of unreasoning euphoria, I smiled into my sleeve and mumbled louder, "Need to sleep now."

Silos unknotted the ropes and tossed them aside. I giggled like one of my little sisters.

"Too late, *plebeiu*. Prince Osriel's man has arrived earlier than expected." He shook me again.

Eventually his insistent prodding stole my good feeling. Dully I dragged my cold, heavy body to sitting. As my hands were yet cocooned in silken cords, I persuaded Silos to help me take a piss in the jar. He refused to wipe the crusted drool from my face.

"You should not have frightened off your valets," he said, his mouth curled in distaste. "Though I suppose you'd best learn to groom yourself anyway. I doubt the Bastard Prince will provide you a bodyservant."

Stupid Silos. What did he think I'd been doing for twelve years? Of course, I'd had my hands to use. Perhaps this prince would just cut them off. I pressed my wrist against my mouth to contain my rising gorge. No, no, the Bastard *wanted* my magic. He was paying for it.

Scarcely able to stay upright, I straightened my garments with my el-bows and wiped my face with my sleeve . . . three times before I realized the offending substance remaining on my face was merely my skin. The open-necked purple and black tunic hung loose over my wool shirt, and they had provided me no belt.

When Silos held up the silver half mask, I could not summon control enough to disguise my loathing. And pride seemed unutterably foolish at the moment. "Ah, *domé*," I whispered, begging, "not that one. Please, I cannot breathe in it."

"Your new master provided a silk mask for the journey and a standard pureblood cloak," he said apologetically, "but, as you are yet under Registry restriction, you must be delivered wearing this and the *recondeur's* yellow. Your protocols within Prince Osriel's house will be his choice, of course."

No protections in a *recondeur*'s contract. My master could require that I wear this mask forever. My stomach clenched. Sweat dribbled down my back and sides as the pressure of Silos's hand on my shoulder buckled my wobbling knees. He latched the band about my neck and secured the strip over my head, leaving me half blind, half deaf, and completely muted. Suffocating.

I panicked, trying to clear my clogging nostril, trying to suck enough air through the exposed half of my tight-bound mouth that I would not die. I scraped my arms across my face as if I could dislodge the hateful metal, and when I could not, I slung my bundled fists wildly into Silos, dug my feet into the rug, and lunged forward. My grandfather's whimpers and screams drifted through the open doorway as they did in every hour in that house.

"Settle, *plebeiu*," said Silos. He grasped my flailing arms and shoved me down again. "Settle. You've plenty of air, if you'll just calm down."

His firm assurances eventually slowed my heart, and my gratitude almost set me weeping. He knelt to shackle my ankles, then hoisted me up and propelled me through the door.

The unending symphony of madness from the corner apartments accompanied our journey through the courtyards and arches. *Poor devil.* I sniffled like a sentimental drunkard. *I'm as mad as you, Capatronn. They'll lock me up in my own filth, too.*

Ssst . . . Silos. My sister beckoned to us from a grape arbor threaded with dead vines. *We're here to save him.*

Silos did not turn his head. I slowed, glancing over my shoulders. Seeing with only one useful eye made everything seem flat and out of proportion.

I bumped Silos's shoulder and nodded toward Thalassa, who now crouched behind a statue of Erdru with his goat's legs. Or were they *her* goat's legs?

The temple guard prodded me to keep walking. I stepped in front of him, forcing him to stop, grunting, jerking my head, and pointing my hands toward my sister. *Look at her. Are you blind?*

Silos paused and spun in a slow circle, stopping only when he faced me again. "Stop playing, *plebeiu*. I don't know what you want."

I whipped my eyes back to the statue. And then to the arbor. Thalassa had vanished. Far behind me, my grandfather cackled. Frenzied, the voice of my fear sealed behind the metal half lips of my mask, I dodged in front of Silos again, pounding my bundled hands on his temple badge and then on my own chest.

"No, *plebeiu*. I cannot take you to the temple."

Grasping my shoulders, he turned me around and gave me a gentle shove toward the main house. Halting again, I tried to show Silos where Abbot Luviar perched beside a crow on a lichen-covered column. Then I pointed out Gildas, grinning from behind a dormant tree.

"What is it, *plebeiu?* What's wrong with you? Move along."

I hobbled forward. Blinked. The garden was empty of all but me and my jailer.

One more glance over my shoulder. The naked man sat cross-legged, tucked into the frost-glazed shrubbery, his gleaming dragon sigils silver in the morning haze. Eyes the crisp gold of autumn aspen observed us. Curious. Disdainful. The world blurred as I turned away, my throat swollen with grief. *Illusions. Visions. Not real.*

We passed through an arched gate and into the house.

Crystal lamps chased the gray morning from the columned reception room. I blotted my damp face on my sleeve and forced myself calm, trying to grasp what was real. No visions here. I was surrounded by the familiar—the richly colored tapestries that my ancestors had brought from Aurellia, the luminous marble statue of Kemen and his belt of stars, wrought by some Pyrrhan master centuries ago, and the enameled urns and gilt caskets brought from exotic Syanar and set here on pedestals shaped like bundles of reeds. Beneath my feet gleamed the silver and blue mosaic tiles that my grandfather had salvaged from a ruined temple on the isle of Caraskan, shipped to Navronne, and reassembled here to display the order of sun, moon, and earth.

Just beyond the vulgar and exotic display of my family's wealth shone the burnished breastplates of four well-armed warriors who flanked the doorway to the outer courts. The warriors stood at attention, lances at rest, their surcoats the rich, dark green of holly leaves and blazoned with the silver wolf of Evanore, a white trilliot under its paw.

Silos closed and locked the inner door behind me. *Holy gods . . . whoever you are . . . please wake me from this nightmare.* Where were distracting visions when I needed them most?

"This is he?" The words scoured skin and soul like windblown sleet.

The speaker walked in alongside my father. Though the mailed forearms that bulged from his holly-green surcoat were formidable, and his thighs might have been piers for Caedmon's Bridge, it was his face that caused my bowels to seize. Where half of mine was encased in graven silver, half of his was fleshless scars, leathery creases and ruptures surely caused by burning oil or systematic beatings with hot irons that destroyed flesh and sinew and underlying bone. The eye buried within this horror was but a dark slit. The other, fathomless in its emptiness and limitless in its disdain, briskly scoured my sorry turnout.

When Silos prodded my back, I bowed ungracefully to my father and the visitor at once. The planets beneath my feet spun in their paths.

"Magnus Valentia de Cartamandua-Celestine," said my father. "A male pureblood of seven-and-twenty years, his bloodlines registered before birth, witnessed and verified through ten generations. Contracted for unspecified service to His Grace, the Duc of Evanore, for lifetime duration."

Of course, this grotesque man was not the prince. Osriel was the youngest of the three brothers, close to my own age. This man's hair, trimmed close to his skull, was mottled gray.

He clasped his gloved hands behind his back, well away from the sword sheathed at one hip and the Evanori battle-ax ready at the other. "Recalcitrant, you said. Incorrigible. But I did not expect shackles in his family home. Is he violent, mad, or merely undisciplined?" He did not sound as if he cared which.

"Not mad," said my father. "Undisciplined certainly. The hand bindings prevent his triggering any spellworking. The shackles prevent him trying to escape his duty. He has willingly participated in armed combat, so I would put no violence past him. Mardane Voushanti, I clearly spelled out his history when we spoke yesterday."

Unfair! I yelled inside. *To hint at violence to this stranger when I can't defend myself.*

"It is no matter," said Voushanti, returning his gaze from my father to me. "My lord imposes his own discipline. He anticipates training a pureblood to his service, a pleasure he has not yet indulged as he has always found the standard contracts too restrictive. Now if your documents are in order . . . we are in a hurry."

At a small desk of polished rosewood, my father unrolled the scroll he had sealed at dinner. Mardane Voushanti flicked a finger at one of the warriors, who opened the door. A servant carried in an iron casket and deposited it on the desk. The Evanori lord accepted the scroll. He exchanged bows with my father. And thus was I sold like a slab of meat. Silos's iron hand gripped my arm, else I would have run, shackles or no, flaccid limbs or no, madness or no.

An excruciating cramp shot through my arms and shoulders, followed by a wash of heat and a shuddering release—an instant's euphoria before my spirits plunged to the depths, as if an uncrushed nivat seed had only now dissolved to work its perverse magic. One rapturous sensation, swept away in a heartbeat, leaving me dizzy . . . hungry. The doulon, unmistakably. I had never experienced such a momentary burst, more than an hour after the use.

Matters moved quickly. The lord refused wine. They murmured farewells. My father did not speak to me, but watched calmly as the four warriors brushed Silos aside and herded me into the weak and frigid daylight of the outer courtyard.

The warriors unshackled my feet and lifted me onto a horse, binding my wrists to the pommel and feet to the stirrups. A groom sawed at reins and halter as the demon beast thrashed and bucked. Every one of the grooms and warriors cursed and swore until the mardane himself came and laid a hand on the vile equine's head, quieting it for the moment.

Even before we rode away into the midday gloom, the door to the house was shut and the lamps extinguished—as was all light within me. No one had come to my rescue.

The shock of noise and activity as we left the secure walls and wards of my family home was almost enough to banish my waking stupor. Bells clanged in frantic warning from every tower. Panicked citizens mobbed the streets, loading wagons, herding children, geese, and pigs toward the lower city, as if they might escape the coming change, or toward the citadel, as if their missing prince might magically develop a spine and save them. Bayard's hammer was falling.

Voushanti rode in front of me, his snow-dusted back stiff and straight. One Evanori warrior rode to either side and two more behind. Wind blustered and whined through the streets, carrying the scents of ash and offal, stirring up eddies of new snow on stoops and walls, frosting every brick, splinter, and twig, whipping Navronne's white trilliot that yet flew alone on the heights, two days after Perryn's fall.

Few in the crowds wore Ardran purple. For the first time in three years,

Bayard's pikemen roved the city, their scarlet and blue badges spread like a fungus through every square, along the promenades and the grand steps that linked upper and lower city, and at every major street crossing. The orange head scarves of their Harrower allies colored the streets like splashes of sunflowers floating on rivers of brown and gray. Like a plague of locusts, those wearing the rags wrought destruction far beyond their size: smashing windows and doors, toppling carts and statuary, throwing burning torches into gaping shop fronts. Bayard's men, better armed but outnumbered, made no move to stop them. The Harrowers believed cities corrupt. Given a free hand, they would level Palinur.

As we crossed the heart of the Vintners' District, three men wearing orange rags upended a barrel into the public fountain. Acrid steam billowed and hissed. The black water heaved, sluggish, oozing. Three tar barrels lay empty beside the stained stonework.

Twelve districts. Twelve fountains. Valves and conduits bearing the city's lifeblood.

Black smoke billowed from at least three directions. The three men lifted another barrel. No one stopped them. No one attempted to stay the burning.

I wanted to scream at those running away: *They'll not stop with the city! Vineyards. Villages. Aqueducts. Bridges. These lunatics will bring the end times.* But spelled silver sealed my lips. My pleas and warnings bore no more sense than the snarling of a beast.

I clung to the saddle, my head rattling like a tin drum in a hailstorm, every sinew complaining as if I'd fought a ten-day battle. Twice more a rapturous burst took me away from the misery, only to abandon me in the same instant, sicker than ever. Never had I felt so wretched after a doulon. Had I told Gildas to wait until the fumes vanished? Or how many seeds to use? Holy gods, what if he'd used all of them? The desire to touch the green bag, to reassure myself that the supply was intact, soon became a torment. My hands twisted against the implacable silk that held both touch and magic at bay.

"Hold!" Voushanti drew rein sharply as we approached the broad causeway that led from the palace gates into the upper city. Drums rattled in the distance.

My horse balked and whinnied. A warrior grabbed my mount's halter and dragged his head around, while I gripped the pommel with my wrists and forearms until my shoulders burned.

Hoofbeats approached, keeping cadence with the funereal drums. Leather creaked. Harness jangled. Not a hundred quercae in front of us, ranks of Ardran knights rode slowly down the causeway, past the fallen statues that ringed the palace precincts. Swords sheathed, bereft of lance or mace, hundreds of them passed . . . the palace garrison . . . and behind the knights, mounted officers herded the massed men-at-arms, stripped of pikes and halberds, heading for the city gates. For surrender.

Here and there a wail of mourning rose in concert with the whining wind. *Yes, mourn for Ardra*, I thought, besieged with images of fertile vineyards and golden grain fields and the glories of long-ago summers. *Mourn for Navronne. For our children's children to be birthed under the Smith's wreckage.*

Yet what did all this signify if Navronne was returning to the primeval forest . . . if all cities were to end? As the mardane and his warriors led my horse back the way we had come, I hunched forward over the pommel and looked no more upon Ardra's shame.

"By the night lords!" The mardane spat the oath through clenched jaw and reined in again.

A party of Bayard's soldiers, bristling with lances, blocked the end of a narrow lane behind us. I blinked. At the head of the party rode a square-faced knight. At his side rode an iron-visaged woman, wearing light mail and a brown surcoat blazoned with orange.

"Identify yourselves, and declare why you should not stand down and yield your arms," said the leader, his voice young and brash. The single blue band on his scarlet baldric proclaimed his inexperience. When the baldric began to crawl across his breast like a striped snake, I begged it silently to stop.

The few citizens abroad in the lane vanished into the side alleys and doorways. Voushanti rode forward on his own, stopping just short of the Moriangi. "I am Voushanti, Mardane Elestri, commander of His Grace Osriel of Evanore's household guard, escorting my lord's retainers. You've no cause to hinder us, young sir."

"The Bastard does not honor the Gehoum," snapped the woman, before the young knight could respond. "These men must disarm or pay forfeit."

"His Grace of Evanore has maintained neutrality throughout this petty dispute, sir knight," said Voushanti, his words as crystal hard as the icicles dangling from the sagging balconies. "And he expects his officials to move unhindered throughout Navronne as they have since his father's death. Perhaps this . . . warrior . . . at your side does not comprehend the protocols of royalty or that my master's displeasure is not incurred lightly, even by his royal brothers or their favored priestesses."

A faint green luminescence rose from Voushanti's sword and from the shipped lances of his own four warriors. The Moriangi shifted backward, so perhaps more eyes than mine saw it.

"Lord Voushanti, m-my apologies." The young knight held his ground beside the woman, though his teeth rattled like the Ardran drums as he waved his men backward. "Pass, as you will."

"Blasphemous weakling!" The woman hung back as the lancers marched away. Then she wrenched her mount's head around and vanished behind them into the smoke and gloom.

"Quickly! This way," said Voushanti, pointing down an alley scarce wide enough for his warhorse. "She'll set an ambush."

He led us through the maze of broken streets and crumbling arches under the causeway. These remnants of some early incarnation of Palinur had been exposed when the new palace approach was built by the Aurellians. In normal times the narrow, stinking lanes served as a haven for thieves, cutpurses, and very large rats.

We emerged from the ancient warren into the wide boulevards of the Council District, streets of small, elegant palaces favored by the king's household, royal relatives, high-ranking clerics, as well as the foreign embassies that had sat abandoned since Eodward's death. Just ahead of us, a party of six or eight Moriangi troopers rammed a hitchpost into the door of a fine house, bursting it open in a shower of splinters.

A little farther down the street, another party, blazoned with scarlet and blue, dragged a writhing man from a house and threw him onto the pavement next to several mortally still swordsmen. A woman in servants' garb stood watching. Calm. Quiet. The soldiers closed in around the man and laid into him with clubs and feet. As his screams tore the air, the serving woman tied an orange scarf about her head and strolled away. I could not but wonder how many Harrowers served in wealthy houses, silent, deferent, behind the wards that families like mine believed impregnable.

Another turning took us out of the din and into a muddy back lane between gated walls where servants and delivery carts would travel on better days. The only sounds in the dim alley were the breathing of our own beasts and the jingle of harness. At the second or third break in the wall, a tall gate of black iron swung open soundlessly. No grind of gears or squall of hinges accompanied the closing, once we had passed inside it. My clammy skin itched beneath the layers of wool, silk, and fur.

The back of the house stood bleak and unwelcoming. Small windows pocked the tall gray wall, stained with rust and soot about gutters and empty torch brackets. A stone kitchen house lurked dark and shuttered, its chimneys cold. An empty cart had been shoved into a corner of the yard. Dead leaves and dirty snow filled watering troughs. I lowered my eyes, afraid of what phantasms I might see lurking in these shadows.

Mardane Voushanti dropped lightly from his saddle and waved a gloved hand at me. "Get him down."

The warriors released the horse and me from our unhappy partnership. When one of the men knelt to reshackle my ankles, I shook my head frantically and pounded my bundled hands on his shoulders. But for the silver mask that forbade speech, I would have abandoned all pride and begged him not. To face this life . . . this master . . . bound and shackled . . . fear came near choking me. The lock clicked shut. Two of the warriors grabbed my arms and almost carried me down a short flight of steps into a musty corridor. Everyone was in a hurry, and neither my mind nor my feet could keep the pace.

We threaded a maze of empty storerooms, of laundry rooms furnished with rusting tubs and a few stiff rags hung on suspended frames, past coal bins and linen rooms that smelled of moldy herbs. From the servants' halls, we emerged into a grand foyer, poorly lit and shrouded with cobwebs and dust.

Voushanti halted before a tall door. Every finger's breadth of the dark wood had been carved with beasts and symbols and set with slips of gold and chips of gemstones. Its centerpiece was a snarling wolf with smoldering garnets for its eyes.

"A warning, pureblood." The mardane gripped a strap of the metal mask and pulled my face close to his, forcing me to look into his eyes . . . black, bottomless, one spark of red fire at the center, chilling me to the marrow. No past, no future in those eyes. "His Grace dislikes liars and gaping fools. Remember it." As if I weren't rattled enough already. When he looked away, I almost wept in gratitude.

One of the warriors dragged open the door. Another shoved at my back. I stepped through, trying to hold my head high without falling on my face.

The cavernous room was as dark as a well of tar. A few threads of gray sketched tall narrow windows, but heavy draperies barred what modest illumination the overcast morning might provide. Across the room lurked the wolf from the door, grown huge, its fist-sized eyes of garnet pulsing with life. I stepped back, blinking in dismay. But this phantasm was no more than pulsing coals in a cavernous hearth.

No sooner had I exhaled than a streak of blackness darted between my legs. Claws scrabbled on wood. Then, slightly above my head, disembodied in the dark, no wolf, but a cat blinked—its yellow eyes sharp and gleaming like faceted citrine. My sluggish heart thrummed like the Ardran drums. *Saints and angels, fool, take hold of your mind.*

Voushanti's hauberk gleamed in the crimson glow as he tossed a rolled parchment on a table and bowed in the direction of the most profound darkness in all the gloom, the end of the room to our right. "The pureblood, Cartamandua-Celestine, Your Highness. The contract is in order. He is your bound servant until the last breath departs his lungs."

Wherever the warmth of the gleaming coals went, it did not touch me outside or in. A lung-frosting chill and a faint medicinal odor pervaded the room. I needed to bow to him. *Curse the damnable doulon.* Why could I not gather my senses? Of all days to have this horrid reaction. Of all hours. I fought my roiling belly, pressed my fingers to my forehead, and concentrated on keeping my knees steady as I inclined my back. After a suitable interval, I rose again . . . slowly . . . using a glimmer of red on the wood floor as a touchstone to prevent my spinning head losing all orientation. I could manage this. A thousand times I had passed myself off as sober when muddle-headed with mead.

First, stop the damnable shivering. The silver mask would reveal my tremors even in the minimal light of the dying fire. I could allow him to think me wary and disciplined, or carefree and ill behaved, but he *must* not think me weak or afraid. My future . . . my freedom . . . depended on carving out a position in this household, a position of respect if I could manage it. Yet here I was, near drooling. I inhaled, deep and slow, and forced my body rigid.

"Have you presented his task?" Low. Clear. Large and deep. Larger than the room itself. Rumbles and echoes and nuances beyond hearing. *Not human . . .*

I shook my head sharply, trying to stifle fear with reason. Of course he was human. Somewhere in that unnatural dark were a man's head, body, limbs, eyes. Crippled, so I had heard. Deformed. Surely he was but an ugly sorcerer with ugly habits—like members of my family. His eyes would be watching me. I summoned every discipline I knew. My soul would not go easy into his grasp.

Voushanti clasped his hands at his back in a military rest. "My first concern was getting him here safely, my lord. The streets worsen by the hour. I knew you wished to interview him before his assignment. Perhaps you even wish to give the commands your—"

"Do as I commanded you, Mardane." The voice was a lash.

The mardane bristled, but swiveled to address me. "Your first duty for your new master will be to locate two prisoners in whom he has an interest. The two were taken from their beds earlier today, but are held neither in palace dungeons nor city jails. Tracking a person from a known location should be a minor exercise for one of your bloodline—even one minimally trained, as we understand you to be. Our lord prince will accept no excuses for failure. We shall remove your restraints, of course, and provide you garments less noticeable. Do you comprehend?"

Making sure not to look at Voushanti's dreadful face, I bowed very slightly in acknowledgment. My mind raced—or at least plodded as fast as was possible through knee-deep mud. Freeing prisoners . . . not so bad a task as I'd feared. And I was to be loose in Palinur, my hands unbound. I knew a thousand hiding places . . .

A whipcrack split the murk; a fiery lash encircled my ankles. The shackles shattered into pieces and clattered to the floor. The hobble chain dropped with a loud clank, almost stopping my heart.

The half-faced Evanori stood to one side, inspecting my cooling ankles, his hands clasped in relaxed unconcern behind his back. When his unsettling gaze slid upward, expectant, I squeezed my eyes shut, afraid even to breathe. This whip was not leather, but magic, and the hand that wielded it was hidden in the darkness.

Another whipcrack. I bit my tongue so as not to cry out. This time the fire encircled my neck and the top of my head, as the metal neck and head straps broke away and the silver mask clattered to the floor. Quickly, I lifted my bound hands and stretched them well away from my belly.

This time the bolt of power flew silently. The air shivered as if a giant sword had whisked by me, its speed and ferocity making it invisible. I blinked. The silken bindings stretched and drooped from my fingers, then frayed into threads of gossamer that floated to the floor. *Free!*

But the mardane quickly gripped my arm and shoulder in such fashion that he could lay me flat should I blink wrongly. My moment's exaltation snapped like a dry twig. The unruined half of his face twisted slightly. "It is certainly as you surmised, my lord. His nature is true. The rebellious spirit does not forsake him."

"Erase any thought of escape from your mind, Magnus Valentia," breathed the voice from the shadows. "Do not think I cannot reconstruct these restraints or provide more . . . restrictive . . . ones should they prove necessary. Though obedience is required by your contract, I know you disdain the rules of your kind, as well as the ordinary courtesies of honorable men."

I tried to reclaim some dignity in word if not posture. "My word, given unreserved, is inviolate, Lord. But I do not honor promises given by others in my name."

"Fair enough. So you will understand why we hold surety for your good behavior."

The door opened, and one of my escorts led in a prisoner. His slender wrists were bound behind him and silk scarves shuttered his eyes and mouth. A tiny sound issued from his throat. Not a sob. Not a wail. Only the choking sound of terror tight reined, of constricted throat and bound heart, of determined courage. Jullian.

"Damnable cowards!" I yelled, rage exploding from my being's core. "What kind of lord . . . what kind of *man* . . . holds a child hostage? How dare you——?"

Voushanti deftly shifted his grip, snaring my right arm in a shoulder lock, bending my neck forward so forcefully I thought it must snap.

"I do only what is necessary to compel your obedience," said the voice from the darkness, cold and deep. "Fulfill your contract, and the lad will survive . . . this day."

I wrenched free of the mardane and dropped to my knees beside the boy. Fear and anger flailed the cotton wool within my skull, so that I could scarcely articulate words. They had brutalized this boy on *my* account. "Jullian, it's Valen here. Have they hurt you?"

The boy shook his head sharply.

"His safety is in your hands, pureblood," said Voushanti, his voice stark as midwinter.

In my hands. Indeed. I gathered the rigid boy close, turning him until his back lay against my chest, laying one hand on his ruddy hair and one hand on his breast. His heart fluttered like a rabbit's throat. "I want him free."

Voushanti snapped, "You have no—"

"Free and healthy as he is right now," I barked into the midnight where the master lurked, ignoring the treacherous servant. "You can throw me in a pit dungeon and lock the trap for a thousand years before I allow him to be your pawn." I could not consider complexities or strategies, but only a certainty that swelled greater than the doulon craving—this outrage could not happen. "Your *word*, Lord Prince, or I do nothing for you *ever* and your contract gold is wasted."

"Free, then, and unharmed, once today's task is done." The voice breathed malice that settled like a cold snake alongside my spine. "But not you, pureblood. Not ever. You claim your given word is inviolable. So swear to me of your own will—without reservation—that you will not run. Prove it this day, and you will have my word in exchange: I will not ever use the boy against you."

Good that I could not hold more than one thought in my head at a time, that I was too dull witted to weigh the balance of this bargain. Yet he was not asking an oath of obedience. Only submission. I spun Jullian around to face me and gripped his narrow shoulders, quickly before I could reconsider.

"I vowed to protect you, Archangel. Do you remember? And so I'll do. My master is noble Eodward's son, thus we must assume he is a man of his word as well. So have courage and say your prayers. While I'm off doing his bidding, you can practice your Aurellian verbs, for I know you have difficulty with them. *Teneo, teneas, teneat . . . teneamus . . .* eh?"

The boy's chin lifted ever so slightly. And then he nodded.

I rose and faced the massive dark in the corner of the room. How does a man yield his lifeblood willing, slit a vein and watch the scarlet flood sap his strength and sentience, silence the music of the world, still his feet? Madness—this foggy mantle the doulon had laid over me that allowed naught of sense, only anger to burn through—that was the only explanation. I bent one knee, inclined my back, and touched my fingertips to my forehead. "You have my word, lord prince. I will not run. Not ever."

"Without reservation?"

"Without reservation."

"Very well, then! Be on your way."

Voushanti bowed to his lord, pulled me to my feet, and hurried me out of the room. "I will outline your morning's task as we go," he said when the door had closed behind us. "Speed is of the essence . . ."

Chapter 28

Blood is unique. Pureblood families insist that each child's blood is identical either to the father's or the mother's, and that the only variance that prevents one of us growing into an exact copy of that parent is malleable "nature." But those purebloods gifted to follow routes and tracks must surely know better—that blood bears the imprint of a singular being who loves and hates and quivers in terror, who sings psalms or grows parsnips or strips pigs—because blood lays down an excellent, unmistakable path to its source.

Though I had no idea whose blood it was, the clotted mess in the sooty, brick-paved courtyard was sufficient to trigger a magical response when I applied my mind to the problem. If only I had more mind.

"Which way?" demanded Voushanti, his voice muffled by the hood that draped his mutilated face. His hand encircled my upper arm with the grip of a pawnbroker holding his last citré. The engravings on his wide gold wristband seemed to writhe in nauseating rhythm with my pulse. "Where were they taken? A month you've squatted here staring at this puddle. We've—"

"—no time. I know that." I pressed the heels of my hands to my eyes, trying to focus on the whereabouts of the unnamed captive whose blood had been so callously shed in this deserted yard. But as quickly as the route to his present location took shape in my mind, the lines and turnings faded again, as if I'd drawn them in breath frost on a window glass. Twice more in the past hour on our way through the chaotic streets of Palinur, I'd felt the shattering explosion of the doulon and the almost simultaneous disintegration of sense. My mind was in tatters. "West, I think. Toward Riie Doloure. There's an old fortress . . ."

Was this a true impression or was it only that talk of missing prisoners recalled a tale I'd once heard about a private jail? Aurellians had inflicted cruel torments on Navron prisoners, not allowing guilt or justice to interfere with retribution, and certain Navron nobles rued the day King Eodward had proscribed such practices. A young thief had once told me of his escape from a grim lockup such men used for torturing "grudge prisoners"—those who bore their especial ire or contempt. Determined to spread word of the dread place before he could be recaptured, the youth had spat out his gruesome story, clutching his burnt, empty wrists to his belly while a fellow vagabond dressed the poor sod's whip-gouged back with goose fat. I'd had no other comfort to offer a lad of fifteen, facing life with no hands.

"Riie Doloure—are you sure?"

I shook my head to clear it and pressed my palms to the pavement beside the dark sticky pool. Icy water dripped on my hands from the cornice that sheltered the unseemly blotch. *Hold the lines this time. Ink them on your senses. The Bastard Prince has Jullian until this task is done.* The traces were so faint. Brick and cobbles did not hold impressions like bare earth. And Palinur bled from every pore this day, confusing me even more. Time crawled by, stretched like a waking cat, and then sagged into a filthy puddle. "Riie Doloure. Yes."

Voushanti dragged me up and shoved me past broken statuary and trampled herb beds toward an elaborate iron gate dangling from one hinge. An aingerou, tucked under the brick arch, spat snowmelt onto the uneven cobbles. I tried to step over the puddle but misjudged the distance and stumbled right into it. Slush seeped into my boot.

"What's wrong with you?" said Voushanti, jerking me through the gate and into the deserted lane. "Your family vouched you were in good health. Said you'd never had so much as a boil on your bum in your life. Are you drunk?"

"No sleep," I said, hurrying alongside him, grateful I was free of shackles and mask at least. "No food. Doesn't promote my best work. I'll not warrant—"

"Sick, starving, or dead, pureblood, you *will* locate these prisoners. Our master has an *interest* in them."

"You should have scraped up the blood and brought it with us, then," I snapped, refusing to meet his glare. I could almost forget his eyes' unnerving lifelessness if I just didn't look at them. "I could sniff it for you like a hound on the scent."

He would not tell me anything—neither the two captives' names nor why Prince Osriel cared about them nor who had dragged them from this house with deadly force. Unfortunately, he understood that names or reasons would not help me locate them. Only a physical link could do that; blood served best.

We hurried round a corner into choking smoke and worsening chaos. A troop of Moriangi men-at-arms entered the square at the same time, and Voushanti retreated a few steps to let them pass. We wore poor men's cloaks that hid my good clothes and his mail shirt.

As we waited for the soldiers to have their fill of shoving and bullying, inspecting bundles by ripping them open and scattering pots, statues, aprons, and blankets in the filthy snow, men's voices rose in plainsong from the court-yard we had just visited. My sluggard mind snagged on the oddity—plainsong here in the city. The melody was familiar, a setting used only at the Hour of Sext—noontide. And then my thoughts drifted back to the blood-splashed yard. The design wrought into the ruined iron gate had been a solicale. A Karish household, then.

The soldiers soon moved on. But as the mardane and I crossed the square and followed the turnings my instincts laid out, an urgency that had naught to do with Voushanti propelled my steps. Our search for these un-named prisoners had begun at a Karish house where men sang the Hours. And noontide was the hour of execution.

The crumbling square called Riie Doloure had likely inherited its mournful title from the squat, ugly edifice that overshadowed it. Plain round towers pocked with arrow loops marked the four corners of Fortress Torvo and the walls of the blocklike keep. In the style of ancient Ardra, no creneled battlements, but rather steep conical roofs of lead topped the four great tow-ers and the two lesser ones that flanked the gatehouse.

On this day *doloure* took on added meaning. Half the squalid houses and shops that lined the cobbled square were smoldering ruins, the other half still burning. Dark smoke billowed in evil clouds, abrading my throat. The snow melted into black slush that soaked my feet and numbed my toes. A jubilant rabble crammed the space before the gray stone walls and gate tow-ers, cheering and shouting over the roar of the flames as ash and embers showered on them like unholy rain.

"The fortress? Inside?" The voice boomed in my ear.

"Yes . . . yes . . . maybe." Clutching the scratchy layers of my plain wool cloak over mouth and nose, I closed my eyes and scrabbled through the denser fogs and smokes inside my skull to find the traces. No good.

"Be sure, pureblood. This is no feast-day frolic to venture. Hurry."

I found a patch of unpaved ground, dropped to my knees, and pressed palms into the ash-rimed muck, seeking a stronger link. *Focus.* My fingers squelched in the filth, and I fumbled with the pattern in my head. Awkward. Slow. By the time I grasped the life thread strung from the clotted blood at the Karish house, my skull felt switched wrong way out, raw and throbbing.

"Beyond the wall," I whispered, wiping my hands on my cloak. Beyond the impossible crowd.

My eyes itched and watered. Voushanti hauled me up, and we skirted the surging mob, dodging shattered stonework, trampled grain sacks, and fallen beams that pulsed with dying embers. Snowflakes transformed to raindrops in the heat, then vanished in a hiss when they struck hot ash or stone.

The throng shifted and surged like a living beast, and though only a few orange scarves peppered the crowd, guttural cries for purification pulsed like its heartbeat. "Give us blood to cleanse the filth! Fire and blood! Slay the blasphemers!" Faces shone with mad fervor. Surely naught of Palinur would be left for Bayard to claim. As for the people captive in this wretched place . . . prisoners . . .

"Who are we hunting?" My voice, harsh and strained, could have been a stranger's. "Why won't you tell me?"

Voushanti squeezed forward along the narrow boundary between a ruined shopfront and the mob. "Because the answer should make no difference."

Sila Diaglou stood atop the fortress walls. Not dressed in a warrior's garb today. Her filmy orange robes flared in the wind like more flames, gifting the willowy, pale-haired woman with a majesty and magic that infused the scene with purpose, as if she were the carved prow of a great ship. She raised her spread arms to embrace the scene of smoke and chaos. "*Sanguiera, orongia, vazte, kevrana,*" she cried. "Bleed, suffer, die, purify. Die to the world. Abandon those who cling to your old self, and live henceforth in repentance for as long as the streams of time carry you forward. Harrow the earth, that the Gehoum shall be appeased."

A savage roar rose from the crowd. "Sila! Sila!"

To either side of the priestess, stolid and proud, stood three I'd seen at Graver's Meadow—the doe-eyed girl, the man with the dog's face and dagged purple cloak, and the man with the oiled black curls. Perhaps the needle-chinned man had died of my blow. Other ragged men and women cavorted along the parapet, waving orange rags, garlands, weapons, and other things round and heavy that they tossed into the crowd. Another cheer shook the ground. Glee and greed and an insatiable hunger surged through the pressing bodies like an incoming tide. A certain darkness, the foulest bile, ate at my throat. Heads . . . the round heavy things tossed from the walls were human heads, now passed from hand to hand atop the mob, evoking new waves of cheers.

Great Kemen Sky Lord . . . holy Iero . . . whatever your name . . . guard us from madness. No prayers for Sila's Gehoum, though. I invoked no powers that took pleasure in headless corpses. Evil rioted in that courtyard. If we could save some poor wretch from such a fate, I would league with Magrog himself. Perhaps I had.

"Inner bailey, outer bailey, or belowground?" The Evanori's voice grated in my ear, interrupting my sudden hesitation. "Speak."

"Not belowground. But inner or outer? I don't know." If I could just think . . .

"By Magrog's deeps, man, what *use* are you?"

He scanned the mob. As suddenly as a judge's hammer falls, he grabbed a scrawny man in a ragged coat from the edge of the crowd, bundling him into his massive embrace. "Gert, old friend! Our day has come at last! The earth shall be cleansed. Harrowed!"

He thumped the bewildered fellow on his chest and then shoved him back into the river of people bereft of his orange scarf.

"Tie it on," he said, cramming the damp rag into my hand.

I tied the scarf about my neck, while he absconded with one for himself. We shoved our way through the heart of the press, Voushanti digging his fingers into my flesh, while waving his free hand and chanting the same words as the rest.

The gates stood open, guarded by Moriangi warriors, spears leveled and ready. But the mob was restrained by their own discipline, not the threat of the warriors. Ten men and women, dressed no differently from their shabby fellows, stood in the front rank, hands stretched to the side as if withholding the pressure of the hundreds. Each one of them wore an orange scarf.

When we came up behind these ten, Voushanti grabbed my chin and pulled my ear close to his mouth. "When I give the word, you will follow me. Stay close. Do not slow down. On your life and the boy's, speak no word until I tell you. Do you understand?"

A bellow of agony rose from the fortress and rippled along my spine. Only its beginning timbre identified the victim as a man. I nodded.

Raising the engraved gold band that he had slipped from his left wrist, he clasped his hands in front of his face. "Ready?" he cried. "Now!"

A glare of red brilliance shattered the gray noonday. The whole world paused for that moment; shocked faces turned upward toward the light, shouts and laughter sheared off in midvoicing. I thought I had gone deaf. What in the name of all gods had he done?

The big Evanori sped toward the gate, his gray cloak flapping. I raced after him, agape. Voushanti and I existed between breaths, between swings of the great pendulum that ticked off our lives. No human eye perceived us. No human hand could halt our passage . . . across the short bridge . . . through the tight gatehouse . . . and into the courtyard of hell.

A grim, narrow, smoke-filled slot of a yard squeezed between inner and outer walls of undressed granite. Ruffians armed with pikes and swords stood behind three seated men wearing the red robes and wide-brimmed hats of judges. Flame soared and dark smoke billowed beyond the walls behind them, as would befit Magrog's own tribunes.

Though Voushanti and I existed in profound silence, events inevitably moved forward. A cage of iron poles against one wall bulged with battered men and women, and under the whips of two filthy guards, a stake-cart vomited more human refuse into the cage. Guards dragged a bloodied prisoner from the cage and threw him on his knees in the dirt before the tribunal. Words were exchanged.

We heard none of it. And no one marked us as we dashed across the yard.

A soundless hammer fell, witnesses waved their hands gleefully, and the silently screaming man was hauled toward the blood-slathered gallows that stood in the center of the yard. A bare-legged man and a silk-gowned woman already dangled from the crossarm—the woman crook-necked and very dead, the man in his death throes, his hands scrabbling weakly at the rope choking the life from him. Lashed to a frame at the end of the platform, a second man slumped dead in his bonds, his steaming entrails newly spilled out across the bloody hands of his executioner.

I halted, aghast, not so much at the brutality of this tableau, for such

vileness too often passed for justice in this world, but at seeing the faces of
the damned. The woman, mercifully, I did not know. But the man in the last
agonies of strangulation was Brother Victor, the small scholarly chancellor
of Gillarine, and the one whose life lay splattered so casually on this altar of
savagery was Abbot Luviar.

O mighty gods! My heart stopped. My gorge rose. My clenched fists
slammed my temples as if the blow might jar my sight to look upon a different truth. Luviar, the passionate heart of Gillarine, the one man I had ever
met who could make a jaded soul feel worthy of a god's notice, butchered
like a beast. Helpless grief and impotent rage stole breath and voice and
filled my soul and limbs with lead. And guilt . . . oh, gods of night, if we'd
arrived but moments sooner . . . if I'd had a clearer head . . .

Voushanti raced up the steps, motioning me to follow. Surely it was the
force of his will that stirred my feet, for I had no will, no strength, no courage to face such ruin. He waved and stomped his foot. He grappled the dangling body and supported Brother Victor's splayed legs, lessening the strain
on the slender neck. The little monk spasmed and heaved a violent breath,
breaking my paralysis. He lived.

I flew up the gore-slick stair and snatched the blunt, curved blade from
the hand of a bull-necked man beside a headsman's block. He gaped, bewildered, at his bare hands. At the limit of my height, I stretched and slashed
the rope above Brother Victor's head. The monk slumped into Voushanti's
grasp.

Spinning in place, I scoured the yard and the cage, searching for another
familiar shaven head and dark brows, sure that he, too, must be a victim of
this outrage. "Gildas!" I bellowed.

Noise and confusion fell on my head like a collapsing mountainside. The
executioner's bewildered gaze met my own, then blazed with understanding.
"Treachery!"

"Useless ass!" Voushanti screamed in fury. "Run! *Now*, or the boy dies!"

Voushanti hefted Brother Victor over his shoulder and raced down
the steps, his threat piercing the thunder of astonished outrage that surrounded me.

Spurred more by rage than fear, I leaped from the platform and sped
after him, slashing randomly at any hand or blade within my armspan. If
Voushanti's own neck fell foul of my blade, I would not weep.

We were most of the way across the yard when the Harrowers on the walls finally grasped what we were about. Sila Diaglou stretched her orange-draped arm over the milling horror and pointed straight at us. "Those three! Seize the blasphemers who dare defy the Gehoum!" she cried, her rich contralto as cold and deep and relentless as the tidal currents in Caurean Sea caves.

Sharp commands rang from the Moriangi troop at inner gate, and a half dozen warriors pushed through the crowd around the gallows. We dashed into the gatehouse tunnel.

"Halt and drop the blade," snapped Voushanti, once we had passed into the dark. "Now."

My hands and feet obeyed the command, whether by his will or magic or my own choice, I could not have said. I saw no possibility of escape without his connivance.

A warm limp weight was thrust into my arms. "Stay close. If you have a hope of life, do as I say."

"Can you work the spell again?" Gildas could easily be the next to have his bowels ripped out.

Red light flared dully from his hand and then faded. "No."

"But the others back there . . ."

From beside me came the unmistakable sound of a sword sliding from its sheath. No doubt the ax he wore strapped to his belt had found its way into his alter hand. "They have no hope of life."

The warriors were on us then, great looming shadows in the dark—distant daylight outlining their bulk. The tight passage restricted Voushanti's opponents to two at once, preventing a quick slaughter. I kept to the deepest shadows behind Voushanti, positioning Brother Victor's slight body across my shoulders while the Evanori efficiently dispatched two, then four, then five pursuers in a blurring flail of sword and ax.

"Now," he gasped as the sixth man fell, "run!"

I bolted. I could have carried two of Brother Victor without slowing, yet we had no route but through the mob. Those outside the walls could not know we were the objects of Sila Diaglou's wrath, and so it was not deliberate opposition that forced us to a standstill, but merely the crush of overexcited bodies.

"Stand aside," shouted Voushanti, over and over, forcing a path through the press, angling toward the side where the crowd was thinner. "Our brother . . . wounded by raiders . . . by Karish infidels . . . Let us through!"

Voushanti's ferocity and our orange scarves gave us passage. But the mardane's cloak had been torn halfway off. We had reached no more than halfway across the square, when a woman noticed the Evanori blazon on his surcoat. "Damn all, he's the Bastard's man!"

Haggard, starving faces, alight with manic fever, closed in, pressing us toward one fiery border of the square, crowding between us and our escape. "Who are you?" yelled a hollow-cheeked man. "What are you about? Who've you got there?"

"The Bastard defies the Gehoum . . . thinks to rival them . . ." The murmurs grew hostile. "Don't trust him."

Voushanti waved them off, spinning a half circle with his fouled ax and the bloody tip of his blade. Yet inevitably they pressed us backward, ever closer to a row of blazing houses behind us. Even through the layers of wool, my back blistered. Brother Victor moaned and shifted in my arms. In moments the mob would devour or shove us into the fire, unless the Moriangi soldiers who had begun slashing a ruthless path through the mob got to us first.

I closed my eyes and imagined my hands penetrating the muck beneath the cobbles, summoning the ruined landscape I had touched with mind and magic: *the fortress like an angry wound on the world . . . the dingy remnants of lives lived solely in its vile shadow . . . the present devastation—half walls, scorched rubble, fallen beams, blazing tenements leaning sideways at precarious angles now that their supporting neighbors had collapsed . . . and the past—ancient stones, broken and buried beneath centuries of filth . . . beneath shifting land and blighted building. Necessity . . . desperation . . . escape . . .* Certainty flooded into my bones.

"This way," I shouted into Voushanti's back. I whipped my heavy cloak over Brother Victor and my own head, leaving only enough of a gap to see my way. Then I turned my back on Voushanti and the mob and dashed straight through the wall of fire.

"Wait, fool!"

Veils of red and orange and blue snapped and roared, engulfing the tall house. To my dismay, we found no sanctuary beyond the dissolving timbers. Flaming debris and flared ash rained down as I clutched the limp body and leaped over a blazing beam. I had no hands free to knock away the embers that singed the back of my hands or set the damp wool of my cloak smoldering. My boots stank of scorched hide, and my feet screamed in agony as I waded through coals and ash. I could not hear for the belching thunder as another wall or bench or barrel exploded into flame, could not think for the suffocating smoke and fear.

Where was the safe, secure stone? I felt it here. Its pattern lived in my mind. Instinct told me we needed to go down. Smoke and garish flames made the patches of darkness too deep to penetrate with watering eyes, yet I dared not slow enough to hunt. To the right the hillside angled sharply upward. To my left a half-timbered wall groaned and sagged as moisture boiled away. Behind me, Voushanti yelped and cursed as an exploding barrel shot burning staves into the air like the brands of Syan fire jugglers. I had to let my feet guide as they would . . . and, in moments, my boot skidded on the brink of emptiness. Littered with charred debris and rills of flame, an ancient stone stair plunged into the earth. Unhesitating, I sped downward.

The stair led into a stone-lined trench. A sewer, I thought at first, so narrow I almost cracked Brother Victor's head on the wall. But as the way angled across the hillside and behind the rows of burning houses, worn steps broke the walls here and there, leading off into jumbles of stone and earth that might once have been far older houses. So perhaps this was an ancient street, its worn base and shoulder-high walls laid with native stone, only this bit of it exposed.

Though fire raged beyond the walls on either side, air flowed gently through the trench, just enough to shift and cool the falling ash without fanning it to flame. The lane widened slightly into a small high-walled court-yard. In its center a stone ring encircled a gnarled apple tree, astonishingly untouched by fire. By the time I thrashed through a snag of dead brush and half-frozen offal and stumbled into an abandoned tanner's yard, all traces of the ancient stone had crumbled into the hillside rubble, and we had left Riie Doloure well behind.

Coughing, gasping, welcoming even the lingering stench of a tanner's vats, I sank to my knees and untangled my cloak. I threw it down on a crusted drift of snow and laid Brother Victor on top of it. His cowl and gown had been stripped away, leaving only his torn and bloody shirt that could neither keep him warm nor cover the vile evidence of his battering. A painful shudder racked his frail body with each wheezing gasp. Broken ribs, like enough, but at least he breathed. His abraded neck had swollen around the arrowed gouge of the noose, but not enough to choke him. One eye socket had been crushed, the eye now little more than pulp.

"We can't stay here," said Voushanti. The warrior was bent over a few steps away, hawking and spitting, one hand planted on his knee. His left arm dangled slack, blood welling from a filthy wound just above the elbow. "Get him up. We have to go."

Brother Victor's hands and body jerked frantically, as if he were trying to defend himself, and his lips moved in a constant soundless stream of words. I bundled the charred edges of my cloak around him. "Easy, Brother," I whispered, wishing I could tell him he was safe. What could Osriel want with a holy monk? "I'll try not to hurt you."

"Valen?" His undamaged eye blinked open—a bruised hollow overflowing with pain. "Iero's grace, you've come."

The spark of hope in his bleak face stung worse, by far, than my seared skin. The implication of his greeting, that his god had somehow ordained me to make things right, choked me with bile. I needed to be designing some strategy, constructing some spellworking to protect him, but the events of the morning floated and churned in my sluggish thoughts like refuse in an oily backwater: Gildas and nivat, blood and fire and Jullian, Bayard's vengeance and Osriel's inscrutable purpose. How could I rescue a man from the Harrowers, only to turn him over to Osriel the Bastard?

A quick glance over my shoulder revealed Voushanti well across the yard, plunging his sword into an ice-crusted drift that still displayed some areas of white through its mantle of soot and ash. His fouled ax lay on the ground beside him. His wounds and heaving exhaustion had eased an unspoken fear that he was something other than human. Perhaps, if I could divert his attention and retrieve the ax before he picked it up . . .

I grabbed a scrap of old hide from the ground and began shaping a divexi—a noisy or frightening illusion designed to ensnare a watcher's attention. But I stumbled through the steps. How did you determine what manner of beast had worn this skin? I could not remember, and without knowing, I could not steal its noise or motion to infuse the spell. I floundered with the interlocking threads of enchantment.

Across the yard, Voushanti pulled the cleaned blade from the snow and wiped it on his cloak, awkward as he favored his injured arm. He sheathed the sword and snapped his head around to look at me, a spark of red piercing the gloom. He raised one hand, and a flare of red light blinded me. I blinked and squinted and turned the scrap over and over in my hand, trying to remember . . .

"Can you lead us out of here, pureblood"—Voushanti squatted beside me now, sword sheathed, clean, dry ax snugged in the strap looped over his belt. With one hand and his teeth, he finished tying off the bleeding wound in his arm with the strip of hide that had been in my hand—"and not through a conflagration?"

My stomach heaved at the unnerving gap in my perception. How had he gotten here so quickly? A blast of wind pelted my face with snow. I wrapped my arms tightly about my churning gut. No pain this time. No answering ecstasy. The raw threads of my spell lay in my mind unquickened as I'd left them.

Voushanti tilted his head, watching me, his half-mutilated mouth twisted upward. "Our master waits. Or is your word as valueless as your family insists?"

I gathered the scattered bits of sense enough to speak, not daring to look at his eyes. "I swore I would not run, Mardane, and I will not. But I never said I would drag others into slavery with me. What does your prince want with him?" Osriel, who stole the eyes of the dead.

"This is not the time to discuss our master's intents. Care you so little for your Karish brother that you would abandon him untended or drag him into this battle that rages around us without hope of succor?"

Melting snow under my knees soaked my wool hose as I feverishly discarded one plan after another. My father would not allow me past his house wards; neither would any other pureblood answer a *recondeur*'s plea. Certainly not on this day. Thalassa would likely help; she knew the little chancellor. But the temples were halfway across the city, and if the sacred precincts were not already burning, they would be overrun with wounded and frightened people. The others I knew in Palinur were tavern keepers, whores, alley rats, many of them kind and generous, yes—I had ever called them friends—but none knew more of me than my name and favorite songs. On a day when every man and woman's survival was in balance, how could I command enough trust to shelter a man snatched from the gallows?

Voushanti scrambled to his feet and extended his hand, the gold wristband gleaming brightly in the murk. Brother Victor lay wrapped in the cocoon of my cloak, struggling to breathe. Of all the facts in this failing universe, one stood clear and invariant. The monk would die if I did not get him help soon.

Cloud and smoke had grayed the midday to little more than dusk. Wind flapped my soot-grimed sleeves, drove flying snow down my collar and up my billowing tunic, and stung the burned patches on my hands and legs and face. Without my cloak, I was already shivering. My mind was numb, my reservoir of schemes barren. "You cannot expect me to believe the Bastard Prince will heal him. He must have some use for him."

Voushanti whipped a knife from his belt. I jumped, but he threw it on the ground in front of me. "I have risked my own survival to preserve this monk's life, which should demonstrate something to a man with limited choices and half a mind. Have you some other plan to save him? If not, then take my knife and one simple thrust will save him from my master's depredations. A second thrust will take care of your own problem." Cold, blunt. He did not care what I chose.

Every tale of Osriel's depravity swirled in my head, yet he had sent me to rescue good men from a terrible fate. Voushanti himself had shown naught but courage in the fight. I could read nothing from his dreadful visage save icy challenge. Perhaps it was weakness or another consequence of my shameful state, but I trusted his word.

He nodded as if I'd spoken it aloud. "The storm has come early upon us, Magnus Valentia, and much of Palinur has yet to burn. We'd best be moving before we are consumed." The Evanori scooped Brother Victor into his powerful arms, handling him as gently as Brother Robierre would have done. "Now, tell me the way out of here."

Osriel had an interest in Brother Victor's life, and for now my master's will would prevail. As for later . . . we would see. Pressing forehead and palms to the fouled earth, I reached out to find a path through the dying city—through layer upon layer of building and burning, of births and deaths, of commerce and art and piety, of cruelty and war, the footsteps of centuries. A simple route revealed itself. I raised my head and pointed down an alley that would lead us back to the house where the Duc of Evanore waited.

Indeed my course was clear, as nothing had been clear in all my life. The day had scribed two images on my soul, images that demanded I answer for my ill choices: Jullian, quivering in his silent terror, and the wise and passionate abbot of Gillarine splayed and gutted like a beast. Both my fault. Because I could not think. Because I could not act. Because I had clung to mindless pleasure to dull the pain of living. Always I had insisted my perversion harmed no one but myself. Who was there to care if Magnus Valentia de Cartamandua-Celestine, dull-wit *recondeur*, burnt out his senses or locked his useless mind away in a ruined body?

I clenched my fists and wrapped my arms about my eyes and ears, miming that deadness as if to silence conscience for one last time. But Jullian's terrified silence and Abbot Luviar's cry of agony gave my shame a voice I could no longer put aside.

And so, as I stumbled to my feet and followed Voushanti out of the tanners' yard, I left a litter behind in the filthy snow: a fragment of a mirror, a silver needle, a linen thread, and a few black seeds that rapidly vanished into the muck. I threw the empty green bag into a smoldering house. Never again. Ever.

Chapter 29

"You are not forbidden illumination, Cartamandua." The lamplight from the passage set Mardane Voushanti's freshly polished mail gleaming, delineating his bulky shadow in a bronze glow as if he were Deunor Lightbringer himself. The warrior quickly dispelled the illusion by stepping out of the doorway, only to return with one of the passageway lamps, giving me full view of his half-mangled face and worn leather. He displayed no sign of bandages or discomfort from his wounding.

Illumination. Upon our return to Prince Osriel's dismal dwelling, Voushanti had whisked Brother Victor away, declaring the monk would be cared for, while two of Osriel's warriors had deposited me into this fusty little chamber. In the hours since, as the gray daylight faded beyond the slot window, I had sat with muddy boots propped on a dusty clerk's desk, and unshaven chin propped on my curled fingers, seeking illumination. The woolly tangle that had snarled my thoughts and actions throughout the day had at last unraveled, and the mysteries of past and present now surrounded me in stark, immutable stillness like a ring of standing stones: my grandfather, my master, the Danae, Gillarine, the end of the world.

"Unless you've brought me dinner or answers, I would prefer you take your lamp and go," I said, too tired to mask bitterness and self-loathing. I did not expect answers any more than I expected word of Jullian's fate or Brother Victor's health. Everyone I'd met since Boreas had deposited my dying carcass outside Gillarine had excelled at keeping me mystified and on edge. Tonight, though I had defined and bounded these myriad puzzles, I could declare none solved.

"You've not cleaned yourself. Are these breeks not fine enough to cover your pureblood arse?" Voushanti prodded the stack of neatly folded fabrics he'd brought along with a water basin and towel soon after our arrival. A mardane, a landed baron and warrior of more than average skill, both military and magical, serving me like a housemaid—one of the lesser standing stones, but a curiosity, nonetheless. Why was I so sure that deeper investigation would reveal this man had no home, no family, no history or ambition that linked him to anyone but Osriel?

"Tell me, Lord Voushanti, was the spell you worked at Riie Doloure of your own making, or was it Prince Osriel's work?" I believed I had deciphered the answer to this particular puzzle. Quickened spells could be attached to objects and keyed with a triggering word, allowing those with no magical talents to use them at will—but only once or twice without a new infusion of magic. Voushanti's limited usage of the spell in Riie Doloure made me doubt he was the originator. And his gold wristband would be a perfect spell carrier.

"Our master will answer questions or not, as he pleases. Just now, he requires your attendance in the proper garb of a royal advisor. So dress yourself or I'll do it for you, and I am no genteel manservant."

Though for once in my life I desired no company but my own, I had to answer this summons. The last doulon interval had been but eighteen days. I bore no illusions about what was to come. Even if I survived the ravages of the doulon hunger long enough to shake free of it, sooner or later the disease that gnarled my gut and flayed my senses, prompting me to seek its comforts, would leave me a drooling lunatic. But in the past hour I had vowed to Luviar's shade that for as long as I had wits, I would give what aid I could to those who fought for his cause. For now, my hope of illumination lay with Osriel the Bastard.

Voushanti remained stolidly beside the door as I stripped off my scorched and bloody garb and used my shirt to scrub the soot from face and arms. The water in the cracked basin was long cold. The tiny coal fire in the rusty brazier could not have kept a rabbit warm.

Where was reason and the proper order of the universe? Abbot Luviar, a man of vision and passion, hung from the gallows with blowflies feasting on his bowels, while my worst injury from the day's events, a deep burn on the back of my hand, had already scabbed over. And Brother Victor, a man of intelligence and reason, lay fighting for breath, while I was to parade as a royal advisor in a house run by spiders, feral cats, one mutilated mardane, four warriors . . . and, ah, yes, one prince who stole dead men's eyes, brutalized children, and salvaged tortured monks.

Was fortune no gift of a harried goddess, but rather purest chance? Perhaps the Harrowers had guessed the truth, that the universe was naught but chaos, and mankind, fearing the impenetrable, uncaring powers of night and storm, had only imagined these kindly mockeries of ourselves that we called gods.

Luviar would have refused such a hopeless premise. Given voice from the grave, he would argue that a beneficent Creator had instilled in humankind the means to shape our own destiny. In the throes of such guilt as plagued me this night, I desired desperately to believe that. The abbot had given me the grace of his trust, and I had failed him. Now I had to find some way to make amends. My meager vow was all I could devise.

The clean clothes were plain, but fine—a silk shirt of spruce green, a pourpoint of blood-red brocade. I swiped at my hair to remove flakes of ash and splinters.

The mardane handed me the claret-hued cape and mask. So, ordinaries beyond Osriel's household were to be present at this interview. This day had left me beyond surprise.

Voushanti guided me through the winding passages back to Prince Osriel's chamber. Though night had fallen, I could see more of the house than I had in the morning's confusion. Tiered candle rings veiled with cobwebs lit the domed foyer, a circular space cold and bare of any decoration save massive pillars, weighty arches, and a dozen elaborately carved doors. Two Evanori warriors guarded one pair of doors and swung them open immediately upon our arrival.

"His Grace awaits," said Voushanti. "You are on trial here, pureblood."

The mardane pivoted smartly, drew his sword, and took up a guard stance, face outward between the two warriors, leaving me to pass through the open doorway alone. His remarks but confirmed my own conclusions. Jullian's presence, my oath not to run, the hidden identities of our day's quarry—I had been on trial all day. How had Osriel known how to manipulate me so thoroughly? And to what purpose?

Myriad teardrop-shaped lamps of colored glass illuminated Prince Osriel's chamber—a grand hall, hung with thick tapestries of dark reds, greens, and gold. Above the hanging lamps the high, barreled vault hosted lurid depictions of the netherworld—scenes of naked, writhing humans being herded by grinning gatzi toward a lake of fire. In one broad panel a triumphant Magrog, crowned with ram's horns, presided over a charred desolation from his throne of human skulls.

My eyes could not linger on the fantastical paintings above my head. The focus of the great hall was a vaulted alcove to my right, where the impenetrable darkness of the morning had yielded to shifting shadows. In front of a curved screen of wrought gold sat an elaborately carved chair of squared oak, knobbed spires rising from its back. To either side of the chair, fire blazed in great brass bowls that rested on the backs of gray stone statues depicting chained slaves twice my height. The chair was occupied.

Considering the size of the chair, I estimated its occupant to be a person of a man's moderate stature, though the voluminous folds of a hooded velvet gown, colored the same spruce green as my garb, left sex, size, and demeanor indeterminate. Yet that person's presence was immense. No storm building over the river country, where the turbulent air of the mountains clashed with hot wind from the eastern deserts and the moisture of the Caurean Sea, could have such monumental force pent in its clouds as the power shivering the air about Osriel's throne.

"My Lord Prince," I said, "or at least so I presume."

Even as I made my genuflection, touching my fingers to my forehead, I fought to control my fear. This house and its macabre trappings were designed to intimidate.

A slender, refined hand gestured me up. A man's hand, bearing a single heavy ring of graven gold, almost too large for the finger that bore it.

"See, now, that I am a man of my word, Magnus Valentia." The voice from under the velvet hood hinted at the first stirring vigor of the storm wind. His ringed finger pointed behind me.

I spun in place to discover a goggle-eyed, unscarred Jullian standing roughly in the place I'd left him that morning. He was unbound, his thin shoulders firmly in the grasp of a wary Brother Gildas. Rarely had I felt such a rush of relief and pleasure.

I had feared Gildas lost at Riie Douloure—the lighthouse Scholar, the hope of a kingdom rapidly destroying itself, my friend. The irony struck me that my need for nivat had likely saved him, removing him from the priory before the assault. And Jullian . . .

The boy's anxious eyes searched, taking in my cloak and mask and the looming presence on the dais behind me. Then his clear gaze slid past the eyehole of my mask, met my own eyes, and as a nervous sparrow finds a branch to its liking, stayed a while. His face brightened. I smiled and nodded and breathed a prayer of thanksgiving, wishing he did not have to hear what I had to tell.

Reaffirming my vow to guard the lad and his cause, I turned so that I could both address the prince properly and assure myself that my two friends would not vanish in candle smoke. I crafted my words carefully, estimating what might be expected or permitted in this room, assessing what might be my master's purpose, and cataloguing the news I wished to convey to the remaining members of the lighthouse cabal. "My lord, I appreciate your generosity in permitting me to share this fulfillment of our bargain. Were poor Brother Victor brought in to be released to his brothers as well, with the painful results of his ordeal at Riie Doloure well healed, then I could ask no better return for my submission."

Gildas stiffened, shock and dismay carving their very sigils on his brow. "Victor alive . . . captive . . . here?"

"You must improve your bargaining, Magnus Valentia, and learn to discipline your loose tongue," said the man in the chair, his voice sinuous as an adder, smooth and coiled with danger. "Here I've given you a gift—releasing the boy to his Karish friend, rather than setting him adrift in the sea of Palinur's destruction as your ill-considered pact would have allowed—and you express your gratitude by sharing our private business with a stranger."

Prince Osriel's displeasure settled on my shoulders like a cloak of lead. Yet no flaming bolts flew across the room to set me afire. No muting spells were triggered in my silken mask. After the magics of the day, I expected anything. So I pushed farther. A limited future gives a man certain advantages in such a game.

I bowed toward the prince again. "My apologies, lord. Clearly you knew of my association with the monks of Gillarine when you brought these two here. As our venture to rescue their brothers from Sila Diaglou's clutches was so nobly wrought, I assumed that the fate of the two captives, certainly to the summary of one salvaged life and one grievous . . . most grievous . . . death, would not be hidden from them."

Jullian's face drained of blood. Gildas, now holding his emotions close, did not seem to notice, but the chalk-faced boy would surely have dropped to his knees had the monk not maintained such a firm grip on his shoulder.

The swirling shadows darkened, and thunder rumbled just at the edge of hearing. The prince waved one hand at the door. "Brother—Gildas, you called yourself?—please take your young charge and go, bearing with you my sincerest cautions as to the dangers of the streets. Charming as it is to encounter an actual Karish monk, my sorcerer and I have important business to attend, and it seems I must school him beforetime."

Without voiced command, the outer doors swung open. Gildas, his dark brow knotted, inclined his head to the man in the chair. As he urged the shocked Jullian ahead of him, he glanced over his shoulder, pressed the backs of two fingers to one cheek, and jerked his head at me. The two fingers were the monks' signing speech—an admonition to use thought before speaking. The jerk of his head and the granite set of his mouth were a more universal language—a promise that he would do what he could to set me free. Such a small gesture to put steel in a man's spine. In my deepest heart, I blessed him.

As the doors swung shut, and I was left alone with the still figure in green draperies, all warmth fled that hall. I imagined frost rime spreading on the slave statues and ice spears growing on the corbels and brackets. The shadows deepened, as if their very substance had increased, as if all those who had ever stood in this hall had been sent away empty, their darkest thoughts and fears kept here as the price of their release. By the time my master spoke, I could scarce contain my shivering, though I mustered every shred of control I possessed to stop it. I was *not* afraid of him. Not anymore. What could he do to me that was worse than what I had brought upon myself?

"You tread a crumbling verge, pureblood," he said ever so softly. "Do you think that because my bloodlines are impure, and my body less than perfect, my mind is also flawed?"

I clasped my hands behind my back. "Your Highness, my awe of your talents grows by the moment. To create a cloaking spell such as Mardane Voushanti wielded this morning at Riie Doloure is the work of a skilled sorcerer. To create this aura of terror"—I waved to encompass the hall, feeling proud that my hand did not tremble and my teeth did not chatter—"is the work of a masterful perception."

I strolled to the foot of the dais, striving to prove that fear did not paralyze me—as much to myself as to him. "As I have not observed your physical imperfection for myself, I could not possibly judge it as a source of weakness, though you are clearly not the horned giant of rumor. And as you have surely been told, I take neither pride nor pleasure in my bloodlines, so I could hardly view another man as 'lesser' for not sharing them. If I were ever to sire children of my own, I would as soon throw them to wolves as submit them to the Pureblood Registry. What is it you wish from me, my lord? You seem to know a great deal about me, whereas I know naught of you but tales and the single fact that you dispatched me to save two good men from the gallows." For what? That was the question whose answer was the key to the man in green.

A movement of his hand and the shadows parted, exposing the bronze-inlaid marble steps in front of him. "A brash mouth you have, Magnus Valentia. More sober-minded than I expected. I was told you were an ignorant buffoon who made jest of all things serious, including your own talents. But then again, this day's events must sober even the most slack mind. Come closer and we'll talk a bit about your friends. And, Magnus"—I shuddered at his particular enunciation of my name, as if he had catalogued every mote of my being and tethered it to his discipline—"always remove your mask when we are alone."

I climbed the few steps to the dais, tugging the silk from my face and tucking it in the glove loop on my belt. Whatever Osriel's game, subtlety played a far greater role than crass brutality.

Moments passed before the prince took up the conversation again. He propped his elbow on the wide arm of his chair and rested his chin on his hand. Relaxed, it appeared. The man seemed as changeable as sunlight in the river country. "Your friend, the Chancellor of Gillarine, fares as well as could be expected of a man who came within a heart's thump of learning the truth of his god. His injuries have prevented my use of him, but they will heal, given time enough."

I could not disguise my astonishment. "My lord, I thank—"

"Do not *thank* me," he snapped, slamming his hand to the chair arm. "You cannot feel gratitude when you suspect I have unsavory motives for snatching the monk from the Ferryman's slip. I prefer honesty from my servants, not mimed groveling, as if I were some simpleton to be swayed with pretense. *Actions* that counter my wishes reap my punishment. Not thoughts."

The colored lamps swayed as if a wind teased them. Weakness raced through my veins and sinews. "Of course, my lord. I only—"

"What would be the pleasure in having bound servants if their thoughts did not resist my own?" Though the prince had not moved, and we were alone, these soft-spoken words emanated from the region of my shoulder, as if the hooded man crouched behind me, his pale lips not a finger's breadth from my ear. "The delight of power is not commanding an army of sycophants, but rather bending one resilient mind beyond its comfortable boundaries."

I suppressed a shudder. Refusing to look over my shoulder, I inclined my head to acknowledge his point—and to compose my expression. I could not allow him to see when his tricks unnerved me. "I appreciate your desire for honesty, my lord. Naturally, I am concerned for Brother Victor's safety and future in the care of a powerful lord I know only from dread rumor. Nevertheless, I *am* grateful to hear news of his state. Accept my thanks or not, as you please."

"Tell me about the lighthouse," said the prince, reversing tone again as if he were two men at once hidden in his robes. This simple request might have been an inquiry about the weather beyond his walls. Yet it startled me out of measure.

That he might have discovered the existence of a collection assembled over so many years was not so unexpected. What other circumstance would send me on a chase for members of the cabal with Jullian held hostage? I did not believe in such weighty accidents of fate. But I did not expect so direct an assault or so prompt. My promise to keep Luviar's secrets left me scrambling for a response. "The lighthouse, Lord Prince?"

The prince's hands hooked on the squared oak arms of his chair and pulled his body slightly forward. The air between us compressed my chest. "We are not here to dice, Cartamandua." Each syllable pronounced precisely. "I know these monks have built a great treasure house, a cache of books and riches gathered from all the known world. I have uses for such things. Only two men have ever known how to open the way into the vault. One of those lies dead; the other lies unspeaking in my guest chamber. Events will not wait on healing salves and poultices. Thus I remember something else I've heard: An initiate of Ophir's order was allowed to visit this treasure house, an initiate with sorcerous powers of his own. A promising development, is it not? If this sorcerer cannot provide me with a monk to open the way, then perhaps he can open it himself."

Damnation! The detail that I had visited the lighthouse was quite recent and quite specific. If he could read thoughts, he'd have no need for my answers. Thus, either he had twisted the juicy tidbit from his captives—Jullian or Brother Victor—or someone else in the cabal was telling tales.

No one had told me the full membership of the cabal. I refused to believe any of those I knew a willing betrayer. The nature and power of their beliefs colored them virtuous in my eyes—even Thalassa, now I looked at her deeds with my childish blinders removed. Then again, if the past few days had taught me anything, it was that I was no good judge of character.

The possibility of an informant gave me little hope of deception; thus I was left with no choice but to test my master's dictum here at the beginning. "Clearly I cannot maintain pretense with you, Lord Prince. I am sworn to silence about the lighthouse and must hope that my promises to you gain credibility from my refusal to break my vow." I rushed onward, hoping to forestall his explosion. "And before you pass judgment, let me also state that neither honor nor intent makes one flyspeck of difference in this case."

His attention threatened to crush both mind and soul. "How so, pureblood? If your intent is disobedience, then it makes a great deal of difference. You'll not enjoy discovering how much so."

I worked to maintain a measured tone, as if on any day I might be found denying the wishes of Magrog's henchman. "Your diligent informants have reported that my undisciplined childhood left me untrained in sorcery. They must also have reported that I lack the basic skills of an educated man. But perhaps the implications were not made clear. I cannot interpret the spells of others. I have no background even to guess what any complex working might be and no trained intuition to know how to go about discovering the answer. I cannot read books of magic, even if any pureblood family would allow a *recondeur* to touch their most prized possessions. So I cannot possibly unravel this spell that opens the brothers' storehouse for you, even if"—I hesitated only briefly before throwing down the gauntlet—"I chose to do so."

Footsteps and voices beyond the doors distracted the prince before his gathering wrath could break upon my head. When the door opened to Voushanti, I found myself able to breathe again.

The mardane hurried across the room, not bothering to bow. His heavy cloak was dusted with snow. "Skay has confirmed that Prince Bayard's men control the city gates this hour. The guards are stretched thin and shitting their trews for fear of the Harrowers. I've transport ready."

"Excellent. Have Saverian see to the monk while I ensure my pureblood's good behavior."

"We'd best be quick, my lord. We caught three Harrowers trying to climb over the wall. Our . . . inquiries . . . revealed they were hunting the little monk." Voushanti bowed and left.

"Alas, we shall have to continue our discussion another time." The prince rose from his chair. Not short, not tall. His voluminous velvets prevented me deducing more of his size or shape. He pointed a finger at one of the blazing bowls atop the slave statues. The fire bloomed scarlet, then vanished, dropping an inky mantle over his left shoulder.

"I believe the time has come to bring my fractious brothers to heel," he said. "Thus I've decided to remove my valuables—including my very expensive pureblood—south to Evanore, far from this precarious city. Until we meet again, you will remain in Mardane Voushanti's sight at all times and obey his commands as if they were my own. You will strictly maintain your pureblood discipline. And you will not discuss this day's business—my business—with *any*one. Now tell me whether or not you *choose* to obey these orders. If you think not, we can just get on with the necessary unpleasantness."

His mild-spoken menace did naught but inflame my curiosity. He had some use for me. To make the best use of my position, to protect my friends and aid their mission, I needed to learn of my new master or, at the least, prevent him interfering with the cabal. "Does not my duty require me to be at your side, lord? I should protect—"

"*Honesty*, Magnus." The second bowl of fire bled and died. My skin felt the flash of heat.

I bowed and touched my forehead. "As you command, Your Grace . . ." Though, *honestly*, I would prefer the freedom to choose my own course.

Chapter 30

We rode out within the hour. In the kitchen courtyard, where Voushanti had first brought me to Osriel that morning, three of Osriel's warriors waited beside a mule-drawn wagon draped in mourning garlands of dried laurel and black ribbon. A stone coffin occupied the wagon bed. *Brother Victor—*

"The little monk sleeps, pureblood," said Voushanti at my mumbled curse. "But not his final sleep."

I gaped at him, unable to contain my horror. "You hid him in a *coffin?*"

"The Moriangi will not inspect Lord Osriel's dead. Now, mount up." He pointed at a beast waiting patiently behind the wagon. "We've found a docile steed for you tonight."

Prince Osriel did not see us off.

Palinur lay eerily quiet as we plodded toward the city gates. Winter held the world fast in its grip. Ice sheathed toppled statues and charred wreckage, and hung in great spikes from gutters and balconies. Churned, filthy snow lay deep in the byways. Hunched figures scuttled into alleyways as we approached and darted out again only after we passed.

No Moriangi gate guard dared so much as glance at Prince Osriel's pureblood or his "fallen knight" in the coffin, not when a warrior of Voushanti's complexion growled hints of the Bastard's retribution should they do so. But neither did anyone want the responsibility of violating Prince Bayard's order that no one breathing was to leave Palinur that night. We were passed from one guard captain to the next—the events a blur of torchlight, waiting, repeated stories, and anxious, stuttering progress. I rejoiced that I was not expected to speak. Exhaustion weighed on my limbs like the burdening ice.

Eventually Voushanti convinced Tiglas Volti, a seedy-eyed senior guard captain, of the mortal risks in insulting Prince Bayard's neutral brother—a brother whose vaults of gold, once opened, would likely dispense their contents as far spread as the Bastard's goodwill . . . even so far as senior guard captains. Eventually, the portcullis slammed shut behind us, and we rolled into the night.

"Get out of the tent or you'll be folded up in it." Voushanti's ugly face poked through the slit in the canvas for the third time since he'd called me out of a dead sleep. The patch of sky behind him was a sunlit blue.

I slipped on my mask and crawled toward him, every bone and sinew complaining, breathing through my mouth to avoid the persistent stench of old sweat, old ale, and old vomit woven into the shelter's fabric. I'd never known a tent that was aught but cramped and stinking. "If you don't give me time to stretch and take a piss before I climb onto that devil horse again, I'll make both sides of your face look equally ugly," I mumbled, as he backed away from the entrance.

I had no idea how far we'd ridden after leaving Palinur behind. I had fallen asleep in the saddle, waked only long enough to break a drover's nose when they threw me into the wagon bed. I'd thought they were going to put me in the coffin. I didn't remember being stuffed into the tent.

Voushanti awaited me in an alder thicket frosted with new snow. Pale sunlight glittered through the crusted branches. "Just beyond these trees lies a party of His Grace's retainers," he said as I unfolded my stiff limbs like some great chick from too small an egg. "We'll be traveling with them. Remember your orders. Keep to your pureblood practices. Once you've relieved yourself, follow me."

"Voushanti!" I called after his departing back. "What of Brother Victor?"

He paused. "My lord yet has hope to extract some return for all our trouble to get him."

I took that as good news. "Where are we going? What does the prince—?"

"South." He vanished into the trees. A flurry of blackbirds scattered and circled above the thicket.

I saw no sign of horses, wagon, monk, or coffin in the vicinity of the brown and white tent. But scents of woodsmoke, burnt porridge, and horses wafted through the leafless trees, along with the muted clatter and bustle of an encampment. My most urgent needs met, I followed Voushanti down the well-trod path into the brake.

The busy camp sprawled across a broad clearing. Soldiers moved among the horses, leading them to water, cinching saddle girths, and picking ice and stones from hooves, while servants collapsed tents, rolled blankets, and stuffed packs. One very large tent yet stood in the center of the trampled snow. The green and white colors of Evanore hung limp from its center pole, along with several other pennants of various colors.

Beside the large tent, a group of well-armed men and women encircled Voushanti, their craggy faces contrasting sharply with their jeweled rings and brooches, gold-etched sword hilts, and fur-lined cloaks. Evanori warlords—at least five of them among the small group—each a petty sovereign in his or her own right with bloodlines far older than purebloods, bound by oath to Caedmon's line since the kingdom's founding.

". . . while he attends to his business," the mardane was saying. He might have been a toad addressing a gathering of eagles. "Prince Bayard is not yet seated in Palinur. Our spies report he is paying calls on several noble Ardran houses before announcing his victory, while Harrower raiding parties spring from the brush like grouse before beaters . . ."

The lords seemed attentive, but not deferent. Voushanti was clearly not one of them. Though his manner and accent witnessed to his Evanori blood, his mardane's rank was an Ardran grant, not Evanori inheritance. His authority was strictly Osriel's.

"His Grace will see you at Ygil's Moon. Do *not* disappoint him." Such woe and ruin as Voushanti's tone promised would have sent Magrog running from his throne of skulls.

The proud warlords dispersed slowly, eyes hooded, mumbling among themselves. A round-headed lord in a steel cap and tall boots glared at Voushanti as if to argue, only to think better of it. He tightened his mouth in disgust and turned his back sharply. Perhaps more warlords than Stearc of Erasku viewed Eodward's youngest son as an abomination.

Two of the Evanori turned to intercept the man in the steel cap, thereby facing me straight on, not ten paces distant. A flood of pleasure warmed my veins, and I fought to keep from laughing outright, which was a wholly unreasonable reaction to encountering a warrior who would prefer me dead and his daughter who had betrayed me.

Elene controlled herself well. After one startled blink, she averted her gaze. But little more than a touch of her father's arm drew Thane Stearc's eye my way. The frown lines about his mouth and hawkish brow deepened. He, too, glanced away quickly.

Though a sword hung at her waist, Elene no longer stood as Stearc's squire, but as a woman of Evanore, a descendant of warlords like these. Her wide-legged trousers were suitable for riding, her breasts unbound beneath her copper-colored shirt and fine-linked habergeon, her cropped bronze hair now grown long enough to twist in numerous tiny braids laid flat to her head. I might have been looking on the goddess Mother Samele herself, the exemplar of the earth's health and strength. My hands ached to touch her cheeks, flushed with the cold, and stroke the hips that filled her trousers so delectably . . .

Great gods, I felt like a witless pup, after a month imprisoned, with no hopes to spare for pleasures of mind or body, and before that a novice vowed. Of a sudden my grievances with the woman seemed of no more substance than the frost vapors rising from the sunlit tents. Somehow I found myself willing to believe that she had acted out of devotion to her cause—at least while I stood so near that tantalizing flesh and bright spirit. So much had changed since I'd seen her last.

The man in the steel cap snapped orders to break down the large tent. Elene stood by as her father and Voushanti exchanged stiff courtesies. No love lost between those two men. Stearc's arched nose flared as they spoke. When Voushanti moved on, Stearc began arguing with a bearlike man about whether their party should travel together or take separate, shorter roads to their strongholds. Elene joined in, her cinnamon eyes flashing. No demure maiden she.

As custom and protocol prescribed, no one spoke to me or acknowledged my presence with anything but sidewise glances. Only a pureblood or his contracted master could initiate interaction with ordinaries. Pureblood discipline required me to maintain that distance. After his pointed warnings, the mardane would surely be watching. And these two . . . I could give no one cause to suspect their divided loyalties. No matter their opinions of Osriel, I had no illusions that others of these fearsome folk conspired to preserve books and tools in preference to their duc and his gold mines.

I tore my attention from Elene and wandered through the rapidly dwindling camp, seeking any sign of Brother Victor. Cheered to discover the emptied coffin abandoned in the trees, I drifted toward the three wagons. One was packed with household goods, one with hay and grain sacks. A stout woman in a shabby cloak was helping the older servants climb into the third wagon. Before I could sidle close enough to peer inside, the woman looked up—and did not drop her eyes. Her look of scorn near torched my cloak. Donning my own best disdain, I strolled on past her and her charges, hoping she cared more for Karish monks than purebloods. I'd have wagered my prick that poor, battered Brother Victor lay among the bags and bundles in that wagon bed.

I retreated and sat down on a fallen tree. Elene stood listening to a tall woman with iron-gray hair and cheekbones as angular as the crossguard on her sword. Happy for once to be ritually ignored, I stared at Elene and imagined and yearned until her rosy flush expanded to her neck and ears, and she yielded me a sidewise glance. Ah, if only we were back under that dolmen in the rain . . .

A dark-haired man bundled in a thick black cloak hurried out of the great tent, lugging a worn leather satchel. He caught sight of me at once. Of course, Gram would be here, too.

I winked and twiddled a finger at the sober secretary. Gram whipped his glance around the company until his gaze settled on Voushanti's back. He raised his eyebrows and flashed me a quick grin, then ducked his head and moved on about his business.

I buried my grin in my hands. How fine to discover friends here. I'd no expectation of seeing anyone I knew ever again—save perhaps Brother Victor. Of a sudden I found myself anticipating the coming journey with excitement. Somehow I'd find a way to speak with them.

When Gram strode past her field of view, Elene scowled at his back. No softening of that enmity. For some perverse reason, that consideration cheered me even more.

By the time the cumbersome party moved out, some fifty of us altogether, the rare blue sky had skinned over with clouds, and snowflakes flurried like dandelion fluff. "Stay close, pureblood," said Voushanti, as I tried to find the right combination of knee and hand, curses and cajoling to prevent my beastly mount from shedding me. "I'm charged to keep you healthy."

The mardane moved into the vanguard beside the iron-gray woman, the lord in the steel cap, and Stearc. They scarce looked at him. Someday I would insist someone explain why Voushanti's presence made a man's bowels churn.

Elene rode two ranks behind, alongside two younger men who eyed

Voushanti's back with a mix of awe and terror. Over the course of the first hour, I maneuvered my balky mare to her side, close enough we could speak with little risk of being overheard. "May I ask where you are bound, mistress? 'Tis a wretched season to trade hearth fire and good company for a perilous road."

"My father and I have business southward—a Karish school in which he takes an interest." A glance my way, quickly controlled. "And then, as do all those loyal to the Duc of Evanore, we return home for Lord Osriel's warmoot, the first he has summoned. We're curious to learn if Evanore's position of neutrality in this vile conflict is to change. Perhaps his pureblood advisor could enlighten us?"

I imagined Voushanti's ears straining to hear my disobedience. I kept my eyes on his broad back. "Alas, I've no leave to discuss my master's business. In truth, having been in my lord's service only a single . . . unhappy . . . day, I'm not even sure of our destination, save that it be south—which seems to leave half of Ardra and all of Evanore a possibility."

She bit her lip and bowed her head, which made me believe she knew of Luviar. "My sincerest apologies, sir. I'm not accustomed to pureblood company, or what is proper to ask. So often we can give offense . . . hurt, even . . . when *none* is intended." Her voice shook a little. "I'd suppose you bound for Prince Osriel's great fortress at Angor Nav or, perhaps, his smaller house at Renna."

I nodded with as much aristocratic dignity as I could summon. "My life has changed dramatically of late, mistress, and I find life more pleasant when I forget unintended slights. You know, though we've not been formally introduced, you resemble a lad I once knew—a squire of marginal talents, but exceeding fair for a boy. I would not be surprised to see his position vacant."

She kept her eyes on the road, snowflakes dusting her flushed countenance. "Indeed, sir, the portion of your face that I can see resembles that of a man I once knew—a monk of marginal piety and excessive interest in matters he had forsworn. I would not be surprised to see his habit uninhabited."

"Thank all gods that men grow wiser as days pass." I could smell her even in the cold . . . fennel and lavender and leather. But for the snow, one might have imagined us on a pleasure outing in happier times.

Impelled by dreary wisdom, I left Elene and dropped back to ride in the fourth rank for a while, sharing curses of weather and Harrowers with a new-bearded youth who rode as if soul bonded to his mount. The weather worsened by the hour, blowing snow and increasingly cold. We passed several villages burnt to ash. Other cots gaped open to the weather, perhaps one in five showing signs of habitation. In the distance, dark shapes—wolves or wild dogs—loped across the snow-covered fields, which did naught to soothe our unhappy horses.

Gram rode several ranks behind me, his cloak and hood bundled about him. At every stop I tried to draw him aside, hoping he might hint at what use the cabal would make of my grandfather's story, but we were able to exchange only a few empty words. The warlords demanded his attendance. His bottomless well of facts about Navronne's history fueled the lords' never-ending arguments of politics and war. By evening, the rigors of the journey had sapped all conversation.

We sheltered that night in a burnt-out inn, its broken walls blocking the wind. I maneuvered a seat next to Elene as the company shared out hard bread and bean soup. "The boy and the Scholar," I mumbled into my bread. "Safe?"

She bobbed her head over her soup.

"And the book?"

Elene turned to the iron-gray Thanea Zurina, who sat on her right. "No matter how difficult the journey, I'm happy my father chose to leave Palinur," she confided. "When one sees both Temple priestesses and Karish practors deserting the place, one must think the gods themselves have given up on it. With so many clerics, the roads south should be safe enough for children!"

I smiled and drained my bowl. Thalassa had book, boy, and Scholar and was taking them south.

On the next morning, once we persuaded the horses to move out of their huddle, four of the seven lords split off and headed west on the Ardran high road, taking all the wagons and two-thirds of the soldiers. I had caught nary a glimpse of Brother Victor, but assumed he traveled with them. The rest of us, perhaps twenty in all, continued on the less-traveled way that led south past Gillarine toward Caedmon's Bridge. We kept a slow, steady pace, stopping only to water the horses or pick ice from their hooves. Just after midday, one of our scouts reported a disciplined cadre of orange-blazed Harrowers bearing down on us, he said, like Magrog's chariots of doom. We spurred our mounts and fled.

For a day and a night of driving snow and merciless cold, we forced our way southward across the rolling, frost-clad barrens of dead fields and vineyards. Every time we believed we had shaken the pursuit and slowed to ease the strain on our mounts, scouts raced from the rear with the news that they had come up on us again. Fifty Harrowers, the men said, led by a squat, ugly man with a face very like a dog. Voushanti forbade me to go back with the scouts to confirm that he was Sila Diaglou's henchman—one of Boreas's executioners. The warlords were spoiling for a fight, but the lord in the steel cap agreed with Voushanti that Prince Osriel would wish neither his neutrality compromised nor his noble supporters slaughtered in a useless confrontation with lunatics.

The relentless pace and ferocious weather took a toll on all of us, but most especially Gram. The cold flayed him. Skin gray, his features like drawn wire, he rode with back bent and head dropped low to deflect the wind. At noontide on the third day of our flight, when we stopped in a snow-drowned glen and scattered grain for the beasts, he clutched his mount's mane and whispered hoarsely that he'd best remain where he was unless Prince Osriel's pureblood could magically transport him from the saddle and back into it again. Stearc pressed him to drink some medicament from an amber flask, but he waved it away. "I'd rather have my wits," he croaked. "I can hold until we find shelter. All the way home if need be."

We had little prospect of shelter. The towns of Cressius and Braden had refused to open their gates to us. No village had defenses enough to withstand a Harrower assault while we slept. Everyone was exhausted—save perhaps Thanea Zurina—and we'd had three horses pull up lame that morning. I feared for Gram's life if we didn't ease up. And if the Harrowers took Stearc, Elene, and Gram—saints forbid—what would become of the lighthouse cabal or their hopes of appeal to the Danae? Not an hour later, a solution presented itself on the horizon.

"We divide our forces," I said, sketching a map in the snow. "While a few of us lure our pursuers into Mellune Forest, most will remain out of sight at the forest boundary. There's good cover and Lord Voushanti is very skilled at . . . hiding . . . people for short periods of time. Once we've got the Harrowers into the wood, the rest of you can continue on the road south at a more reasonable pace . . . stay alive . . ."

Even Aurellia's imperial road builders had declared Mellune Forest impassable. A snarled swath of beeches, pines, and scrub, inhospitable Mellune traversed a jagged ridge that split Ardra into the wine-growing plateaus of the west and the dry, rock-strewn grazing lands to the east. Its unstable land-forms, altered by frequent avalanches and raging floods, provided no reliable markers for guides. Except, perhaps, for a Cartamandua.

Using my bent to devise a route, I could divert and delay our pursuers, keep them on a short leash while getting them thoroughly lost in the wood. After a suitable time, I would abandon them to find their own way out of trackless Mellune, and lead my companions off to rejoin our company for the remainder of our journey to Evanore.

I thought Voushanti would split his hauberk. "You've no leave to go off on your own," he snapped, when I stopped to take a breath. "Prince Osriel—"

"—would not wish Thanea Zurina, Thane Stearc, or Thane Gar'Enov's only son and heir to fall captive to Harrowers," said Gram hoarsely. "Will you tell us that a single pureblood has more value to the Duc of Evanore than three of his warlords? If so, then offer us a better plan. Even if you leave *me* to rot at the roadside as you ought"—scarlet spots stained the poor fellow's pale cheeks—"you'll be but fourteen men and two women against fifty. And the scouts say these are no rabble, but Sila Diaglou's disciplined fighters."

The mardane had no answer. The snow kicked up by the onrushing Har-rowers swirled on the stormy horizon. Unwilling to allow me off on my own, Voushanti insisted on accompanying me.

Before a whore could have her skirts up, I was kneeling in the snow, pressing my hands to the frozen earth, and releasing magic through my fin-gers to seek out the beginnings of our route. When the guide thread took clear shape in my head, I sat back on my heels and looked up at Gram and Voushanti standing over me.

"I don't like this, pureblood," said Voushanti. His wide hands flexed and fisted. The red core of his mutilated eye pulsed like coals. A red crease at the corner of his mouth looked like blood. "Only fools split their forces."

"Complain to Prince Osriel," I said. "I won't see these people—his people—run to ground."

The mardane stomped away toward the gully where Stearc, Elene, and the rest had taken cover. His three warriors awaited Voushanti and me at the forest boundary. Only the secretary lagged behind.

"We'll see you in six days at Gillarine," said Gram. He offered me his hand, feverishly hot, and steadied me as I got to my feet. "Unless . . . Perhaps the gods have sent you this opportunity. With your skills and the weather to hide you, you could take your own road at the end and stay free of the Bastard. Osriel treads perilous paths, Valen. No one knows his plans or the extent of his power."

"I've given my oath not to run," I said. "It was necessary; Gildas can tell you. But my soul has acquired stains enough all these years without my sitting on Magrog's lap. So you can be sure the Bastard will have little good of me. Godspeed, Gram. *Teneamus.*"

"*Teneamus.* I'll not forget this, my friend." He turned his back and trudged slowly toward the gully, his shoulders racked with coughing. Wind and snow and failing light erased his footsteps as if by a sorcerer's hand. I shivered and headed into the trackless wood.

Chapter 31

"Up with you, pureblood. The hounds are baying. No time for sleep." The hand on my shoulder shook me so hard, the blanket slipped off my head. Bitter cold bit my cheeks and plumed my breath as I squinted into the night. Trees. Snow. Unending trees and snow.

"Leave off the bone rattling, Mardane," I said, groaning. "As if a man could sleep with his blood frozen and his backside raw . . ." . . . and his hip-bones throbbing from too long astride, and his stomach devouring his liver for want of a meal not eaten on the run, and his mind a roiling backwash of questions, mysteries, and anxieties that neither misery nor exhaustion could quiet. Not the least of which mysteries was how to shake the fiendish Har-rowers, now the time had come to leave them behind. We just couldn't seem to move fast enough.

When I had suggested this diversion scheme, I never expected it would mean six god-cursed days of lacerating briar tangles, ice-coated avalanche snarls, unending hours in the saddle, no fire, no sleep, no respite. We'd had to keep our pursuers close, but not too close. If we got so far ahead as to discourage them, or they realized too soon that we had split our party, they might double back on their tracks to escape the forest and hunt down the others. Gram. Elene. Stearc. Every hour I could give them was a boon. But next time I had such an idea, I would stuff a boot in my mouth.

"We can't wait for Nestor." Voushanti's proffered hand hauled me to my feet. "The orange-heads are already coming up the gorge. Maggot-ridden halfwits must have legs like mountain goats. I've sent the last of the horses downslope, but that won't confuse them long. So let's make an end to this. Lead us out of this tangle and onto high ground, where these two and I can take them on, and you can run like hell's own messenger to join the others."

Voushanti's temper sounded far more equitable than my own. The crash of brush, grunt of horses, and shouts of oncoming Harrowers bounced through the darkness from tree to thick-boled tree from every direction at once, clawing at my already shredded nerves.

Philo, one of our three companions, snatched up my blanket and stowed it in a rucksack before I could wipe the sludge of unsleep from my eyes. The missing Nestor had gone in search of water to refill our depleted flasks, as we could not afford a fire to melt the snow. The third warrior, Melkire, stripped weapons and food packets from our abandoned saddlepacks and stuffed them in our belts, rucksacks, and pockets. We'd ridden our horses to frozen, quivering uselessness. Now we were afoot. I could only pray our pursuers fared no better. Deunor's fire, there were so many of them.

I dropped to my knees and scraped away crusted snow until I could touch my palms to the forest floor and heed only the sounds of Mellune: the snap of frost-cracked limbs, the sough of overburdened pine fronds giving up their load of snow, the beating hearts of burrowers. Delving deep, I inhaled the faint aroma of the earth warmed by my hands, tasting pine resin and galled oak, dirt and mold on my tongue. As magic flowed from fingers through earth, my mind reached south and west through rotting trees and frozen soil, shearing through buried stone and dense thorn thickets, seeking a path to Gillarine's valley and the wide River Kay that fed it. *Tell me the way*, I said as I examined the landscape unfolding in my head. *Reveal your paths.*

Perhaps it was the unaccustomed practice, or the fact that I no longer hoarded magic against the demands of the doulon, but my route finding had grown more assured over the past days. Or perhaps the need to accomplish something of worth in my life had at last forced me to fully accept the bent of my blood, no matter its connection to my parents. Or perhaps it was only that Mellune Forest and I had become intimate acquaintances.

The grim woodland straggled straight down the spine of Ardra, grown up in thin, sour land, broken by sills and ridges of limestone, its trails choked with briars and snakevine since ill weather and disease had all but exterminated its game. Deadfalls, snarls, sinkholes, and gullies had diverted us constantly, making my carefully laid course of southward-spiraling circles resemble the route of a headless chicken. Our purpose was delay and confusion, but for our pursuers, not ourselves. I prayed I could get us out before we starved.

The route took shape in mind and body, a gray pattern of fading game trails, a dry watercourse, a logger's track, long abandoned. High ground, Voushanti wanted. So I shifted the thread slightly here and there, searching for a more elevated way.

Beyond the southern boundaries of Mellune the land opened into the rocky pastures of upper Ardra. A single modest hill, crowned by a scarp, and a few scattered protrusions of dense black rock presented the only defensible positions. The mountain drainages—the upland valleys like the vale of the Kay where Gillarine lay—would give us much better cover, but the inexhaustible Harrowers would be stripping our bones before we made it so far afoot.

"Come on," I said, scrambling to my feet.

Snapping branches and spitting snow, I broke through a wall of snow-laden bracken to find the narrow streambed that would lead us up a seamed ridge, heading the direction my gut named southwest. A chorus of terrified whinnies said the pursuit had discovered our blown horses.

The blizzard had abated on our third day in the forest, which worsened the cold, but lent us more light. Above the canopy of trees the stars shone clear and bitter, providing illumination enough to reflect on open snow and depositing inky shadows under trees and scrub.

An hour along the way, my purposeful spiral took us along the bank of a pond. There we found the signs of a Harrower camp and all that was left of Nestor. The thirsty fool must have walked right into their hands. The Harrowers had shredded his flesh and staked him to the earth as they had Boreas. I blessed all gods I had not eaten that night. Nestor's mouth had been packed with dirt to silence his cries as he bled and died.

"We leave him lie," said Voushanti harshly, snatching up Nestor's water-skins that lay abandoned in a willow thicket. His boots and weapons were missing. "We've no strength to spare and no time. Move out, pureblood."

Closing my eyes, I sought my guide thread, happy I did not need to touch the ground here. "This way," I said and moved westerly.

Philo joined me, whispering the Karish prayers for the dead. Voushanti followed, mumbling curses with the passion of a lover scorned. But Melkire dropped to his knees beside the savaged body. I held up to wait for him, then blurted a malediction as the warrior dipped his thumb in Nestor's blood and marked a spiraled circle on his own forehead.

"What the devil are you doing?" I said, anger and disgust raising my bile. The Harrowers had licked Boreas's blood from their fingers.

"Nestor is a son of Evanore," said Melkire, rising, his eyes hard and fierce in the starlight. "The mark binds my memory, so that I can bring a full account of his deeds and his end to his family."

I walked on. I had to find them a place to make a stand.

"I've not heard an untoward sound for an hour," said Philo, passing Voushanti a waterskin. We had climbed to the brink of a limestone scarp to rest and drink. "We should get away from here and make camp, else we'll not be able to move by morning."

"No," I whispered, plastering myself to the ground and peering over the edge of the scarp into bottomless darkness. The creeping up my back felt like an army of spiders. "They're still coming. I need to understand how they can stay so close on our trail in the night." I had my bent to guide me, but how could the Harrowers determine which crisscrossing trail of churned snow we had trod the most recently?

Voushanti hushed the two young warriors and wormed up beside me. "I sense them, too."

Before very long, yellow light blazed from the wood—a torch, I thought as it moved through the trees. But the wind neither shook nor snuffed it. The silent procession passed below us like wraiths. Perhaps forty men. Fewer horses. They had muted their harness with rags. Only their tread in the snow and the occasional whuffle of a beast marked their passage.

Their leader bore the light—a gleaming ball of piss-yellow brilliance that emanated directly from his hand. And as he walked, he held one hand in front of him, fingers stiffly spread, and he turned his head from side to side, sniffing, his nostrils flared wide like some great hound. Sorcery. *I knew it.* As he vanished into the thicker trees, a gust of wind swept down the scarp to flutter his cloak—worn purple velvet with a dagged hem. The dog-faced man had tasted Boreas's blood, watched the priestess lash Gildas's back, and stood on the fortress walls with Sila Diaglou as Abbot Luviar was gutted. I prayed he would rot in this demon wood.

"Come on," I said through gritted teeth. "We need to move faster. That one might have other skills." He was Sila Diaglou's companion in slaughter, either a pureblood or a mixed-blood mage powerful enough to create light in this overwhelming night.

Though purebloods were unmatched in native talent for sorcery by virtue of their untainted Aurellian descent, any ordinary with a trace of Aurellian blood carried potential for the bent—as did Prince Osriel by virtue of
his pureblood mother. Most mixed-bloods became market tricksters, potion
sellers, or alley witches, like old Salamonde, who had taught me the doulon
spell. Registry breeding laws had assured that little talent remained outside
pureblood families, but always a few took their talents seriously, training and
testing with others of their kind, calling themselves mages. Purebloods disdained them, of course, and named mageworks trickery. Prince Osriel had
already taught me elsewise.

Another day. Another night. The rapacious cold cracked bone and spirit,
dulled the mind, and transformed limbs and heart to lead. Using my aching
hips and legs to break a trail through thigh-deep snow, laced with broken tree
limbs and frozen bracken, became purest misery. Sticks snagged my clothes
and flesh. Pits or sinkholes beneath the crusted snow left me floundering on
my face at every other step, clothes packed with snow, arms scraped raw.
No part or portion of me stayed dry, and the sweat of my exertions froze
beneath my layered garments.

I clung to the gray guide thread in my mind, checked and rechecked
it, pouring magic into each test to be sure I followed true. My companions
dragged me up when I fell, brushed me off, and trod carefully in my steps.
We had to persevere. We had to lose these devils, else they would follow us
to Gillarine. Stearc's clever choice of a rendezvous now seemed incalculably
stupid.

We pushed onward across a broad meadow, an unexpected relief from
the oppressive trees. It troubled me to find a clearing where my instincts
said none should be, yet I dared not stop to assay another trial of magic, lest
I freeze there in the open. It might have been a single hour or ten sunless
days that we traversed that meadow, and then we were in the wood again,
the wind thrashing leafless branches as if angered it could no longer claw our
skin directly.

My head swam with sleepless confusion, my frozen flesh no longer
able to feel the pull of north or south. Southwesterly should take us higher
in Mellune Forest, so that we would emerge, a day or so from now, atop
Pilcher's Hill where Voushanti could mount a defense. Yet every instinct
cried that safety lay downward. And downward did not feel like southwest.

Thoroughly muddled, I fell to my knees at the bottom of a long slope and scrabbled in the snow.

"Where are we?" gasped Voushanti, even his leathern toughness on the verge of shredding. "We'll have no feet to stand on or hands to wield a sword, if you don't find us a place to make a fight."

"Just need to find the blasted hill. This terrain is all wrong."

My fingers might have been wooden clubs for all I could feel of them when I touched earth. I poured magic from my core but sensed nothing of the land. *Which way?*

An owl screeched from atop a spindly pine. I rubbed my frozen hands together. Breathed on them. Stuffed them under my arms, trying to warm them enough so they could feel. Another shriek and a spread of dark wings drew my eye to the treetops. And there, shining in yellow-white splendor between the branches, hung Escalor, the guide star. North and south settled into their proper positions in my head.

"Mother Samele's tits!" Sitting back on my heels, I laughed aloud at ignorant fools and their earnest blindness.

"Spirits of night, lunatic, will you be quiet?" Voushanti would have throttled me if he'd not been doubled up by a spreading beech, his lungs wheezing like a smith's bellows. "Never knew a man could move so fast in such cursed weather and still have breath to cackle like a gamecock."

I pressed my wet, filthy sleeve across my mouth to contain the hilarity that simple sense could not. Bound up in pureblood sorcery and earth-borne mystery, it had never crossed my mind to look *up* for guidance. I offered a prayer of thanks to the forest and the owl whose dark wingspan ruffled against the starry night.

As I pleaded with my aching legs to unbend and bear my weight again, I watched the kindly bird preening. Thus I caught the glimmer of sapphire brilliance in the leafless branches of a giant beech nearby. I held breath and dared not blink. From the snarl of twigs and branches, an arm scribed with blue fire reached out to host the wing-spread owl's claws for a few heartbeats before the bird took flight. My heart came near stopping.

Twice in the past six days I'd believed us irretrievably blocked, facing the choice to be overrun by our pursuers or reverse course and meet them head on. In both instances escape had come by seeming chance. A falling rock, dislodged by some scuttering animal, had exposed a stairlike descent of an impossibly sheer scarp. A bolting fox had revealed an unlikely passage through an avalanche slide the size of half a mountain. Now I wondered. Chance had never been my ally.

We could not linger. But I touched the earth once more and sent my whispered gratitude into the roots and rock, hoping that the one who aided us would hear. Would he have a dragon scribed on his face? Were his eyes the color of autumn aspen? Was that arm the same that had offered me refuge in an aspen grove as I fled Gillarine? Earth's Mother, how I longed to know.

Of course, the Danae despised humankind. How could they not, when the Harrowers' grotesque rites poisoned them? Yes, they had driven my grandfather mad, but he had stolen something precious from them. Danae were the essence of magic, the gift of beauty and grace below heaven. Even angels brought down the god's righteous fury on sinners.

We ran. Onward. Downward. Slipping and sliding on wooded banks. The owl arrowed southward ahead of us, as if scribing the path across inked vellum, and my fatigued mind gratefully relinquished the guide thread it had gripped for seven unrelenting days.

Soon the trees thinned, and a flat wilderness of mottled white spread out before us. Darker patches marred the starlit landscape as if unseen trees cast shadows on the snow. Clouds burgeoned behind the ridge we'd just descended, hiding Escalor and her companion stars. Wind gusts brought flakes drifting from the heights. We had to hurry. If any of our pursuers were yet mounted, flat ground would be our end.

The owl glided in a circle above our heads, then soared serenely toward the heart of the wilderness. Instinct affirmed that refuge was near, though perhaps not so directly across the flats.

"This way," I said to the three who had just arrived at my elbow heaving and coughing, their collected breath enfolding us in fog. I pointed to the wing-spread owl. "She'll lead us to safety."

I slid down the last few quercae of the steep embankment and struck out across the flats. In our weakened condition, a shorter distance likely outweighed the increased danger of exposure. Voushanti and the others trudged after, well behind me.

Fifty paces into the wilderness, I heard . . . or perhaps only felt . . . an unsettling noise beneath my feet. Instinct screamed warning. I motioned the others to halt so my dulled senses might register the sound, and I cupped my lifeless fingers over my nose and mouth, breathing out my last warmth to thaw my nostrils. Then I inhaled slowly, felt, tasted, and listened, as my father and grandfather had tried to teach me when I was small.

Water. Mud. Rot.

Appalled, I dropped to my knees and speared my hands through the snow and into the cold muck that lay just below. Dead trees. Rotted marsh grass. Burrowed frogs, cold and still. Old droppings and tufts of animal hair caught on buried willows. A harper's distant song . . . Ever so faintly, the sounds, the smells, and the land's retained memory seeped through the winter's blanket. And nowhere did I find my guide thread. *Fool! Blasted mindless idiot!*

Dulled with cold and yearning for finer magic, I had forsaken my own path to follow the owl. And the Danae, who had no use for humankind, had brought us here.

"Stop! Go back!" I shouted hoarsely, peering at the treacherous landscape through the darkening night. I knew exactly where we were. How could my sense of distance be so far askew? It seemed impossible we could be so far south, but I had traveled here before. "Step not one quat outside our tracks. This is bogland."

"What of you?" shouted Voushanti, wind blunting the edges of his words. "We have ropes—"

"I'll be all right. Go around, stay on the side slope, head straight southward . . . that way. Only two quellae to Gillarine. Hurry!"

Thank all gods, the three were in no mind to argue. Voushanti's beard and eyebrows were frosted pure white as if he had aged fifty years in an hour, and Philo and Melkire might have been but four glazed eyes in unfleshed skulls. They were in no state to fight anyone.

I watched until they had made it back to solid ground safely and vanished in the thickening snowfall. Then I shoved magic through my buried fingers and sought a path deeper into the bog. The trickster owl had vanished, leaving me no choice but to twist its vicious cleverness to my own purpose.

The route fixed firmly in my mind, I wiped my frozen, muddy hands, bundled them in my cloak, and set out across the snow-draped fens. The falling snow would blur my footsteps and mask the inadequacies of my spellworking long enough to close the trap—a snare I believed had been set for every human abroad this night, pursuers and pursued.

An irregular mound, well into the heart of the bogland, provided enough substance and variety for my purposes: a leafless willow, a sheep's leg bone, a rotted branch, a charred stick. I structured two spells, one to serve deception, one to serve fear. Then I waited, stomping my sore feet and flapping my aching arms to keep my blood moving. Dawn was near—as much of it as I was like to see with the weather closing in.

As the moments slid by in abject silence, fear nagged that I had miscalculated yet again. I could scarce muster the strength to shake the clinging snow from my cloak. While I became another stupid beast rotting in the bog, the Harrowers would follow Voushanti straight to my friends.

"Aaaagh!" I yelled in inarticulate fury, yanking my hair to force blood to my head. "Come find me! Any of you . . . come do what you will! Show me your face if you dare!" I shouted and raged, railing at ignorance. At blind folly. At all who desired my death or captivity and, in equal measure, at myself.

My grandfather had warned me. Such torment as the Danae had wrought on him displayed a cruelty colder than this cursed winter. So whence came my sentimental folly that because they were beautiful and magical and caused my knees to grow weak with unfounded yearning, they had a benevolent interest in *me*? Perhaps the one writ with dragons had invited me into the aspen grove the better to destroy my mind.

Though the snowfall deadened my pitiful prating, the anger kept me living. I shivered and coughed and honed my spells, determined they would be sufficient to end this wretched journey.

They came in the purple gloom that passed for sunrise. Harrowers flowed over the ridge like a tidal surge, cries hoarse with triumph and fury when they spotted me in the open. I noted with grim satisfaction that they had dropped at least a quarter of their numbers since I'd seen them last. At their head rode the dog-faced man, his orange scarf flying, the glow of his hands like a bilious sun leading their way.

I fell to my knees and fed magic into my mound of sticks and bones, recalling the appearance of my departed companions to shape the illusions of harried travelers, stopped to succor a fallen comrade.

The yowling Harrowers swept onto the flats without pause, and even the shouts of the first to flounder did not slow the rest. When the yellow glow failed—snuffed by mud or fear—their triumph turned to dismay.

Weary and mind-numbed, they did not think to stay calm and press through the muck to seek firmer ground. Rather, weighed down with mail coats and supply sacks and weapons, burdened with legends of bogwights and sucking ponds and trickster Danae, they felt their feet sinking and their clothes waterlogged, and they panicked, as I had gambled they would. I touched the charred stick and set wispy tendrils of flame adrift from my hand until the cold numbed my fingers and I could conjure no more of them. The gloomy landscape was dotted with winking flames, and the men in the bog started screaming.

Half of the Harrowers killed each other, trying to use their comrades for stepping-stones. Others drowned quickly, pulled down by panicked horses or tangled in dead vines and rotted trees swept down from the mountains in long-ago floods. Some wandered, crying for help in the neck-deep mud, climbing on hillocks only to have them sink under their weight. After a while I could only hear them, for the blizzard rose in full fury, and human eyes could not penetrate past the length of my arm. The cold and the mud would finish them. The memory of Luviar butchered, of Nestor and Boreas condemned to slow agony, of tar-clogged wells and villages burned to ash, crushed what glimmers of mercy blossomed in my soul. These gatzi would have ridden my friends to ground.

I huddled on my islet in the center of the bogland, a driftwood club ready should one of the lost find his way to me. Only when my ears assured me that neither man nor beast roamed the upland banks did I press my hands into the muck to seek the path back to firm ground.

I jerked them right out again, then bent double and retched bile until stomach, chest, and throat were raw. The terrors of dying men and beasts permeated the pools and hillocks, and I could not find my way. I sank to the ground, buried my face in my frozen cloak, and begged the earth's forgiveness for the horror I had wrought.

Chapter 32

Valen *fiend heart!* The mocking cry stung like a tutor's rod on cold
knuckles. Cold . . . what wasn't cold? The world, all life, and certainly every part of me was frozen. No one ever listened when I said
how I hated the cold.

I trudged onward. One step. Then a rest. Another step. Hip-high drifts
covered the path that would take me away from the treacherous bog. Perhaps
the insulting name, a relic from childhood, etched itself so vividly in my
imagination because I longed so fiercely to believe that another living person
existed in this wintry desolation.

Fiend heart . . . Soon I'd be imagining I heard *iron skull* or *lead wit* or *gatzi
prick,* though the damnable girl would lob that last stone only outside adults'
hearing. I smiled . . . more of a grimace, I imagined, as I could not feel my
face. *Lassa, please be real.*

My sister had once enspelled a connection between her favorite insults
and my ears, so I would never fail to hear them. I'd never learned the skill,
but on one precious occasion, I had managed to reverse her spell and bind
one of mine to her. "Toad witch," I mumbled into the folds of my cloak for
the fiftieth time on this dreadful afternoon. If she were within ten quellae,
she would hear.

"Magnus! Magnus Valentia!"

"Brother Valen!"

I paused and surveyed the gloomy distance. No one in sight. I pulled my
hood tighter and fretted that these faint voices, too, were naught but wishing
dreams.

Hellish dreams of mud and ice and suffocation had clung to me like draggle weed as I had crawled out of the bog hours and hours ago, too tired and too afraid to walk, unable to bear another route seeking lest I buckle under the weight of guilt and horror. That I managed to reach solid earth, that I was not drowned or dead, astonished me. I had dug a snow cave to wait out the blizzard and had drifted in and out of sleep, dreaming of long limbs marked with blue sigils embracing me, choking me, setting me afire.

The wind mourned over the frozen fens. Did beasts feel this way after emerging from their winter sleep, as if ice crystals flowed in their veins? I feared the oncoming night. *Find me, someone. Please. I hate the cold.*

Lights moved around the hillside toward me. Torches. Spits of gold against a sky the color of ripe blueberries. I sank to the ground, closed my eyes, and rested my back against a boulder. Let someone else break the path through the drifts. Friend or enemy, wraith or bogwight, I didn't care.

"Gracious Mother, Valen, what have you done this time?" My breathless sister's painted eyes swam huge and worried from her fur-lined hood. "This Voushanti said you were facing fifty Harrowers alone in a bog, and that you'd saved Stearc and Gram and these Evanori lords. But they couldn't find you in the storm. I called and called— No one believed when I claimed to hear you, but I knew. How is it you're not frozen dead, fiend heart?"

"B-been thinking w-warm thoughts of you, *serena* toad witch. Whatever are you doing in the neighborhood? Did you bring them my boo—?"

She hissed, pressed her hot hand on my lips, and jerked her head backward. Several shapeless figures approached from behind her, one leading a donkey.

"Watch your tongue, Valen. And I do mean that. The answer is yes." She glanced over her shoulder. "Listen carefully: I came to continue my negotiations over new sheep pastures for the Temple and was shocked to discover the shambles. Do you understand?"

"Shambles?" I croaked, wretchedly confused.

But she had squeezed her painted eyes shut, and her words kept flowing, so softly no one but I could have heard them. "Who or what is this Voushanti? I See naught but death about him—blood and fire and torment. He says he's taking you to Evanore as soon as the weather breaks. Bound to the Bastard . . . Holy Mother, Valen, I cannot help you more. I must return to Palinur immediately. With Luviar lost, Victor captive, and what's happened here, the lighthouse may depend on my office."

The aura of her divination tickled my spine, as the newcomers joined us, their faces taking recognizable shape in dark wrappings. Indeed, Voushanti brought an ill odor with him everywhere. But I was more confused about her passing hints. "Lassa, I'll be all right, if I c-can just get warm. But what shambles—?"

"Silos!" She snapped, jumping to her feet. "He needs hot wine! And get a mask on him before I report him to the Registry. Good monk, bring your linens. No diviner is needed to see to the pitiful whiner. Lord Voushanti, take up your charge, though even my scoundrel brother is unlikely to run today." Excessive sisterly sentiment would never burden Thalassa.

Voushanti loomed over me like a frost giant, but he said naught as the others ministered to me. A somber Silos took Thalassa's place and offered me a steaming wineskin. My fingers couldn't grasp the leather, so he poured the stuff down my raw throat. *O, great Mother Samele, grant my glorious sister a place at your side!* Silos's masked face drew up in disapproval as I hooked my elbow about his, preventing him from removing the skin until it was half empty. "Careful, *plebeiu*. You cause everyone trouble when you're out of your head. Have you a mask with you?"

He pulled the half mask of purple silk from the pocket I indicated and slipped it on me. Cold, wet . . . it felt like fish skin.

Thalassa threw a blessedly dry cloak about my shoulders as Brother Anselm, the piebald lay brother from the Gillarine infirmary, examined my hands and feet. I despaired of ever being warm, shivering uncontrollably as he marveled that I showed no signs of true frostbite after crawling in the snow for most of a day. Voushanti refused to consider a fire, though I assured him that the dog-faced man and his Harrowers were no longer a threat. I could not bring myself to tell him why.

They insisted I ride Brother Anselm's bony donkey back to the abbey. As the monk led the plodding beast along the embankment, I looked out on the flats—still and silent, the horrors of the morning hidden beneath the mantle of fresh snow. My sister walked alongside me, and her gaze followed mine. "What happened out there, Valen?"

I shook my head and shuddered. "Just don't walk there, Lassa. Don't ever."

"When did they strike?" I said.

Brother Anselm, the donkey, and I slogged up the last slight rise between us and Gillarine. I had dismounted the balky ass. Walking eased my stiffness and kept the blood flowing in my hands and feet. Save for the marrow-deep chill and a general weariness, I'd come out of the day's events astonishingly well. But all relief had fled when the shy assistant infirmarian at last explained Thalassa's references to "shambles."

" 'Twas on Saint Eldred's Night, Brother Valen. You were not a fortnight gone from here. Some hundred or more raiders, both Moriangi and Harrowers, come twixt Matins and Lauds. Their fire arrows and torches took the scriptorium first. Then the church. Then the rest."

"Great Iero's mercy!" We had reached the top of the little rise, and the sight took my breath. The windows of the abbey church, whose brilliance in sun and candlelight had spoken of angels' wings, gaped black as hell's maw; the groins and buttresses mimed the naked ribs of a skeleton. The wooden buildings—infirmary, brewhouse, stables—had vanished, their remains hidden beneath a pall of gray snow. Gillarine Abbey stood broken and dark.

"We were blessed our walls were stone."

But the slate roofs had fallen when the supporting timbers burned—a pureblood firemaster attached to the Moriangi raiders would have seen to that—smashing at least a third of the inner courts to jagged ruin. Only the gatehouse and walls stood unmarred. The damnable cowards had marched straight through the sanctuary gate to wreak their holocaust.

"What of the brothers, Anselm? By the One God . . ." So many good men lived here: the kindly, skilled infirmarian, Robierre; garrulous Cadeus the porter; old Nunius, who reveled in holy minutiae . . .

"Eleven passed to Iero's heaven on Saint Eldred's Night, three succumbed to injuries since then, and five more fell to lung fever—Abelard and Nunius, the eldest and weakest of us who breathed too much smoke or bent to the cold. Dear Brother Robierre died saving poor Marcus from the fire. With the ground so hard frozen and neither hands nor time to spare for digging, we've had to lay them in the cellars."

"Ah, Brother . . ." The physical ruin paled beside such a loss. What words could express sorrow enough? Neither sympathy nor helpless anger could repair this wound or ease the future it boded. The survivors' trials were only begun. They would yet have more than twenty to feed and clothe. "What of your stores? And, blessed saints, what did they do to the orchard?" The trees still standing looked leprous, not burned, but bark hanging in rags, trunks gouged and seeping, branches broken. More than half had fallen, bare roots frosted like nests of white snakes.

"The undercrofts were gutted for the most. Naught burns like spilled oil and dry grain. We've a few bales of wool left, though smoked and charred, and Brother Jerome, Iero welcome his cook's soul, fell to a Morian blade defending his last root cellar. But the orchard now"—the lay brother's wide face crumpled like an old rag—"that weren't the soldiers. No man, but only the One God himself sent us that trial. A root rot, Brother Gardener said, that spread through the trees at the same time the murrain come to the sheepfold. It's the sickness in the world, as Father Abbot so often warned of, come to Gillarine at last . . . and now we've heard tidings of his own passing."

Anselm's stolid presence faltered but did not break. His gaitered sandals crunched the snow, and he encouraged the tired donkey with a soft pat and an assertive tug on the lead.

"Prior Nemesio has taken us well in hand. And the good God grants us fortitude. To share the trials of his poorest in this land must surely bring us grace. A blessing we've none with *your* appetite to feed." He chuckled softly, then sighed. "We could use a cheerful story adventure as you're wont to tell, though. We rejoice that our brothers live with the saints, and we know that Iero will give us all we need, do we but ask, but truly we feel a dreadful sadness come upon us with this untimely winter."

Sadness. Yes. More than the failing light and ruined buildings. More than so many good men dead. *Gods grant you peace and care, good Robierre, as you gave so many, and Jerome, may you feast at the god's own table.* A pervasive sorrow held the abbey in its grip, a grieving in the stones and earth that felt as if the sun would never relieve this falling night. The thick dry cloak Thalassa had given me felt thin as gossamer.

As Anselm and I led the donkey across the field toward the gatehouse, the shy lay brother continued his stories of the raid and its aftermath. I'd never heard so many words from the infirmarian's assistant in all the weeks I'd lived at Gillarine. Perhaps trials did bring out new strengths in us.

Behind us, on the road that stretched northward toward Elanus and Palinur, Thalassa, her faithful Silos, and her five temple guards had vanished into the darkening forest, determined to reach Elanus before nightfall. My sister's parting kiss yet burned on my forehead. A kiss from Thalassa. She must believe I was going to die in Evanore. Unfortunately, I could not ease her concern. What use would the Bastard find for a mind-dead former doulon slave?

"Thank you for rescuing me yet again," I'd said after she yanked my head down and planted that unexpected kiss. Then I'd stooped to whisper in her ear, "*Teneamus.*"

I'd never seen her smile like that. Genuine. Pleased. Sad. "Hold on to your soul, little brother," she'd said as she mounted her palfrey. "Be well."

"I'd be happy enough with *warm, Sinduria serena.*"

She'd rolled her eyes and ridden away. I was happy she hadn't told me whether I would ever see her again.

"I'll put old Dob to shelter; then we'll find you a bed and a bite," said Anselm as we slogged through the gatehouse tunnel. A snarl of thick ropes and harness protruded from the drifted snow, and the wooden gates lay twisted from their hinges. "I needs must ask Father Prior if you're to be housed in the dorter—which is now moved to the abbot's house as it's got a roof—or in the guesthouse. That new lord's come today is most forbidding, I'll say." He nodded at Voushanti's retreating back. The mardane had hurried off ahead of us to see where Philo and Melkire were bedded down. "Some folk I knew as a lad would call him marked of the Adversary. You've not renounced your vows, have you, lad, or been dispensed from them?"

"Just taken on new ones, Brother," I said, feeling an unexpected heat in my cheeks. "Lord Voushanti is my new master's proxy."

We trudged through the Porter's Gate and into the trampled gardens in front of the dark church. Anselm frowned. "So you'll to the guesthouse, then. We've a fire laid. And you'll need dry clothes. Secular garb. You take a good rest tonight, and I'll put a flea in Father Prior's ear to ask if Lord Stearc might have left some things would come near fitting you. I'll send a posset as well, to stave off chills and damage from frostbite. Not so excellent as Brother *Badger* would have made for you, of course."

Summoning a smile, I clapped him on the shoulder in thanks.

Once left alone, the sad emptiness of the abbey gripped my spirit sorely. Despite the cold, I lingered in the familiar paths and courts. To rush toward fire and food seemed somehow lacking in respect. So, rather than taking the straighter way to the guesthouse, I wandered past the church into the north cloister walk and looked out on the cloister garth—the abbey's heart.

Rubble littered the square, the angular bulk of fallen cornices and corbels bulging awkwardly beneath the snow, alongside the birdcage shape of Saint Gillare's shrine. Though every building showed damage, the primary target of the raid was obvious. The walls of the abbey library and scriptorium had collapsed completely, crushing the eastern cloister walk. Naught was left but heaps of scorched stones and charred beams. The chapter house on one side and the monks' dorter on the other gaped open on the sides that had adjoined the library. Both structures were gutted shells. Of the jewel-like chapter-house windows, depicting Eodward and Caedmon, only one soot-marked pane remained, bearing the outline of an upraised hand.

So what had become of the magical lighthouse and its tools and books and seeds, gathered to sustain humankind past these dark times? Its creators had surely built it to endure through end-times chaos and destruction. Was this raid Bayard's vengeance for the abbey's sheltering Perryn? Or was this Sila Diaglou's handiwork? If she knew of the lighthouse . . . It would be anathema to her, a promise to undo the chaos she worked for. I thought back to her savage attack on Gildas . . . a ploy to "draw out" her enemies . . . and Luviar and Stearc and Gram running for the gate. Yes, she knew of the lighthouse and its creators.

Firelight flickered in the far corner of the cloister, where the great hearth of the calefactory was required to remain lit until Saint Mathilde's Day. As I rested my back on a slender column, a handbell broke the oppressive silence, ten measured rings calling the monks to the Hours, a thin, strident summoning compared to the sonorous richness of the bronze bells fallen from the belltower. The pattern of two, three, and one, followed—Vespers, the Hour of peace. But I felt no peace and could not shake the sense that more than bodies and buildings had been shattered here.

I believed in the gods and their creatures—whether they were named Kemen or Iero, angels or Danae or gatzi. Even a dolt could see that the universe was no soulless clockwork, but infused with life beyond human understanding—wondrous and mysterious, perilous and exquisite. But as to whether the deities truly listened to our prayers or desired our votive gifts or libations or blood sacrifices, I'd been content to leave that study to wiser heads. And never had I given literal credence to the god stories and myths I'd been told—of Deunor's stolen fire that lit the stars or of the Danae whose dancing nourished the world and held it together. Not until I looked on the ruins of Gillarine and knew in breath and bone, in flesh and spirit, that the Canon, the pattern of the world, was truly broken.

Curious, apprehensive, I knelt at the edge of the cloister walk and brushed away a patch of snow. The grass of the garth, so thick and green but a month ago, lay yellow and slimy. I pressed my hands to the earth.

Nothing. No slamming darkness. No piercing light. No music of grief or longing to wrench my soul as it had every time I'd tested this particular patch of earth. I felt only the sickness of the outer world that had intruded here. Plague into the sheepfold. Rot into the orchard. Fire and death into the cloisters.

Wiping my hands on the hem of my cloak, I sat back on my heels. Stories nagged at me. King Eodward had built this abbey on "holy ground." I had almost forgotten the first death. Young Brother Horach had been brutally murdered inside Saint Gillare's shrine, where the holy spring bubbled up into the font. Harrowers poisoned the land's guardians with violated corpses. That was what Sila Diaglou and her cohorts had tried to do with Boreas. I recalled Graver's Meadow, the lush grass and shimmering pond that swelled my spirit as if the angel choirs sang in the abbey's soaring vaults. Easy to believe a guardian had lived there.

What if the legends of Eodward and the angels and Gillarine's holy, fertile ground had given someone to believe the abbey spring a Danae sianou? And what if that someone had tried to poison the guardian Dané with the murdered Horach? The plan would have failed, because the true sianou lay at the spring's source in the hills at Clyste's Well. Clyste would have lived on, locked away for her part in my grandfather's crime, yet still infusing the abbey fields and flocks with her own life and health, a balm to such horrors as Black Night. And then I had opened the way to her holy place . . .

Faces, events, information shifted, twisted, and settled into a new pattern like tiles into a fine mosaic. Gerard had disappeared on the night of my attempted escape, only days after I had led Gildas to Clyste's Well. And only days later, pestilence had come to Gillarine.

I jumped to my feet, horror and certainty wrenching mind and heart. I knew what had happened to Gerard. Tears that had naught to do with the cold blurred my vision. Murdered. Great gods in all heavens, they had murdered the boy to kill the Danae guardian of the abbey lands. I knew it as I knew my own name. And now I understood what crime had been committed, it became clear who had committed it.

I stepped into the cloister garth and spun as I yelled, violating the holy silence and the land's grieving. "Where are you, monk? Gildas, come out here and tell me what you've done!"

Blind and stupid, Valen. Self-absorbed wretch. From the moment I had stepped into this abbey he had played me like a vielle. How had I not seen?

Great Iero, he had all but told me outright. *I belong with the cabalists little more than you,* he'd said. And, *If the cities die, if learning dies, we are sent back to the land, to nights in the wild forest with spirits we can no longer tame with words, to awe of these Gehoum—the Powers who make the sky grow light or dark, whose righteous wrath is fire and storm. Righteous* wrath. *Everyone should be pure like you and Gerard,* he had told Jullian. Horach had been his student . . . and an innocent, too.

The part of me that believed I was unworthy of this place, that bore gratitude and affection for Gildas, who had welcomed me with good humor and allowed me to imagine I could be friends with scholars and men of substance, cried out that I was wrong. But I was not. Not this time. Clyste was dead. And so was Gerard.

"God-cursed child murderer!"

Brother Cantor intoned the opening note of Vesper plainsong as if to correct the abrasive timbre of my shouts, and then the voices—so terribly few—joined in the chant. Perfection, continuity, clarity . . . the music swelled as their procession approached the ruined cloisters.

Sila Diaglou's spy had told her of the lighthouse. But he couldn't tell her how to get into it and destroy its contents, because he was not privy to that secret. And a runaway novice had disrupted their ruse to lure Luviar and Stearc into her clutches with a bloody Gildas as bait. No wonder his hands had been left loose that night; he had *offered* himself to his Gehoum—*a noble sacrifice.* So he had waited until Palinur and given her Luviar and Victor. No wonder Gildas had looked dismayed when I told him Brother Victor had survived the gallows—not only because the chancellor was in Osriel's custody, but because the little monk could reveal who had betrayed him and his abbot.

Where are you, betrayer? I tugged at my hair. Gildas would not be at prayers. The worm would lurk in the heart of the cabal—with Gram and Stearc and Elene. I ran for the guesthouse, forced by shattered walls and rubble to circle south of the lay brothers' reach and past the ruined kitchen. Across the yard. Up the stoop.

"Come face me, gatzé! Tell me how clever you are to fool an ignorant pureblood!"

I slammed through doors and kicked aside the toppled furnishings and soot-grimed couches littering the dark rooms of the ground floor. A single rushlight burned in a tripod holder near the stair. I sped up the narrow, winding ascent. Yelling. Heedless.

The middle floor was dark. I raced upward and burst into a firelit chamber that smelled of scorched plaster and spiced cider.

Stocky, pale-skulled Prior Nemesio knelt by the meager fire, a sooty poker in his hand. He was alone. His startled expression quickly smoothed into satisfaction. "Brother Valen! It's Iero's own blessing to see you safe here again."

"Where is Gildas?" I snapped.

"At Vespers, I would think." Worry carved a mask on his big-boned cheeks. "What's wrong? Brother Anselm said you'd had quite an ordeal. I offered to bring his posset so I could tell you—"

"Where are the Evanori—Thane Stearc, his secretary?" I said. Jullian had vouched that Nemesio was one of us. "I must speak with them outside Mardane Voushanti's hearing."

"That's what I've come to tell you. Thane Stearc and his party moved on to Fortress Groult with the rest of the Evanori. When they saw what's happened here, they dared not stay."

Cold dread bound its fingers about my rage. "Did Gildas go with them? Or Jullian?"

"Brother Gildas thought they would do better to remain here. It's entirely unsuitable that an aspirant run about the countryside in the midst of—"

"Father Prior, Gildas murdered both Brother Horach and Gerard." My hands trembled with scarcely held rage. "We must find him. Confine him."

"What slander is this?" Nemesio surged to his feet, his thick neck scarlet. "Gildas is your vowed brother! The lighthouse Scholar!"

"I'd wager my life that Gildas is a Harrower. He took Gerard to Clyste's Well and bled him to death. You *must* send this news to Stearc right away. Don't you see? Gildas betrayed Victor and Luviar to Sila Diaglou. He knows your identities. I'd give much to be wrong, but to be certain, we must secure him tonight."

"I cannot credit this." Prior Nemesio chewed his full lips. "Gildas is a pious man. Holy and generous. Hours ago, when the Sinduria said she'd heard your call for help, both he and Jullian wished to set out with her at once to succor you. Your sister refused, unwilling to risk his safety. The two of them went straight off to the church to pray for your return."

I glanced about the room, dread and helplessness threatening to undo me. "Father Prior, where is the Cartamandua book? Please tell me that Stearc took it to Fortress Groult."

"No." Nemesio looked up. Uncertain. "Gildas kept it. To study, he said—"
I bolted for the stair.

Plainsong floated on the bitter air, along with the mingled odors of charred wood, of broken sewage channels, of incense and peat fires. The monks stood in a circle about the high altar of the ruined church, under vaults now open to the sky, and sang of their god's joy and care. Depleted ranks of lay brothers stood in a small area of the nave that had been cleared of rubble and dirty snow. Only a few heads moved as I sped through the nave yelling Gildas's name and Jullian's.

The boy was nowhere to be seen, and, as always, the monks' hoods were drawn up, hiding their faces. Knowing the search was futile, I snatched a lit candle from the high altar and intruded on their circle, peering at the hands clutching tattered psalters. Gildas's hands, backed by their thatch of wiry brown hair, were not among them.

I replaced the candle and strode out of the church, cursing. Halfway across the trampled garden, hurried footsteps behind me spun me in my tracks.

"Brother Valen? Is that really you?" The hard-breathing monk lowered his hood. The round head and fringe of gray hair identified my novice mentor.

"Yes, Brother Sebastian."

"The mask makes it difficult . . . and no tonsure anymore . . ." Uncertainty snagged his speech.

"I'm happy to see you alive, Brother. But I'm in a great hurry."

"Well, of course, I knew it was you. Not so many purebloods come here, and none so tall. Brother Gildas said this pureblood life"—he fluttered his hand at my mask and my clothing, giving no impression of having heard me—"has changed you. Secular law forbids me to speak to you, but Saint Ophir's Rule says you are yet my charge."

I stepped back, brittle with impatience. "Excuse me, Brother. Unless you can say where Gildas—"

"Brother Gildas is gone off to Elanus. Left something for you, he did. Said you would come looking for him . . . angry . . . saying terrible things. Said he wanted you to have this." From his cowl Brother Sebastian pulled a thumb-sized wooden box, tied with a string. He laid it in my hand. "And he said to tell you that an archangel would be his shield when the last darkness falls. Brother Valen, what did he—?"

"How long?" I said, scarcely able to shape words. My shaking fist threatened to crush the little box. "When did he go?"

Sebastian hesitated, his unsteady gaze not daring to meet my own. He expelled a sharp breath, as if he knew how close he stood to the blood rage threatening to crack my skull. "Just after Sext I encountered him coming out of the chapter-house undercroft, where we've stored what supplies we've salvaged from the fires. Young Jullian was with him. I remarked that they had missed the service—understandable, as they had just ridden in this morning with the Sinduria. But I said that I would expect to see both of them at Vespers. Our vows must not founder on the shoals of trial and sorrow. That's when he told me they had borrowed a horse from the Evanori and would be off to Elanus right away on Father Prior's business. Then he gave me the box and the message for you. The two of them rode out well before Nones."

"Thank you, Brother Sebastian. Please excuse me." Nones rang two hours before Vespers. I gave no credit to the stated destination. Gildas was taking the boy and my book to Sila Diaglou.

"The night drowns us, Valen," Sebastian called after as I hurried away. "Go with Iero's light."

I ran for the guesthouse. Nemesio would know if the Evanori had left horses for Voushanti and his men. If so, I could ride out . . . use my bent to follow Gildas. But before entering the guesthouse, I paused by the stoop and ripped open Gildas's parting gift. One glance and I launched the damnable thing into the night, scattering its contents into the churn of mud and snow. I could not find a curse vile enough for Gildas, and so I cupped my arms over my throbbing head and leaned against the stone wall, screaming out self-hatred and rage. The scent lingered: spicy, earthy, pepper and mushrooms, lighting an ember in my belly, where lurked a diseased knot the size of a fist. Nivat's claws settled into mind and body, ensuring I could not ignore it, could not forget, could not commit what wit I had to any other cause but servicing my hunger.

Smug, Silos had called him that morning in Palinur, and rightly so. Gildas, the scholar who had surely read about herbs and medicines among all his studies, would have known that giving me too much nivat would turn my head to muck and would grow my craving when the need came on me again . . . and again . . . and again. He had abetted my escape before calling down Thalassa's hunters and then so very kindly had fed my perversion. He knew his service would put the weak and gullible fool in his debt, give him a leash to control the ignorant sorcerer. Who in the world had measure for my folly?

I shoved open the guesthouse door. Harsh reality dispensed with my silly imaginings of riding off on my own to retrieve Jullian. Of a sudden every fiber and sinew of my body ached. Exhaustion weighed my limbs with armor of iron. And Voushanti sat on the stair beside the rushlight, paring his fingernails with his knife.

"So, pureblood," he said, without looking up from his task, "I thought perhaps you had gone wandering again. Lost yourself in the bogs and forgotten your oath."

"I do not break my oaths." Though I too often failed in my striving to keep them. As with Boreas. As with Jullian. Gildas would use the boy to manipulate me, as he had used the nivat. His shield. His hostage. *When the last darkness falls . . .*

I kicked a broken chair out of my way and tried to muster some semblance of a plan. Perhaps I could convince the mardane to let me "aid the brothers" in a search for Jullian and Gildas. "Tell me, Lord Voushanti, is our master Sila Diaglou's ally or her rival?"

"You needs must ask him that yourself. I've had word he'll be here tomorrow."

"Tomorrow? Here?" So soon. I'd expected . . . what? I was too tired to imagine.

"Prince Osriel's plans ripen. He needs neutral ground for an important parley, and this place happens to be convenient." He stood and stretched out his shoulders. "We'll likely move fast after tomorrow. I'd advise you to sleep off these past days' trial while you can."

He would never allow me to go out. I shrugged. "Tell me, Mardane, do *you* ever sleep?"

His face twisted in his grotesque mockery of a smile. "When my duties permit. Tonight, I keep watch." He moved aside just enough that I could squeeze past him to reach the stair. No doubt I would find him there in the morning.

The nagging ache of failure filled my boots with lead as I climbed to the upper chamber. A meal had been laid out on a tray—bread, boiled parsnips, dried apples. Anselm's posset sat in a pitcher by the hearth. Too weary to eat, I pulled off my sodden boots and hose, sat cross-legged on a woven hearthrug, and poked up Prior Nemesio's fire.

A cabal that thought to preserve humankind past the end times. A master who stole dead souls. Fanatics who used tormented spirits to slaughter the land's guardians and unravel the fabric of the world. How in the name of all gods had a man who prided himself on keeping his head down stumbled into events of such magnitude? Stumbled . . . had I?

My thoughts wandered back to Wroling Wood, to the day Boreas and I had given up on Perryn of Ardra and deserted his legion. When we spied the tidy manse, sitting unguarded in the forest outside Wroling Town, we thought Serena Fortuna had at last acknowledged our meager libations. Unfortunately, rodents had found the larders before us, and we had to be satisfied with inedible spoils. We stuffed our rucksacks and ran, arguing about whether to head straight for Palinur or to pawn the goods in a lesser town. I had laughed at finding my book after so many years, crowing that an unwelcome gift could pay me twice over.

Just as we dropped from the outer wall to head for the road, the Moriangi outriders attacked. The arrow strikes pitched me into an overgrown ditch, thick with soggy sedge and brambles. Boreas dived in beside me, blackening the air with his curses. Our attackers, caught up in a blood-frenzied pursuit of hundreds like us, failed to stop and ensure we were dead.

We lay in that ditch waiting for nightfall, hearing the pursuit pass over and around us. I bled into the sodden earth throughout a long afternoon, praying that the rain would not turn to ice and seal my foretold doom, longing to be warm and dry and safe, to be free of pain and feel my belly full. And when I at last staggered out of the ditch, half delirious, my gut and heart and blood had led us . . . driven us . . . here. Straight to Gillarine.

I stirred the coals and asked the question that had squatted in the back of my mind since I'd waked in Gillarine's infirmary. How was it possible that I had traveled ninety-three quellae in two days, starving, delirious, and half drained of blood? I could not answer it any more than I could say why my heart ached so sorely in the cloister garth of Gillarine, or why I wept when I looked on a Dané, or how a man who reveled in impiety and scorned all consideration of family had come to think of a Karish abbey as his home. My fists overflowed with shards of mirror glass, but I could not put them together in any way that made sense. I could not see myself anymore.

Perhaps I must have faith that whatever . . . whoever . . . had brought me here would show me the rest of the way. I dragged the tray of Gillarine's bounty close and poured a generous dollop of Brother Anselm's posset into the fire as an offering for Iero, for Kemen, for Serena Fortuna or whichever god or goddess might welcome it. As the sweet liquid sprizzled and scorched, I wolfed down the food and downed the remainder of the posset, pretending it cooled the fire in my gut. I would need my strength in the coming days, whether or not I chose to run. I would need it for Jullian. For my grandfather and his book. For the lighthouse cabal and the treacherous, dangerous Danae, whom we must beg to help us hold the world together. I had no time for weakness.

Read on for an exciting excerpt from
the conclusion to Valen's story

Breath and Bone

Coming from Roc in January 2008

We trod slowly along the shelf path. Wind had piled snow up against the cliff wall, and subsequent melting and freezing had left small glaciers along the way.

Shivering, uneasy, I gazed back out over the valley of the Kay and the slopes we had traversed, shrouded in snow fog that teased the eye. Drifting clouds mantled the clifftops above us. How could I have been so stupid as to come here? I could not shake the certainty that we were being watched. Only one day ago I had narrowly escaped a trap set by the trickster Danae down in the bogs of the River Kay. And now we were to intrude on their holy place.

Sila Diaglou, priestess of the ragtag Harrowers, who wished to send Navronne back to the days before cities and roads and tilled soil, to a time when women hid in caves and men cowered in terror of night and storm, named all gods false: Iero, the benevolent deity of the Karish, as well as Mother Samele and Kemen Sky Lord and the rest of the elder gods, worshiped in Navronne since time remembered. Harrowers ridiculed belief in Iero's angels, and called the impish aingerou naught but fools' wishing dreams. They also denied the existence of the Danae, the guardians of the land's health, whose dancing defined the Canon—the pattern of the world.

I could not name which gods were real and which but story. Nor could I argue the truth of angels or aingerou, though I spat on my finger and patted the naked rumps of those cherubic messengers carved into drainpipes and archways in hopes my prayers might be carried on to greater deities. But Danae . . . As boy and man I had scoffed at my grandfather's claims to have traveled their realms. But since I'd come to Gillarine, I had glimpsed at least two of them for myself.

"Are you having second thoughts, pureblood?" asked Nemesio, blowing on his rag-wrapped fingers to warm them. "Why would Brother Gildas choose this particular spot to hide a body when any of these gullies would do? Perhaps you'll tell me this is the wrong location after all."

There was no mistake. "He chose this place because killing Gerard was not his object. He wanted to kill the Danae guardian."

Despite their claims to the contrary, at least *some* of the Harrowers believed in the Danae. It could be no accident that their savage rites murdered Danae guardians one by one.

I pointed to a jutting slab of limestone. "The entry is just beyond that."

Legend said Danae lived both on the earth and in it. Everywhere and nowhere, my mad grandfather said. Most times they took human form to walk their lands—our lands, for the human and Danae realms were both the same and not the same. But for one season of every year a Dané became one with a sianou—the grove, lake, stream, or meadow he or she had chosen to guard. The protection of a Dané infused the sianou and the surrounding land with life and health.

Our destination was such a sianou, a pool I had located at the bidding of Abbot Luviar, before I even understood what kind of place it was. I had brought my friend Brother Gildas there, and in the weeks since that night, Gerard had gone missing, blight had infected Gillarine's orchards and fields, and disease had come to its sheepfolds. When I touched my hands to the earth in the abbey's cloisters, I could no longer feel its living pulse. Harrower raiders had left the abbey buildings in ruins, but I believed the cause of its underlying sickness lay here and that Gildas was responsible.

We had to step carefully around the jutting slab. Snow and ice packed the rock beneath its slight overhang. Dob balked and brayed in protest. As the prior slapped the donkey's rump and hauled on the lead, a horse whinnied anxiously just ahead of us.

Startled, beset with imaginings of lurking Harrowers, I hissed at Nemesio to keep silent.

Footsteps and jostling spoke of one man and one beast. "Easy, girl, it's friendly company on the way. We'll be about our business and be off again to hay and blanket."

The quietly persuasive voice brought a smile to my lips. Gram could convince a cat to play in the ocean.

"How in great Iero's mercy do *you* happen to be here?" I said, abandoning the prior to the donkey while I hurried around the rock and along the shelf toward the slender, dark-haired man stroking a gray mare. "Did you get Nemesio's message about Jullian . . . and Gildas? Well, of course, you must have done. That's why you've come—Nemesio must have written that he planned to bring me here. Gram, you must believe me. Gildas has taken Jullian and the book. He's murdered . . ."

I wanted to pass on everything I knew: what I had sensed in the abbey's cloisters, things Gildas had told me through the past weeks that I only now understood, the truth about my damnable perversion and how Gildas had thought to use it to bend me to his will. Ever-sensible Gram would understand the importance of prompt action. The man spent his days as the calm center of the lighthouse cabal, juggling his prickly employer, Thane Stearc, and Stearc's ebullient daughter Elene. But I'd scarcely begun my tale when Gram raised his gloved hand.

"Hold, friend Valen," he said. "We are already moving. Thane Stearc and his men have spent the night scouring the countryside between here and Elanus for the two of them. Mistress Elene leads another search party between here and Fortress Groult. When our old traveling companion, Thanea Zurina, set out west to her holding, we told her that a wayward monk had kidnapped a young friend of yours and asked her to keep an eye out. Though she's not privy to the secret of the lighthouse, your diversion at Mellune Forest impressed her so mightily that she insisted on mounting her own search along the roads west."

The flushed Nemesio joined us, hauling Dob behind him. "What are you doing here, Gram?"

Gram gathered himself and bowed politely. "Good Father Prior, your god's grace be with you this morning. As I was just telling Valen, Thane Stearc has dispatched several parties to search for Jullian and Brother Gildas. As he wished to move swiftly, my lord left me behind at Fortress Groult. So I rode up here, hoping to make myself useful by joining you in this unhappy investigation."

The secretary's pale skin took on a hint of scarlet at this confession. Though no older than I, Gram was afflicted with ill health.

Prior Nemesio shook his head. "Brother Valen's story is nonsensical.

How could a scholarly man such as Gildas give hearing to Harrowers? Even if he be apostate to divine Karus and the One God, which I cannot credit, who but mindless lunatics could imagine that a world without tools or books is what any god intends?"

Sila Diaglou claimed her dark age would be a time of appeasement, a time of cleansing, required because we had forgotten our proper fear of the Gehoum, the elemental Powers who controlled the land and seasons. The bitter wind whined through the crags, as if to answer my skepticism with a reminder of our wildly skewed seasons, and the pestilence and famine that howled at Navronne's door like starved wolves.

Gram stroked the mare's neck and fondled her ears. "Men are driven in such varied ways, Father Prior. Brother Gildas relished his task as Last Scholar, destined to be the holder of humankind's accumulated wisdom. Perhaps—and who can say what is in a man's heart?—he does not relish the task of First Teacher."

Nemesio tightened his full lips. "We have only Brother Valen's surmise. I'll not believe ill of Brother Gildas without some proof. So where is this pool, Brother? We must get you back before the demon prince's heathenish servants awaken."

I'd been to the Well only once, in conditions of light and weather so different I didn't trust my memory to recognize the cleft in the wall. So I crouched down, recalled the passage, the grotto, and the pool, and allowed magic to flow through my fingers into the stone beneath my feet. Cold, harsh, its cracks filled with frost crystals, the stone gave up its secrets far more reluctantly than earth. But I stretched my mind forward, swept the path and the cliff, and after a moment, a guiding thread claimed my senses— a surety something like that birds must feel when the days grow short and they streak southward beyond the mountains toward warmer climes. Such was the gift of the Cartamandua bent, the legacy of my father and grand-father's bloodline—a gift I had spurned because of its cost to my freedom. "This way," I said, moving northward along the shelf path. "Not far."

"You said Prince Osriel himself comes to Gillarine tonight," said Gram to the prior, as they trudged behind me, leading the beasts and sharing a flask Gram had brought.

"Aye," said the prior. " 'Twas only out of respect for good King Eod-ward's memory that I could stomach hosting such a visitation. How could a noble king breed such a son?"

Gram downed a long pull from his flask. "Abbot Luviar himself could not explain the ways of the gods sufficient to that question."

Dikes of dense black stone seamed the pale layers of the limestone cliff with vertical bands. Some twenty paces along the cliff, a wide crack split one of these dark bands. "Here," I said. "We'll find him here."

The gray morning dimmed to twilight in the narrow passage. We stepped carefully. A dark glaze of ice sheathed the straight walls and slicked the stone beneath our feet. Ahead of us a rectangle of light marked the end of our journey. Beyond it lay the little corrie, centered by a pool worn into the stone.

Clyste's Well, the pool was called, named for the Dané who had last claimed guardianship there. On one of his journeys into the Danae realms, my grandfather had involved Clyste in a mysterious theft that had driven humans and Danae apart. For his part in the crime, the Danae had tormented his mind to madness. For hers, they had locked her away in her sianou, forbidding her to take human form again. She had lived on all the years since, enriching the lands watered by her spring including Gillarine. But no more. My every sense insisted she was dead. Murdered.

Heart drumming against my ribs, I bade Nemesio leave the ass where he stood. A few steps more and we reached the entry, the point where the passage walls expanded to encircle the grotto like cupped hands. *Ah, holy Mother . . .* I clamped my arms about my aching middle. I would have given my two legs to be wrong.

Translucent blue-white cascades of ice ridged the vertical walls and sheeted the smooth ground. The pool itself lay unfrozen, dark and still, no matter the wind that whipped the heights, showering us with spicules of ice. Gerard floated on the glassy water, naked, bloodless. Rain must have washed his shredded flesh clean of blood and what scraps of his abbey garments the knives might have spared. The thorough savagery could have left no blood inside him. Iron spikes had been driven through his outstretched hands, tethering him to the rocky bank like a boat to its mooring. But one hand had torn through as he struggled to escape his fate, and now dangled loose in the water. Harrowers left their ritual victims to suffer and bleed, for it was both their blood and their torment that poisoned the sleeping Danae and the lands they guarded. So my grandfather had told me.

Nemesio choked, and I shoved him ruthlessly back into the passage to empty himself, though it was likely foolish to worry about further desecrating a place so vilely profaned. Gram pressed his back to the cliff wall at the entry, his pale cheeks as stark and drawn as the frozen cascades. "I cannot go here," he whispered. "I'm sorry. I can't help you with this."

"No matter. Rest as you need." I retrieved a worn blanket from the donkey's back and entered the grotto. Kneeling at the brink of the pool, I touched Gerard's tethered hand. *Cold. Great, holy gods . . . so cold.* Darkness enfolded me, threaded my veins and sinews, tightened about my heart and lungs until I felt as if I shared the terrifying, lonely end of this child's short life. And with it, the cold suffocation of the dead guardian. The burden of the worlds' end weighed on my limbs and drained my strength. I needed desperately to empty my stomach, too, to cry out my sickness, to run, to be anywhere but this dreadful place. But I could not leave the boy. *Forgive. Please gods and holy earth, forgive us all.*

Stretching out from the brink, I drew him close, then worked awkwardly to wrap the blanket around him. By the time I had carefully pulled his weakened flesh from the remaining spike, an iron-faced Nemesio had joined me. Together we used the blanket to lift the boy from the pool, then wrapped him in an outer blanket and carried him into the passage.

As the three of us tied the gray bundle to Dob's back, a movement caught the corner of my eye back the way we had just come. A glint of sapphire brilliance quickly subsumed in the gray light.

"Go on out," I whispered, still fighting to contain my own sickness. Gram looked ill, and the prior's teeth clattered like a bone rattle. Nemesio and I were both soaked. "I'll be along before you start down the steeps."

Nemesio clucked softly to the donkey. I slipped back down the passage toward the rectangle of light, flattened myself to the icy wall, and peered carefully into the grotto.

A tall, naked man, every quat of his lean flesh ridged with muscle, knelt on one knee beside the pool. Back bent, head bowed, he extended his long arms over the water in a graceful curve as if to embrace the very essence of the pond. Red hair, twined with yellow flowers, curled over one shoulder. Patterns of blue light scribed his skin—a sapphire heron on his back, vines and flowers the color of mountain sky on his powerful limbs, a spray of reeds drawn in azure and lapis along one thigh and hip.

He lifted his head, and a single anguished cry tore through him— echoing from the ice-clad walls, resonating in my bones. And then, stretching his arms to the heavens, he raised up on his bare toes and whipped one leg around so that he spun in place. A quick step and then he spun again . . .

and then again, moving around the pool in a blur of flesh and color and woven light, one arm curved before his chest, one above his head. The very rocks wept with his sorrow. I thought my heart might stop with the beauty of it.

When he reached his starting point, I stepped farther into the grotto. He halted in mid-spin and dropped his hands to his sides. He was not at all surprised to see me. And I recognized him. Three times I had glimpsed this same one of them . . . but never so close. Never in the fullness of his glory.

His eyes glowed the fiery gold of aspen leaves in autumn. On his left cheek the fine-drawn pattern of light scribed a dragon, whose wings spread across brow, shoulder, and chest, and whose long tail wrapped about his left arm. Below the graceful reeds that curved from his hip across his belly, a hatchling dragon coiled about his groin and privy parts. He appeared no more than thirty, but Danae lived for centuries and did not age as humans do.

"I didn't know this would happen," I said. "The man I brought here pretended to be what he was not. The child he slaughtered was an innocent . . . chosen because he was my friend. Never . . . never . . . did I mean to bring this on the one who slept here—this Clyste. My grandfather—" I caught myself before saying more. The Dané wouldn't care to hear that a human wept for her.

"As wolfsbane art thou, Cartamandua-son," he said, speaking fury and grief in the timbre of tuned bronze. "Beauty and poison. Taking life. Giving it back. Speaking the language of land and water, but with words graceless and ignorant. Intruding where thou shouldst not, violating—" He broke off, trembling, and swept his hand to encompass the grotto. "Thou dost lead me here, cleanse the Well so I do not sicken, return it to my memory so I cannot escape knowing what is lost—though I must lose it all over again as I walk away. Is this thy pleasure to taunt those thou dost not know? Dost thou think my love for Clyste can shield thee from the judgment of the long-lived?"

As flint to steel, his indignation sparked my anger, erasing all caution. "I know naught of you, Dané, save that you once offered me a haven in my need, then stood back and observed my captivity as if I were a performing bear chained for your amusement. I know that Danae vengeance has left my grandsire a madman. And I know that you or one of your fellows tricked me and my companions and our enemies into the bogs as if *all* humans were naught but beasts worthy of a slaughterhouse." Naught would ever erase the memory of luring my enemies into the freezing mud to save my companions' lives. Watching . . . feeling . . . them drown. "I once believed your kind to be the blessed finger of the Creator in this world. But you are no better than we are."

"Pah!" With a snarl of disgust he turned away. Kneeling once again by the pool, he scooped water in his hands and poured it over his head. "*Askon geraitz, Clyste*," he said, his voice breaking. "Live on in my heart, *asengai*. Let me not forget thee."

"Kol, don't leave. You must— Please hear us!" I had forgotten Gram. The wan secretary stood framed in the dark band of the passage entry, astonished . . . stammering. "Many of us . . . most . . . despise these murderers. The Everlasting is in upheaval, to the ruin of our land, our beasts, and all humankind. Whatever the cause, we desperately need the help of the long-lived to understand it . . . to make it right again. The guard of the dragon names thee Kol, friend and foster brother of Eodward King, brother to shining Clyste, who danced as none before her. In Eodward's name we beg hearing. Please, take us to Stian Archon or to any who might heed our message . . . our need . . ."

The Dané shifted his gold eyes to Gram. Cocking his head, he flared his nostrils and inhaled deeply. His lip curled. "Human speech is briar and nightshade. Human loyalty is that of wild dogs and weasels. Stripped is Stian of his archon's wreath." His finger pointed to the dark pool. "These evils are the gifting of Eodward to those who sheltered him. Begone! Thou dost bear the stink of betrayal and shalt not pass one step into our lands until his debt is paid." He strode toward the ice-clad wall, but before he reached it, he vanished in a ripple of air and light.

Never had I stood in a place so unforgiving, so empty. Gram might have been frozen into the wall. I gave him a nudge, and we abandoned the grotto.

Shivering with cold and pent emotion, I'd walked halfway down the dark passage when it occurred to me that I likely could have used my bent to follow the Dané, no matter his refusal to take us. I might have thrown away my first and only chance to seek answers to questions that had plagued me since I'd spoken to my grandfather . . . to give Gram a further chance to plead our case. *Stupid, stupid, Valen.*